THE WINTER PEOPLE

BOOKS BY JOHN EHLE

FICTION

The Winter People

The Changing of the Guard

The Journey of August King

Time of Drums

The Road

The Land Breakers

Lion on the Hearth

Kingstree Island

Move Over, Mountain

NONFICTION

The Cheeses and Wines of England
and France, with Notes on Irish Whiskey

The Free Men

Shepherd of the Street

The Survivor

THE
WINTER
PEOPLE

JOHN EHLE

PERENNIAL LIBRARY

Harper & Row, Publishers, New York
Grand Rapids, Philadelphia, St. Louis,
San Francisco, London, Singapore, Sydney, Tokyo

Portions of this work originally appeared in *The Arts Journal*.

A hardcover edition of this book was published in 1982 by Harper & Row, Publishers.

First PERENNIAL LIBRARY edition published 1989.

Designer: Kim Llewellyn

Library of Congress Cataloging in Publication Data

Ehle, John, 1925–
 The winter people.

 "Perennial Library."
 I. Title.
PS3555.H5W5 1989   813'.54   81-47684
ISBN 0-06-080939-6 (pbk.)   AACR2

89 90 91 92 93 OPM 10 9 8 7 6 5 4 3 2 1

To Leon and Connie

Get me to some far-off land
Where higher mountains under heaven stand,
Where other thunders roll amid the hills,
Some mightier wind a mightier forest fills . . .

THE WINTER PEOPLE

1

About an hour before sundown, she saw a man moving through her deadened woods, coming toward her house. Nobody who lived around here would walk through a tree-girdled forest, where limbs fell at random and trunks tilted like named corpses, their black arms scraping against one another, dropping bits of themselves. A woods like that would still the muscles and chill the blood, and she was instantly cautious about anybody who would enter into one.

She laid her baby in among the pillows on her bed. "It's all right now, Jonathan," she assured him. He was too young to understand the words, but since he was her only companion, she talked to him often. She got her butcher knife, hid it behind her dress, knowing even then that she would never be able to hurt a person with it, and stationed herself just inside her open doorway. She was a strong woman, able to protect herself within reason; she was twenty-three, her birthday had been last month, October, and she was tall, was agile. Also, she was pretty; everybody had told her so, and this was not the first time a man had approached her place, although this was the first one to come through that woods, to come to her from off the mountain.

The man was not alone, she noticed. Two people. Yes, there she saw two people in the woods, making their way through and past the fallen limbs. It appeared that a woman accompanied the man, either a woman or a girl, twelve, thirteen years old. The man was carrying a bag strapped to one shoulder and had a crate perched on the other. The girl was dressed in a simple print dress and was leading a dog by a leash. Neither of them was dressed for outdoors in cold weather, especially the weather up on the mountain.

They stopped just downhill of the woods and the girl brushed flecks of bark out of her hair, off her clothes. He was a short man, not much taller than the girl. Well-built, athletic-looking, slender. Appeared to be a handsome person, although with a need of a shave. They moved toward her house, stopped just uphill of the chickenhouse. They were looking over her holdings, the two-stall barn built decades ago, the old rock room that had once been a springhouse; they were considering the road which led on down the cove to the mill, to her brother's house, as she knew, to the community where the rest of her family lived. The two people were standing still in the failing sunlight, murmuring to one another.

Somewhere off on the mountain a crow sounded its lonely, mocking call. He was commenting on their visit, she thought, relishing the bitter mirth he reserved for human affairs.

The man was perplexed, the girl appeared to be frightened. The man slowly lowered the strap off his shoulder and set the bag down. He called to the house suddenly, a long, tenor heeeelllllloooooooo.

She made no move at all. He came a few steps closer, now set down the crate, in which he had nothing in the world but three game chickens. The little girl stepped forward and stood beside him, as

2

if to help protect him. That girl had a pig on a leash; when Collie saw that, she almost laughed out loud. She remembered as a girl having a pet pig for a little while, a gentle few months of her life, but it had proved to be a messy pet, not one she would care to sleep with. Up to that time she had always slept with her pets, had let them lie on the covers at the foot of her bed, cats and even dogs. Now here was a little girl with a pet pig.

Collie moved to the open doorway, let the sunlight reveal her to them.

The man raised both hands at once, instinctively showing he was unarmed. He bowed in a half-bow, appeared to be embarrassed to have to discuss his predicament, or maybe he was aware of the ludicrousness of his party's appearance. He paused in his presentation to brush stinging, dead bark off his neck, from under his collar. "Was up on the ridgecrest," he began, "and I saw smoke—we saw it together, and I brought Paula down the side of the ridge to ask you to let us warm, and maybe feed us."

The man was looking her over carefully, she could tell that. Well, she thought, he's looking at a lonely woman dressed in a brown wool dress, with a world of worries under her blond hair, and a useless knife in her hand.

"We lost our way on that ridge," he began once more.

"There's been others lost up there," Collie said. She could tell he was a mild person, and indeed he was handsome, with a high forehead, which her father had always said was a sign of intelligence, and broad chin, a sign of courage. "People who are lost usually go back along the ridgecrest till they come to the Campbells' road," she told him. "They don't come down the side of the mountain."

"We saw the wood smoke, and I didn't know where—"

3

"Don't walk through a deadened woods loaded with chickens and a pig."

That made him smile. He was a pleasant, harmless person, all right, a city fellow venturing away up here in the deeper mountains for some reason or other. Only a few had been coming up here, ever since the depression started in the outlands.

"Was heading toward Tennessee," the man told her. He came a few steps closer, and his daughter moved up to stand beside him, as before.

"No, you can't go to Tennessee that way," she told him. "You missed the turning." Over her shoulder she called, "Did you hear that, Jonathan?" She meant to leave the impression that there was a man inside the house. "They're going to Tennessee by heading up that northern route to Virginia."

"I missed the turning," the man explained.

"You missed it, indeed you did," Collie assured him. "That road you took becomes a trail, not much more than that."

"I noticed," he said agreeably.

The pretty girl beside him was still wary, was conscious of every falling leaf, of the crackling of tree limbs above her head, the sudden grunt of a pig, the approach of the milk cow. "Where you come from?" Collie asked.

"Up south of Philadelphia," the man replied.

"Why'd you leave up there?" She was asking the same sort of questions her father would have asked. She had a keen, assertive way of speaking, softly attacking most of the words, but at the same time she clothed them in a musical, considerate tone. Nothing in her manner was allowed to aggravate or challenge.

"My wife died in the spring," the man was saying. "Paula and me had a world of cares all the sudden, being reminded of her, so we decided to try a new place."

4

"What you do for a living?"

"I'm a clockmaker."

She had not expected that. In all her days she had never met a clockmaker before. "They need clocks in Tennessee, do they?" she said, a smile working at the corners of her mouth.

"Why, I heard about Tennessee, that's all."

"Everybody's heard about Tennessee," she said, "but not everybody goes there."

He laughed appreciatively, once he noticed the smile on her face. "I tell you, lady, if you'd let us warm, I'd be grateful to you."

"What's your name?" she said, again proceeding as her father would.

"Name is Silas Wayland Jackson, but I'm usually called Wayland."

"You kin to any Jacksons up this way?"

"No."

"You know Lester Jackson, for instance?"

"No."

"What family your wife from?"

"Staples," he said. He shrugged helplessly, trapped by the series of questions.

Collie thought she ought to send them on down the road to the community. She shouldn't endanger herself with strangers, and she shouldn't endanger that man this way; Jonathan's father wouldn't like any man being here, even for a while. She ought to send him along, but he was a tame, gentle man, and his daughter had a pet pig, and all they wanted was to warm. After all, it was her house, her time, her loneliness, which had been an all-day plight for her, and it was her right to offer him hospitality. "You both come in to warm. Tie your pig to that bush, Paula," she told her. "You can leave that coop where it is, Mr. Jackson. These chickens are pets, too, are they?"

Wayland plunged into the house and crouched on the hearth, hands held up to the flame, his shoes

5

touching the edge of the coals. Paula shoved in beside him, tried to get into the fireplace with him. Probably were about frozen through, up on that mountain, Collie thought, where the wind comes howling across, full of stings and meanness. "You might put some more life in that fire, Mr. Jackson."

"Lord, thank you," he whispered. "Once we got lost, we became scared as rabbits," he admitted. "We're new to this mountain country."

"Were you walking, or in a wagon or truck, or what?" Collie inquired.

"We left our new truck up there with another flat tire. I bought it earlier this year, it's a '32 Ford pickup."

"People freeze up there," Paula informed her. "They do of a night."

"Yes, I've heard of people freezing in the mountains," Wayland said. "And we saw smoke from your chimney, so that was the nearest hope."

Collie didn't know whether she really ought to feed them anything or not, but she did put the kettle on the stove. "Now if you'll move out a few feet, Mr. Jackson, I'll get to the fire and rustle some heat into it. I see you don't know how to tend it. And Paula can go for wood. The best is stacked by my rock room."

Paula at once leaped forward and darted out the door, anxious to please.

"Your husband not going to come out to meet us, Mrs. what-ever-your-name-is?" Wayland asked.

"Name is Miss Wright," Collie told him at once. She noticed him flinch, as if the "Miss" had struck him peculiarly. He had doubtless seen the baby on the bed.

"Your husband back in there, is he?"

Collie shook the stove's grate. "No, there's nobody in there."

The man said, "Is he off working?"

6

Collie shook her head.

"Did you say 'Miss Wright'?" he asked.

Collie closed the firebox door. "I had a dog with me till last week or so," she said, "and Papa's offered me another one, but I had it in my mind maybe to leave here for a while. My young brother promised to bring me money enough to take a trip."

The man was staring at her curiously, as if he had never known a woman simply to take off talking on her own this way.

"The McGregors' dogs killed my last one. They come at her with their teeth showing. I kicked one so hard it landed sideways in the creek, and they all turned back to think things over. There I was, wearing Papa's boots, just as I am now, for they don't let the water through as bad as my own shoes do..." She went on talking about the dogs and her boots and her papa, and the new man listened carefully, she noticed, a quizzical smile playing on his lips, as if he had never heard a woman talk in a steady stream before.

When finally she hushed, she moved a chair nearer the fireplace, sat down and began nursing her baby at her bare breast. Well, that seemed to surprise him, too. Did he think she was going to sneak into that dark back room to feed her own child, at her own house?

"That's the prettiest baby I ever saw," he told her, moving to a chair across the table from hers.

"There have been others say so," she said, smiling at him, then proudly at the baby. He had a round face, reddish-tinted hair, big blue eyes.

Paula came in with a load of wood and set it near the hearth.

"What's his name? Paula, you see the baby?" the man said.

"Jonathan, and we call him by the full name, Mr. Jackson. Jon Wright is too abrupt a name, don't you

7

agree, is like two spikes set for driving, while Jonathan Wright is somebody to be accounted for."

"I can see that," Wayland told her, sneaking another look at the hungry baby.

"He's the least trouble," she said. "I raised my younger brother, Young, and he was a minute-by-minute bother, was always into everything. Now, that's a name that's too short and blunt, I think, my brother's, Young Wright. His name is William Easter Wright, but of course he never would put up with Easter, and my father is William, so he was called according to his age."

He was staring at her, and concentrating on the lilt and sway of her words. "I remember being called Silas as a boy. I didn't answer to it."

"Nobody calls this one Jon, if I can help it."

"Your husband not here at the house, you say?"

Collie noticed that the question caused the girl to look up suddenly, then to turn to stare at the room and at the open doorway to the back room. "No, he's not here," Collie said simply.

"He's off working, is he?"

"The boy's father is not here, Mr. Jackson."

"But he has a father?"

"All children have fathers, Mr. Jackson," she said.

He nodded, readjusted his body to the chair. "The Miss in your name surprised me," he admitted.

"Well, you're not the first to admit it." Carrying the baby, she moved to the wood range and busied herself there. "Paula, you come take Jonathan and watch over him." The girl was afraid to take hold of him. "Here, he won't break. He was crawling at three months. Now, you'll need to get that firewood off the floor, Paula, stack it in that box, or he'll be into it and have splinters an inch long. Here now, Mr. Jackson, don't put that poplar log at the back." She had noticed he was adding wood to the fire. "Use a hard wood that'll reflect heat." When he had served the fire pretty well, she said to him, "No, Mr. Jackson, I have a father and three brothers close by, if I need help of any sort. I have no husband here at all."

He returned to his chair and made himself comfortable once more. "Did your husband pass on?" he asked.

Persistent man, more than modestly curious about her situation, Collie realized. She smiled down at him, met his gaze with her own, not the least bit embarrassed to have him interested in her. And who are you, she thought, how did you come here on this certain Thursday of loneliness, where are you going, or will you stay? "I have a tea leaf or two, if you're interested?"

"Well, I'm sure interested," he said.

She made tea from spicebush cuttings she took from a wall bag—her walls were covered with small bags of herbs and teas, strings of dried beans, and other goods, and with clothes hanging on pegs. The three of them drank tea, sitting by the warm fire, the front door open. "That cold air makes the fire feel warmer, more welcome," she told them. "And I love light, don't you, can't abide darkness, and there's but the one window in this room. I leave the door open until the coldest weather arrives, which it will soon." They huddled close to one another, Jonathan sitting on Paula's lap, playing with her chin, her nose. Collie said, "I need you around the house to help me take care of him, Paula. I carried him all the way down to Papa's, then came back to Papa's store, then carried him to see my brother Gudger's wife, who was a Grindstaff before she married, and I learn more about the Bible by just being with a Grindstaff than Saint Paul ever knew. Do you know anybody, Mr. Jackson, who only talks about the Bible?"

"I've met several like that," he replied. "My cousin Elizabeth—"

"I'd say to her it's too bad my dog got killed, and she'd say we are coming into the last days and Jesus is due. And I'd say I had a time digging a grave for him deep enough, for the other dogs might try to dig him up of a night, and she said there'll be earthquakes and pestilences, which I take to be flies and mosquitoes, in the last days."

"I know people like that," he said, "up where I'm from—"

"She looks up from her sewing every once in a while to see if Jesus is in the sky."

"Well, I know," he said, laughing, as was Paula.

"But listening to her's better than loneliness, Mr. Jackson, or leaving here, which is all the place I've ever known."

They finished two cups of tea apiece, then went outdoors so Collie could do her late evening work. She clomped about the yard in her big boots, chasing chickens from before her. She put the cooped chickens of Wayland's and Paula's in the shed near the barn and shelled corn for them.

The hinges on one of the double barn doors was sprung, Wayland noticed, so he brought a length of a sapling and placed it for the door to ride on until it could be hinged properly. Collie threw ears of corn to her pigs, then to Paula's pet pig. She threw each pig an apple as well. "Give them more than one," she explained, "and they'll do nothing but lie around waiting for more apples."

Wayland helped her haul water to the pens. "My papa brings me what corn I need," she told him, dropping grains of corn for her chickens. "He has big fields of it in the valley, this side of the river. My brother Young put me in a patch last spring so we'd be more independent of Papa, but Young's so flighty about work, keeps changing his mind about everything, so the groundhogs ate what they wanted of the crop, and a cow bear and two cubs finished it up."

"Bears come down here?" Paula asked.

"If they want to," Collie told her.

"Pretty stand of stock here, Miss Wright," Wayland said, "except for some of your chickens."

"Why, they're preyed on by everything. Look back to the north, Mr. Jackson. That woods rolls up on those far mountains and goes beyond several miles and over another range. It's the North Woods, or so my family always has called it, and it's full of bears and wolves and weasels and foxes and Lord knows what all. Last winter I heard a cat, a bobcat or maybe a panther, crying back in there. It was in the dead of night and was as shrill as a woman's voice. I'd not heard the like since childhood."

He slipped a sliver of wood behind the upper hinge of her chickenhouse door to secure the hinge more tightly. He closed and opened the door a few times to test his work. "Gap's too big under the door," he told her. He brought stones and closed the gap.

While she milked the cow, he sat on a stump nearby, considering her, no doubt wondering about who she was, what sort of person, and looking over her house and holdings. She said to him, "A penny for your thoughts, Mr. Jackson."

"I was thinking you're a pretty woman," he told her. "And I like to listen to you talk. I'll bet you could say something mean and it'd sound sweet as syrup. You ever get angry?"

She laughed. "Lord, yes, I'm known to want my own way, Mr. Jackson. Growing up with three brothers, and with no sisters to help me, and with a sick mother, I had to represent myself."

She led him and Paula up on the hillside a short way, where they could look out over much of the valley. It was bounded by humped-shouldered mountains, blue in the evening light, with tinges of orange at their crests, reflections of the sun setting over in Tennessee. The mountains rose half a mile from where they stood, she told him, and were clothed in all the trees of the country, with Canadian firs on their tops.

"I came back in here wondering about myself," Wayland told her suddenly, awed by the grandeur of the place. "I said to Paula yesterday, I said to her we've broken our life cord to the world outside, we've come too far to go back again. It's almost like dying, is a closed door. Does that make sense to you, Miss Wright?"

"Dying makes all the sense in the world, but coming up here is not like dying."

"It's far off and different, has its own air, different from the others, and the creeks wash, rush more than rivers, seem to be beating themselves on the rocks and laughing at us. I tell you, it's almost beyond my own thoughts."

"Well," she said helplessly, watching him with amusement, "I hope it's not like dying, that's all." Across the river, she told him and Paula, lived the Campbells, Scottish and clannish, tough, died-in-the-wool Protestants; they owned the rocky, steep side of the river valley for ten, fifteen miles, every stone and root and wild beast and tree and drop of water, all the way to Tennessee. On this side of the river the Wright family still owned major holdings, although over generations they had sold parcels to other families, unlike the Campbells, who kept all their land in one deed, listed just now in Drury Campbell's name, he being the chief person of the family. In the valley, particularly on this side of the river, were substantial houses, as Wayland and Paula could see, perhaps twenty in view, and a church for the Wrights and their friends, and one for

12

the Campbells, and a school for each, Collie said, down under the trees. And there were more houses between here and Tennessee.

She poured the milk into clean jugs, which she set inside the stone room. Paula came with her, watching every move she made. Paula saw there was a rope-spring bed with a thin mattress set against one wall of the room.

"That was my brother Young's bed before he got a house of his own," Collie explained. She led the way to her own house, where Wayland was stacking firewood. She paused near the doorway to survey the yard, to reassure herself that everything was tight enough, to admire the work done, the safety attained, the comfort of living here with her own holdings, everything dependent on her; the idea of leaving this place appeared strange to her at this moment, although it had been dear that afternoon. She watched, smiling, as Wayland lifted the top off her one beehive and looked inside. "Honey enough for them?" she asked him, knowing there was.

"Might be better to move the hive some distance from the house, Miss Wright. Be less annoyances for them."

"Well, all right," she said. "We can do it whenever you like."

Rain was beginning to fall in big drops. Paula said she had never seen drops as big. One landed on her nose and she blew it off with a little laugh, then Jonathan laughed at her. He tried to hold the raindrops. "Papa, look how he does," Paula called, delighted with him, with her new toy and friend.

"Must have some hail in it," Wayland said, holding his hand open to receive the drops.

No place to wash up except the kitchen sink, Collie told them, thinking about getting ready for supper, but Wayland went down to the creek, knelt on a rock at a pool and splashed water onto his face and neck and arms. Collie trailed along, wondering what he was doing. He blubbered and blew through the water, finally shouting out in exhilaration. He loved cold water, he said, had always swum in winter as well as summer. Swimming had been since childhood the one diversion from shop work which he had permitted himself. His mother, whose parents had been born in Norway, had said he was part fish, as all her people were, that he swam before he walked, that he was born under the sign of the fish. He was kneeling there at the creek edge, water pouring down out of his hair, rain pelting him, explaining all this to Collie, who stood nearby under a spruce pine, marveling at him, at herself as well, two children in an unreal world.

The family sat before the fire and dried off. They watched the fire lick the oak and hickory logs and sniffed the aroma of potatoes and a chicken, which was splattering and sputtering in the oven. "So you decided to leave home, did you, get up and go?" she asked him.

"Paula suggested it, didn't you, honey?" he said.

"One morning I said let's go live somewhere else, and by evening we were on the road," Paula said.

"I bought a new truck, packed the best clockworks I had, took a few tools, sold the furniture—"

"We were on the road by evening," Paula said.

"Place to place," he said, "trying to find somewhere unlike where we had been. You ever travel much, Miss Wright? Did you ever want to?"

"Here lately I've been thinking I might go see my Uncle Charlie."

"Is he way off?" he asked.

"Lord, yes. He once wrote us from San Francisco. Before that he was in Portland, Oregon. Or go visit Aunt Amanda in Asheville."

"Paula and me tried to settle at a town in eastern

14

Virginia, but there was no interest in clockmakers there at all. Found no shop space in Raleigh. Then somebody said Charlotte would be a clock town, but we went on through the place, finding nothing. Third generation, that's what I am, of clockmakers. Too late to settle for repair work, or being something else."

"Are you?" she said, impressed. "Three generations? Well, my people have been here storekeeping and clearing the land longer than that, I'd say."

"I don't order the clock parts assembled, Miss Wright. I start with wood and metal and make a creature that has a face, a heart, a voice, that knows to chime the hours, has a personality, has work to do and can be counted on."

She liked his enthusiasm. Men around here would often show anger, but held closer reins on other emotions. She liked his manners a good deal better than those of the men who had grown up with her, and she began to wonder if indeed he would decide to settle here in this community. "I was saying to Paula about that stone room, Mr. Jackson, it has a bed in it, and if you need a bed for tonight..." She had tried not even to utter the invitation, but it had come out naturally, and, in any case, there was no special reason to believe Jonathan's father would arrive here tonight, or any certain night. The man was watching her, trying to read any special, personal invitation in her offer, she suspected. "Tomorrow you can find a place to stay down the road," she told him.

"Don't want to be a nuisance," he said.

"No heat in that room, but it's about half buried, so it's not so cold. And the bed's small."

"We'd be pleased," he said, watching her thoughtfully.

Collie, trying to break the spell that was holding them closer, suddenly said, "Now, here I sit, talking

15

away, and I've not even thought to offer you a drink." One hand fluttered out before her, toward his arm. "Do you ever touch liquor, Mr. Jackson?"

"Now and then," he admitted, a big smile opening on his face.

"Sit here talking without remembering the basic needs, as my papa would say." She unlocked a wooden chest, using a key tied to a chair post, and produced several bottles and jugs. "Now, what do you want?" She brought two cups. "I'll take a few drops but not enough to get Jonathan intoxicated."

"In the town where I come from, they say a woman who drinks will do most anything," Wayland said, smiling up at her.

"I'm surprised you didn't come down here sooner, then, Mr. Jackson," she said at once, "where women can be sociable." She let him taste the whiskey, then the apple brandy. He chose the latter. "Now you sit down and make yourself at home," she said, "and we'll have our supper, then you and your daughter can sleep in that rock room for the one night. You can start sewing up those tears on your dress right now, Paula. You'll find thread in that chest."

He chose the rocker, but took two of the pillows out of it, since they crowded him. "You sure we won't put you out, Miss Wright?"

"I'm not going out, Mr. Jackson," she said.

"No, no, it's a manner of speech. 'Put you out' is a figure of speech."

"Don't put me out, Mr. Jackson; it's raining even more now." She hurried outside, let the cold rain fall on her upturned face. She held out her hands to the rain, embracing it and the whole wide world, happy with a world that could change quickly, completely, so that a bitterly lonely person one morning could have a life renewed, a few changes offered by suppertime, maybe a hope better than a change or two.

They were in no hurry while eating their meal together. She had hot biscuits, potatoes, fresh butter and the chicken, and he drank brandy while she and Paula drank milk. After supper she sat in the rocker and nursed the baby for a short while, then Paula took Jonathan outdoors to listen to the water flowing down, making words inside the rainspouts, which her brother Milton, the smith, had made. Collie and Wayland sat beside the warm hearth, now and again their gazes meeting, both mildly embarrassed by their secret thoughts, their lingering signs of interest. He asked her, "When will Jonathan's father be coming home, do you know?"

"I don't know when. He didn't bother to say."

"Then you do know who he is?"

She leaned her head back against the rocker and considered him kindly. "Yes, I know."

"And he knows?"

"Yes. I told him, but I've not yet told anybody else."

"Must have had others who were curious."

"My father, my mother, my three brothers, and that's the mere start. But it's a secret I have to keep privately."

"You won't marry him?"

"He's not a marrying type. And he's still rough on everything that's dear. You appear to be a gentle man, Mr. Jackson, but there are not many gentle men around here, except elderly people."

"Has he asked you to marry him?"

"No."

"Will he ask you?"

"I don't know."

"You've not inquired about it?"

"Yes, I've inquired about it." Her keen blue eyes watched him thoughtfully, kindly. She didn't know whether she ought to resent his inquiry or not, but she knew she did not resent it, that she welcomed

17

any interest he felt for her.

"I thank you for telling me as much as you have," he said suddenly. "There's a world of people who go mincing about a birth or a love affair as if they're bushes that need circling, and it's a pleasure to meet a woman who has a mind of her own, and I thank you."

"You're welcome," she said. What had he thanked her for? she wondered. Maybe he was mildly drunk by now. He did have a manner of stretching out his sentences, of meandering, which was a sign of intoxication among her brothers.

Suddenly, seeking to arouse himself, he said, "The mill next down the road is your brother's?"

"Papa gave it to him, but Young won't work it, I'm afraid. He's not even put the millwheel together, has it strewn all about the ground."

"I'm the world's best fixer," he said, watching her. "You want me to put it together?"

She was not prepared for an offer of help, but welcomed it. "I know Papa would appreciate it. Young probably would, too. He's gone to Asheville, was expected back today, but he's not here yet." She felt kindly disposed toward Wayland's offering to be helpful this way. "I do hope you'll have the chance to assemble it, Mr. Jackson," she said.

It took all her spare blankets and quilts to get the two of them comfortably housed in their bedroom. She gave them the lantern, said firelight would do for her and Jonathan. The stone room was dry and cold but wind-protected. The spring which once had served this house had deviated; only a bare trickle of water flowed along the channel now, merely enough to fill a small pit near the doorway where two milk jugs were kept.

Wayland brought in more wood for the fireplace before finally preparing to leave her house. Even then he lingered at the door, said goodnight several times. She listened to his footsteps fade away on the clanking yard boards, then sank down gratefully in the rocker, her baby in her lap, and tried to recall bit by bit the evening.

Now and then her hopeful thoughts would be muddled by a reminder of danger, but she tried to set that aside. She clutched the baby all the closer, pressed his little mouth firmly into her breast, moaning to him, and murmuring baby-talk words. The baby was all she had, along with such evening thoughts as she held of the new man and his daughter; they were the three divisions of a single need she felt just now.

She crept into her bed, the baby still at her breast, and drew her knees up close to the baby's diapered bottom. "Well, tomorrow I'll send him along, put him on the road to Tennessee," she told Jonathan. "I'll not endanger him," she promised herself. "If I do cause harm, I'll stand for it," she told the child, "I'll answer for it." She pulled a quilt close around their shoulders. "Ought to get up and heat bed bricks for us," she whispered, but she was comfortable enough, she decided. "I hope you'll never need to be lonely," she whispered to him. "I hope you'll never have your own life broken," she told him.

She had broken her own life herself, in a sense, she realized, and had involved Young, his life, as well, taking risks she need not take, encouraging him to do the same. She had him leaping off the high rock at the falls at age of four; she had allowed him to keep going to see that teacher, knowing it wasn't proper. She had always led the way into any door that opened, welcoming risks that were offered, accepting them along with the new chances. "You're a strange woman, Collie," her mother had told her repeatedly, always with astonishment.

Well, she wasn't one to accept life on somebody

19

else's terms, she would admit that, until all the ways were closed to her.

Next day the rain continued. It kept promising to stop, but abruptly would gather strength and renew itself, robbing the higher sky of moisture. Most of the morning the family spent indoors, talking about their lives, the death of Paula's mother, for instance, informing one another about a few personal matters and relationships. Collie taught Paula how to sew a patch on her dress, how to bake cornbread. Now and then the group would troop out to do chores, to feed stock or gather eggs or watch Wayland work on the sheds, which seemed to attract him because of their contrariness. He was a quick, sure worker; whatever action he took was definitive and successful, she noticed. "I'll move that beehive when the rain stops," he told her. "The way it's set now, a truck or wagon coming up your drive will pass through the bees' lane of flight, and that'll irritate the devil out of them." They discussed where to put it, deciding on a spot next to the barn, and he constructed a stand there, using locust saplings, driving four legs into the ground, bracing them. Then, even in the rain, he picked up the hive and moved it, stationed it securely.

Now and then Paula would ask about getting the truck off the mountain. No, it's raining, he would tell her, the roads are slick. Indeed, nobody wanted to interrupt the magic of the morning, the casual talking and touching and working together.

In late morning a group of horsemen rode through the yard, men dressed in furs, riding tough mountain horses, with pack horses trailing loaded down with furs and other goods. The men made no excuse for coming through the yard, nor did they pay much attention to Collie or Wayland or Paula. They appeared to be moving in a world of their own interests, were content to wait for an act of destiny to relate them to others, to involve them.

"Campbells," Collie said, whispering their name.

That afternoon Wayland was bound to go for the truck. He and Collie and Paula, with Collie carrying the baby, walked down the road, stopping at the mill long enough for Wayland to count the mill-wheel pieces and move them under cover. "I can assemble that, all right," he told her. Collie called down the hill to Young's house, called his name, but he didn't show himself, wasn't back from Asheville, apparently. "Be back by tomorrow noon, has to be," she commented. "You'll like Young," she told him.

They chose a little twisty lane that led up the hill to the east, meandering alongside a branch that was littered with tin cans and debris. Pretty soon dogs came to greet them, to bark and snarl at them, but Collie, turning the baby over to Wayland, picked up a stick and slashed out at them, sending them fleeing to a safer distance. At the three huts of the McGregor family, silent children waited in the yard to see who was approaching, the children watching with dull disinterest as the family walked by. Some of the girls had on new dresses, Collie noticed, which surprised her. The McGregors, as she told Wayland and Paula, were a shiftless mixture of Scotch-Irish, German and Indian bloods, with a few drops of French, and the combination had resulted in a shiftlessness unmatched even by the Plover family. The McGregors were squatters here, had been inhabitants for some decades now on Wright property, which they had cut over, walked over, denuded, eroded, and now swept with homemade brooms, living with dogs and hogs and chickens, hunting furs for what little cash they needed.

At the truck site she and Wayland and Paula worked together to get the goods back on the truck; the tools and the clock parts had been hidden in the laurel. They realized finally, only near the last of the effort, that most of his clothes and some of Paula's were missing. Wayland appeared not to mind about that. "There are the tools," he told her, "we have the tools and the clockworks I need." When she insisted they go back to the McGregors' and ask about the losses, he said he was newly arrived here and meant to start as little trouble as possible and he would not worry one bit about old clothes.

They tried the truck out there on the ridgecrest. It coughed because of the high altitude, the lack of oxygen, but it chugged along. The outlands lay to the east, to their left as they cruised back along the ridge; they could look out over rolling hills stretching for many miles, shimmering in the sunlight, with now and then a wand of smoke rising from a cabin or house. To the west side of their high road were black hulks of mountains, big, brooding mysteries, with mist rising from them, from their crannies and warts and bleeding branches and streams, like hot breath.

Collie directed the way on the return home, choosing the same little road that led past the McGregors'. Of course, there was a better way, but she had it in her mind that the clothes must be retrieved. As the truck approached the three huts, they could make out three McGregor boys dressed in Wayland's clothes and a few girls wearing Paula's. Paula, who was standing in the truck bed, abruptly shouted for her father to stop this truck so she could jump off. Apparently she intended to retrieve her garments on the spot. Wayland speeded up the truck. "Not going to have trouble," he called back to her.

Paula continued for a mile or so to complain mightily about the loss, but Wayland remained adamant.

Collie thought about suggesting they drive to the

inn, where he and Paula could get lodging, but she found herself hesitating to make the thought known, and when Wayland turned his truck up the hill to return to her house, she said nothing. She decided she would ask them merely to have a cup of tea with her before venturing forth once more, but Wayland began drinking liquor right away, and became talkative, explaining about the depression he had suffered when his wife died and how here, in this high place, he was shaking off that sadness at last, so they both talked about being alone in the world. They did the outdoor chores together, and she cooked supper.

After supper Paula bathed Jonathan, put him in the washtub there in the kitchen and used creek water mixed with kettle water. He was a handsome fellow, was beautifully built—as was his father, Collie knew—had sleek, firm flesh without a scar. Paula was lathering him with the soap Collie's sister-in-law Gloria had made the previous summer, a soft soap she had scented, perhaps overscented, with pine.

"You might as well bathe next," Wayland told Paula. When Paula said no, she wasn't going to strip naked and bathe in this tub, he said, "Well then, Collie can bathe next." It was the first time he had used her first name.

Collie strangled on a piece of biscuit she was eating. She had been taking the food off the table. "No, thank you."

"I tell you the truth," Wayland said, adjusting his body to the rocker, "I've had a nice supper just now, or I'd go in that creek."

"Why, that water's cold as ice," Collie told him.

"I can last maybe a minute or two, even in winter ice water," he said. "The cold stiffens you, slows your heart, did you know that?"

"I'd say it'd stiffen me, all right," Collie said.

23

"I might go in sometime later," he said. "It'll kill you, you know that, Collie? Cold water'll kill you, given half a chance."

"Then don't you risk it, Mr. Jackson," she advised him.

Now and then she and Wayland would touch each other, a hand would rest on a hand, which surprised and thrilled her. Several times she noticed him watching her, and she found herself looking at him, seeking him out as well, with questions in her eyes. There was no certain question.

Paula took Jonathan to the back room to dry him, to roll him in towels and powder him and diaper him, and it was during this spate of privacy that Wayland said, "The horse that's been in the barn, Collie, was it yours?"

"No," she said at once, a tightness coming to her throat. "I have none."

"Small riding horse, I would judge from its prints. Was stabled there briefly."

"What horse is that?" she said, frantically trying to get her mind to settle into a form.

"In your barn, Collie," he explained simply. "There's been a horse kept there. Was it your brother Young's?"

"No," she said. "Young stables his riding horses at Papa's barn."

He poured himself more brandy and put a splash in a cup for her as well. "Was it the other man's, the one you don't discuss?"

Collie glanced away uneasily. "Why, I don't know."

"Well, there's been a horse out there, that's all I mean," Wayland said.

She did feel that indeed his comment had been casual, that he had not attached special importance to it at first, but now was alerted by her evasiveness. If he had become angry, or had been upset about her secretiveness, if he had gone stomping away, she re-

24

alized, her hopes would have shattered like a teacup in a thunderstorm. She waited expectantly to see what direction his mood would take.

"There's a man's razor back of that pitcher on that shelf," Wayland said, nodding toward the northeast corner of the room. "Is that his, too, Collie?"

"What razor?"

"Why, Collie, it's on the shelf there. Go look, if you want to."

"No, I don't want to look at a razor. Why would I want to do that?"

"Well—" He turned to stare at her, to seek meaning from her.

"I told you before all that's to be said, Mr. Jackson," she said, speaking in a tight voice. "My brothers ask me every time they get the chance, and of course my mother is angry with me and my father is hurt, as he'll admit on any invitation. It's been the beat of him, he says."

Paula brought Jonathan into the room, and Collie at once busied herself at the sink, but Wayland sent Paula outdoors to get his pipe from the rock room, then he somewhat apologetically said to Collie, "I didn't know the fellow had come here to your house, you understand, Collie, that's all. I had an idea of your meeting by chance, or your being forced to it. But this fellow came to the house, did he?"

"Why, I never said."

"I'm not trying to pry, Collie, but I didn't know you cooked for him, same as me. You make bread for him, I suppose, the same way?"

Her hands were trembling so that she thought she really might break a dish.

"I didn't know you'd sit around with him, drinking liquor, as now," he said.

"I've been known to drink with him, Mr. Jackson. My father permits a woman to drink if she isn't bearing or nursing, though I was never served as

25

much as my brothers, seemed to me."

"And he would get drunk, like I am getting drunk now, Collie, here in your house, that's all I meant."

"Young taught me first to drink. Young and me always have been explorers of everything around us."

Wayland said softly, "The man has some rights. That's all." He made his way to the brandy bottle and poured some more into his glass.

Thoughts twirling in her head, Collie returned to her chair at the fireplace. "Maybe if you have a clock in your truck, sometime you can mount it on that wall, Mr. Jackson. I can move those coats out of the way. I miss hearing a clock tick. Not home without a clock ticking, not to me." She glanced at him uneasily. He was lost in thought, was frowning down at his brandy glass in his hand. "No, it wasn't in this house, Mr. Jackson, that I first met with him," she said, speaking directly to him. "I moved up here just before Jonathan was born. I came up here and swept out the place while I was carrying Jonathan. My mama would cry so much, and the baby was— She had wanted me to try to lose it. And she kept leaving open Bibles in the room, to save me from the devil, I suppose. I don't know."

"Your mama believes in devils, does she?"

"She believes in anything she reads about in the Bible, whether it's manna from Heaven, or flooding the earth, or spirits, or anything in between. She told my brother Gudger that Jonathan's father must have been the devil himself."

"Gudger is your oldest brother?"

"So I said no, it wasn't the devil, though the devil had tried on numerous occasions to win me over." She laughed quietly; even so, there was strain in her manner. "I said he had tried on three different walks during last summer to grab me, but I outran him."

"Outran the devil? Don't think she would believe that."

"Gudger is my brother that has the store. He's taken over most everything else, too—the fur trade, the herbs, has even started selling gasoline, says it's all part of the store, which makes Milton and Young sick to their stomach. Milton says any part of the store is worth more than the smithy when it come to making a living up here."

The room was glowing with light and was warmer than a woolen bed—that bed there, her bed, where as she knew she had often lain with her lover, had often made love there, including a few weeks ago, the night he told her he was leaving, was going up to Kentucky to see a piece of land he was interested in, then he would meet two men in Tennessee and hunt game on his way in. He said he would see her again in good time.

"I see a pretty woman," Wayland said to her.

The words slowly took hold. "You mean me, do you?"

"Pretty woman."

"Wonder where Paula is."

"Probably got the point and stayed in our room."

"What point is that, Mr. Jackson?"

Just then Paula appeared at the door, put his pipe and tobacco on the table. He told her she could go on to bed, which surprised her, but she obediently washed her face and hands at the sink, then started out, pausing at the doorway to see if he had changed his mind. "I'm scared out there by myself," she admitted.

"No, you're not. Jesus'll take care of you," he said. "Haven't I told you that?"

She closed the door behind her and could be heard walking slowly, a measured step at a time, along the yard boards. "Just blink a few times," Wayland called after her, "and you'll find me there."

Collie started to put away the soap tray.

"Now here, wait a minute," he said, speaking kindly. "I've not bathed yet."

She turned on him, surprised. "You intend to bathe tonight?"

"Thinking about it, in a little while. I've been sweaty. Don't want to offend you."

There was a quaint, almost shy smile on his face which she couldn't quite interpret. "What you thinking? What do you mean, offend me?"

"I have a few personal thoughts," he admitted. "Only thoughts a man might have of an evening in a fire-lighted room with a woman he's...attracted to."

"Is that a proposal, Mr. Jackson?" she asked simply.

"I suppose men around here would do differently, would simply take hold. Am I doing it wrong?"

She slid the soap tray onto the shelf, then paused. She turned to look down at him, weighing the matter. "I'm not going to deliver another baby, Mr. Jackson. That would be a tragedy for me, as you can understand."

The playful smile was fading slowly.

"That's one reason Jonathan's father and me fall out so often; he won't understand. I'm still trying to recover my senses since he was here last time. I told him looks like all you want is my bed." She hadn't meant to say all that, and she wasn't sure where she had left herself in his thoughts, either.

"I understand what you're saying," he told her.

"I'm really a private person, and have always been."

"Yes," he whispered, nodding. "Even so—"

"No need for me to claim to be a virgin, but there's only one man I've ever been with. I want you to know that. I'm not what's called a loose person."

"I didn't mean you were."

She came closer still, stood close to him and looked down into his face. She leaned forward and kissed him on the lips, the gesture soft and mild and dear, and even while she backed away to the other fireside chair and sat down, her gaze still met his. "I'll have to say no, Mr. Jackson." When he nodded, she said, "I'll shave you now, if you like."

"Yes, it'd be all right," he said.

She heated water and mixed up a froth of lather, using the scented soap. She took down the razor from the shelf without comment. She pulled a towel around his shoulders and moved him to a chair nearer the hearth. She lathered his face, working the lather into his several-days growth of beard, her fingers lingering. As she shaved him she plopped the wads of lather into the hearth ashes, but her eyes were always on him, on examining his face as she worked, nodding as the razor revealed the contours of it and the small scars. She shaved his neck last, the razor raspy on the growth there, then she used a warm towel to soothe his skin. She dried his face carefully and rubbed his face with her fingertips, all the while watching him, letting him know she cared about him.

He drank more brandy; she kept pouring more into his glass. About nine o'clock he got to his feet, somewhat unsteadily, made his way to the shelf where the soap cup was, made his way to the door, the cup in one hand and his brandy glass in the other. She called out, surprised, "Where are you going, Mr. Jackson?"

He turned slowly, cast a thoughtful gaze on her, then went on out.

She gathered up two towels, borrowed the lantern from the stone room, where Paula was asleep, and followed his path to the creek. She found him standing behind a rhododendron bough, having discarded his shoes and shirt. He asked her where the

29

deepest pool was, and she replied and said it was about three feet deep, that was all. In the yellow lantern light he began to drop his other clothes, item by item at his feet, until he stood naked.

Below them the flashing creek water was aflame with lantern light. Abruptly he flung his body forward and shattered the creek's surface, spraying water, and shattering the light, his voice shouting out, defiant of all of life's incredulities and challenges. He barrel-rolled in the water, found a footing, stood up yelling, enraged, shocked, renewed, burned clean. Collie began laughing out of relief. "Soap," he said. "Where's the soap?" She held the cup so he could scoop out some of the soft paste. He lathered his body, entertaining himself with her laughter and his own chuckling and occasional shout of sheer joy.

Paula came running from the stone room, asking what on earth was the matter. Collie set her to work washing out her father's shirt and pants, soaping them quickly and tying them to bushes where the creek would flow through them. Abruptly Wayland once more barrel-rolled in the water, rinsing himself, and walked toward the rock where they were standing. He was waist deep in the water, the lantern light yellow on his skin, and was talking about how warm the air was. His chest and head were in an oven, he said.

He wrapped towels around himself as he climbed onto the blue rock where they stood, where the lantern was set. "Where's my clothes, where'd they get to?" he asked, looking through half-closed eyes at Collie, clutching the towel around his waist. "Collie, I feel clean now," he told her, suddenly smiling. He saw his clothes soaking in the water. "Hey, hey," he called out, "hey, where are you, what you doing?" He began laughing. "They look like big fish down there." He felt his arms, his chest. "Air'll warm you," he whispered, staring about.

Collie said, "I'll give you one of my gowns to wear tonight."

"Oh, hell," he said. "A gown?" he roared.

"Well, it's nothing but a nightgown, in its own way. Your clothes will dry on the hearth by morning."

"Oh, to hell with it." He was renewed, he was warm. "Ahhhhhhhhhh," he moaned contentedly, drugged of mind, dizzy as he began moving barefooted up the slab of rock.

Dressed in a white gown with blue lace at the neck, he sat by the fire, Collie and Paula hovering over him. "Be many a trout in that creek wake up surprised, once that soap strikes their nostrils. Be pine-scented trout by morning. Soap's going to clean all those trout skins, make them shine." Rocking, laughing, he didn't even need to drink. He had passed into a world crazy on its own. "Going to wash those fish and perfume them with pine, you hear?" Suddenly he took a new tack. "Collie, I'll never bathe again. That is the last bath I ever mean to take. That's it for me."

Collie plopped into a chair, rocked back and forth, laughing.

"Never bathe again. I'm Samson shorn of hair."

She poured more brandy for him. "No, you've just been shaved, Mr. Jackson. You were shaved already, so I can see how pretty you are."

Laughter possessed him again, new peals erupting whenever he looked at her. Paula was laughing with them. Lost somewhere in the mighty music of their voices was the reason for them to laugh at all. Never bathe again. How pretty he was. Three or four words could set him off again, or merely a look, his showing off his profile or his gown-clad figure. Blobs of fireplace shadows were moving, tilting.

Finally quiet came to them, rest, the fire popping

drops of water into steam as his clothes dried on the hearthstone. How silly we are, she thought. Will we ever again be as silly as tonight? When was I silly last time? About—oh, about two years ago, seemed like, sometime before I fell in love. Pretty man in firelight, handsome face. "Have more brandy?" she said.

"Where's the soap cup? Down at the creek?"

"I don't know," she admitted.

The empty brandy glass slipped from his hand. "I'm tired," he said, and smiled at her. "I'll go to bed," he said. But for a while longer he sat there in the rocker smiling at her. Giggles, giggling, laughing with each other, all three lonely children at the edge of the wild forest, their lives meeting here in firelight and shadows.

2

Gudger, the big storekeeper, the oldest of the three brothers, was making his rounds about this time of night. He was a big-boned, heavy-set man, handsome and sweaty, and he had with him his bird dog, Preston, a small dog with fine vision and a good nose, possessing the added advantage of being quiet. After a busy day at the store Gudger valued solitude.

As he walked he liked to allow his mind to dwell on family matters. In the main they were old worries, and were companionable. He was well aware that others in the family found him grasping and possessive; he had examined himself and found that he was protective. While others found him to be overbearing and commanding, he found himself to be dedicated to good order. While others found him jealous and guarded, he found himself to be suspicious of surprises and changes. Take Young, for instance. Young was given to changes. One day he was interested in a mill, so a mill was built to replace the various tub mills and the horse-driven one at the Crawfords' back lot. By the time the mill was built, and a dam constructed, and a sluice made, and the grinding stones hauled in, and the belts and pullies and gears installed, Young had lost interest entirely. So that was Young, the community's miller.

Gudger and his dog stopped beside the widow's inn and listened for conversation from inside. Not even a whisper tonight. Probably the hot-blooded lady was in bed, seeking sleep. A hard-working woman, indeed, she had quality in all she did, and was attractive, too, had a special, appealing nature. Nobody denied that. Whether she could at her age snare Young, well, Gudger wasn't at all sure of that. She had known Young for four or five years, since her start at schoolteaching. Her teaching had appeared to Gudger to be more amorous than academic, in Young's case. They were in the hay together, or at least on a bed of pine needles, less than halfway through Shakespeare, and Young a mere sixteen.

He and the dog moved on, approaching Young's house slowly, not meaning to intrude on an occupied dwelling. Gently he pushed at the door. He called out. No answer from inside. He struck a match to an oil lamp, set the wick and carried it before him into the back room. Nobody here.

In the main room he set the lamp down before the fireplace and rolled a cigarette. The lamplight flickered life into the dozen animals old Jed Marshall had carved across the mantelpiece, and seemed to make them threaten and connive. The biggest beasts were the bear and the mountain lion. Gudger had suggested that elephants and tigers be included, but Young had insisted on confining the display to animals native to the North Woods.

A noise outside. Gudger in a swift swing crushed the cigarette and blew out the lamp. He moved stealthily to the front window.

A sow came out from behind the fence and sniffed at the gate.

Gudger grunted, relaxed. Why had he become so nervous, anyway? Always had been easily frightened. All his life, since he could remember, always conscious of danger.

He chased the sow off, sending a rock bounding after it, and walked on up the road toward Collie's. He never went all the way to her house, was well aware that she preferred privacy; in fact, he rarely went past the edge of her lot; however, he noticed there was a light on in her main room, that heavy smoke was filtering up from her chimney and he heard a man laughing. Sounded as if a girl was laughing as well. The sound of the laughter chilled his blood, confused him, so that he stood entranced, the unlit lamp dangling from a trembling left hand. He knew as a girl Collie had always tried to keep up with him and Milton, her older brothers, and had led Young into devilment, but she had been severely hurt because of the recent birth of Jonathan and would not entertain a strange man, surely. Even the Wrights couldn't flout the ways and wills of God and the community without suffering consequences.

He told his dog to stay, and moved farther into Collie's clearing, stopping each time he heard voices. Carefully, slowly, he moved past Collie's pigs' pens, so as not to arouse them. Yes, a man was laughing, a girl was giggling, Collie was laughing. He moved up close to the lower room of the house, where the baby slept, as he knew.

Everything was quiet all of a sudden. Then he heard a man talking. He could not make out the words, but he knew it was a man talking. He heard Collie speak.

A pig squealed. There by a bush a pig squealed where no pig was expected to be, and Gudger leaped back, scared, angry to be announced. The lantern striking against his hip and leg, he quickly made his retreat down the hill past the other pig lot, where these pigs were now squealing and grunting, alarming the world. He heard Collie calling; she was calling out from the house, saying who is it. Damned pig wasn't supposed to be tied to a bush. What sort of pig was tied to a bush?

On the way home he and his dog stopped at Milton's house, a five-room cottage made of rough-hewn lumber. Gudger found that Milton was asleep, but Gloria, his wife, was wide awake and, as always, was eager for chatter. She was a pert, strikingly pretty woman who was always being told she ought to be in picture shows. Gloria was not bothered by a deep mind, but she had instincts easily awakened. "Didn't know whether you'd stop by tonight or not, it being later than usual, but I've kept the water hot for tea," she told him.

He was still nervous because of the pig squealing and Collie calling after him. Of course, she didn't know for sure who it was prowling near her place, but the experience had unnerved him nevertheless. He chose a ladder-back chair one of the Plovers had made locally, moved it to a spot near the hearth where he could poke at the fire, stir it into colored pictures.

"I just got all my brood to sleep," Gloria said. She asked if there appeared to be any guests at the inn tonight.

"No, but there are people at Collie's," he announced simply.

Gloria responded with a shocked gasp. "Who's up there? A man up there? Are you and Milton going to allow that?" Often she referred to what Milton might do or allow, as if decision-making in the family needed to include him; in practice he rarely exerted himself. "She's become a whore, Gudger?"

"No, she's not a whore," he said. He drank tea and studied the fire. "I imagine Young will be back tomorrow and can find out who's up there."

"You didn't try to find out?"

"No, I don't want to spy on people."

Gloria studied him thoughtfully. "You think it's the man who fathered her baby?"

"Don't know," Gudger said. "Sounded like a man and a girl. Maybe there are others as well."

Gloria watched him thoughtfully, anxious to find a sign of concern in him. "You think she'll ever say who fathered her baby?"

"I imagine the father will show up. Had a new idea about that the other day, but the man I have in mind wasn't the one laughing and talking up there tonight."

"Who is it? What idea do you have?"

"I'm not saying yet, Gloria. I'm not certain yet."

"It's Young that loves her more than anybody else."

Gudger stared at Gloria for a moment, then smiled. "You're getting mean, Gloria?"

She shrugged. "Did you ever ask Young about that baby, if it was his or not?"

"Yes, I asked him," he admitted.

"What did he answer?"

"He answered no. Then he knocked the hell out of me."

She laughed, giggling. "Hurt you?"

"Hell, yes. I saw him fight Cole Campbell this summer—this was when they fell out from being friends—"

"A less likely pair ever to be friends—"

"They near about killed one another. Took place at the meadow barn, in the horse stalls and the yard and against the fences. They tore up the place trying to kill one another. I told you about it."

"I wish I'd been there," Gloria said, her eyes alight.

"Papa said very little, except that he never did like Cole, but old man Drury Campbell sent a hell of a

37

warning, said Young ought to be sent off somewhere."

"Was it Cole I saw at the store this afternoon?"

"No, he's traveling, I've heard. He's away somewhere."

They talked for a long while, she a willing audience interested in whatever he had to say. Only his
own mother listened to him with the same rapt attention. When at last he was willing to go home, she
helped him pull his wool coat on and she buttoned
it. She had a way of standing close to a man, looking
directly into his eyes and appearing to be defenseless. "Will you stop by tomorrow night?"

"You know I will." Awkwardly he kissed her on the
cheek, then suddenly hugged her tightly in a burst
of affection.

When he got outdoors, he ordered Milton's new
bear dog to leave his dog alone. No end to dogs
around here.

Normally he would go on home about this time of
night, but he was still nervous, was far from relaxed
by his walk. He stopped by the church to close the
doors. Almost every time he had ever checked on
them, they were open. There was something about
people up this way that preferred church doors to
stand open. He moved into the cemetery, his dog
growling as customarily he did near graves. Just
there was the grave of Tinker Harrison, the oldest in
the cemetery, buried with a slave to each side and
his wife at his feet. That combination afforded him
minimum staff, Gudger suspected. Harrison had
been a slave owner, the only one around this region,
and when he died, all his slaves were sent away except two, who were allowed on his orders to live out
their lives in retirement and then were buried near
him—so they could wait his table and make his
bed, do whatever slaves did, Gudger supposed. They
were house servants, not field hands, so presumably

Harrison wasn't planning to have a crop of any sort.

Over there lay the grave of the first Wright, who married Harrison's daughter Lorry and lived in the house, in fact had built the house that Collie used now, built it over a hundred and fifty years ago, about 1780. How much life had gone on since then, Gudger speculated, impressed with the weight of life and death.

He crossed the trade lot and stopped by his store to listen for any intruders. One night as a boy he had stood just over there, the night he saw the store ablaze. He was probably the first person to see it. All in a moment the back side of the store flared up like an oil torch, then in another instant it was burning on the side wall as well. Gudger saw his grandfather trying to get the front door open. The boy ran closer, answering his grandfather's cries for help, but stopped short, paralyzed. All this while the fire was coughing black smoke into the air. His grandfather, aflame, came onto the porch, stumbled down the steps, a moving, tottering torch, his arms held out to Gudger, his voice crying for help. Gudger couldn't move, his muscles were frozen in place, he was a mere dumb stump dug into the ground. His grandfather, pain engulfing, devouring him, sank down, burning, not ten feet away from the lad.

Tonight, as he often did, Gudger walked close to where the porch of the old store had stood. He could imagine himself kicking open the door, rolling his grandfather on the ground to put out the blaze and turning the rain barrel over, splashing water on him. Tonight he imagined being a hero, but actual life had not been that way.

He sank down on a bench at Milton's forge and bent forward on his stiffened arms, his hands cloaking his face, covering his eyes. Why did his memory so often try to kill him this way?

His wife, Helen, was in bed reading her leather-backed Bible, which he had given her for Christmas, the third such gift since they married. He admitted to having little imagination about presents. She was doing the book of Ezekiel. Why the Book of Ezekiel? he wondered. "That little print'll put your eyes out," he told her stiffly. She was always reading the Bible, had worn out several.

She said, "Did you see her?"

"No, what you think I am, a sneak, to go at night around other people's houses?"

"You did go to her place. I know you better'n that."

"No, I did not. That is, I didn't go close." He debated whether to tell her what he knew or not, decided he had better admit it all. "There was a man and a girl and maybe some other people at her house tonight."

His wife pursed her lips. "What man is it?"

"I don't know yet."

"Are you going to allow it?"

He ran a heavy, fat hand over his face. "Why ask me to change the ways of the world? What am I, the family's keeper?"

"I'd better go up there tomorrow and talk to Collie myself. She was here yesterday afternoon, sat in that chair, never mentioned a man might visit her."

"You wouldn't climb the hill," he said.

"I'll go first thing in the morning."

"Now, you stay out of this. My family won't concern you."

"Your family concerns both of us all the time. It's a full-time job worrying about your family."

"I'll talk to Collie tomorrow, if I have to go back up to her place."

"It's my family, too, did you know that?"

"No, it's not your damn family, either. Your family is Pattersons and are bedded down by this time of

40

night dreaming of finding money alongside the road."

"Don't you talk about my people," she said fiercely.

"Let me handle my own. Papa and me will handle this. We might come to need this man, whoever he is."

"Need him?"

"Collie needs a husband, if ever a woman did. She's not one who can go long sleeping by herself."

His wife was aghast; only gasps came out of her.

"Papa and me'll have everything straightened out by tomorrow noon dinnertime."

"You and your papa," she murmured, turning away from him.

"I know, I know." He took his shirt off and washed his hairy chest and under his arms, standing before the kitchen sink. He needed to wash his crotch as well; all day he had caught whiffs of his musky odor while working, but he wouldn't strip naked while his wife was awake. Even married to her all these years, going on sixteen, he didn't feel comfortable stripping naked at the kitchen sink and washing himself.

"What's that widow a-doing?" she asked.

"No business tonight," he said.

"Young not visiting her, either?"

"No. He's still in Asheville, I suppose."

"Better talk to him, too, if I was you."

"How in hell can I talk to everybody all in a wave? I'm not my brother's keeper."

"Then just stand aside and let everything take its own way. Be your father's man."

"Thank you," he said.

She looked over at him, surprised. "For what?"

"For being so helpful," he said.

In their cold bedroom, which his youngest daughters shared, he turned down the quilts and flopped his big body across his and his wife's bed to mutter his prayers, the same ones he had been taught as a boy. That was easily done and didn't get his mind thinking about his sins; he preferred to be clear of worries, at least as much as possible, so that as soon as his head struck the pillow his dreams could commence, and would be comforting.

3

At first Collie had thought it was Jonathan's father come home, and her blood had run cold, her breath had almost suffocated her with fear; however, he would have come pounding his way into the house, no sneaking away down the hill for him. If it had been Campbell hunters on their way home, as often happened, they'd stop to explain; Campbells were not secretive people, were always willing to declare their actions, except for Skeet Campbell, who was sneaky, but he was not altogether sane, either, seemed to her. It wouldn't be McGregors sneaking about at night; they sneaked about of a day, as a rule, and talked and drank at night, preferring their home fires to anybody else's. No, it was doubtless Gudger himself. Whatever star that brother had been born under, it was a guardian angel's; he saw himself as the protector of the family. Her father loved him, that was the trouble; her father always had favored his oldest, so Gudger had immense authority.

First thing in the morning, she was up and dressed, and with Jonathan on her hip was on her way. She was standing near the store before her father arrived there. Gudger was probably indoors by now. Somebody had stoked the wood stove; the chimney smoke was billowing. Probably Gudger was in there counting all his goods to see if anything was missing.

She walked quietly up the steps and pushed the door open. A little bell tinkled and she saw Gudger swing around at once to see who was entering. He was standing near the pay-out counter, was pulling an apron string around his heavy waist.

She went on inside, shifted her baby to her other hip. She opened a fresh box of saltine crackers and ate two of them, crunching them as loud as she pleased, knowing it irritated him—both her opening the fresh box and the crunching. She kept looking at him as if daring him to say anything to her.

Abruptly he began to laugh. "Who you got up there, honey?" he asked her.

"Come a man out of the woods, off that mountain," she said honestly. "And his daughter, name of Paula."

"Come in yesterday, did he?"

"Day before," she said, staring at him defiantly.

Gudger winced. "Leaving today?"

She opened a package of cheese, cut off a sliver and made a cracker sandwich. "Haven't had time for breakfast yet," she said.

"You have to expect the family to watch after you," Gudger explained reasonably. "You were inside there laughing, or I'd 'a come on in, but when you kept laughing..." He allowed the subject to dribble away out of thought.

She moved to the back window, waited there, showing her baby the birds at her father's bird feeder, among them a beautiful cardinal. Only when she saw her father leave his house, which was over at the far side of the field, did she walk the length of the store, step out onto the front porch. Without a word to Gudger she hurried toward the big field.

"We can tell him together, if you come back here," Gudger called to her from the porch.

She began to run, smiling to herself. She waved to her father, who waved back at her. He was wearing his heavy homespun suit, first time this winter, the one he had bought from his servant, Mavis Campbell—he had always used a Campbell to wait on him, having a Campbell for a servant appeared to please him immensely. He had paid a high price for the suit, claiming it was the best weaving he had seen since his mother passed away. She recalled many a time when he had embraced her, had held her as a girl, the soft wool of that suit caressing her. Her father was in his sixties now, a tall man, slender—he had watched his weight, arguing that no mountain person had a need to carry extra pounds up hills all his life. He had a mustache and had sported, until recently, a beard. He had shaved it off Christmas as one of the gifts to his wife, who had hoped he would try to look younger. He was a pipe smoker and cigar smoker, so he smelled of tobacco, but he smoked less and less these days. He was quick of mind and hand, but was careful in expressing opinions. He rarely argued an issue, merely stated his own view and let the world go its way.

They met in the field. He took both her and the baby in his arms and held them close for a long while, talking to her and Jonathan, saying it had been two days since he had seen them, and so many hours, and he had worried about them, had wanted to see more of them, that he loved them. He walked along with them, holding Collie's arm, carrying the baby, and listened as she told him about a new man coming off the mountain, mentioning her stone room, Gudger's visit, stolen clothes, a tumbling of ideas rushing out of her. He listened, saying nothing, only now and then nodding or making any other acknowledgment, his gaze on the ground before him as he walked.

At the gate to the trading lot, there near the store,

she stopped talking. They paused. For a while he thought over what she had said. Then he told her the man ought not to stay at her house another night, though she might want to keep the daughter there to help with Jonathan.

"I like him, Papa."

"Well, likes change from time to time." When he noticed that reply hurt her, he said, "I'm sure he likes you."

"Papa, I lay awake most of the night, worrying, and I have a request of you. I have one, that's all I have."

He nodded, waited.

"I want you to offer him a corner of the store, to start repairing clocks in."

The idea was like a hot wire touching him. "I couldn't take Gudger's store away from him."

"Papa, you've given Gudger the store, Milton a forge, Young a mill, and I'm your only other child—"

"I have that North Woods for you, for you and Young—a part for Young—"

"Papa, I need a corner of the store."

"Now, you're not going to have it." He touched the gate latch and the gate sprung open. "No, no." He went on through, turned to hand her Jonathan.

Obviously, he was finished with the matter, she could tell that. "Papa," she said defiantly, "I want a corner of the store for a week or two."

He started on, his shoulders hunched now, as if he were leaving an adversary.

"Papa, don't force me to leave here," she said, pleading with him.

He turned slowly. "I worry about you more than any child I have, Collie. Always you're into something I can't understand. You always plow your own furrow, get in trouble, get others in trouble. Your life is so complicated, and so secretive—"

"I'm trying to solve all that, Papa." Tears came to her eyes, which she resented. She fought against them desperately.

"You—" He hesitated, was himself almost in tears. "Your mother is deeply hurt. I admit I am, too."

"For a week, two weeks, a corner, a corner of the store."

"You make it sound so reasonable. But I don't even know this man, and you have him living at your house." He shook his head in pain.

"Papa, I am asking. I've not asked you for anything else, have I?"

"You've never asked for much."

"You told me once you wanted me to ask more of you, to let you help me."

"Not with a man I never saw, come off a mountain."

Jonathan started crying, and she put him to a breast, let him suck.

For a while Wright waited, debating the matter, silently. Wearily he considered her, an adamant daughter cut in his own hard image, nursing his grandson next to the field gate, tears in her eyes. "Well, I'll do what I can," he said, and moved on toward the store.

He stopped at the porch steps, she noticed. He held his hand on his chest, as if a pain were bothering him. She had not seen him do that before and it panicked her. She walked slowly, apprehensively toward him, stopped only when she was within touching distance of him. She put her hand on the hand he held on his chest, and she felt his heart beating with a fierce pounding.

"Does it hurt?"

"No, not a bit, but it beats hard at times, Collie. It's not serious." He patted her hand, pressed it against his chest. "We all have reminders of our bodies at times." He patted her hand, smiled at her.

47

"I'll arrange for the corner nearest the door, Collie. You send him down here with his tools. I know he'll be all right, if you like him so much."

She tried to find words to thank him. "I know Gudger won't like it."

He laughed suddenly, and the tension was removed, all in a moment. "No, I'll say not," he admitted, and went on up the steps without turning back.

Later that morning a reluctant Wayland approached the store. He had rarely felt a lack of confidence in himself; most all his life had been spent in familiar territory. Here he was at ten o'clock, tools in one bag, lunch in another, Collie and Paula bracing him one to a side, each of them appearing to agree that he was about to enter a lion's den.

For them he would do as ordered. For his own part, he would as soon park his truck some place and repair clocks on the truck bed, if repairs were wanted. Lord knows, he thought he had explained to Collie his reluctance to get involved with clock repairs at all.

Collie was once again telling him about Gudger, saying not to pay undue attention to Gudger, who got his feelings hurt easily, and to be respectful of her father, not to argue with him, nor with any customer, all of whom were armed, all carried pistols in their pockets—at least all the men went about armed, she said.

Several people in the trading lot had noticed this strange three-person group huddled near the bell tree, where the church bell was dangling from a low limb.

He approached the store with determination. As he moved into the store, a bell announced his arrival. Gudger—Wayland knew him on sight by his huge size—arose at once from a stool in back of a counter, his face reddening perceptibly as he tried to arrange a greeting. Wayland put his lunch bag aside, held out his hand to him.

Gudger looked him over with the practiced eye of one accustomed to evaluating strengths and weaknesses of strangers. He shook Wayland's hand, but without commitment. "I don't have a place ready for you yet," he said petulantly. He took off his apron. "Papa said you were to be set at the north window." He moved around the far side of the counter and approached the northeast corner of the store. Cans of paint had to be moved, a table had to be cleared of hardware. Gudger fell to work at once, Wayland helping, following his example.

"I'll pay you twenty percent," Wayland told him, trying to make conversation.

"Twenty-five," Gudger said at once. "That's for parts as well as labor?"

Wayland hadn't intended to include the value of parts, but he considered, said yes, he would include parts and labor.

"If that's what you think is fair," Gudger said, accepting without revealing any concessions of his own.

"I'm not a repairman by trade," Wayland explained, defending his prestige and emphasizing the temporary nature of the arrangements. "I'm a clockmaker."

Gudger shoved paint buckets and tools into piles near the yard-goods section. He wiped off the table, ran a cloth over the shelves, brought Wayland a chair. All in all, he did as well as anybody could, and quickly, too, then paused to survey the work. "Two weeks," he said, returned to his counter stool and at once busied himself with his credit ledgers.

Wayland had his tools arranged and was drawing a sign on a paper bag, one announcing his shop's purposes, when Mr. Wright left his favorite chair at the stove, moved past Gudger's counter without comment, came forward to introduce himself. He spoke kindly. He stood in the pool of sunlight near the front door of the store, uttering words of welcome, speaking in a perfunctory manner about this being an isolated village, away off from centers of trade; the store was the one center of trade, he said, so those who had clock needs would be able to make ready contact with him. All that while he watched Wayland, appeared to be estimating his value, seeking out any flaws. Once he took hold of a box of bolts that had been left under Wayland's table; he shoved that down the aisle to get it out of his way. "That'll make more room for your feet," he told him. After the brief visit he retreated to the wood stove, where he had a rocking chair, and began talking to a few elderly men who had gathered there to warm, to discuss politics, to trade.

"Your mother was fussing this morning about being left alone," Mr. Wright suddenly said to Gudger, speaking over his shoulder. "Where is Mavis? she kept asking me. I told her Mavis was often late, was getting old, like the rest of us, couldn't get her blood warm of a morning." He packed his pipe with tobacco, proceeded to puff gray smoke into the air. "Come a time when your mother'll have to grow up."

A Mr. Weaver came in, as Wayland noticed, took a chair near the stove and began to talk about land for sale just over the Tennessee line, about four thousand acres with several bold springs, a fair house and a four-stall barn. He was obviously inviting Wright's interest in the offering, but Mr. Wright was uninterested. Later to Gudger he said, "We have to take noon dinner today, soon as Young's back. We need to catch up on business for the week."

"He might be back today, it being Saturday," Gudger said.

"Gudger, you tell the new man to come eat with us so we can talk about Collie," Wright called.

Gudger looked up sharply. "You want strangers there?"

Wright got partway out of his chair, managed to focus his eyes on Wayland. "You come eat with us at noon, if Young's back," he said. Then to Gudger he said, "Send word to Mavis to fix for us."

Wayland had arranged a few tools on the table and had posted his handwritten sign. As the store's customers came and went, a few expressed curiosity about his work. Through the north window he could see Collie and Paula in the trading lot, Collie talking to first one person, then another, and he had no doubt she was trying to discover their clock-repair needs.

About eleven o'clock, after a miserable hour of in-activity, a Mrs. Starnes came up the steps of the store carrying a mantel clock, an Eli Terry, its pendulum and weights in a flour sack. This needs fixing, she said. She mentioned Collie had assured her he could fix anything. At once, three of the old men near the stove came forward to watch Wayland's procedure. Here I am, Wayland thought, the new boy on the block, with an audience for my first effort. He broke down the works so swiftly that the old men gasped. He sorted through the parts, discovered the problem, was able to make repair without difficulty. When he reassembled the clock, the steady ticking sound assured them that all was well.

No sooner was the woman out of the store than Mr. Wright approached the front, nodding to two customers who had ducked inside. He spoke to them graciously, with compliments, and stopped beside Wayland's table, his eyes glistening with curiosity. "How much did you charge her?" he asked.

Wayland shrugged apologetically.

The smile slowly faded. "You didn't trade with her, did you?"

"She offered me a chicken," Wayland admitted. "I told her it would be all right to wait until later, when she had the money to pay me."

"She won't pay you later."

"She won't?"

"No, she has you in her debt now. You want something from her, she doesn't want anything further from you." Grumpily he said, "I thought you knew your business."

"Repairing, no, I don't know that."

"Collie wanted you to have a place indoors. Now, indoors you can insist on money in payment. Out in the trading lot you have to settle for a trade. Most any out-of-doors place requires that, but if you are under a roof you get money for your work." He frowned critically. "Also, you work too fast, make it look too easy, Mr. Wayland."

"Sorry," Wayland said, smiling in spite of the seriousness of the incident. "The name is Jackson."

"Well, whatever it is." Wright took several pieces of stick candy out of the jar, broke them into pieces and passed them out to children on the porch, then he sought out his spot near the stove.

Not anything more for Wayland to do, it seemed. Collie and Paula worked their way near enough to the store that he could motion to them and they could talk to him through the glass. Collie said a man had gone to get his clock, to bring it in for fixing. From his window Wayland could study the faces of the other people in the trade lot, generally satisfied, healthy-looking people, all of them lean, the women especially pretty, maintaining their smooth skin and rosy coloring into old age. He watched one lady, eighty or older, walk spryly across the lot, bringing a quilt to trade for furs that were offered by an elderly man and his wife. She trooped into the store and sold the furs to Gudger in order to buy with cash sugar, salt, flour, vanilla extract, chocolate and five glass jars of snuff.

The store was about sixty feet long, Wayland estimated, and thirty feet wide. The main counter was to the right of the entrance, about ten feet from it, and another fifteen feet from the stove, placed near the middle of the room. There were shelves on both side walls, floor to ceiling, boasting a host of items, among them canned and bottled foods, boxes of shells, bars of lead for use in molding one's own bullets. There were rows of gleaming glass lanterns, as well as lamps and lamp chimneys, and wicks tied in lots of a dozen. There were hats and caps, folded jeans and work shirts, shoes and boots. There was a wall display of pottery jugs, plates, cups, saucers, bowls, serving platters, pitchers, all of them made locally, Gudger said, or nearby. There was a single bookshelf, chiefly for copies of the Bible, but also Wayland found a few copies of poets, among them Keats, Poe and Shelley, and five complete works of Shakespeare's plays. There were stacks of paper tablets. There were nineteen china plates imported from England. In addition to the shelves, there were bins for nails, screws, bolts, staples, and the like; there were rolls of barbed wire and two rolls of chicken wire. On the south wall were stretched hides, even now curing, and stacks of cured furs awaiting shipment—bear and deer were the majority, but there were all manner of small animals, including mink and beaver. Also on the south wall were several stuffed animals, in various states of challenge or repose, displays done by a Campbell in-law, a friend of Mavis, who claimed special knowledge of animals' coloring and habits. There were tables on which bedding was stacked, including muslin sheets and both down and feather pillows, made locally. There were two small areas for furniture, a chest of drawers that Mr. Caesar Plover had made from cherry wood, a corner cupboard, a pie safe, a kitchen cabinet with enameled work surfaces, a few chairs, two different sizes of bedsteads, all well made, most of them of solid woods, a few with veneered surfaces, and there was one example of marquetry, which Wayland examined carefully. All this, except the kitchen cabinet, was done locally, Gudger confirmed. "No, not by the Campbells," Gudger told him, ridiculing that idea. "They hunt and timber. When I say locally or nearby, I mean here or just downriver." There were leggings, saddles, hame strings, gauntlet gloves. Then there were various toys for children—not many, and those were well worn from use in the store. There was a box of artificial flowers, which Gudger had written the word *Germany* across; they didn't look like German flowers to Wayland.

The store had only two small windows in the back wall; the main windows were in the front, facing north, offering views onto the trading lot. The church supported the east side of the lot, the cemetery the west, and the main road traced the north edge of the lot, with wallows and deviations caused by traffic, hogs and the frequent rains. Off behind the church was Milton Wright's house and blacksmith shop. The windows at the front of the store were tall ones, perhaps twelve feet high, and had sections that could be opened at the top. Ladders were provided for that purpose, as well as for reaching merchandise on the high shelves. The store left the impression of being immense, far too large for one or two men to work successfully, but the customers seemed to know what they wanted and where items could be located, and they brought what goods they chose to one of the long counters for payment or credit entry. They pretty well waited on themselves, unless the goods had to be weighed, such as coffee beans or sugar, or had to be cut to size, as in the case of lace or calico or cheddar cheese.

Wayland saw Collie standing near the church doors, Paula nearby holding the baby.

He ordered a pair of pants, 28-inch waist and 28-inch inseam, from Gudger, and considered buying a few shirts, but decided to ask Collie's and Paula's opinion of them.

Finally, a Mr. Fletcher parked a 1930 Chevrolet coupe near the butcher tree, which was where the butcher in winter displayed his meats, and brought into the store a wall clock, which he presented to Wayland, the weights and pendulum still dangling inside. "How much will it cost to fix it?" he asked breathlessly. "It's been broke four years."

Wayland set aside the pendulum and weights, punched out the frame pens and removed the wood works. He saw the trouble at once, and so did Mr. Fletcher. Sometime or other, mice had built a nest of threads inside it. Wayland pulled out the nest and set the works into place once more. He put the weights and pendulum in a paper bag for easier carting. "That'll be—" The apprehensive face of Mr. Fletcher deterred him. "No charge," he said.

Mr. Fletcher let out a gasp. "Well, charity's not necessary."

"You just didn't know about the nest," Wayland explained.

"I'm not a charity case," Fletcher said, gathering up his possessions and angrily leaving.

Pretty soon Mr. Wright roused himself and came forward, peering ahead through the dusty air, his bright eyes finally fastening on Wayland once again. "Four years broke, is that the gist of it?"

"Four years. But it was never broke," Wayland explained.

"Four years is worth four dollars minimum," Wright said.

"There was nothing wrong," Wayland repeated.

"There's been something wrong for four years," Wright said. He appeared to be bothered by another matter, which he broached indirectly. "When I was a young man I made some spare money repairing pistols, and I found it wise to take in a broken pistol for private examination and repair, agreeing to return it fixed in five or six days. In some cases I could fix a pistol in five minutes, but since only I knew that and had kept it five days, the owner was prepared to pay a decent fee." He wandered on back toward the belly of the store, commenting to Gudger on the way. "He works too fast, I'm afraid." Beyond the main counter he paused to pay attention to a Mr. Ezra Tomkins, who wanted to buy the right to log black-walnut timber from the North Woods. "No, we'll save the North Woods for now," Wright told him. He waited on an elderly lady who wanted wheat flour and fresh yeast. He kept calling her Aunty Smith and measured out a generous weight, then let her sign for the payment. Once he had returned to his chair near the stove, Wayland, who was nearing the end of his patience, who never had been able to abide inactivity, approached Mr. Wright while he was rocking and conversing with his friends.

"You want me to assemble that millwheel for you?" he asked.

Wright's gaze swept up to him at once. "You know how?"

"Yes, I can assemble it for you."

"Wouldn't take more'n a few hours to do it, would it?" Wright asked, moving into a bargaining position.

"It'll be one day for me, and half a day each for two helpers."

"Helpers, what helpers?"

"Collie and my daughter."

Wright laughed. After a moment he said, "Collie won't be much help with a baby on her hip. Be a waste of money."

"Paula, my daughter, will watch the baby for her."

"Well, I'm paying her to help *you*." Wright spit into the sand box at the base of the stove. "You have noon dinner with me today? We'll talk about it then. Young'll be here. It's his mill."

That was the way they left the matter, but Gudger came over to the clock table in a few minutes and asked what his father had decided, what reply he had made about the wheel.

"It's all there, all the parts are there," Wayland assured him. "Not like making clocks, when you have to start from scratch."

"What sort of clocks you make?"

"Most of them are long clocks."

"Long clocks?"

"Long-case clocks. For hallways or parlors—"

"Grandfather clocks?"

"Except I don't put so much glass in mine. I leave the clock its privacy," Wayland said.

Gudger laughed about that, and later repeated the remark to a customer.

The business about the millwheel must have preyed on Gudger; he couldn't help accosting his father about the matter, even while others in the store listened.

"Who?" Wright demanded of him. "You say I've already hired somebody to assemble it?"

"You hired a man," Gudger assured him.

"I never hired anybody. That new man is the first to ask," Wright replied from his chair. "Milton a time or two promised to look it over—"

"Your son Young, you hired *him*. Your son Young is to operate the mill, and he's done nothing. All he

57

has to do is work there, instead of running all over the countryside shooting off his cock."

Wright gazed forlornly up at the store roof, where a bird was perched on a rafter above the winter-rye seed bins, and began quietly to utter speculations about the meanness in one man's heart for his brother.

"Ain't no meanness in mine, Papa. He's off drinking and lolling about, and he'll come back and charge us for his time delivering furs while you pay for his other work not being done. He'll let you do it all and go off courting old women—"

"Old women?"

"That inn widow Frazier is old enough to be his mother."

Nervously Wright retreated to the glass counter, pushed panes back out of the cutting area. "Does he still see her? You telling me he sees her after my talk with him?"

"God knows, it's unfair," Gudger said. "Of course he does."

"Well, it might be unfair," Wright admitted. "It just might be, Gudger. You've made your point." Murmuring, he wandered over to the gun section, returned three guns to the racks, locked the racks and stuck the key in his pocket. He moved on to the rear of the store, to a window offering a view of his house and the river. "Mr. Wayland, is that you at the gun racks?" he asked.

"Yes. I'm following you," Wayland admitted.

Wright grumbled to himself, his words lost in heavy feelings. Abruptly he called to Gudger, "I don't see how you can contend that a millwheel's not part of a mill, Gudger."

"Now, Papa, I'm only saying what's right," Gudger told him.

"You are telling me what you see to be right, but in my eyes the wheel is part of the mill. Two months

58

ago I paid for logs to be brought, a splash dam made—"

"It's not been part of the mill these last seven weeks. The wheel's in pieces up there at Young's house, in his yard."

"Now, once the mill is finished—"

"Papa, you try to give away, give away to Young, and you keep setting back provisions for Collie as well, while Milt and me work to get ahead, even to hold our own."

"Well, God save you, Gudger, I never provided anything for Collie except what's—"

"You said the other day to write a codicil for her new baby."

"Well, it's her baby, it's my grandson."

"But a baby in order to inherit should be legal. Let her first say who the father is, by God."

Wright threw up his hands in exasperation. Of course, the conversation had been overheard by Wayland and the men sitting about the store, but neither Wright nor Gudger appeared to mind. "Well, Lord," old Wright murmured, then winked at Wayland. "He told me once he never got jealous."

"It's only right, Papa," Gudger called out to him. "A person not legal ought not to receive a grand-child's legal portion."

"That old rule has to do with blood kin. The child's blood kin enough. He's certainly Collie's baby. It's who else he's blood kin to that I would give a pretty penny to know." He left the back win-dows, entered the fur section.

Wayland followed, curious about him, attracted to him, to his mixture of strength and softness, posses-siveness and generosity.

Wright turned to him abruptly. "Mr. Wayland, we've paid the price a hundredfold for allowing that clan of Campbells to settle across the river there." He had stopped to stare out a window at their land.

"They work hard, they timber the best you ever saw, have been known to construct a flume several miles long and shoot logs down it, some of the logs five feet through the middle. So they're a capable people, but they live without books, without any other comfort, so far as I can tell. They're a hand-to-mouth people. They keep their word, except they promised my father to sell their furs to our store and they've not done it since the fire. Old Drury, he got angry back then because somebody claimed he and his father had set the fire. Well, I never thought he would do that himself, but we did trace footprints to the river afterward."

"I understand," Wayland murmured.

"That was a time of the deepest feelings, the time when my father burned to death."

"Yes, sir," Wayland said, respectful of the sorrow in his manner.

"Is that Collie out there at the field gate?" Wright asked suddenly.

"She's been hovering all about this morning," Wayland said, amused by her frequent appearances.

"I've often thought she ought to be invited to the noon dinners on Saturday, you know it, Mr. Wayland, but here men don't bargain with women, never have. Is that the English influence, the Scotch-Irish, or the German—what is it? My mother never even sat down to the dinner table with her husband and sons, nor did my sisters."

"Mr. Wright, if I were to make clocks away back up here, where is the nearest shipping point?"

The elderly man turned slowly, stared at him.

"I make clocks, that's my living," Wayland said. "You have wood craftsmen up here who could make the cases—"

Wright said, "I have relations in Asheville who

run a store. They might be willing to ship for you. Young knows all of them."

"Do they visit up here often?"

"No. My niece had people living in a cove nearby, but they're dead now, as of a few years past. People who leave rarely come back. When Papa died in the fire, my brothers and sisters and cousins returned for the funeral, then they all went away again and I was left with it. They didn't need it, they said. They didn't want to be tied down here. Of course, we've always had a family tradition that those who leave do not inherit any of what's here." He began wandering about once more. He returned two pair of boots to boxes, straightened out the medicine shelf, which stocked patent medicines, coughing cures, aspirin, paregoric....He paused to stroke Othello, a black cat, then spoke kindly to a blind dog named Chester.

At eleven-thirty Collie came indoors. She had left Paula at the church, sweeping, she said. She opened a jar of pickles and offered Wayland his pick of them. "I saw you outdoors, saw you from time to time," he mentioned to her.

She opened a can of potted meat and a loaf of bread, pointedly rejecting Gudger's critical stares, and offered them to Wayland. He explained about being invited to eat his noonday meal at her father's house, which surprised her, as he could tell. She made sandwiches for herself and Paula.

After she left, Gudger stuffed slices of bread back into the cellophane bag she had opened. "Comes in here, takes whatever she wants," he murmured.

Just before noon Wayland rejoined Mr. Wright, who was sitting near the stove. "Ever think about putting a clock on the church?"

Two of the other men sitting nearby stopped their conversation, and Mr. Wright lifted his gaze to consider Wayland speculatively. "We have no steeple," he said. "What we need a steeple for? my papa always said. Buy more Bibles and hymnals instead. That was his view."

"I can put a church clock in a steeple," Wayland said, "but I can't do that to a hymnal."

Wright smiled. "Bring it up at noon," he said agreeably. He turned to look across the store to see if Young had arrived. "Where the devil is he? He knows not to miss a Saturday."

"If you have a steeple made—" Wayland said.

"It might be too dear for this community, Mr. Wayland."

"I can put three or four faces on it," Wayland said.

Mr. Wright occupied himself with his pocket watch, opening the gold cover, holding the watch face up to the stove light. "Bring that up to the meeting, too," he said disinterestedly.

"Milton can make faces for it, as well as hands and a pendulum."

"Well—you can use Milton, you say?" Wright asked.

"I'll make the clockworks at Collie's barn, or wherever I set up shop, and we can cast the faces, the pendulums, the weights at Milton's."

"I— Can you use Milton, for a face? I worry about Milton's doing so much routine work, shoeing horses, repairing mowers. A man's life dozes when it has too much dull work, just as it flies off crazily if it has too little."

"Yes, we need Milton," Wayland assured him.

Wright at once moved to the front of the store to get a look at the church. He even stepped out onto the porch for a better view.

Wayland followed, watching him, realizing Wright was interested. He stopped close to him at the porch rail. "Mr. Wright," he said quietly.

Wright was concentrating on the situation, was imagining a steeple and clock. "Yes, Mr. Jackson? What do you want now?"

"I can make it strike the hour," Wayland said.

4

Young Wright swung out of a friend's car at the bridge; the store's pickup truck had run out of gas four miles away, and he had hitched a ride. He walked toward his parents' sprawling house, along the riverbank which he loved, past places he had swum when a boy, climbing pasture fences often crossed before. At his father's stables he stopped to give each horse a friendly pat and a share of grain.

He was crossing his parents' yard when the maid, Mavis Campbell, let out a yelp from inside the house. She came running to greet him, her arms extended, a formidable, big-boned, somewhat hefty woman, half bald from sweating over a kitchen range all her life. He hugged her, tried to lift her, finally got an arm under her knees and carried her, staggering, or at least pretending to stagger, to the house, calling out for everybody to come to their wedding, that he was marrying Mavis Campbell today.

A boisterous spirit, Young's was; he was a handsome man of twenty—no, not even twenty for another few weeks, a genuine, independent, wasteful, celebrating spirit.

His mother received him with eagerness mingled with melancholy sighs, with moaning reminders that she wasn't well, had not been well, was having some trouble with her back, her shoulder, her leg.

"You're a multiple invalid, Mama," he told her, ushering her into the kitchen, the warmest room, and to her favorite chair. "Rocking is the best exercise," he told her. "That's reviving for every muscle in the body." He stood back from her, told Mavis to stand back as well. "What a pretty woman. Look at her, Mavis. Don't even talk about age. Most women look old by the time they're Mama's age, but not a wrinkle on her face. Look at those red cheeks. Going to put you in a magazine, Mama, doctors come up here with cameras to see you, but they won't be able to represent you well enough to suit me."

"Oh, my Lord," she moaned, pleased beyond bearing, even though she knew Young was part show. "Young, why are you so late getting home? Your father—"

"Fountain of youth, that's what my mummy's found."

"She *is* pretty," Mavis agreed, leaning back against the sink, arms folded across her breast. "You had her eyes, Young, looked like her even as an infant."

There he stood, three inches over six feet tall, as well formed a figure as had ever been seen in this country, and she was recalling his helpless infancy. He beamed at her, his eyes crinkling, just as his father's did sometimes, as if he were amused at his own amusement. "Go on, Mavis, tell me about myself."

His mother, irritated by his attention to the maid, said, "Now sit down there, Young, and stop talking. I want to tell you about your sister."

Young received that warning guardedly. "Pregnant again?" he asked dryly.

Mavis let out a surprised laugh, which she tried to subdue, but Annie Wright struck the arm of her chair angrily. "Don't you joke about anything as serious as that little boy. He's not going to be a happy child, I can tell that already—"

Young humbly sat down across the hearth from her. "Go on, tell me about the disasters ahead for him."

"Collie's taken in a new man," Annie Wright said sternly.

The news affected him, all right. His smile folded slowly, as if being pinched, leaving him solemn.

"Helen came to tell me."

He moaned in his chest. "I don't believe this."

"Why are you so nervous all the sudden, Young? I've never known you to clam up so sudden. Well, I'm glad to know you do care about your sister, at least her, if nobody else."

"Who is it, Mama? Is it someone I know?"

"He's given to laughter, Helen tells me."

"Well, damn it, does he have a name?" Young asked sharply.

Mrs. Wright withdrew into her shawl. "See how he's afraid for her?" she said to Mavis. "See how scared he is?"

When word reached the store that Young was over at the house, promptly Gudger and Mr. Wright put on their coats. Wayland stacked his tools under the table, and the three men started across the field. Wright and Gudger began talking at once, personally, intimately. "Kill the prodigal calf," Gudger was saying. "Prepare for the return of the son that was lost."

"It's not a prodigal calf, but a prodigal son," his father corrected him. "Young's not been gone but five days. A man's not considered lost in only five days."

"Mavis will have food stacked up high as the second shelf."

Mr. Wright unbuttoned his coat, let it flap as he

walked. Middays were sometimes warm, even though the nights were bitter. "Mavis loves him. Mavis loves him because Young's beautiful as a human being. So was I once. So were you, though not as beautiful as Young."

"I cut off my curls, Papa."

"I love to see him dash about. Ours is a small bowl for him, I'm afraid."

At once Gudger became considerate of his father's worry. "You think he'll leave here, Papa?"

"What a loss," Wright said. "Mr. Jackson, do you ever dream of being in your teens again? I dream sometimes of being a mere boy, and whenever I do, it's about him I dream. Not about myself, nor you, Gudger, bless your heart, whom I love more than anybody else. It's true, Gudger. You and I have been in that store together for fifteen years, arguing life along. I argue with you more'n with your mama. However, I *dream* about Young; I smile at all the women, I scythe the weeds of the world, I change wrongs to right, I walk only the high roads, I cross rivers with dry boots."

"Papa, what do you say?" Gudger said, embarrassed.

"I wouldn't go back to being eighteen, nineteen again if I had to be as insecure and hurt as I was then, but what if I could go back to being like Young at nineteen? There you are, there you have the difference."

Milton had left the forge. Wayland could see a man pulling on his sheepskin coat as he hurried across his yard.

"Mr. Jackson, you like to dream?" Mr. Wright asked, taking hold of Wayland's elbow, pulling him forward to be in step. "I long to get to it of a night."

Young came into the back yard to greet his father. There was special affection between them, Wayland could tell, but neither man touched the other in greeting. They were guarded one of another, and respectful. They talked about the furs Young had delivered to the King Store in Asheville, uncritically discussed the transaction. Wayland was introduced as Mr. Wayland, a clock repairer. He tried to mention that he was not a Wayland and was not a repairer, but Wright began talking about the church steeple, a new church clock being in prospect.

Young showed little interest, anyway. "Gudger, you've lost weight," he said, poking gently at Gudger's belly. He led the big man indoors. "Mama, I've brought you your best-looking son," Young announced, introducing Gudger, who sputtered out an apology for his brother's well-known exuberance. "Mama, turn around in that chair and look at this figure of a man. Gudger, don't step back." He brought Gudger up before the fireplace. "Look over the body on this man," Young said to Annie. "They make bodies in Detroit that are not as big as this. In Norfolk they float ships—"

Gudger broke out laughing. "Don't pay any attention to him," he told Wayland.

"Weighs about four hundred fifty pounds, would you say?" Young said to his mother. "This was in you once, Mama."

"Oh, Lord," Gudger moaned. "I weighed—last time I weighed was two hundred thirty-five."

"Look at those feet. Walk a hundred miles in a few steps. Look at that right thigh. Well, take either one of them, right or left. Must be two feet around."

"Ah, Lord," Gudger said, amused, embarrassed but pleased.

"Look at that waist. Does it still bend, Gudger?"

Gudger laughed out loud. Obviously he didn't mind being made the center of attention, regardless of the reason.

"Chest that makes oak trees look scant. See here, Mama, see the tits through his shirt." He pulled

Gudger's coat back to show her. "Look at that neck, like the bull you had, Papa—what was his name, the one that drowned himself? And best of all, here, see that pretty face, Mama."

Gudger's face had a silly grin on it just now, pride mingled with defiance.

"Well he *is* a handsome man," Annie admitted.

"Gudger, turn your face more to the left, that's it. What you say, Mama? Now turn it to the right . . ."

Mrs. Wright was staring up at her son, not sure whether she found the matter serious or amusing.

"Mama, you've got here the prime example of a man born out of a woman's womb, and it was your own womb, Mama. Stand up, Mama—" Young said.

"My womb—"

"Here, come stand beside him."

Guardedly she took her place beside Gudger. She was a foot shorter, a foot or so thinner; she was a slight, frail bird indeed, beside this one.

"Papa, look what you helped do. All in a few seconds, too. See that pair, would you?" He began to laugh, overcome by his own ingenuity. "Papa, set that picture in your mind. Let it be a warning to you."

Everybody began laughing, guardedly at first, then boisterously, even Gudger and his mother, the laughter bubbling over their defenses, everybody except Wayland, who was mystified. Mavis even began striking a pot with a spoon, her way of sharing excitement. Poor Gudger, flustered, proud, didn't know quite how to remove himself from the shackles Young generously had put on him.

Milton arrived, came poking his way past Wayland at the door, exhaling deeply of the chilly air. When he came upon the family display, the daguerreotype in real life, the picture of his frail mother and his more than ample older brother, he stopped, stymied in place. "What in heaven?" he said, speak-

69

ing mildly, as was his habit.

Then it was over. Suddenly the event was flat, life-less. Young himself deserted it. He busied himself at the stove, tasting Mavis' food. "How's the store doing, Papa?" he said.

Wayland was introduced to Milton and Mrs. Wright, not as Collie's friend, but as a new clock man. Wright himself led Wayland into the dining room off the kitchen, where the big, round oak table was set for five people. The table already had on it dishes of honey, butter, preserves, sugar, a pot of thick cream. Mavis brought in a basket of biscuits, then went back for the beef, the boiled onions, and the other dishes she had prepared. Wayland took a chair beside Mr. Wright's. Milton came in, hung his sheepskin coat on a wall stob. Gudger, after washing in the kitchen sink, came into the room, drying his hands on a towel. Young could be heard in the kitchen, laughing, complimenting Mavis. Finally, he joined them, greedily surveyed the food before him. Only after he sat down did he notice Wayland. "You a lawyer?" Young asked him.

"No, not that I know of," Wayland replied.

"You a doctor?" Young asked.

"No, no," Wayland said. "I'm a clock man."

Young's smile widened. "What time are you?" he asked.

"I make clocks," Wayland said.

"You passing through, is that it?" Young asked.

"I once thought so," Wayland admitted.

Young unfolded his linen napkin. His gaze rested on Milton's coat. "You still wearing that coat, Milt, when you know how fast a ram can run?"

Milton laughed out loud; all the men started laughing fit to be tied. As their laughter died out, Wayland thought he heard Collie's voice in the kitchen. Yes, it was Collie, just beyond the doorway, talking with her mother, he was sure of it.

The men were passing the dishes around, serving themselves. Young said, "Collie ought to be invited to these meetings, Papa."

"A woman's mind is different from a man's," Gudger said.

"She has as much right here as I do," Young said.

"Probably would make as much sense," Gudger admitted.

"You've not had a bastard baby," Milton told Young, and winked.

"Not a joke, not about that boy," Wright said. "Every time the door opens at the store, and a man comes in, I wonder if he's Jonathan's father. I can't go to church without looking out over the pews, thinking which one of the men was it who got to her. A young fellow came to the store last Monday—was it Monday, Gudger? He asked for a loan to buy a used car he found in Burnsville. He's Tison's oldest son, but it wasn't Ed he was asking. Why not ask his own father for it? I wondered. Ed's not a poor man."

"Hell, no," Gudger said.

"Why ask *me* for it? I asked the young man that and he replied that he thought I would understand. Now, did he do it or not?"

"Buy the car?" Young asked, a devilish grin appearing suddenly.

"You know what I mean. Did he seduce Collie and she have his baby, or not?"

"I'd say not," Gudger said. "I don't believe he could handle her."

All this while Wayland was conscious of Collie being outside the room, talking with Mavis and her mother. He couldn't, from where he sat, understand what the women were saying, and he hoped they couldn't understand what her brothers and father were saying. As for himself, to hide his concerns, he leaned over his plate and ate.

"Young knows who the father is," Wright said.

"I never have claimed to know," Young said, surprised.

"You told me once who it wasn't. You went down a list as long as from here to that door."

"Only my opinion, Papa."

"No, it was more'n that. Who was it, Young?" He had laid his fork and knife down and was staring at him, pleading with him.

Young calmly returned his gaze for a few seconds, then shrugged. "Some say it was me, Papa."

Wright struck the table, slapped it so hard dishes were jarred. "Don't say that again."

"You've heard it, you know what's been said."

Wright himself got to his feet and shut the door. "I don't care what any Campbell says."

"No, sir, but it's not a secret what they say," Young said.

"I paneled the windows on my south side to keep from looking at the bastards—"

"We're just now talking about our bastard, Papa," Young said firmly.

Wright considered lashing out at him again, but instead settled back in his chair and slowly raised a little brass bell and rang it, signaling Mavis. "We're talking about my grandson as well."

Mavis took his order for a glass of buttermilk, which he told her he required in order to settle his stomach. "And shut the door when you leave," he said.

The business session began while the men were eating. Wright brought up several matters for disposal, among them two loans that were overdue. It was decided that Young would visit the delinquents and arrange a settlement.

There was a difference of opinion about a boundary between Wright and Turner land, and Milton said he would look into that. He had a basic knowledge of surveying and owned a transit.

There was a feeling on Gudger's part that the McGregors were selling many of their furs elsewhere. It seemed unlikely to him that they could have spent the season hunting and had so few pelts to show for it. "What they do is run up a big bill all year at the store, then come cold weather take the best furs to Tennessee, to their own people, so we have no way to collect what's owed."

Milton said, "Too late to put them off the land, is it?"

"Too late by law, whatever law there is up here," Gudger said.

"We've made two mistakes, both because of furs," Wright acknowledged. "One's called the Campbells, and the other is called McGregors." Everybody seemed to agree with him on that. "Mr. Wayland here has started repairing clocks," he announced, referring to a list of items on a slip of paper, "has rented a corner of the store—"

"Name is Jackson," Wayland reminded him.

"Mr. Jackson has repaired a few clocks, using a corner of the store. It's a temporary arrangement for twenty-five percent—"

"Wants to make a clock for the church," Gudger said.

"Steeple clock," Wright said, "over the church."

"How much it cost?" Gudger asked Wayland, chewing as he spoke.

"Depends on how many faces it has," Wayland said, "and whether it has a striker on it."

Gudger stopped chewing, his body stiffening. "Striker?"

"Like in London, Gudger," Young told him.

Gudger said, "Could strike once a day. That's enough so people can set their watches."

Wright turned to stare critically at him. "Would prefer day-long striking."

"Strike one o'clock in the afternoon, that would be enough," Gudger said.

"Wake me up if it struck at night," Milton said. "I live right close, remember."

"Now, listen here," Wright began, "we are going to have it strike all the hours, or none."

Gudger grumbled. "We have these meetings to make such decisions, don't we? Not to hear reports on decisions already made. I never have agreed to order it made at all, not yet."

"I hope we'll agree to order it," Wright admitted. "I don't deny I'm partial to the idea. Listen to me, I mean to use it for the rest of my life, which is not so many years—"

"Oh, Lord," Gudger moaned. "Don't start dying on us, Papa."

"Well, my grandfather lived to be ninety, that's so, and that's natural," Wright said. "I've noticed that a man, when he dies, he's asked—his relatives are asked what he died of, and if they say he died at the age of ninety, then that's answer enough. If he died in his seventies, then he died of heart trouble, or a stroke, pneumonia, or a wound or whatever. No reason needed for the nineties."

"So you only have another twenty-five years to use the clock," Young said, smiling at him.

Wright reflected on that, finally smiled. "Exactly so."

"Well," Gudger said, waving one hand in the air as if shooing away arguments, "we'd all have agreed, anyway, to some sort of a clock."

"With a striking mechanism," Wayland added. "It'll take a month or two for it to be cut and the weights cast and the face and hands made—"

"How many faces?" Milton asked.

"No need for a face to the back, over the roof," Wayland said. "So I'd suggest three."

"I'd vote for two," Gudger said.

"Now listen to him," Wright said, annoyed. "I was about to suggest three, and here comes Gudger with two."

"No need for the back nor the front," Gudger said, amused by his father's criticism. "Nothing's out front, except the cemetery, and what does a dead man need to know the time for?"

"You don't know what the dead'll need," Young told him, "unless you've been one."

Gudger winked at Wayland. "Not a polite family, I'll tell the world that."

"Let the dead have a face," Wright said. "Three cost not much more'n two, I'd imagine."

"Not much more at all," Wayland said.

Wright told them he would ask the Cranshaws to construct a steeple.

Gudger said the Wright family was not the only one going to use the clock, was it? "We going to pay for it all, Papa?"

"We're going to ask for help from others," Wright agreed.

"Lord knows, others will make use of it," Gudger said.

Young said, "I tell you what I'd rather have, that's a bell tower, something nice, with chimes—"

Gudger, his mouth caught open in the act of chewing, began moaning, apprehensions multiplying inside him.

"Start with an eight-sided base, then graduate to four, which has the clock in it, then put a ball on top. Construct it out in the open, between the road and the church, near the old spring. Have a pool of water—"

"My Lord," Gudger whispered, seeking relief from the torrent of ideas.

"Why eight sides?" Milton asked.

"We'll need a big base for the track," Young said.

"What track?" Milton asked.

"For the bear," Young said blandly, not a sign of facetiousness about him. "The bear," he repeated. "In Europe a bear comes out when the clock strikes."

The family and Wayland were stone silent, stunned. Young, perched on the edge of his chair, his hands demonstrating, began describing the path around his clock tower, where every hour or so a carved wooden bear would move in a circle. As he talked, Gudger covered his face with his big hands and peeped out through spread fingers. Milton, hunched in his chair, slowly began smiling like a possum, aware that the scheme was about to topple of its own weight. Once Young stopped explaining, imagining, there was silence for a while, broken when Gudger leaned heavily back in his chair. "This bear, will it be life-sized?"

"Yes," Young replied, "life-sized."

"All-foured, or on its hind legs?" Gudger asked.

"Hind legs."

"Black or brown?"

"Black, like bears around here."

"With paws and all?"

"Yes," Young replied.

"Claws?"

"Yes, we can have tongue, claws, tail—"

"Slobber or not?" Gudger asked.

Young sat back, considering that. "Might hook up the spring in such a way—" he began.

Wright struck the table a blow. "Now, damn it, are you serious or not? What are you asking for, Young?"

"I thought I told you," Young said, hurt, drawing into himself.

Wayland began busying himself with his food, realizing that the debate among the brothers was too dangerous for him to engage in.

Wright spoke up. "Do you propose, Young, that we have such as that?"

"What do *you* say, Papa?" Young replied.

"Well, I'm still trying to see it in my mind's eye."

Silence for a while. Wright abruptly called to Mavis to bring some more bread, and he said he wanted another glass of buttermilk. "Mr. Jackson, I recommend buttermilk to you. I made a survey of the ages of people who had died on our side of the river, and there were seventeen men and fourteen women in the study who used buttermilk, and a similar number used whole milk, or no milk at all. Well, sir, we found that the buttermilk people lived an average of four years longer."

Nobody thought to challenge the findings or enlarge on them. The brothers ate, nobody saying anything, until finally Young began talking gently, saying he would like to live in a community that had a proper clock tower with a striker and chimes as well, and that in the tower provisions should be made so a bear could be added later. "My opinion is that my brothers aren't ready for the bear yet."

Nobody denied this. "Mr. Jackson, can you even make a bear?" Wright asked.

"Yes."

"Can you make a tower for a bear to be added?"

"Yes."

"Can you do chimes?"

"Yes."

Mavis brought in a pie, which Milton cut.

"Might as well put the bear off for now, I agree," Wright said.

"I understand," Wayland said.

"But make a tower rather than a steeple."

"A tower'd be easier to build," Gudger admitted. "That church roof won't hold much weight."

"Eighteen-inch faces big enough?" Wayland inquired.

"Whatever you decide about that," Wright said. "Now then, what comes next to discuss, gentlemen? Is it Mr. Jackson himself? We need to have an idea of your background and intent, Mr. Jackson," he said quietly. "If you're to live here among us, we need to have confidence in you." He paused briefly. "What's your faith, for instance?"

"Episcopalian," Wayland replied at once.

Wright studied him critically, coughed into his napkin. He sipped some buttermilk. "Lord help us," he murmured.

"Let the new minister convert him, Papa," Milton said, winking at Wayland, "whenever we get one."

"Can't find one that Papa will allow," Gudger said. "Has to know the Bible by heart."

"Ought to know the details of it," Wright admitted. "Send young men that have scant knowledge of it. There's only three revelations God ever made to man, Mr. Jackson. There's the earth and heavens, which declare the glory of God and show His handiwork. There's the Bible. And there's Jesus, the final revelation. There's not been another one since Jesus."

Chewing on his food, Young said, "Heaven and earth, the Bible and Jesus total four."

"At least Wayland's not a Pentecostal, Papa," Milton commented.

Wright said suddenly, "I know there's Episcopalians in the world who believe the same as the Methodists, but they don't seem to get around to it as often. In any event, maybe we can revive you. Now then, you have a trade to work at, don't you?" Wright said. "That clock matter. And I suppose you farm a little as well."

"No, I'm not a farmer," Wayland admitted.

"Suppose you mend rifles and pistols, such as that?" Wright asked.

"No, I don't," Wayland said.

78

"You'd have more business in firearms than clocks and watches around here," Gudger told him.

"Don't do watches, either," Wayland said.

"You're not going to have much work, just repairing clocks," Wright told him.

"I'm not a clock repairman," Wayland admitted.

"You only want to *make* clocks, do you?" Wright said.

"Start with wood and metal and make a clock. My uncles and my father had a clockmakers' shop, all three of them working in it, and when my father passed on, I took his place myself, at the age of eleven. I've never done much in my entire life except clocks. Some people say I tick when I move."

"How do you make clocks?" Young asked, suddenly interested.

"Order cases from local people, make the works yourself, maybe a dozen works at a time, make the pendulums, weights, faces, put it all together."

"Do everything, that's the way," Young agreed emphatically. "Lord 'a mercy, this could be a savior. I'll do it with you."

"Now, just a minute," Gudger said, afraid a new enterprise was getting away from him.

"You stay out of it, Gudger," Young told him. "You have enough—"

Gudger said, "We're here to discuss this new man, not you—"

Mr. Wright broke in. "I'm trying to find out what Mr. Jackson is going to do for a living, assuming he settles here. Now, Mr. Jackson, you propose to make new clocks?"

"I mean to do that somewhere," Wayland said.

"A factory?" Wright said.

"No. To me each clock has its own way of being. My uncles' shop finally got so big it was a factory, and they lost interest in the clocks themselves, became money people, borrowing at the bank and hiring labor at the door, trying to get more floor space. They lost it all, finally. They'd order the clock cases made in one factory, order the works ready-made—"

"I understand," Wright said respectfully. "You'd be smaller."

"A clockmaker can make great clocks, or else he can turn out clocks by the score," Wayland said. "I've recently made a long-case clock that can correct for changes in humidity and temperature. Maybe most people don't care about a few seconds a day—"

"Wayland and me will do it," Young said emphatically. "I'll help do this. I know what he's saying."

"He will need bookkeeping," Gudger said, "needs markets—"

"We don't need your help, Gudger," Young said bluntly.

"Do we need *you*, that's what I'm wondering," Gudger said. "What you mean to do?"

"Get the cases built, sell the clocks for him," Young said.

"Milton can make the hands and pendulums and all that," Wright contributed.

Gudger demanded, "You going to allow them to exclude members of the family, Papa?"

"Now, let's keep calm," Wright advised. "Tell us, Mr. Jackson, what each one can do. As I see it—"

"It's not for Gudger to do a damn thing," Young said angrily.

Gudger laughed, then shrugged helplessly. "Brotherly love," he murmured.

"Papa, you keep his big fat hands out of this, you hear?" Young said. "This is the first thing around here that I like—"

"Now, I'm trying to find out what Mr. Jackson can do to make a living up here," Wright said.

"He can make a living if he'll just get out of Young's way," Gudger said, laughing.

Wright laughed as well, then Wayland laughed. Then Wright said the factory idea must wait for the next meeting, in a week. "You can meet with us then, Mr. Jackson? It's too hot for us to handle."

"Is that all?" Milton said, preparing to push his chair back.

"No, I have two other brief items. Let's see, here— they pertain to Mr. Jackson. It seems his arrival has created a long docket. One is the millwheel. He proposes assembling it for us."

Silence. Each son waited for the others to comment. Young at last said, "I'd let him do it."

"'I'd let him do it'!" Gudger said. "Young ought to *pay* him to do it."

Young stared at him, dismayed. "Pay him?"

"It's your wheel," Gudger said. "Papa gave you the wheel. It's your wheel. It's your problem."

"What the hell business is it of yours whether that wheel—whether it's my wheel?" Young was tongue-tied with anger. He threw a biscuit at Gudger, then threw another one.

Gudger said, "What the hell's the matter with him?"

Young pushed the table against him. He was in a state of hurt and anger that was clearly unbearable.

Wayland stood. "I'll do it for nothing," he said, speaking quite loud enough to catch their attention.

When Wayland resumed his seat, Milton gently mentioned the need to keep tempers in check, to remain brotherly. "After all, we all are blood kin," he told them.

Wayland said, "I'm going to do it free, Mr. Wright."

"Very well," Wright said simply, "suit yourself." He looked over his list of items, cleared his throat meaningfully. "The final item has to do with you and Collie."

"What about Collie?" Young said, preparing to protect her.

"He's been visiting her," Wright told him simply. "Living at her place."

Young started to speak, faltered. A cloud settled on him. "Mama said something about—Is he the man?"

"Mr. Wayland seems to have got himself involved in this family in many ways," Wright commented.

"I wouldn't stay up there," Young said to Wayland. "No, I wouldn't do that."

Wayland stared at him, astonished by his open show of jealousy.

Wright said firmly, "He can stay here at the house, if he likes. I have a parlor room, Mr. Jackson, with a big bed in it."

Wayland sat frozen in his place, staring at the family. He took a deep breath, started to reply, or to protest, but said nothing.

Wright pushed himself away from the table, sighing deeply, wearily. "You can stay here or at the inn, Mr. Jackson. I'm going back to the store, Gudger."

Milton followed, then Gudger. Wayland remained at the table, he and Young. "You can stay at *my* house, if you prefer," Young said.

"She's let me use that rock room. It's the old springhouse," Wayland told him.

"I know the place," Young said. "She told you to use it?" he asked incredulously.

"I've stayed there two nights with Paula," Wayland said stiffly.

Young watched him carefully. "I wouldn't use it any longer."

"No?" Wayland accepted his interest as friendly, helpful. "I'll talk to her," he said.

Young was almost whispering. "You want me to go up there with you?"

"To stay?"

"To ask her?"

"No, I can ask her." He stopped in the kitchen to thank Mavis for the meal. Collie had gone over to the store, Mavis told him. In the yard, he patted the friendly dogs. A few hunting dogs were caged and were anxious to get at some prey or other, were mean and watchful, but the pet dogs were friendly.

Young walked beside him. They walked across the torn field, the wintering rows crunching under their feet. He could see Collie waiting for him near the store. "I'll ask Collie," Wayland said, doggedly determined not to be pushed about.

"Don't want you to get upset over this," Young said. "You won't run off, will you? We have our clock works to do here."

"No, I won't leave," Wayland said.

Young chose a path, one too narrow for them to walk side by side, so Young walked behind. He said, "I been thinking about leaving, but not after today. If we start a clock place, I can stay here and help you. But I can't stay buried under Gudger all my life."

"A lot of weight there," Wayland admitted. "We can work it out." He waved to Collie.

"I've never been anywhere else," Young said. "Went off to school, left there. I just couldn't take the day-to-day exercises. I want to be a great man, Jack."

Wayland stopped, turned to face him, attracted by the claim.

"I want to be a great man today, not wait it out, and I don't know how," Young admitted.

Wayland studied him for a while longer, intrigued by the sincerity of the fellow.

They went on across the field together, and it was near the gate, as they approached Collie, that Young said, "I don't want you to stay another night at her place, Jack."

Time after time he would fall into laughter as he tried to tell about that family meeting, repeating the details to Paula and Collie, explaining about the bear clock time after time, then more seriously, excitedly explaining about the clock tower he was to build, perhaps with chimes as well as a bell, and the millwheel they were together to assemble. Already he had plans soon to disband his clock-repair work; he was about through with all makeshift measures. But I'm not through with you, young lady, he thought, recognizing in Collie the one who had manipulated him and her family, all to his advantage, and he liked to think it would come to be to her advantage as well.

He became more and more strongly attracted to her every day, that was the truth of it. Each of the next several nights he would troop down to Young's house to sleep, leaving Paula to sleep in the stone room, but each morning he was back to wake them up, to share breakfast, to work about the place before going off to the store. He was building a fish trap for the stream so that they could have fresh trout whenever they wanted. He set the trap in her creek, but later moved it just below the small dam near the mill, which fed water into the mill's sluice —a dam only three feet high, intended to channel enough water to turn the wheel.

They worked on the wheel every evening for an hour or so. This was before supper. Then at Collie's he and Paula would draw sketches for the clocks that were to be made, discussing the width, the height; these mountain rooms had lower ceilings than rooms in the North, and even though he meant to export most of the clocks, he did mean for them to be usable at home. For several nights they entertained themselves with such designing. They would round the hood, narrow or widen the trunk, change the trunk door from two panels to one, change the

84

size of the dial, add columns, then erase them, change the break-arch top to a Parthenon one, reduce the height to seven feet ten inches, then reduce it an inch more. One evening they even added a pagoda to the design, a pagoda with ornaments.

In one of two final versions, as Paula drew it, the door of the trunk had three panels; the edges were to be beveled, with an inlaid braiding of holly along the case edges, a light wood to contrast with the walnut from which the case was to be made. This design, as well as a less decorative one, was sketched on different pieces of paper, and these Young gave to three different families, urging them to quick, hard labor in order to finish a few cases, if at all possible, before Christmas.

5

Winter enveloped them now. It began biting hard at the chimney tops. Winter would strip these mountain forests completely, except for the hemlocks and the spruce on the highest peaks. Winter storms were noisy battles in these high places, resembling wars of gods and spirits. Last year, lightning struck that black tree near the road, Wright told Paula. "See how the jagged teeth marks are left along the side, moving halfway around the tree; that's where the hot fire bit into the wood."

Winter made judgments, he told her. It righted wrongs. Winter would tear at any tree or other creature that was exposed, or was enfeebled by age or injury. Jeffrey Marshall's cattle froze on the night of December 18 last year, seven heifers and a young bull, eight dead next morning when he braved the winds, the animals frozen bunched together in a glistening hecatomb, all except the bull. He had his hooves frozen to the ground. Marshall said the warm daytime preceding this freeze had left a mire of the creek bottom, and the bull's hooves had been frozen in place. The dead bull stood like a sentinel, bravely watching over his frozen family.

Such wolves as were left were likely to pack in the coldest part of the season. Wright recalled that a pack of five came down January first, last winter, on

Coffin Taylor's yard, killed most of his chickens and geese, tossing the limp bodies about. They attacked both of his Jersey cows, at which point his wife came at them with an ax, chasing them off. Those two cows were hers, she said. Then there were wild dogs as well as wolves. They attacked one of Milton's cows near his shop, with him working at the forge, almost in sight of them.

Of an average winter, as Wright judged it, many people went hungry—it wasn't only the wild animals. Usually if a family had salted down pork, they could get through until cress grew once again in the fields and fish were easier to catch. Old people had the worst of it. They would eat a bite of salt pork and drink buttermilk and break off a piece of cornbread and huddle near their fire. Of course, we all die and death prefers no single season, but winter deaths were much more common up here, which is why the Jenningses, who were from stern German stock and usually dug the graves for the community, would dig two or three graves each autumn while the ground could be worked. To keep rain out, they covered the holes with bearskins, as had their fathers, which they spread out and staked at the four paws.

That explains how the worst winters were here on this high floor, an isolated room for life with walls of trees and earth, pockmarked with caves and crevices where wild beasts were listening, with winds feeling their way along the river, where a hundred or more families of Scotch-Irish, German and English stock lived alongside a few Swiss and French.

"My great-grandfather never would have come here to settle if he'd knowed about all this meanness," Mr. Samuel King once said. "Why, frost will get the apple blossoms one year in three, and last year we had to replant the corn in June. Have to build fortresses of rock and logs to hold the beasts out. Nobody would know if we all died away back up here."

Can dream of kinder places, the widow Benie Frazier thought. She recalled a favorite dream, of floating down the river, which was strangely smooth and silky, even at the rapids. She was floating west toward Tennessee with her lover, Young Wright, who lay beside her in the boat, his hands gentle on her breasts, his face close to hers, and he was telling her that he was lonely and wanted her for his wife.

The hunting season was fading to a close. Three of the McGregors returned from the North Woods, three little pack horses laden with pelts, some of which they nailed to house and barn walls to cure. The McGregors had meat to eat these nights; even their dogs had all the meat they wanted.

"We go to get us a bear about this time ever' year," Gudger told Wayland, mentioning a subject he had begun bringing up virtually every day. "You court my sister, you ought to dare come with us."

"What has courting your sister to do with it?" Wayland asked.

"Let's see what sort of man you are."

"I'm not curious about it, Gudger," Wayland told him.

"Don't want just anybody with my sister, do I?" Gudger replied. He was halfway joking; however, the rite of bear hunting and the duty of inspecting Collie's suitors did appear to be wedded in his mind.

"What if I got up there in the woods and ran from the bear?" Wayland asked him. Which, indeed, he might do, he supposed. He knew nothing about bear or guns or hunting, and wasn't anxious to prove himself in any such way; at the same time, he was rather confident of doing well. When Young came to him and quite seriously invited him to accompany them on the hunt, to accompany Gudger and Milton and two or three others, Wayland found himself accepting.

Perhaps he had accepted, he later told Paula, because Collie didn't want him to do so; he confided in his daughter to that extent. He had to maintain a degree of autonomy. "And I suppose it's an exercise of some sort," he told Paula.

"As in school?" she asked.

"When *is* school, by the way? When do you go to school?"

"They're closing down now till after Christmas. The widow says she won't teach this next year, though."

"Who'll teach you, then?"

"I don't know. Mr. Wright is said to be looking for a preacher who can teach."

"And farm," Wayland said dryly. "And repair guns and run boundary lines, I imagine."

"And hunt bears," Paula said bitterly, revealing her own unhappiness about the hunting situation. She hoped he would decide not to go.

Collie told him he had hurt her deeply, agreeing to the hunt. "Why do you want to be like them?" she asked him. "Why do you want to go off with Gudger and kill a bear? Wayland, I'm asking you something. Now, answer me."

No adequate answer came to mind, really. He had leaned toward wanting to go. It wasn't a driving force in him. He was curious about it, and about himself, and now he reveled in Collie's and Paula's disappointment in him. He felt somehow superior to what he had been, or at least different, separate, because he was going, even though he knew he had put a great deal in jeopardy.

The evening before the hunt he set aside the clock parts he was cutting—he did part of his clock work here in her house of a night, even though the light was dim—took Jonathan from Paula and rested him on his own lap. Casually he mentioned to him, as well as to Paula and Collie, who was washing the dishes, that once in his experience in Pennsylvania there had been a cross between a bear and a pigeon, with the bottom part being the bear. "He was most all of him hams, you understand, and he lived with his mother in the biggest pigeon nest the flock could provide. Even so, it was not much larger than his fanny when he sat down."

Paula smiled fondly at him; she knew this one of his many stories by heart.

"That bird-bear ate more than the rest of the flock combined. Had to eat continuously to get enough food through his beak. And water—had to drink twenty-three hours a day, off and on. Had all the pigeons in the flock hauling food and water for him."

"Mr. Jackson, I do wonder about you," Collie said.

"So the flock held a meeting at the meetinghouse, which also served as the Methodist church, to see if they ought to put the baby out of the community, for it occupied sixty-three nests."

"Mr. Jackson, I—what a story!"

"But his papa came to the meeting, cleared his throat and said that instead of putting him out of the community they ought to put him in charge of the fire department, make him responsible for protecting the houses and buildings and nest." Wayland paused to await a reaction. Firmly he met the gaze of Collie, then Paula, allowing the crisis to be savored by everybody; meanwhile, Jonathan was drinking in the sight of his face and exploring it with his fingers. "Several arguments were presented against such a notion," Wayland continued, "most of the pigeons not understanding the suggestion until the father gruffly worded his argument this way: 'My son,' he said, 'will surely be able to piss out any fire.'"

Collie disappeared behind both hands, tears forming in her eyes, and Paula rocked on her haunches, giggling delightedly, and only Jonathan seemed to understand the seriousness of the story, and to appreciate the victory that the pigeon-bear's father had attained.

Wayland washed for supper at the sink. He took his shirt off to keep it dry, and by the time he reached for it again, soap in his eyes, Collie had it soaking in the washtub nearby.

When Paula took Jonathan into the back room to put him to sleep, the two adults sat at the table, sipping coffee. "How old are you, Mr. Jackson?" she asked him. "I never asked you that, did I, and we've talked about most everything else."

"I'm thirty-four years old."

She wet her lips, pressed them tightly together. "I'm twenty-three," she said.

"So you were already getting along in age at the time of your baby."

"That's so," she said.

He smiled kindly. "Where did that man get you, Collie?"

She blinked with surprise. "Why, what do you mean? He got me in the only place there is. There's not but the one, is there?"

He laughed. For a minute or so he chuckled about her reply. "I mean to say, where were you living back then?"

"Been living at Papa's all my life, except when I visited relatives, and that was when I was fourteen and Mama took me with her, said she wanted to breathe somebody else's air. We went as far as Durham. Traveled on the train. I recall that everything I sought to secure myself to was moving along. Papa later said I could go off to school, and he gave me catalogues to study and pick from. I picked Weaver College, because it had a lake. He laughed about that for the longest time. Young didn't want me to leave him; he cried every time it was mentioned. I raised Young, and Mama'll admit it. She never did pay enough attention to Young. He needs a world of attention, too, let me tell you. Mama blames me for Young's obstinacies, says he takes after me. So I've been a bone of contention in her house all along, a deep worry. Then Papa began to ask about the father of the baby, bringing up one possibility, then another, working some man's name into a conversation to catch any change in my expression." She twisted about, huddled inside her crossed arms, seeking her thoughts. "What was I trying to tell you?"

"About every man in the community being a prospect."

Her eyes flashed. "What you mean by every man in the community?"

"You were telling me your father had to consider everybody—"

"I didn't mean...I didn't mean every man was a prospect, Mr. Jackson."

"Well, Collie, I didn't say he'd think you had—had received every one of them, but how was he to know which one had got to you?"

"What you expect me to do, Mr. Jackson, tell him who had got to me, as you term it, when it would only break his heart?"

Here they were once more at the same impasse, except now it held new shading for him. "Well, it doesn't matter tonight," he said, although he didn't feel that way about it.

"You keep asking who Jonathan's father is, Mr. Jackson," she said. "I'll say this. He'll very likely come by to see me before long, and I want you to understand I don't have any affection for him left, and didn't have much, if any, before you arrived. I want you to know I'm going to send him away. It's a decision made days ago. I'm tired to death of depending on him."

"Sometimes a person's life changes. I know how it is," Wayland began. "My wife, Ruth, changed ever' so often, once she saw death ahead, even changed her name. This was just before she passed away. She walked into the sea to end the pain, Collie. Did Paula tell you that?"

"Let me tell you something as sure as the stars are light, Mr. Jackson—"

"Had the name of Dot for a time. Then wanted Lyn. I said, well, I'll call you Lyn, honey, but she said later that week to call her Mary. Nobody knew all this about her, except me. Paula knew some of it."

"Let me tell you something, Mr. Jackson—"

"Then we were at the beach and she got a fierce pain below her stomach, down in here, and she walked into the water one evening. I was on the porch of the cottage working, paying no attention."

"Let me tell you something, Mr. Jackson—"

"What's that, Collie?"

"He won't walk into the sea."

Wayland went out to the barn, got the parts of his master clock, carried them in a wood box to the house and began assembling them so that he could hang it on the north wall. It would make her feel that he realized he belonged here. Collie soon became interested in the brass works, the enameled face, the shining pendulum. "Don't have a case for it," Wayland explained, "but I can attach it to the wall itself, for now."

He called Paula in from Jonathan's room to wind the clock and swing the pendulum for that first time, and the three people sat near the fire watching the pendulum catch sparks of light and return them to the walls, to the ceiling, to their own faces. They listened to the steady heartbeat of the beautiful instrument.

Once Paula went to the stone room to sleep, Collie decided to shave Wayland, "to tidy you for the hunt," which amused him. He consented, of course, and she set his chair near the fireplace and lathered his face. She bent close to him as she worked, and he began nudging her breast with his chin. "You're getting soap on my dress, Wayland."

Her complaint contained more amusement than criticism, he noticed. "I can fix that," he said, and pulled her over to the bed, where he kissed her and held her, the soapsuds gettting on the pillow, the sheets, her dress, her naked breasts. The two lovers began clutching at one another, loving one another in the warm light. The clock on the wall went on counting, counting, evenly counting.

He would not leave her tonight, not yet, he decided. He could not. He belonged here, with his face buried against her breast, his arms around her. They were as close as one person—no, not that close, not joined; the woman was not yielding herself completely to him, she was protective, was still a guardian of herself. Even so, she was not hesitant about the love she made to him.

The property that was to be used in the hunt was the stretch of mountain range at the Tennessee line. In fact, the border of the two states, Tennessee and North Carolina, possibly passed through the middle of the one-room hunting shack that some years ago had been thrown up there. This ridge was steep on the Tennessee side, falling down through laurel slicks and hells, which the bears liked well, where they could den in safety. There were always bear to be found here if a man was willing to risk all he had to get them.

It was Gudger's insistence that the brothers hunt

94

once a year together, and this year he included the senior Crawford, who had been an excellent bear hunter over the years, especially able before he put on an extra thirty pounds of weight, and the senior McGregor, who had the best dogs, all of them full-blooded Plott hounds. This year there would be only this small party, the three brothers, the two friends, and the prospective brother-in-law. Six bunks were in the hunting shack.

On the morning the men were to leave, Gudger went around the store humming and beaming at everybody, measuring out cornmeal and cutting off slabs of bacon, wrapping them in wax paper. He poured a pound of coffee into a leather sack, broke three dozen eggs into a glass Mason jar. He washed out three jugs, each half-gallon size, and filled one with whiskey, the other two with peach and apple brandy, and stashed them in a shoulder pack, which he said he would carry personally. Since McGregor didn't usually drink—he got wild whenever he drank, Gudger said—there was enough here for five men for three nights, which was as long as a hunt ever ran. "Might get a bear tomorrow and decide to come on back Sunday," he told Wayland, "but you never know. Hell, I'll stay till I win." He put dry matches in a tin. He stuck squares of toilet tissue in his pocket. "If you need paper, take your own," he told Wayland. "I don't supply paper." He cleaned his rifle, a .32 Winchester, and put a box of rounds in his pocket. He oiled his pistol and filled its clip with rounds, then put another eight rounds in a small cardboard box, with cotton to keep them from rattling. "Now, this rifle will shoot through a bear, but the pistol won't, not usually," he told Wayland.

Wayland had been following him around, watching everything, offering no opinions.

"So if you shoot with a rifle, you have to be sure a

dog's not on the other side, or you'll shoot your own dogs."

"I understand," Wayland said.

Mr. Wright came in carrying a .30-.30 carbine, a World War I Luger and a knife to loan to Wayland. He laid them on the counter side by side. Wayland didn't know how to load them, so Wright showed him. "Now you have eight and six rounds," he said, and filled a box with additional bullets. Wayland tried to put the pistol holster on his belt, but Mr. Wright showed him how to put it over his shoulder, the pistol carried under his arm. "It's a bit hard to get out," he said, "but you usually have all the time in the world on a hunt, anyway."

Wayland put the knife sheath on his belt.

"You going to the Devil's Saddle?" Wright asked Gudger.

"To the very place," Gudger said happily.

"Say hello to him for me," Wright said, smiling. He took a chair at the stove and watched Wayland as he weighed the rifle in his hands, getting the feel of it. "See the ghost of my dog Harry, say hello for me," he told Gudger.

"I remember him, Papa," Gudger said.

"My best one. Harry was cautious, but he never gave up. Had a sow bear treed when I got there, and she come down the tree fast as a falling stone and landed on top of him, crushed him. I shot her, and then she come at me, and I held my second shot till she was nigh slobbering on me. Wayland, are you listening?"

"Yes, sir."

"Not many people appear to listen to my hunting stories."

"I was listening."

"Look like you're thinking about making clocks, or something."

"No, no. Mr. Wright, that millwheel is ready to hang now."

"Shot her finally, and she fell backwards and her claws scraped the shirt front off my body. Riiiiiiiipppppppppp. Never touched me. She fell backwards, you see, was carried back when the last bullet hit inside her skull."

"Take eight men, I'd say," Wayland said.

"Buried Harry. Held a funeral, and I put eleven rocks on his grave, one for each year of age."

"I understand," Wayland said.

"When I come to the age of seventeen, my papa took me up on the mountain, told me it was my time, that I had it to do."

"I never killed anything," Wayland admitted suddenly. "I don't know," he murmured, glancing warily at Gudger, who was moving toward the tea chest to rob that of a supply.

Wright said, "My papa said, it's your time, William. I'll not say I wasn't nervous, for I was. Then the hunt was all around me, dogs and noise and the bear coming down a hickory where he had gone to rest, then he saw me and Papa and took off running. Next thing I knew, I was running after him hell bent for leather, the dogs in front of me, and I never gave danger another thought. Gudger," he called, "you got bacon and cornmeal enough?"

Gudger said, "Enough for a bite or two, till we get bear to eat."

"Salt?" he called out.

Gudger quickly added a half-full box of salt to his pack. "Yeh, have that," he called back.

"Pepper? Bear meat without pepper is inedible, Wayland."

"Got that," Gudger called out, pouring pepper into the same box, mixing it with the salt.

"Matches?" Wright called out. He satisfied himself finally.

"Got that."

"Then you're ready to go." Wright reached up and took firm hold of Wayland's arm. "So are you, Wayland," he told him.

Milton brought along to the store a big dog he had bred and was ready to try out. He had used a pure-bred Plott sire and a cur bitch. He had always done that way, crossing a Plott with more common animals, he explained to Wayland. The Plott breed had been bred here in the mountains for bear hunting; it had been developed out of German boar dogs a few generations ago, and there were those who swore by Plott dogs and would have nothing else. Milton enjoyed cross-breeding, however, seeing what mixture gave the best starter, the best tracker, the best attacker.

Young arrived, and he had a bitch he had traded for, had got from Roy Campbell's nephew Horace, who lived near Tennessee and who owed the store money and wouldn't pay, but would give up this scarred hound. Not a square inch of her hide but had been ruptured at one time or another. She was a bundle of scars. Campbell said she could beat any dog ever born, was three-quarter Plott and the rest German boxer and bulldog. She was broad-breasted, narrow-hipped, looked more like a male than a female; one of her eyes was about half closed, where a five-hundred-pound bear had raked his claws across it in a fight near Collins Crossing, Tennessee. Her name was Sally. Well, Young had taken to her, though he admitted he didn't quite like her, didn't know that he wanted to go to sleep with her in the same shack with him. He said owning Sally was like owning a piece of lore, a legend still breathing, that he could look at her lying there in the store by the stove, where she'd plopped down in everybody's path, and imagine all sorts of fights she had had, won and lost, for he supposed she was not above losing occasionally if death was the alternative. She was his dog and he was the proud owner of her, he claimed, but Wayland noticed he didn't touch her. Petting Sally apparently wasn't in prospect.

So there was this young dog that Milton had, and this veteran, Sally; then McGregor arrived from across the trading lot, walking in the loose-jointed, bent-shouldered manner acquired by some mountain men, limber and patient, never pushing beyond a conservative, even gait. The big rifle in his left hand, dangling there, was an appendage of his body, one grown into his bones. He also carrried a pistol in his under-arm holster, perhaps one he had liberated in France, where he was said to have taken a number of prisoners, more enemy soldiers than anybody else in his company. Shifty-eyed, wary, he paused before the store, considering Milton, who was waiting on the porch, and Milton's fresh, new dog, which had bristled at the sight of McGregor's three bear dogs, all of them veterans with scars to prove it, all of them buckskin-colored with some black striping on them. "Hain't he purdy?" McGregor said to Milton, and spat tobacco juice into the dust. "He wants to go, too, does he?"

"Name of Sandy," Milton said.

McGregor studied the dog, evaluating him as if weighing him on a scale, measuring by sight matters of girth and breeding. "Why, hain't he purdy?" he repeated, smiling, spitting, giving the hound low grades; being pretty wasn't much of an accolade for a bear dog. "You boys let hit in, you hear me?" he told his own hounds, and they appeared to understand well enough, to consent, though not without growling and shivering.

Out of the store, onto the porch came Young, with his Sally on a chain long enough to give Sally room, for if she didn't want to go where Young wanted her

99

to go, he would compromise. Sally on first seeing the three McGregor dogs leaped forward down the porch steps, dragging Young behind her into the pit of snarling, snapping jaws and McGregor boots as that gentleman stomped and stormed about, cursing his own dogs, kicking at them.

Peace and quiet at last, Sally sitting squarely in the place the other three dogs had occupied, the other dogs giving her room.

So there were five dogs with an uneasy truce among them, and the dogs were one by one called into Wayland's truck bed, along with McGregor and Young, then Gudger climbed onto the truck bed as well, which weighted it down at the left rear wheel. Crawford arrived, his wife beside him, adding directions. He unloaded his rifle and dropped the bullets into his jacket pocket, gave her a peck on her cheek. "All right, all right, Nanny," he told her.

"You be back Sunday," she told him.

"I don't know when it'll be," he told her.

"You come back Sunday," she said, her voice quivering.

"You should be so lucky," he said, and winked at Gudger. He accepted a hand as he climbed onto the truck. He looked about at the five dogs, studying Sally particularly, asked their names, said they ought to do well enough, he thought. He sought an adjustment of his body so he could cushion his pistol holster. "I need this trip," he said to Gudger, wanly considering his wife. She was waving to him.

"We have pork enough?" Young asked Gudger.

"Enough till we get bear."

Wayland handed his rifle to Young, then swung into the driver's seat. He had bought at the store two cans of green beans and a quart bottle of milk, which he carried in his blanket. He waited for Milton to climb into the passenger's seat, then they were off, jolting out of the trading lot past the beginnings of the stone clock tower which Wayland had under construction. Several people waved to them. Paula and Collie from the church door called for them to be careful, for everybody knew they could be injured; now and again a man went off this way on a hunt and didn't come home at all. Take Horace Fletcher, went up there to the Devil's Saddle when he was getting over an illness, disappeared entirely, never came back. A stray dog arrived at the trading lot four days later with a forearm in its mouth. That might have been Horace's.

Years ago the shack had been built by Gudger, Crawford and four other men in a few days' time, from logs cut on the place. Men had cornered the logs as they were handed up, then the group had packed clay in the cracks between. Gudger often claimed they would have made it taller, but light on the second day of work waned, dark was coming on, so they threw roof rafters on six-and-a-half-foot walls. Next day they shingled the roof, using wood shanks split off oak logs, and threw up a wide-mouthed assembly of rocks for a chimney.

The cots were built against the wall, with double bunks against the south wall. There was a chair—one chair. Of course, a man could sit on a cot or a log or the floor. There was a table. There was a kettle and a frying pan and a big pot for stew.

Wayland had had a hard time on the hike. There was a path to follow, but it had grown over and briars were everywhere. Then, too, there were several steep places where the men scrambled up over rock, holding to laurel boughs, trusting their weight to them. Now and then they had to walk around massive fallen trees. Here he was, Wayland thought, thoroughly out of place, high on a mountain at a windy gap, with the world at his feet both to east and west, under an ancient forest of stooped hardwoods, rock-rooted trees stunted by high altitude, the wind just now sweeping across them making whines and moans and gusty whispers as real as spoken words.

He stacked his milk and green beans on one of the high bunks; he would prefer being above the floor as far as he could get, away from the dogs. He climbed up there now and sat with his legs dangling, drinking a swallow of milk, complaining to himself about his foolishness in being here. Already he missed Collie and Paula and Jonathan, that was part of it.

McGregor's dogs swept into the room and with a few warning snaps assigned themselves territories. Milton's young dog, Sandy, came in and slipped under a cot. Sally came in and plopped down before the fireplace, where Gudger and Milton were busily striking matches to leaves and bark, blowing on the promises of a fire, saying gentle prayers to the spirits in charge of blazes.

"Where's the state line?" Wayland asked McGregor.

McGregor looked about the room, orienting himself. He waved a line down the middle of the room, north to south.

"Am I to sleep in which state?" Wayland asked.

"You're in Tennessee," Gudger told him.

"Was going to Tennessee once," Wayland commented.

"Well, you've arrived," Gudger told him, straightening, brushing hearth ashes off his pants. "Where'd I put the liquor?" he said.

"Tennessee looks very much the same," Wayland commented.

They drank from one of the jugs. "Needed that," Gudger said, after downing a swallow. "Been needing that. Best to wait till you get to the shack to drink. It don't help with the hiking one bit."

Crawford drank down a long draught, then shook the jug and smelled it; he poured some of the whis-

102

key into a chipped snuff glass and shook it, studying the bead. He sniffed at what was in the glass, passed the jug along to Milton, who took a little chew of it, as he called a drink, which he held in his mouth, letting it burn as he swished it against his cheeks and tongue. He passed the jug back to Crawford, who served himself again, then gave it to Young, who gave it in turn to Wayland, the dogs watching this hand-to-mouth, hand-to-hand occupation, concentrating on it. Somebody asked who remembered where the nearest spring was and who was going to go for water. Nobody responded. Nobody was in a hurry now, they were enjoying being settled in, were enjoying seeing the fire grow. "The bears heard us, did they?" Gudger said to McGregor.

"Oh, they knowed anyhow," McGregor said. "They knowed we'd come."

"Come back for another year," Gudger said, snickering, pleased immensely.

"Been hoping fer'it," McGregor said, taking a place on a cot and rubbing his hands between his pants legs to warm them. "Now, look at that there dog," he said, indicating one of his dogs lying near his boot. "She's not been well, and she come up that mountain same as the others. She lost nine pups two weeks ago tomorrow." He patted her head, contented himself with being near her.

"Why did she lose them?" Wayland asked.

"I wished I knowed. Some devilment of my boys, I'd say."

"What were you going to do with nine pups, Greg?" Young asked him, using the name that the older man most often answered to.

"That's a fair question, but I can't answer hit," McGregor said, chuckling.

"Jesus'll come back soon," Crawford said, "then there'll be no more pup deaths."

Whether Crawford was serious or seeking to be

amusing, Wayland couldn't tell.

"Jesus want a dog?" Young asked.

All the men paused to ponder this.

"He never had one," Crawford said, sitting down on a cot, which creaked and groaned under him. "Was surrounded by people there for a while; before that, was alone in the desert for three year. I never saw a desert with a dog in it, have you, Gudger?"

"No, I ain't," Gudger said, drinking in the older man's satire like a thirsty man drinks water.

"Dog could have tested the water for him," Crawford said.

"Water on a desert?" Young asked.

"Oh, there had to be some water, though nothing like we got around here," Crawford said.

"Now, who is going for the water?" Gudger asked.

Nobody volunteered.

"It'll be dark soon." Gudger untied his boots to let his feet breathe, as he said.

"A good dog might have helped him with Judas," Crawford said.

"Walk on the water," Young suggested, "go to walk with him."

Crawford winked at Wayland. "Could keep him warm of a night. You know, he never had a woman."

"Well, he was so long getting grown," McGregor said. "Was thirty afore he started work. Hell, I had a teenager by then."

Young began giggling, even while trying not to.

"He did a world of walking," Crawford said, "and a dog is company. I mean, you know, if you're needing to walk ten, twenty miles, you click your fingers and you've got yourself a companion."

"Are there ary dogs mentioned in the Bible?" McGregor inquired.

The men silently considered that.

"Must have been two on the ark," Milton said.

"Serpents," Crawford said. "Mostly serpents in the Bible."

Young laughed out loud.

"Well, I'll go get the spring water," Crawford said, a dry smile on his face, the smile slowly opening as he went out carrying the big pot.

"Bring enough for the washstand as well," Gudger called after him.

There were beginnings of a dogfight when the pork was put into the skillet, and a few sharp words ensued between McGregor and Young, McGregor claiming his three dogs had been lying on their bellies minding their business when Sally bit his Charlie. "Hit's that'n I mean," he said, speaking adamantly, poking a forefinger at Sally. "She's a-going to get herself chewed up here directly is what I'm afeared of." Obviously he was relishing witnessing that very event.

Young didn't appear to be the least bit apprehensive.

"That there coffee's boiled enough," Gudger said, speaking more to himself than to anybody else.

"Bit him on the tail," McGregor complained fiercely. "Pshaw, look at that." He poured a drop or two of whiskey on Charlie's tail, which sent him into a mighty howl.

The men fed the dogs fatback and cornbread, then made cornbread for themselves, using the frying pan and hot fireplace rocks. When a piece of bread was brown enough, they cut slabs of it in two and lathered them with bacon and bacon drippings, satisfying their hunger in that way, drinking down the black coffee, emitting gusts of mist from their mouths, now and then drinking a nip of corn whiskey to cool off with, belching, going for another share of meat and bread.

Wayland sat on his bunk, drinking milk out of the

jar, eating green beans from a can he had opened with his knife—about the only use he would have for it, he imagined.

After supper, which caused considerable belching, the men sat about discussing bears, what the bears would be doing now, whether they slept with a paw in their mouth or not—a big argument between Crawford and McGregor—whether they bedded down alone or in company, whether the most dangerous ones were those weighing two hundred and fifty pounds when full grown, or three hundred and fifty, or five hundred. The night wove a friendly carpet; even the dogs were relaxed and content. "Boys, when we going to give Wayland our advice?" Gudger asked finally.

"We going to advise Wayland, are we?" Crawford said.

Gudger, his face red from fire heat and liquor, looked around at the circle of faces, pausing at Wayland's. "He's courting my sister, boys."

"Is she spirited, Jack?" McGregor asked dryly, not bothering to take his gaze off the fire.

"Why, I'd say she must be," Gudger said.

"He's been married before. Wayland, you been married before?" Young asked.

"That was in the North," Wayland admitted, sitting up on his bed.

"Even so," McGregor said. "Don't women have nary pussy in the North?"

"If you've been married, you ought to have learned something," Crawford said. "Tell us what you learned."

Wayland grinned. "Usually was dark," he said. "Never saw much."

Crawford said, "Dark or not, I would expect you to feel around. When you come to something that feels like wet silk inside, has fur out, then you're right there at it," he told Wayland in all seriousness.

"Now, it's not always wet," Milton said. "Have known a dry piece."

Crawford laughed and slapped his leg with his cap. "Lord, listen to him."

"Did you ever have ary bit with sand in hit?" McGregor asked.

"No, not yet," Crawford said.

"Hit's got a little man hung on the outside of the doorway, like a latch," McGregor said to Wayland, "and you tickle that there man. Don't you know how?"

"I never said I didn't know how," Wayland protested.

"Hit'll open most ever' time," McGregor said. "Hit'll slit just as pretty."

Young began laughing.

"Used to get so many hairs atween my teeth, I'd need a wire brush," McGregor was saying.

Crawford was laughing so loud he startled Sally, and she snarled at him.

"Also, tits are good to chew on," McGregor allowed. "Some men are more for tits than ary other part."

"Oh, I don't think so," Gudger said.

"And they're a sight easier to get to."

"No, I don't think so," Gudger repeated.

The whiskey jug kept going around. They talked some more about their experiences, advised Wayland liberally, and all the while he sat on his bunk, a grin on his face. "Just don't wear yourself out, boy," Crawford advised him. This was something along toward the bottom of the jar, when each man had drunk so much his words were slurred. "I look at it this way," Crawford said, expressing himself solemnly. "Did you ever see men driving a pole into the ground? Did you, Jack?"

"Yes, I suppose," Wayland said guardedly.

"Did *you*, Gudger?"

"You mean drive a pole into the ground to make a hole?"

"Yes."

"Lord, yes, I've watched that," Gudger said, "have done it."

"Have you, Young?"

"Yes," Young said.

"Did you ever see the hole wear out before the pole?"

As the meaning sunk in, the men all fell about, laughing. "It's the pole that wears out," Crawford bellowed, and laughed louder than the others, until the dust lifted off the sills and drifted down all around them. The dogs were looking from one man to the next, testing their skill at deciphering human meanings. First it was Sally who began to howl, then Charlie, then one of McGregor's males howled as well, and all the dogs pretty soon were singing along with the men, who were laughing fit to be tied, all of the men and dogs lost inside the music, the mighty sound filling their ears, embracing their bodies, with Crawford now and then calling out over the bedlam, "It's the pole that'll wear out before the hole."

The men were awakened in the middle of the night by Gudger calling, "Breakfast, breakfast, breakfast."

They stumbled about, rubbing their eyes, complaining, bumping into cots and boots and rifles. "Where is it, then?" Milton demanded of Gudger. "Where's breakfast?"

"It's to be cooked," Gudger told him. "Get up and cook it."

Milton returned to his cot and pulled his shirttail over his head, but Wayland was down off his cot by now and stood by, sleepily watching Gudger scramble about a dozen eggs. He had fatback as well, and

108

pones of cornbread were browning.

"Everybody wants to be waited on, have done for them," Gudger complained.

Wayland's foot crackled the frozen twigs as he walked to the washbasin, which was a half-log held up by forked posts. He broke the ice in the basin by hammering it with a rock and tried to wash his face clean; it was about as satisfying as lying in bed scratching flea bites and listening to the snoring of Gudger and the dream-talking of McGregor.

He dried his face, using his shirt sleeves. Now the sleeves would freeze, he imagined. Cold as winged death up here. Nearby, beech-tree limbs were crackling like rifle shots from the intense cold.

Here at the gap, the saddle of the divide, he supposed, he was at something over six thousand feet elevation, about five thousand above the Tennessee valley just below and three thousand above the North Carolina one. The air was thinner than he was used to. Also, because of the peculiarity of the place, he could hear a dog bark in a valley miles away, and a man call out. Probably this was an excellent place to listen to the dogs during the hunt, and prepare for the appearance of the bear.

The bears denned on that steep side, the Tennessee side, Young had told him. Just beyond this washstand was the tip of that near-mile drop into the valley. The bears lived in Tennessee, but did their feeding behind the washstand in North Carolina, where the nut trees were sun-warmed of a morning and mast was much more plentiful.

He ate half-raw bacon and a hunk of fried cornmeal dough for breakfast and thanked the good Lord for coffee. He stayed indoors, kept warm while Gudger and McGregor left with the dogs. They went down the North Carolina side with all five of them, intending to come up from below the bears, to pick up their trail. Bears are nighttime creatures, they had said. A while later Young took up a listening post to the north of the shack. Wayland said he would wait nearby as well. He selected a spot behind a big rock, secure from the coldest winds, his rifle near at hand, his bottle of milk dangling from a limb. He was conscious of a mild headache caused by the wood smoke in the room, from that and lying awake, listening to a bear described as being faster than a horse, more athletic than a cat, able to ball itself up and roll down a mountain, able to slither through laurel hells. Might be able to vanish as well; invisible bear, bred in one state, fed in the other.

Of more consequence, he wondered how Collie and Paula and Jonathan were.

Once as a little boy he had learned to make turkey calls, and he tried that now, but the sound was wobbly and unattractive. He kept trying, however. Once, away off he heard the dogs start yapping, but after a few minutes they were quiet.

Only signs of life at dawn were the nervous squirrels. They must be trying to determine what creature he was, whether dangerous or not. He spoke to them and they stopped chattering. I am a hunter, squirrels, he thought. I'm a great hunter, well armed, full even yet of a fair amount of whiskey and smoke, with just a little bit of cornbread and bacon. I am here to kill bears. I mean to kill a few, skin them with my borrowed knife and hold their hides up by their ears as high as I can reach while I stand on their tails. I am a Philadelphia hunter, just now coming into my powers. I have dogs out there somewhere, and soon they will smell a bear and let out their horrendous noises. I am waiting for them.

He saw Young. He was leisurely walking toward the north. Now he paused to consider streaks of gold in the east. A holy morning, suitable for worship. Wayland walked over to the edge of the divide, to an

110

overlook, with the North Carolina mountains stretching to the horizon. This morning clouds had slept late, were still filling in the valleys around the peaks, so that the peaks resembled toes of a prone giant.

There was a single hawk on the wing, bathing in sunlight. Now it dipped down into the clouds to moisten its wings. Now it rose into sunlight again.

Cold. He built a small fire and warmed his hands over it, then he stretched out in the sun, hoping that would keep him from freezing. He dozed off, awoke with the sun higher in the heavens, so high he supposed it was midmorning. He lay still, listening. Out the corner of his eye he located his rifle. He could hear the ground and tree squirrels working, chatting among themselves. He propped himself up on one elbow. A groundhog was sitting on a broken tree stump not twenty feet away, staring at him, whistling a tune, its nose quivering. Astounding, the ways of nature, the living procession, so that this dumb animal will manage to breed others of its kind, and they, on and on, to live here in this windy cathedral peopled by squirrels and an occasional invisible bear, by hunting dogs and hunters in season, and a skunk, like that one just there, wandering about, inquiring of the morning what was in store for today.

He drank his milk and ate a crust of cornbread. Still hungry, and lonely as a wordless song, he went walking toward the north to join Young.

He found Young lying on the ground, his rifle laid across his belly, singing bits of old verse as they occurred to him. Young knew all the words and tunes he had ever heard in his life, a companionable talent which served him well at times like this, and just now he was singing verses of "I'll Hang My Harp on a Willow Tree."

111

Oh! Who's going to shoe my pretty little foot, foot, foot,
And who's going to glove my lily-white hand,
And who's going to kiss my ruby lips
When you're in a far distant land?

He reported that earlier, down somewhere on the flank of the mountain, Milton's dog had let out a feverish yelp, then had begun his song, chasing something or other. Since none of the other dogs chimed in, Young decided Sandy had left the pack. Anyway, the hound had chased something into the east, had faded out finally. "We'll have our bellies pulled tight against our backbones if we don't find a bear before dark."

Wayland sat down nearby on the ground and tried making a turkey call.

"You get us a turkey and you'll be remembered," Young told him. "Oh, you'll be remembered for it. No more talk about your being tender."

"Last night did McGregor say he had known a hundred and fifty women?" Wayland asked.

"Don't think he can count that high." Young said. He sang:

My Pa's going to shoe my pretty little foot, foot, foot,
My Ma's going to glove my lily-white hand;
I know who'll kiss my ruby lips
When I'm in a far distant land.

Wayland was getting the call down pretty well by now, although Young didn't appear to be impressed. "Can cut a reed and do better," Young told him.

"Don't have a reed," Wayland said. "Left all my reeds behind."

"Not many men can do a call with their mouths alone."

Wayland kept trying, anyway. "You hungry?"

"Lord, yes," Young said. "Had a little bit of nothing for breakfast."

112

"It's not much sport, is it?" Wayland said.

Young smiled, cushioned his head with his hands comfortably. "When you're old you'll tell people about your big bear hunts."

"I doubt it," Wayland said. "What will I say?" He thought about that for a while, then began laughing.

"Well, I know," Young said.

Later they talked clockmaking. "How's Plover doing with the new cases?" Wayland asked. "How are the Marshalls doing? How many clocks will we make by Christmas?" Wayland wondered. "Two or three?"

Suddenly breaking across the winter land came the clear voice of a hound, maybe Sally, probably Sally, an assertive, assured note of mean music in the wasting, waiting world, and almost at once another hound joined in. This was coming from below them on the east mountain, from down the hill and off toward the northeast. The hound music, four distinct voices, swept across the mountainside, echoing crazily. Young was on his feet at once. "Come on here," he said to Wayland, and grabbed his rifle and went running along the ridgecrest toward the north, Wayland scrambling after. The two of them tore through thickets and briars, rocks flying out from behind.

A fifth hound voice chimed in, and Young took his hat off and waved to Wayland. "That's Sandy back," he called.

The music was a massive commotion which echoed up and down the valley. When the voices changed to angry snarls and yelps, Young let out a yell and went charging down the mountainside toward the noise, then turned, reconsidered, waved Wayland on along the crest of the ridge. "They've caught up with him."

Now baying again. The chase. Young began running for all his might toward the north, was passing

113

through a stand of oaks when his feet went out from under him and he took a tumble, cracking his head on a tree. Wayland called to him, then ran down the mountain to where he was lying and helped him to his feet.

"Damn acorns everywhere," Young said. "Have to run heavy, like a horse."

He had scraped across the ground for about twenty feet, landing against a black oak, and was holding his head between his hands, his face pained. "Wow," he whispered. "There, you see what a bear can do to you."

The bear was crossing on over the ridge by now; they could hear the music disappearing as the dogs chased it into slicks and hells.

Wayland helped Young up to the ridgecrest, where walking was easier, and they moved slowly to a stark, rocky lookout where the music of the hounds was full and strong, rising from off in Tennessee. They saw McGregor come pushing along, bent forward. He waved his hand at them, went on toward the cabin. It was too late to start another bear.

They sat around the night's fire, discussing bears, fussing about them. Only enough fatback left for tomorrow's breakfast, so it would be plain cornbread and whiskey tonight, Gudger decided. "Bread and water fer me," McGregor said.

Gudger was trickling water on his legs, which were cut and bruised, especially the shins; his pants legs were about half torn off.

The dogs came in, Sandy first. There were no severe cuts on him. McGregor's three came in, one of them injured on the shoulder. Probably he had been bit there by the bear. McGregor washed the wound out. Young from the yard kept calling for Sally, who was not with the pack, was still in the slick, and here it was growing dark. Every once in a while he would call her name.

The apple brandy was passed around. Wayland finished his milk, rinsed out the jar and filled it a third full of liquor, enough he thought to do him. "Last night I lost count," he explained.

"We have this jug for tonight, and one of peach for tomorrow night," Gudger said. "Got it in my suggin, and nobody's to touch it. If we don't get bear tomorrow, we'll not have anything else."

They fed half the cornbread to the dogs and ate the rest. Then when it was all gone, here came Sally scratching at the door. She entered like a village queen and flopped down before the fire, taking Gudger's customary place. Young examined her, said the worst injury was to her paw, where her flesh hung down a couple of inches, and he said there were two holes in the top of her head.

"Bear's tusks tried to crack her skull," McGregor told him. "Big 'un," McGregor said, considering the distance between the marks. "And he never treed, spite of them closing in."

"Anybody see him come by?" Gudger asked.

Nobody had. "He'll be back tomorrow to take his revenge," McGregor said. "They like a commotion."

"Now, I tell you what you do tonight, boys," Crawford said, speaking confidentially. "We have a bear to get tomorrow for sure. There's this bear out there. He's damn near killed Sally. Look how sweet she lies there, with nothing to eat."

Young mixed a bit of cornmeal with water and laid it on a hot rock, where it sizzled near her nose.

"Tell you what to do," Crawford said, "everybody dream tonight of food, of red meat."

"Can't help doing it," Milton said.

"Dream of bear meat, of having a hunk of bear meat about the size of a hot-water bottle, all to yourself. Are you listening?"

"I'm listening," Gudger told him. His stomach growled. "Not even got a deer. Got nothing. I'd eat a crow."

"Listen, boys, dream of having all the bear you can eat."

"I'm in favor of it," Milton said.

"When we raise that there bear tomorrow, when those dogs give us the word, we have to be sure to catch up with him. No failing this time."

"That's right," Young said. "No failing or falling." He nodded to Wayland.

They talked about bear feasts held in this very room, Gudger remembering any number of feasts where the men had chewed on the meat of the tenderloin, boiling it, baking it, frying it, until they were stuffed. "I could use some little bit of meat," Young admitted. The men savored the meal they wouldn't have tonight, speculated about tomorrow night, discussing bear.

The men blanketed the fireplace each time they needed to open the door; that is, four men held a blanket across the fireplace so the draft wouldn't pull the ashes and smoke into the room, while the other two ducked out to gather wood. Of course, the door was closed tight while the men were gone and was opened only when they had wood stacked at the door. Once the door was open again, they tossed and kicked the wood inside, thinking nothing of hurling it against men and dogs, beds and table, then they slammed the door, even as the blanket began to scorch and smoke.

"How fierce is the wind?" McGregor asked them.

"You can stand up against it," Milton said.

"Hit'll increase like pneumonia fever, I imagine," McGregor said.

"I've known many a time when a man had to crawl to wherever he was going," Gudger said proudly.

They huddled near the fire, watching Sally eat her supper. She ate it in a few gulps, steaming as it was, then lay back on the floor and allowed the firelight to reflect in her big eyes. "She's thinking about him, that there bear," McGregor said.

"Kill him, kill him, she's thinking," Gudger said. He was lusting for the bear, he was slobbering for the bear.

"That there Sandy took out after something," McGregor said critically to Milton.

"Maybe he's not learned yet what to hunt," Milton said, rising to Sandy's defense.

"That dog ever fight a bear?" McGregor asked.

Milton shook his head.

"This beats clockmaking, don't hit?" McGregor said suddenly, turning to Wayland.

Wayland laughed.

"A world of hits own," McGregor said. "People say to me, why do you hunt, and I tell them that's just the wagon I climbed aboard, a man has to do something."

Abruptly there came a warning from outdoors, a splash of wind that appeared to be as heavy as a wave of water, which set the cabin walls to trembling and alerted the dogs. It was probably a whisper, not the shout of a storm itself. An unsettling brew was mixing over in Tennessee, McGregor said, judging by past experiences up here at the Saddle; it was sucking strength from the lower reaches of the valleys, filling its belly, gathering together all its meanness in a ball of clouds and thunder, and they would be wise to watch out for the unleashing of it. "God's mercy," McGregor said and chained his dogs. "You better get that Sally chained," he told Young.

A minute or so later the crash came, terrifying Wayland, who had not known what to expect; a shudder of the heavens smashed against the shack walls and against the land and rocks on which the

117

shack was set. The roof rose a few inches, the walls strained to be freed, the men and dogs were blinded by dried mud from the chinking.

As the storm exploded around them, the light of the lightning emblazoned the hearth itself, made glow the open spaces between the logs and seeped in around the roof shakes.

"Hit's nigh on top of us," McGregor shouted, and tried to crawl under a cot. One of his dogs was under there.

Alternating drives of wind slashed at the cabin, moving in and retreating much like waves at the beach.

The men were awakened sometime in the night by Gudger, were ordered out of bed for breakfast. "What day is this, is it Monday?" Wayland asked McGregor. Outdoors he smashed at the wash-up ice with a frozen rock, which in turn burned his hand. "Want to be home," he moaned. "Hey, Young, you going to get that bear today?" he called.

Young grinned. "You getting a hunting fever?"

"I might as well," Wayland said. "Nothing else going on around here."

Mist everywhere, floating about in the lantern light, fingers of gray touching his face, moving on by. He knew that trees had fallen around here, but in the dark he couldn't see them; he had heard at least one tree crash during the storm.

Breakfast was being announced. Wayland ducked back indoors, where firelight coals were all that lighted the place, and found his way to the frying pan. "There's coffee in the kettle," Milton told him. Wayland climbed up on his bunk to get away from the dogs, and ate, catching the crumbs on his lap. He was wearing the same clothes he had hiked up the mountain in, hadn't seen a piece of soap since he had arrived, but didn't feel too dirty to live. There was no mirror in this place, nor any other feminine niceties. No woman would stay up here, no child would ever be born here or could survive here, he imagined. It was a male place, and he was beginning to accept, admire it as such. Some instinct long buried inside him was responding to it.

Crawford talking: "Bears are left-handed, all I ever saw are left-handed, and you have to watch for it, for when a bear swipes at you with a left paw, you're knocked unconscious, certain as the world spins round."

"Bears are like Gudger in that respect," Milton commented.

"Does the world spin," Young asked, "or turn?"

"You believe hit's round, do ye?" McGregor said, looking over at him skeptically.

"I always heard that," Young said.

"Believe everything you hear, do you?" McGregor said. "I allowed you had better sense."

"Now, he'll be waking up about now, won't he?" Crawford said.

"He's out from under the bresh by now," McGregor said, "is moving to where he's going to eat breakfast."

"How you know it's a male instead of a female?" Wayland asked him.

"Sow bears are probably denned by now," McGregor told him. "I saw yesterday a place where a boar bear had him a den, had tore up laurel, so much hit wouldn't all go inside this shack, and had stacked hit in the middle of a thicket so thick hit'd scrape skin off a snake back, and then he'd got under it, don't you know, slept there."

"But he wasn't to home," Crawford said.

"No, he was out hunting just then. They travel a sight of miles a night and day. I've known my dogs to follow a bear for twenty-five mile."

"Yesterday's bear crossed at that chimney place,"

119

Gudger said, "so he might be there looking for us, will want to eat that dog of Young's that bit him."

"Sally?"

"They don't like to be annoyed," Gudger grumbled.

"He probably got a taste of Sally," McGregor said, "liked her."

"Well, let's go," Crawford said impatiently.

Outdoors Wayland was cold as ever in his life. Only a few trees were down, mostly oak, Young reported. How he could tell in the dark, Wayland didn't know. Squirrels had made a nest in one such tree and were now huddled near it, fussing about the alterations the storm had made to their quarters. Wayland could smell honey, so he supposed one of the fallen trees had had bees in it. Honey was a night smell, he decided, was particularly delicious and mouth-tingling to have floating around in the air in this black crispness. Bear come along, break open the fallen trunk, fill his belly with honey...

That thought struck him with a chill, and he sat flat down on the ground and stared about, glaring at the fire-lighted door of the hunting shack, considering his new idea, thinking about honey and the bear, wondering if he were to be the one first to see the bear, if this honey were to be the strangeness, the attraction of the day, and he, the newcomer, the outlander, to be the benefactor, the slayer of the bear. He wanted it. He wanted it, could sense the thrill of being the one among this company who killed the bear. He needed it. Only he among the six needed it. "Honey, honey, honey," he whispered, and crouched low to the ground, his rifle in both hands. He had not thought it possible until this moment for him to kill the bear.

An hour later his muscles were worn thin and

complaining, so he stood up and walked about a bit. By now the smell of honey was less pronounced anyway, seemed to him; either that or he had grown accustomed to it.

Soon after dawn a shot sounded far down the mountain, way off in the pits of North Carolina, then he heard a man shout something or other, then silence. Later a man was heard calling from that same direction. Sounded like McGregor. Later Wayland heard two men shouting to one another, but their words were indistinct.

Quiet. Deathly quiet, except for the leaves and the noise of everyday existence on this mountainside. Not much wind now.

Having heard voices made him sense his loneliness all the more. He was, he realized, the only man left at the hut, the lone representative here of these other five men, of his company. Rarely had he experienced any such sense of responsibility. Usually he had been his uncles' nephew, the one who works in the shop, the uncles in charge, or his mother's son, the mother in charge, or the husband of that ill woman, the lady in the chair on the hotel porch who always has her way. He had not been prepared for a mission with danger in it and to have others depend on him. War must be like this, he thought, men waiting, complaining, eating whatever they can find, talking about women, cleaning guns, depending on one another. He cocked his rifle, just to feel the weight of metal and of the danger in his hands. By God, he could kill a bear.

A sudden noise, a whistling in his ear, something close hurtling by, the sound of a bear's paw here— Terrified, he swung around, sought the ground, only to realize it was a bird, that bird there turning on the wing, looking back, cackling derisively. "You son of a bitch," he uttered between his teeth.

The crow was laughing at him.

Imprison dead men in those birds' bodies, put them on the wing, he thought, pour their souls into those black bodies and let them haunt the living. My God, it had scared him.

Midmorning. He ate what cornbread he had brought with him. The sliver of fat meat was juicy in his mouth and he licked the taste off his lips greedily. Nothing to drink it down with, no water anywhere around here. Get a handful of honey, if he knew where it was. Ought to go along the crest to find Young, see what Young was doing with his time, but no, he held his own place, anxious for a bear; not going to share it with Young either, if he could shoot it himself.

The hounds, first one of McGregor's males, then a chorus, almost in a single instant ruffled the air, the dogs directly below him not half a mile away, making eager music. The hounds were running now. He could tell the dogs were just down there below, not more than half, a quarter mile away, and they seemed to him to be coming up the slope.

He leaned back against a hickory tree, waiting, and stared down through the staggered rows of trees, where all the squirrels had flitted into their nests, all animals had fled or buried themselves in holes. The world was preparing for an assault, as for last night's blast of storm, the whole mountain was shivering as much as the leaves on the trees. The bear.

There was the bear, galloping with enormous power, the dogs at his heels, moving up the mountain toward where he stood, the tree to his back, Wayland waiting until the bear was so close he could see the slobber from his mouth, the redness of his eyes. A massive form he was, amazingly graceful, running like a galloping elk up the mountain.

A rifle fired. The sound stunned Wayland. The rifle was smoking in his hand, his own shoulder was hurt

122

where the heel of the stock had been braced. The bullet had entered the bear's chest and the bear had stopped, surprised. A trickle of blood was coloring red the black hair of his chest.

The bear swung away, heading north across the side of the mountain, one of the dogs holding to his flank, being dragged by him.

"Hey," Wayland called to the bear, "hey, where the hell you going?" He felt deprived, denied; he took off running, shouting for the return of the bear. He went crashing through a stand of rhododendron, being spun by limbs, tearing his way, being torn, hurled to the ground by it, crawling desperately, anxiously striving, the rifle filled with litter and soil. He cursing the rhododendron, snaking his way through, abruptly falling, the earth having ended, falling twenty feet onto other rhododendron, finding himself bedded by branches, held up to the sunlight like an offering, the round sun looking down on him, his rifle landing with a plop somewhere below. He lay there staring upward, a smile on his lips. "Hey, come back here!" he called, loud as he could.

Noon. Hounds were just now far off to the north. He could hear them while he was stumbling around on the side of the mountain. How many times had he fallen to the ground, rolling on nuts and acorns, slipping on wet rocks, finding that moss would give way under him? First he would hear the dogs over to the north; the bear was treed, he would decide, and run in that direction. Then he would hear the dogs coming back toward the south, baying. North to south, south to north, treed and untreed, dogs baying and yapping and snarling as suited their endeavors, he thoroughly exhausted, left without energy enough to think even of climbing back to the saddle of the divide.

But he had shot the bear. Let the world know that.

Nobody could take that away from him. He had seen the deep red color sop the chest of the bear.

The hound voices changed to snarls, and he supposed the bear had stopped to fight. Somebody was calling out, maybe two men were calling. Had he traveled three miles, ten miles from the place where he had shot the bear? Was he lost? He thought he must be.

The voices of the hounds were music once again, so the bear was moving. Wayland stopped to listen, stared dumbly at the woods all about. He looked down at his clothes, torn and ripped. There was no pants leg left below the knees, and his legs were streaked with blood.

The bear was coming this way again.

"Very well." He waited. "Rooster," he murmured, remembering to cock his rifle. The sound of the hounds was a rising, tumbling noise from just up there. The bear was crossing above him.

A shot sounded. Somebody else had taken a shot.

The bear must have stopped and turned on the dogs, to judge from the racket. The bear was just up there a ways, was fighting the growling dogs, and popping his teeth. Wayland moved toward it, pushing himself up the side of the mountain, moving faster, anxious to be present, the racket of yelps and barks and growls loud and ominous. He heard Young shout, and he thought he saw Young higher on the mountain, moving down. Wayland pushed through dogwood branches and came upon the battlefield, a narrow ravine in the mountainside with the bear at the pit of it, his back to the rock wall, the dogs before him, snarling at him and each other, dogs getting in each other's way, the bear tossing a dog off whenever one came close enough. As Wayland drew near, one of McGregor's dogs leaped at the bear's arm, dug his fangs into the arm, and the great bear swung that arm high, trying to hurl the

124

dog into the air. No, it was not McGregor's dog, it was Milton's new dog, Sandy, and Sandy went sailing through air and landed yelping, running off through the woods. The bear's paw now mauled a McGregor dog, opening him down the stomach, then the bear received the frontal attack of Sally, who ignored the shouts of Young to stay off the bear. Young was now stationed above and behind the bear, on the rocks. Sally bit into the jaw of the bear, managed to get hold of the lower jaw, which caused much grunting and growling from the surprised, greater animal. Young gave a shout and leaped down to the floor of the battleground, landing behind the bear, perhaps twenty feet away from him, and the bear, sensing new danger from that quarter, with both paws took hold of Sally's body and sought to pull her free of her hold on his jaw. Failing that, the bear bit into Sally's own upper jaw and ripped her head open, hurled the body aside, the dog dead instantly. The bear turned to face Young, Sally's lower jaw and part of her head still in his mouth. Young fired directly at the bear's head. Two of McGregor's dogs, the only two left, leaped on the bear's back. He brushed them off with side blows as he waded toward Young, furious to be so often offended. Wayland shouted a warning to Young, and then to save Young he leaped upon the bear's back, dug his hands into his fur and tried to pull him back, Young shouting at Wayland to get the hell out of the way. Young even crouched down, trying to get a safe shot at the bear, which was dragging Wayland and one dog toward him. The bear, weakened by wounds, was still powerful.

A rifle shot, a single singing bullet plopped into the bear; the bear collapsed, Wayland falling forward on top of him, still holding to his fur, the bear's head landing only a foot or so from where Young stood, pistol in hand. Gudger came swaggering forward and told Young he could put his pistol away, told Wayland he could let go of the bear. "What you have in mind, anyway?" he asked Wayland.

"Keeping him off Young," Wayland replied.

"Yeh, Lord," Gudger said. "Had to shoot from the side. Young, you can put your pistol away, honey. Now chain them dogs, the two, before they get to fighting."

Wayland stared about at the mound of fur, then at the dead Sally. One of the McGregor dogs crept close to the bear, flopped to its belly, took a bit of the bear's tail in its mouth to show it claimed the bear. Gudger tied the other dog to a dogwood, then nudged the bear with his boot and sat down on the body and gave a yell, the rebel yell of the long-ago war. He sat there on the bear's body giving that rebel yell.

It was almost dark by the time the three men started to the hunting shack, leaving most of the meat for portage home tomorrow from the spring-water bath where they left it. They toted with them the tenderloin roasts and the liver wrapped in laurel. Along the way they called out their presence, announced their victory generally, and now and then shot off a rifle. The two remaining McGregor dogs were with them, and Sandy was always just over there, skeetishly moving alongside. Sally and a McGregor dog were left behind, buried under rock not far from the bear.

Sunset was fiery, and the sky was alive with rumbling thunder, mostly off over Tennessee, throat-clearing thunder, merely practice, some assembly of heaven's dwarfs preparing their throats for song. Whether they were getting ready for a major performance or merely passing time till dark, Wayland didn't know.

The three of them, Young, Gudger and Wayland,

reached the shack about five o'clock, and Gudger stripped some of the fat off the roasts and fried slices of liver for the dogs. He kept referring to the bear he had killed. Of course, at least three men present had shot the bear, but they knew how Gudger was, that the composition of his flesh and bones was about half boastfulness and the rest hunger for praise. "You have to stay back from the bear so other men can shoot, damn your hide," Gudger said to Wayland.

"I was trying to keep him off of Young."

"Young couldn't fire, either," Gudger said. "You lay all over the bear's back, so if Young fired and the lead went through the bear—"

"Leave him alone," Young said, conscious that Gudger was hurting Wayland. "The bear's dead," he said.

"Thanks to me, coming in from the right," Gudger said.

"I had my pistol out by then," Young told him. "Pistol bullets wouldn't go through the bear."

"Stop a bear with a pistol?"

"He was about dead. You were the undertaker, Gudger."

"Undertaker my ass. My God. I come in there and saved your life and what you say? Why, you say leave Wayland alone, that's all. Hell, he has to learn."

"You never saved my life," Young said. "I had a pistol, I had a knife. Hell, he shot the bear first, before you had even finished your morning shit."

"By God," Gudger said, his voice trembling, "by God, is that it? Is that the story?" His hands were trembling so much he could scarcely stir the fire. "Ah, God, thank you, Mr. Gudger, for saving both our lives. There we were, one naked before the bear with a stone wall to his back, the bear advancing, and the other riding the bear, taking the air, without

127

even a saddle under his ass or a blade in hand."

"Shut your damned mouth," Young demanded.

"Now, you don't tell me what to do. Not another word from you, Young." Gudger got to his feet, his fists clenching, unclenching. He was hovering, was ready, and Young came up like a spring off the floor and struck him under his chin, then kneed him as Gudger swung out a big left fist that caught Young beside his head and spun him, sent him sailing backward against a set of double bunks, dogs scattering. Wayland, trying to get between the men, was hurled against a wall brutally. "Now wait," Wayland said, taking up his rifle and aiming it at Gudger. "Now wait, damn you," he said.

Gudger backed away before the rifle until the wall was to his back. He belched, then slowly smiled, staring at the rifle and at Wayland. "You going to kill me?" he said, his voice goading.

Wayland stashed the rifle on his upper bunk and buried his head in his arms there, his back to the big man, and Gudger kicked the chair out of the way and shifted his attention to Young. "You want some more?" he asked.

Young was still dazed. He was not steady even yet. Clearly he was not able to do more fighting just now. Gudger shrugged, knelt before the fireplace and ran a stick around the edges of the pot, stirring the bear meat in its water. He put the iron lid on the pot to hold the steam inside. He belched again. "Sorry, Young," he said.

"Yeh," Young said. He righted the chair and sat down weakly at the table.

Gudger kept belching. "Wish't I had some buttermilk. Get drunk, by God, that'll help. Might give you men a little sip or two. How about it?"

"Keep your damned liquor," Young said.

"You speaking just for yourself? You want liquor or not, Wayland?"

"Yeh," Wayland said.

"He'd crawl from here to the spring and bring water back in his mouth and wash my ass with it for a drink of liquor, and don't you doubt it, Young." From his pack Gudger took the one remaining jug of brandy and drank a long, slow drink, then set the jug on the table across from Young. "Don't you want some?" He appeared to be perplexed, there was no animosity evident in him now. He had won the fight, as was customary, that was what had happened, and the decision was that he was in control. If he was in control and everybody knew it, he could relax and be generous. "Go on, Young, wet your whistle."

Milton arrived. He was always a soothing influence on the family. He arrived when darkness was so thick it resisted the meager light the cabin offered, but he had been able to see to get home, as he said. He smelled the meat cooking and saw the jug was open, so he settled down on a cot near the table, pleased beyond bearing. He took a long drink and nudged the jar toward Young, who took a swig and passed it to Wayland, who drank from it and set it on the table. Milton said his day was so much up and down and across the mountain to no effect. "One shot is all I got, and it was from a goat distance."

"How far's that?" Wayland asked.

"You just waste it," Milton said.

Young went outdoors and called Crawford and McGregor. He kept calling and finally he earned a response from Crawford, from somewhere down on the Tennessee side. "What the hell you doing down there?" Young called out. "Hey, Crawford?"

Crawford came crawling up out of Tennessee, tired to death. "Shot a turkey, winged him, had to run him down." He held up the turkey at the shack door, a plump hen. "What say to that?"

"Why, you come on indoors, then," Young said.

"Went through laurel for a mile," Crawford told him. He told the others, too, crouched before the fire warming. "Damn fool thing to do. Minds get crazy, like the wind does, up here."

"Been men lost in laurel, starved to death," Milton told him.

"Oh, I know that," Crawford said. "Always think it can't be me, but I was lost for better part of an hour, was fighting laurel, got to combatting it, aggravated to death by it, using my last strength."

"What you mean, last strength?" Gudger said.

"Couldn't hear or see anything." He drank deeply from the jar. "Said goodbye to my family." He grinned. "Who shot the bear?"

"Wayland shot him," Young said at once.

"Wayland did? Did Wayland shoot it?" Crawford said, surprised.

"Shot it in the chest, and after that he was just following along to let it fall," Young said, watching Gudger, who was squatting at the fireside near Crawford.

Gudger grumbled, cursing. "Was alive when I shot him."

"Shot him in the chest, did you, Wayland?" Crawford said.

Wayland took a drink out of the jug, a long drink, enough to do him for a while, then climbed up on his bunk.

Young said, "And I shot him twice. And I think Gudger might have shot at him as he fell."

Gudger growled angrily. "When I got there, he was alive enough. It'd 'a killed both of them, the way they kept doing."

"Wayland's got more courage than anybody I ever saw," Young said. "He couldn't shoot, since I was in the way on the other side, so he leaped on him."

Crawford was hanging his turkey from a ceiling

130

hook to keep the dogs off of it. "Jumped on him?" He stared at Wayland. "Takes a born bear hunter to wrestle a bear."

"He has more courage than the rest of us combined."

"Craziest thing I ever saw," Gudger said, grumbling. "Was riding the damned bear—"

Young gave the jar to Crawford, said to celebrate his turkey with another drink.

They were eating when McGregor arrived. He was so tired he thought he'd take one drink of liquor. He had been delayed because he had found a bear trap set in a path. "I wondered why the leaves was so out of order, so I poked them with a stick and the leaves reared up like Gabriel and snapped that stick between them steel jaws. Hit was God's kindness that hit never got my leg, just God's kindness that I noticed them leaves."

"Why did that delay you so long?" Gudger said. "Punching a trap—"

"I had to bury the trap so'it couldn't be found. Hit won't be used again," McGregor said.

"You mean you missed the bear fight so you could bury a trap?" Gudger said.

"One of them Campbell traps, I'll bet you that's whose hit is, and they'll not get hit back when they come. Hit's down there deep in the ground."

"You missed the hunt, Greg," Crawford told him.

"Buried hit, that I did," McGregor said, satisfied with his work. "They had hit set right there where I would have stepped."

Young had a bruise rising at the place on his face where Gudger had struck him, but since everybody was cut up and damaged, nobody noticed. When he got up to go outdoors "to finish up for the night," as he said, Wayland came with him, and they urinated on a big tree near the door. It was pitch dark tonight, couldn't even see each other. "Don't let

Gudger rile you, too," Young said. From here the hut resembled an animal with striped sides; the stripes were where the glow of the fire shone through the spaces where the chinking was gone. "I meant to kill that brother years ago," Young said suddenly.

"No, don't say that," Wayland told him.

"I've fought him half a dozen times and never have beat him. Twice I stood him off."

"Well, what does it matter?" Wayland said.

"It's easy to hit him, he's so slow, but when he hits you, then it's the end of the play."

"Was funny anyway, me jumping on that bear," Wayland said. "If I had had my knife, or anything whatever—"

"No time to plan," Young said. "I was getting down low so I could shoot up and miss hitting you, do you understand? I could have killed him with the pistol, I believe."

"One blow of his paw, then where would you be?" Wayland said.

"Or his foot, you mean," Young said. "Get low, they kick you."

When the men returned, Gudger was telling about how he had come upon the two infants and the bear and had killed the bear with a shot from the side. Of course, he was the savior of the two of them. Wayland pulled himself up on his bunk and listened from there as the group of men drank and questioned and confessed and argued. He had no need for claiming more credit, nor denying anything, either. He was the one who first shot the bear; nobody denied that. He was too weary to talk anyway, and the brandy had flown into his body, so that he felt giddy. "They say a bear hunt is the best thing in the world for a man," Milton told him confidentially, stopping beside his bunk. "It purges him. Did you know that?"

"I felt something," Wayland admitted.

132

"Take all the guilt you have and lay it on the bear. Then kill the bear."

"I'd say it's hard on a man's clothes," Wayland said, examining the tears in his shirt.

Gudger said, "A bear fights back. No lamb about him."

Coffee was boiling now, and what was left of the cornmeal was baking. The meat wasn't tender, but was hot and chewy and rich of taste. The dogs were fed well and were drowsy. Smoke rose in the room from the fireplace and from Milton's Camel cigarette. "That dog Sally was a great dog," Young said. "Sorry about your dog, Greg."

"Sorry what?" McGregor said. "One go on home?"

"No, we rock-buried him down in a vale," Milton said finally.

Tears came instantly to McGregor's eyes. "Oh, my God," he whispered. He sought out his dogs, pulled them from their places under Gudger's cot. "Lost Jim," he said. "Why'd you let that bear kill Jim?" he asked the dogs. "Here, what you got on your head, Stem? Is that a deep one? Where did the bear get your brother?"

"Stomach," Young told him.

"A suffering pity, by God. Stomach him, you say?"

"Ran off dragging guts till he died."

"Ah, God," McGregor moaned. "Was in on twenty kills if ary one, was the brother of this'n, the father of that'n there. Your papa's dead," he told her. "You listening?" He got to his feet, stood on his limber, rubbery legs. "Did they whimper ary time?"

"They sniffed around him," Milton said. "One howled."

McGregor complained mightily about the loss. "I thought they was all under the bunk," he said. He brushed big tears out of his eyes.

"I been left out of the new clockmaking company,"

133

Gudger was saying to Crawford. "Suppose you heard about that?"

"Yeh, I heard," Crawford said, winking at Young. He had heard about it often enough, all right.

"Oldest son left out of the new family enterprise, then of course they will come to me for advice about loans and savings and how to get the cabinets built."

Wayland didn't bother to comment. He was done with Gudger, wouldn't accept help from him.

"Don't have a license," Gudger said.

Young stared at him quizzically. "What license?"

"See there?" Gudger said, and laughed. "Put the oldest son out, and him the one that knows business."

"Well, let's change the subject," Crawford said.

"Accounts be out of adjustment first thing you know."

"I imagine," Crawford said. "Let's talk about something else."

"People come in the store, open canned goods," Gudger began. "Or come in for sugar, get what they want, put it on credit, then take a stove chair for an hour, pay nothing for that, go off. It's a social club I'm running ..."

"Evenings Mama wasn't down at the river fishing," Milton was saying to Wayland, "those nights she'd weave. I'd say to her, Mama, fish of a day before dinner, then we can have fresh fish with our bread."

Wayland listened, sleeping through part of the talk, waking up and conversing with them, drinking with them, feeling relaxed with them, really for the first time since he had come to their community.

"We have to stoke that meat tomorrow," Young was saying.

"Lot of trouble," Gudger said.

"Have to divide it into six piles, anyway," Young

134

said. "Might as well blindfold a man to say the owners of each one."

"I don't care," Gudger said.

"Wonder what Wayland will do with the hide."

There was a long pause, then Gudger said, "What do you mean, Wayland do with it? I shot the bear."

"Wayland had about killed it, I'd say," Young said.

"Why, God damn you," Gudger said, "I shot him dead and you was standing there."

"Bears are born weighing a pound each," Crawford said, interrupting. "If a man grew as fast as a bear does, how big would he be when he's four years old, Wayland? Is Wayland awake or not?"

Wayland removed his arm from across his face. "About five hundred pounds."

"No, he'd be two thousand."

Gudger said, "Wayland, this brother of mine says you're claiming the hide."

Wayland said nothing.

"Can't make a clock out of it?" Crawford said, and laughed.

"Paula would like it," Young told Wayland. "Hell, you shot the bear."

"No, she doesn't need it," Wayland said, anxious to avoid more fighting around here. "Maybe Collie could use it."

Crawford said, "Sometimes I think I might go up to three hundred pounds myself. My father condemned to hell any farmer that got bigger'n a thirty-two-inch waist. Doctors and lawyers could go to thirty-four. Sheriffs could go to forty."

Wayland would listen to a spate of such foolishness, then would doze off, so weary he could not even think of standing up, then he would awaken and listen to the talk some more.

"Good bear dogs won't hold to a bear, they'll snap and back off," McGregor was saying sleepily, yawning. "That there dog Sally was too hungry to suit

135

me. A revengeful dog gets killed."

"A wounded bear is always more dangerous, anyway," Milton said.

"Plotts are the best," Young was saying, "but they don't always aggravate a bear enough to make him tree."

McGregor was talking: "Hit would be better, as a man ages, for him to lose his balls rather than his teeth. I sure do need my teeth." Later he said, "If hit was all explained to me how a man and woman go atter'it together, I mean if hit was drawed on a sheet of paper with numbers, I'd not be the least bit interested. I'd think hit was a fool idea. But hit works the best I ever saw."

"Strangest damn thing God ever invented wasn't that," Milton told him. "Know what it was, Mac? It was a tree. Now, you think about that."

Each time Wayland dozed off and awoke, another man had gone to bed, and the ashes were deeper on the hearth, the fire was lower. He heard Gudger saying, "Decided to go ahead and skin him, and I hung him to a limb, using Wayland's belt, and Wayland got to looking at the bear strange, it hanging there to a limb, and I asked him what was the matter, and he said that the bear looks like a man, now that it's skinned, it's a white man. And I said, well, that's so, though its back legs are stumpy for a man's."

"How much fat he have on him?" Milton asked.

"Four to five inches," Gudger said.

He did look very like a man hanging there from the belt, Wayland thought, drifting off into sleep again. Like Collie's lover hanging there, he thought.

It was deep in the night that he awoke to listen to Young and Milton keep the night alive. Only they were left up. He heard Young in his pleasant, relaxed, late-time manner say, "Of course, if I don't marry Benie, I'll have to leave this place. It's one or the other."

"I don't see that you'd need to go anywheres," Milton said.

"I wouldn't want to say no to her, then pass her house two, three times a day."

"Go through the woods, then," Milton said, laughing contentedly. "Women can adapt, you know that. If they wasn't good at that, they'd not be able to put up with men at all."

"She says it'd kill her."

"Well, there'd be many dead that's walking about, in that case."

"She asked me, Milton. Keeps at it."

"To marry her, you mean?"

"Several times she's asked. Wants to have babies before she's too old. I say no and she turns over in the bed and cries the most pitiable you ever heard. So I say this, if I ever tell her once and for all, I'd better go on down the road."

"And leave Papa? Leave Collie and that clock man? He's an interesting, mild sort of fellow, ain't he?"

"He leaves that impression. But I believe if he gets the bit in his teeth, he won't ever let go of it."

"No, I wouldn't leave all of us, and the clockmaking company, just for Benie Frazier, who's got what she wanted for these years now."

"She's not had a baby. She wants that."

"Well, even so."

"Collie said to go."

"No, she never. Collie did?"

"She said to go find myself. That was only a few weeks ago she said it."

"Collie did? Oh, I don't know about that."

"She said if I married Benie, I would be stunting my life here at the start. She said I'd be picking myself green. She said she'd rather I run off somewhere and start over."

"She's not tough enough to mean that."

137

"She said to go find Uncle Charlie. Or go to Asheville and work with the Kings."

"She'd not be able to do anything like that herself," Milton said.

"Yes," Young said simply, "yes she would, too. You've none of you yet seen what Collie's able to do. She's the toughest one of us."

After a while Milton said, "Well, give Benie a baby, then."

"Then I'd be tied for sure, wouldn't I?"

"Then go find you a young girl to marry."

"No, I can't do that."

"Why? It won't hurt Benie so much, once she has the baby."

"Can't do that to the child," he said.

Milton was quiet for a while. "You ever notice how life blocks its own path? One gets these fences set up. My wife and me, why, we fell into the wagon and I never got enough courage to leave here. Take them Campbells, they bed 'em and leave 'em, they tell me. Hell, they trade off wives, daughters." Milton drank from the jug and passed it to Young. "Might as well finish it."

"And it's so, Milton, that Benie gets on my nerves."

"Gloria gets on mine. What you expect?"

"But I've never had another woman to love. You know that?"

"I don't believe it."

"I've been with other women, but not in love."

"When did you first know Benie? How old were you? Gudger says you were fifteen."

"I was sixteen."

"Still young. Gudger told me he thought he'd figured out who fathered Collie's baby."

"Who?"

"He never would tell me. Do you know yet?"

"Gudger's a damn fool," Young said.

"You don't have your life anyway, that's what I see. The only life a man has is what he's not given away, what's not owned by others, and I never seem to have any of that. Of course, the worst form of slavery is being free of everybody."

Young sat up straight and faced his brother. "Where'd you hear all that said?"

"Papa told it to me years ago, when I was meaning to sneak off and go with Uncle Charlie, and Papa found my cloth bag packed with my things, and I had a rope to climb down to the ground from that loft room, and he told me Charlie was lost. I said, Papa, Uncle Charlie's the one that's found the way."

"Did Papa say Uncle Charlie was in slavery?"

"He said the only choice a man ever had in life was to decide what sort of slavery to accept, and that determining to be free was the worst slavery of all."

"So you decided to stay there with him, not go with Uncle Charlie."

"No. I still wanted to go. So Papa did something that night I've never told anybody about. He roped me to my bed."

When Wayland next awoke, he heard Young talking. "I said, what do you tell me, Collie, how can I be mean to Benie? That's what a man does, she said, keeps saving his life, and what a woman does is to give her life." He sniffed at the liquor jar, drained it of a swallow. "I don't know just how."

"Collie keeps giving her life away?" Milton asked suspiciously. "I never noticed it." Sleepily he went over to his cot and stretched out. "Time to sleep or time to get up, which is it?"

"I said to Collie, it'll tear my heart out to leave her, and you know what she said, Milton?"

Milton grunted.

"She said to put my heart on the table there, where hers was." Young was quiet after that. Way-

139

land lay awake, staring at the roof above his head, biding his thoughts about Collie and this place, and himself and Paula, all of them willing prisoners in it. He lay there listening to the boy, Young, weeping.

He drove Crawford, Milton and Gudger to their homes, but near McGregor's his truck coughed and quit, so he wrapped his allotment of bear and turkey meat in brown paper that McGregor's children brought him and left the truck parked.

His leaving appeared strange to everybody standing there in the road. "Just needs gas," they said, and mentioned how far it was to home, and how heavy the meat was, and how cold the day was, all of which deterred him not at all. Lord, he had walked enough in the last three days so that a little more wouldn't matter, and he had the idea firmly in mind to go home the way he had once arrived from off this same ridge.

He walked through the breaking woods itself, made a path through the fallen limbs, just as before, and stopped at the downhill edge of it, where he wiped the broken bits out of his hair and off his shirt, as before, and when he was about a hundred feet from the house, he called out his presence. He had to call again before this tall, slender woman came to the door and shaded her eyes.

"I've been up on the ridge," he told her. "Saw a chimney of smoke, and I need to warm." He moved closer. "If you'd call your man out here so I could ask him to let me warm—"

"He's not home," she said, lingering on the words fondly, watching him kindly. "Wayland, do you have the bear's hide?"

"Then call your children out so they can see how harmless I am."

"Wayland, did you shoot the bear?"

He set the pack down on the ground and she came

closer to him, and they came together, laughing, and that was the way he arrived home that evening, the second time he had come to her house from off the mountain.

6

Up and down along the road, the citizens hung their slaughtered hogs this time of year. Wayland often would ride past half a dozen as he drove out to visit the wood craftsmen, or the old lady, Mrs. Doris Hemstead, who was painting numerals on the steel dials. These hogs, when first hung by the tendons of their back legs, were complete bodies, but quite soon they were cut down the belly and later the backbone, then were parceled into roasts and hams and slabs and pieces. This was a ceremonial time, featuring special foods, with fresh ribs and back-bones for everybody, with liver pudding and spicy sausage made by German recipes passed down by generations. It was the busy time of salting down the hams and bacon, for closing up the bins of sweet potatoes, for making kraut. Over at the Wrights', Mavis had stored exactly one hundred and four pumpkins in one corner of the earthen-walled cellar. She had personally selected each one for size and thickness and color. She had twenty bushels of sweet potatoes stored in another corner, where they wouldn't be near apples, which would make them sprout. Why an apple would make a sweet potato sprout she didn't know, but there were even rarer oddities in the world than that, she realized, and didn't worry about it. William Wright had uncovered his copper still, one hand-riveted in England in the eighteenth century and carefully maintained; he had it set up back of the barn, and the Bolton boys had it fired. He and Milton's boys meanwhile poured soda and water inside the two fifty-five-gallon oak barrels; into each barrel they also dropped a few stones, then stoppered the bung and rolled the barrels back and forth across the yard to clean them out and make them ready for sulfuring and for the new liquor.

Wayland, usually with Collie close by, would spend time every day supervising the building of the clock tower. He wanted the stones laid down, with none of them standing up on their edges, and he wanted little mortar to show. Also, he wanted the stones to reveal only their weathered surfaces. Each day he would criticize the previous day's work, insisting on his own standards, at one point requiring the men to take down one section of the west wall.

The remainder of his time was spent in Young's mill, where the wheel was in place, as were the belts and pulleys. The mill was ready for use, but all the use the building got was to house Wayland's press and clockmaking tools. He had built a big table close to the south window where he would have maximum light, and there he would cut or mold the wheels and gears and arbors, the hammer tails and hammer stems and hammer heads, the balance cocks, the pins and all the rest. Then, too, often at night he would work at Collie's table, her two new hurricane lamps burning beside his hands, would turn over and over the brass parts he had made for the first twenty clocks, selecting and finishing with an Ayr stone. He would use a magnifying glass to examine each part. Sometimes he would discard one, or set it by for possible use later on. "I want these first clocks to be special, that's the way I feel about it," he would tell her. "I want their hearts to beat at the exact time of the world."

Mrs. Davenport made him a pair of pants, using a piece of linsey she had woven years ago, and Collie made him a shirt and some underclothing. The linsey would never wear out, Mrs. Davenport said, and the cotton clothes would see him through the "weakening time," as she called these days of economic depression. "You have to make do today or do without," she said.

"Trust Roosevelt," William Wright advised everybody, but the advice was sourly received by most of the people, who distrusted governments, who had had only unhappy experiences with them. This attitude extended back as far in history as their families could remember, both in this country and Europe. Only William Wright and the Widow Frazier spoke well of the President. "At least he's trying," Wright said one day in the store. "I've been in other depressions. Take 1907. That was a stomach tightener. No government help then. That put people in the grave, Mr. Wayland. I mean you could see grown people weak from hunger. When a fellow had to trade, why, he had to trade his family or his land. If he wanted medicine, he had to trade hard for it. And where was the government? The government was a dog in the manger, that's where."

"When was the worst before 1907?" Wayland asked him.

"About fourteen years earlier. You can figure there'll be one about ever' fourteen years, one that'll be a plague of locust."

"Hit's none of the government's business. Let the poor man be," one of the old fellows at the stove told Wright.

Another man said, "Get its toe in the door, next thing you know the government'll be in the kitchen and the bedroom with us. Ain't that right, Mr. Wayland?"

"Name is Jackson," Wayland reminded him.

"Be telling us how to farm."

"That wouldn't hurt anybody," Wright told him. "There's plenty of farming we don't know."

"Be in here flooding this valley to make a lake out of hit," one man said. "No, I'd rather go hungry a few months out of ever' year than have a government at all."

"Well, you're going to have to have one," Wright told him.

"Why do I?" the old fellow asked, trying to be patient with Wright, who on most matters appeared to be sensible. "Papa never put up with one."

"Well, how did he fight wars, then?" Wright demanded.

"He fought them there at the house, fought whichever enemy arrived."

"We've fought the French, fought the English, fought them Highland Scots at the Widow Moore's Creek Bridge, fought the Indians," one man said, trying to remember who the enemies had been. "They was the meanest to fight. Fought the Yankees and the Rebels both . . ."

"You never fought nary one," an old fellow told him.

"No, I never said I did, but I've heard tell. The Indians would torture a man. They was mean as that Campbell cousin—what's his name?"

"Skeet?"

"He tortures dogs, and such as that, for a fact. He covers their faces with their own skin."

"Well, he's crazy," Wright admitted simply.

"Crazy or not, he's a nephew of Drury and he's in line to inherit a part."

"Well, who cares about the Campbells?" Wright said impatiently. "What were you saying about the wars, Ed?"

145

"I say the Indians hung men on poles and tortured them to death."

"Campbells do that, too. Used to," Wright said. "Mr. Jackson, sit down here next to me. Did you know that some years ago, on an election day, a Campbell man went off with a McGregor girl—"

"Which ain't too hard," one old man commented dryly.

"Took her off into the woods for the day, and then took her to his papa's home, and after three days shaved her head and sent her back to her people. Well, sir, that led to old man Scott McGregor shooting the Drury Campbell boy. What was that boy's name?"

"It was Drury's cousin," a man said. "What *was* his name?"

"Well, sir, the Campbells then went to the McGregors' holdings, which are mainly in Tennessee, and tore up everything they could in the way of furniture and sheds or whatever. And they captured two of the McGregor boys, age about fifteen, took them back to their place as prisoners, and when their mama come up here weeping and praying, they told her if their cousin didn't die they would allow the boys to go home, but if he did die, they'd shoot the boys, starting at the feet."

"At the feet?" Wayland said. "What does that mean?"

"Break the feet, then break the legs, then break the arms, then finally when the boys have been in pain all day and night, they shoot the top of their heads off."

"They wouldn't do that, would they?" Wayland whispered.

Wright said, "Yes, they did it just that way, once the Campbell cousin died. What was that cousin's name?"

"I think it was Clarence, but he was called Buck."

"Oh, yes, that's the way it was. The McGregors finally died, singing 'Amazing Grace.' The Campbells waited till the last verse: 'When I've been there ten thousand years, bright shining as the sun...'" Wright broke into song himself, two of the other men joining him. "'I'll have no less days to sing God's praise than when I first begun.'"

The singing required a period of respectful silence afterward. Wright twisted about on the bench to see Collie, who had come indoors from the lot.

An old man said, "Mr. Wayland, you about done with that clock tower, or we goin' to have it tore up again?"

"We're getting it along," Wayland said, smiling at them.

"I'm a-wantin' to know the time," one of them told him.

"Be cold this winter, Mr. Wayland," an old man said, "cold enough to freeze the creek. Have you finished hanging the millwheel yet?"

"Yes, it's done," Wayland assured him.

"Get down to zero, the chicken combs will turn black, toes turn black and fall off." The old man belched, then took time to spit tobacco juice into the sand under the stove.

Now and then customers would come in and get what they wanted, waiting on themselves and writing out their list on a paper bag. Gudger came back indoors, his face red from the pinching cold. Collie sat down next to Wayland on the bench and warmed herself. He took her hand and warmed it in both of his. After a while Wayland said, "The McGregors ever shoot the men who tortured those two boys?"

"Both sides claim they killed ever so many," an elderly man told him.

"They still don't bother to speak to one another," a man said.

"Well, I don't speak to the Campbells, either, if I

can go around it," Wright said. "But they do work hard, I'll give them that. The McGregors wait for bounty to land in their yard or lap, are a disorganized people, subject to their whims, but the Campbells are regimented. Nobody goes against the old man over there without considering the consequences."

Wright spent more and more time with Paula, because he found that she was curious about the mountains themselves, their age and history. To her, coming from the east, they were marvels, full of wonder, and once he became aware of that, he was overjoyed. Now take Gudger, he kept a record of the changes in daily temperature and knew who owed the store money and whom he owed, but that was the limit of his interest in climatic and historical changes. Young accepted the mountains as a gift he had inherited at birth, and since he had never known any other part of the world, their special majesty and beauty went past him, or at least were lost on him more than on Paula.

Wright told her their age: two billion years. It was a staggering sum, he realized, beyond her or his own comprehension. They were several times as old as other mountain ranges in the country, according to books he had bought, several times as old as the mountains of Asia. "Don't know their height when they were first born," he told her. "They were bigger babies than they are old men and women, though. Wouldn't be surprised if they haven't taken several thousand feet of themselves and broken it into bits with cold and rains and sent them down the rivers to Tennessee, to the Mississippi." He drew maps for her, identifying the ranges, the cross-ranges, the peaks, giving various names the peaks had been given over the years, first by the Cherokee Indians. He told her stories about explorers, among them Guyot and Clingman and Mitchell, all arriving and departing from outside the mountain world itself, all before his own birth, expressing astonishment at the wealth of flowers and plants and bushes and trees, minerals and rock formations, all speaking of the uncountable centuries of age. Paula would listen with rapt expression and, should he ever contradict himself, would correct him at once. Meanwhile, the old men sitting in the store would doze, or look with friendly skepticism on facts unprovable, on estimations, on word-of-mouth lore, most of it beyond their own memories or needs or curiosities.

"Your daughter is a beauty," Wright told Wayland. "Come spring I'll take her into the North Woods to show her the changing of the vegetation, and once it's warm enough we'll climb, or maybe ride, to the peaks. I have a mountain trail pony or two that will go that far, that well, and I'll show her the world waking up with a dozen shades of green. God loved that color best of all, didn't he, Jack? Wouldn't you say so?"

Whenever he saw Paula out in the trading lot, Wright would call to her from the store's porch, if only to say hello, but as often as not he would invite her in to sit with him for a while. One day he gave her several letters from the Civil War days. "Remind me, Paula, to tell you about this later, these letters, and you keep in mind what I say; nobody else knows these stories, and you'll need to pass them on accurately." Day by day they became the closest of friends. He even let her help him with the ginseng drying. He had reserved the seng trade when he gave Gudger the store; he alone took care of the buying of the roots, the drying of those which had not been dried by the men and women who had grubbed them out of the mountain soil, and he handled their sale to wholesalers in Asheville. There was more money in seng than there was in furs, he told her, since the Chinese were so crazy to have it,

149

especially the gnarled seng which grew wild and could be found by people willing to go far enough into the wilderness for it.

The Caesar Plover clock case, made of walnut, was finished on the afternoon of the 17th of December and was delivered to the mill, riding on Plover's wagon, laid on its back, wrapped in bear skins. Accompanying the Plovers were several neighbors who had watched the long case take shape, and a dozen companions they had gathered along the roadside. Everyone stood about there at Young's mill, staring at the polished body standing on its polished feet, waiting for its life. They watched as Wayland mounted the gleaming works he had made, and set the balancing mechanism. He hung the weights. He used tiny brass screws to secure the dial in position. He put on the hands he and Milton had cast, and by the time Milton arrived with the pendulum, the clock was proudly looking out at the world. Bit by bit the people were witnessing the birth of a living being; at least there were those present who felt that way about it: Paula, for instance, was one, and Collie another. Old Wright himself came over, holding to Young's arm. "I suggest a prayer," he said at one point. Collie later said she was never so surprised in her life, that never had she known her father to pray outside a church or a dining room. Wright prayed, thanking God He had sent this man out of the North to show people hereabouts how to make clocks and to bring them together in this special way, and please God let this clock work.

When Wright was done, everybody waited expectantly for Wayland to start the clock. He looked over at Collie, then at the Plover family, who were standing just this side of the mill's doorway, and at Milton, standing just beyond. Everybody was present who had contributed, except the woman who had

150

painted the dial. "All right, then," he said. He moved the minute hand around to the figure XI, then told Paula she could set the pendulum to swinging. Paula came forward, hugging herself, holding in as best she could the delight she felt. Nobody said a word just now. Everybody was listening.

Gently Paula moved the pendulum, started it swinging. The clock ticked steadily, evenly. "It seems to be level enough," Wayland mentioned to Collie, his voice trembling. At four minutes before the hour, the striker mechanism cocked itself. Wayland gently closed the door to the trunk. On the hour the clock struck. "Why, it's pretty," Wright said at once, more to himself than to others.

"Oh, my Lord, listen to it," Collie murmured, sniffling, feeling foolish but not caring, at least not turning away when Wayland looked over at her.

For transporting, the clock was wrapped in the same two bear skins Plover had used. "Just sell 'em when you get to Asheville, and give me the money," he told Young. The clock was laid in the store's truck, on a thick bed of other furs. "He travels like royalty," Wright commented, laughing.

Next afternoon Wayland and Young drove off toward the south to sell the clock. For three full days there was not a word from either one of them, and Wright sent Milton himself to use the telephone in Tennessee, but a snow that evening closed the Tennessee road, so Milton didn't get back. No word from Young or Wayland, either. Wright waited supper over at his house until Mavis had to go on home. He fretted and paced. Collie up at her house had supper ready, too. The entire community was waiting for word. Then, along about nine o'clock, she heard a truck trying to climb her hill, and she and Paula ran outdoors. It must have got stuck, for in a few minutes they saw Wayland trudging up the hill. They greeted him out in the yard, on the frozen ground. Yeh, he had sold it, he told them. "Sold it a time or two," he said.

Sitting in the main room trying to get warm, he said he and Young had arrived in Asheville about eleven o'clock at night, way past the best time, but they had unloaded the furs at the King Store, which never closes, seemed like, then took the clock in its bear skins around to the King house, where Young got Cal King himself out of bed and brought him down to the sidewalk, where the clock was set up under a street lamp. "There Mr. King himself stood in the middle of the night," Wayland reported, "dressed in an overcoat and bedroom slippers, and he stared at the clock, and he stared at it some more, chewing on a bit of tobacco, and he walked around to the other side of it to stare at it, all the while Young telling him that Caesar Plover's family had hand-made the case, and I had hand-made the works, and telling him what Milton had done, and about the painting of the dial. And Cal King kept saying, you did it, did you? Then there would be quiet as he wandered around it again. He looked over at us, finally, seemed to be measuring us against some obstacle he had in mind. 'People around here wouldn't trust a clock made in any such way as you describe,' he told us."

Collie and Paula gasped.

"Well, sir, that took the wind out of our sails," Wayland told them. "Young looked like he had been hit by a brickbat. 'They wouldn't expect it to work more'n the time it took to buy it,' Cal King said. His words were falling like hammer blows, I mean they hurt, let me tell you. Then he looked us over one more time and said, 'Now if you'll forget all that and paint on the dial one word that I can give you, I can sell it.' Young asked him what the word was. Of course, I wasn't breathing by then. Mr. Cal King chewed on his tobacco for a while longer, and then he said, 'On the dial I want you to letter in the word *London*.'"

Wayland threw back his head, there in Collie's main room, and roared with laughter. Collie and Paula didn't know why he was laughing, and they were struck dumb by the possibility of losing authorship of the work they had done together. Their sad faces stared at the laughing man before them, who was recalling the moments under the street lamp that first night. "London," Wayland kept calling out to Collie and Paula, between peals of laughter.

Young was lying naked on Benie Frazier's bed, resting from their lovemaking. They were in the topmost bedroom of her inn. Young was telling her about his trip. "So when he said to put the word *London* on it, poor Wayland grunted as if struck and staggered back to the truck, and Uncle Cal quickly said there were other words that'd do, such as *Edinburgh* or *Shropshire*, and every time he named another one, Wayland would moan again, as if he were hit in the belly with a fist."

Benie pulled a bathrobe on and sat down near him in the bed and kissed his forehead. "Where'd you sleep that night?"

"Might know you'd ask that," Young said, smiling.

"Just wondering. You said you were drunk by then."

"Uncle Cal has a parlor with a bed in it, and he took us in there, lit the fire in the coal grate, sat with us for an hour or so, sorry about the clock, of course, but most often talking about the depression, which is on his mind. Every time I'd ask about Lottie or Kin or Beth, he would be brief in reply, his own thoughts still on the poor people. Finally he went wandering off, I suppose went back to bed, and Wayland slept on the bed in the parlor, and I slept on a mohair sofa for the first and last time of my life." He laughed about that. "Even next day I was itching from it."

"You sold the clock at Cal's store?"

"Tried to. Let it set there all morning. Finally we were offered six head of cattle for it." That amused Young. "You ought to have seen Wayland's expression when that fellow offered those steers. Best offer we had. And Wayland kept wandering off, trying to escape. So finally I wrapped the clock up in a blanket and loaded her. I borrowed a phone book and found a Biltmore Forest address in it, then we drove up to that very door, don't you see, and I called the woman of the house by name, and asked her where the clock was to be placed."

"What are you telling me now, Young?" Benie asked, frowning thoughtfully at him.

"So she said she didn't know of any clock, and I said maybe it's a Christmas present, could that be, and Wayland and me carried it into her house, right past her, and she began to help us move furniture around to make a place for it. We set the clock up for her in the hall, in the dining room, in the living room, and she kept saying she didn't know who would give her a clock like that but wasn't it beautiful, didn't it look wonderful there by the piano? We got its hands set to the minute, then I asked to use her phone to call my office. So I made a call to nowhere and came back and said I was sorry, but this was the wrong house. I told her I felt awful about it, and indeed I did, Benie, once I saw that woman's face. Well, sir, she got to crying and said she liked that clock, and I told her I would get her one in a few weeks if she was sure she wanted one. We sold the clock four times that afternoon, left it finally where it stood in an old man's living room between

154

two French doors." Young lay there smiling up at Benie.

"Sometimes I think you're crazy," she said.

"Rich people don't seem to run out of money, you know it, Benie?"

7

Collie had told Paula and Wayland that Christmas eve was one of the times the entire community would come together each year, and so it was. In the afternoon, out of the coves, along the roads came the Coles and Dettles and Tuttles, the Silvers and Vadens and Carters and all the others, a few of them walking out of the woods for the first time in a long while; particularly was that true of some of the quite elderly people. The families brought their suppers with them, sweets predominating. There were pound cakes, rich with butter and eggs, homemade candies and cookies, sweet-potato, chess and mincemeat pies, applesauce and apple butter; then, too, there were German sausages and other specialties. These various dishes were displayed on planks, makeshift tables placed pew to pew along the main aisle of the church. The doors of the church were closed to keep dogs out, and the people fell to, helping themselves. Children, once served, usually found seats along the walls; the adults chose pews, or stood near the two old Moravian stoves, both made of pottery, that had served the church for fifty years. The men talked smallholder timbering they had done or seen done lately, or cash work they had heard about in Tennessee or Asheville, or winter farming. The women talked about bearing and rearing children, teaching them to read and figure, about the ewes bagging out now and their hope for twin lambs and maybe, God willing, triplets, about cooking, about tending to their elderly relatives. Now and then a hymn would be lined out for the congregation, but more often a family group would move forward to the pulpit and would sing a carol which it had rehearsed, some doing better than others, admittedly; daughters of Thomas Wilson appeared to have the prettiest voices.

A lady from near Flint Rock, Gladys Starnes, came forward, unfolded a piece of paper and read in a direct manner, with a clear voice, a poem she had written for the occasion.

> Christmas crowns the gift divine,
>   Virgin-born Lord Jesus,
> God Emmanuel in flesh:
>   Born to die for us.
>
> Christmas sings the joy of peace,
>   Hope of what will be,
> Light thru death's dark valley, and
>   Life eternally.
>
> Christmas beckons all wise men
>   To the manger scene·
> There, the shadow of the cross
>   By eyes of faith is seen.

At the time "of kindest feelings," as he termed it, Mr. Wright called for the crib to be put before the altar. This crib was a Caesar Plover cantilevered contrivance, one used every year, which would rock more or less continuously as it responded to the slightest motion of the baby lying in it. The crib was installed below the altar, between the stoves, among green boughs, and Wright called for the mothers offering new babies to please stand. Collie stood, hold-

157

ing Jonathan. Mrs. Jeremiah Carter stood as well. Mr. Wright suggested that Mrs. Carter bring her Judith forward first, then the older baby, Jonathan, would be recognized later.

All the lamps were extinguished. Candles were lit. Children flocked forward and knelt as near the crib as possible, and the people fell to singing old carols, as they had for many years past.

> Come hither, ye faithful,
>   Triumphantly sing!
> Come, see in the manger
>   The angels' dread King!
> To Bethlehem hasten
>   With joyful accord!
> Oh come ye, come hither
>   To worship the Lord!

Little Judith didn't appear to trouble herself about the singing. Her mother was anxious about her, afraid she would cry, but Judith was comfortable and was enjoying the gentle rocking of Plover's crib.

After a while Jonathan was brought forth, was given the place of honor, Collie hovering as close as the boughs of greenery would allow.

> Oh, that ever-blessed birthday,
>   When the Virgin, full of grace...

The reference to the virgin caught Collie unprepared and in her haste to back off a few steps she stumbled over one of the Turner children.

> By the Holy Ghost conceiving,
>   Bear the Savior of our race;
> And that Child, the world's Redeemer,
>   First displayed His sacred face,
> Evermore and evermore!

As for his part, Jonathan was fascinated by the candles which flickered close to him, only a few feet from where he lay.

The Bible reading was from the Book of Luke; that was done very well by Milton's second oldest, reciting from memory. He forgot one small part of it, which eliminated one reference to the shepherds —not a dire loss, Wright assured him. Mr. Crawford led a prayer, calling by name the families present, listing all the McGregors as one family for convenience and safety's sake, presenting each to Jesus for renewed acquaintance and attention, his remarks as simply uttered as if Jesus were close by, perhaps standing near a stove.

After the service, bonfires were lit in the yard to help the people see the way to their cars and wagons, those who had brought them, and to the main road. For a while afterward one standing in the church doorway could hear the families, those walking home, singing, their voices growing more distant.

> Watchman, tell us of the night,
>   For the morning seems to dawn.
> Traveler, darkness takes its flight;
>   Doubt and terror are withdrawn.

They sang in order to hold company with themselves and each other. They sang because they had been singing and didn't want to stop.

> Watchman, let these wanderings cease;
>   Get thee to thy quiet home.
> Traveler, lo! the Prince of Peace,
>   Lo! the Son of God is come.

Mr. Thomas Wilson permitted his daughters to walk home with their suitors; they could follow him and his wife at a private distance, but were required to sing all the way, loud enough for him to hear.

Old Mr. Frank Cole was making his way home among the last, drunk as an English lord. He had a ways to go, about three miles, and the moon was only quarter-size; the wind off the mountains was chilly to the bones of an old fellow. He fell down near the widow's inn, but righted himself, insisted he had tripped on a rock, that he was competent. Slowly, very slowly, step by step, he made his way toward his cove road, others passing him, singing, calling goodnight, wishing him a merry Christmas.

He went to sleep at a rock near the Carter holdings and was found there by the Widow Hastings, who was hurrying along home with her two daughters and little boy. They helped him as far as their own house and fixed him a cup of hot tea before allowing him to go on.

Over the years the Wright family had acquired a number of decorative items for their nativity scene, animals and angels and the like, and the first time Young took charge of arranging them, the family parlor became impressive indeed. He had the star in the east, as well as other stars, and several angels hovering in the heavens; he had fully a dozen shepherds on a hillside made of newspapers painted green. He fashioned sheep out of spun wool. The stable was constructed of tiny logs, with donkeys without. Wise men approached, to see the baby in his manger, his mother and Joseph nearby.

The scene was lantern-lit that first night, and the family came together to marvel over it. Nothing quite like it had ever been seen in this part of the world before. Mr. Wright, who was somewhat baffled by the spectacle, and proud of Young, thought to invite Mavis in from the kitchen to view the display. Mavis studied it most seriously for a while before saying to him, "She just had the one child, didn't she, Mr. Wright?"

Christmas Day was reserved for the family, for visiting with one another in the house, and for venturing out in the afternoon to see relatives. Gifts were almost invariably made by the giver: a pan of fudge and another of cookies, which Paula made; a squirrel fashioned out of scraps of cotton cloth, which Wayland sewed and stuffed and gave to Jonathan—"Something for him to chew on," he said; two mated birds carved out of walnut, which he made for Collie; a tan-and-gray dress Collie made for Paula from cloth from the store, and a coat—as yet without buttons sewed on—which she made for Wayland. "The buttons are due to arrive most any day now," she explained.

For Paula, Wayland made a bear about six inches tall which would, once she pushed a plunger, throw a ball through a hoop. At least, the bear would throw the ball toward the hoop, and if the plunger had been pushed with proper judgment, the score would be made. The toy was like one he had seen as a boy, which his mother had brought from Europe with her; rather, which her parents brought when they arrived with their family. The toy was unpainted, just as his mother's had been.

At Christmas there was plenty of cider to drink, both alcoholic and non-alcoholic, and at this season the alcoholic type was still fizzy. There were a few tangerines to eat as a special treat, and Collie and Paula spent part of the day making four loaves of date-nut bread to be given away in the afternoon. There was in most families a good deal of laughter mingled with the special, tender sadness, the type that occurs when believers seek to commemorate the Christian story, the baby born to be sacrificed.

161

Across the river the Campbell men had a turkey shoot at noon, using such midday warmth as was available, and the men and women filled a small casket with written confessions of their sins. Most of the confessions were general: "Forgive me, Father, for sins of pride." That was one. Only a few were specific, mentioning detailed sins. A few petitioners asked God for relief from drinking too much, or from pain: "There's a fair amount of pain on this side of the river, Lord, but precious little medicine or doctoring getting done." All the petitions were put into the casket. Back in Drury's father's time, the casket would be buried, but working with winter dirt was a painful chore, so recently Drury had permitted floating the casket off toward Tennessee.

There was an afternoon ritual at his house. Everybody was invited to come by, and was expected to leave after half an hour or so, in order to afford room for others to get into the house and pay their respects. Those inside could choose from the wild game on the dining-room sideboard and table: roasts of deer, bear, coon, possum, groundhog, rabbit, squirrel, grouse, wild turkey, wild boar, the meats served cold and accompanied only by a few sauces.

A parcel full of food also had been sent to a work party of three Campbells who were tending the sixteen oxen and several mules penned over near Collins' Knob, where the winter's spate of timbering was suspended for the celebrating. There was food sent to Asheville as well, where two Campbell men had on December 20 been arrested for public drunkenness and resisting arrest; they had assaulted three policemen with garbage-can lids, and were seeing Christmas from the ninth-floor cells of the Buncombe County Courthouse. No food was sent to Cole Campbell in Tennessee or Kentucky, or wherever the

162

heir apparent was. He was not here at home, anyway, which his father, Drury, complained about. Possibly he was in the North Woods by now, on his way home. His father had counted five days since Cole's brother Harmon and cousin Skeet had taken pack horses to meet him near the Tennessee line at Flint Top. They were to do some hunting as they made their way home. Well, Cole, where are you today? Drury wondered; how much longer would it be before his son filled the doorway with his powerful body, flashing his big smile, his hands extended to his old father in greeting? Not long now, Drury thought fretfully, before my youngest will be home again.

8

One night about a week after Christmas, a thick snow began falling, and William Wright helped his wife to the outhouse, the snow having made the yard planks dangerous and blotted out the moonlight. He waited outside the privy door, acknowledging her complaining. This was a nervous night, he thought, with irritants and dangers hinted at in its sounds and pauses; the spirits of the dead were restless, hungry. All evening Annie had complained about pain in her back, her legs, her wrist. In the privy she was complaining about living away back here in the woods, where no help could be had for the injured, where there were no doctors or police or roads. She preferred a city, she said, though what city she had ever lived in, he didn't know. She had been born at a crossroads place several miles south of here; of course, it was more of a town than this was, but you'd think she was referring to Philadelphia or Chicago.

When she got herself "put back together," as she phrased it, he helped her to the house, where he had left a lantern burning on the rock steps. "Here, you go up onto the porch and hold both hands," she said. "Don't you slip and leave me by myself."

"Now, one step at a time," he said.

"Slick, rock steps are slick. Wood ones are better."

"Here. Snow's soft as yet, not slippery."

"Lock the screen or the wind'll slap it and scare us to death in the night," she told him. She stopped at the middle of the kitchen floor, and suddenly her shoulders slumped and she began to cry, complaining about her helplessness, and her sons not visiting her often enough, and Collie taking up with somebody from away off.

He put his arms around her, comforting her as best he could. "You want to go to bed, Annie?"

"The dreams I have, I'm almost afraid to go to sleep."

He sat down on his leather rocker and watched her, considerate of the misery she felt. "I dreamed the other night of building this house, you and me planning it, selecting paneling for the parlor, choosing a rug from the Sears, Roebuck catalogue." He could usually distract her by referring to the house.

"I never planned it," she said.

"You chose the rug."

"Dream of winters freezing people on the road, and I see a face that's dead."

"Well, Mama, we all have dreams."

"And I hear a baby crying, and know it's hers."

"Hers?"

"Collie's."

"No, that baby's safe as can be, and healthy, and it's a happy child."

"I'm just telling you what I dream, William."

"You're bound to get into an argument tonight, is that it, Annie?"

"What do you care?"

"Deny everything I say. I say we planned this house, and you say not."

"Oh, hush, William."

"Tired of talking, are you?"

"Tired of myself. What good am I?"

"I've enjoyed our life together, myself. Now, why

do you want to ruin everything?"

"You could have done your life better without me in it. I know that."

"No, honey. Couldn't bear the children, could I?"

"And what comfort are they, I want to know?"

"You said not to have a hall in the house. You said to put the kitchen sink at a window."

"We have a hall."

"No, we don't. Where is it?"

"Through that door there, go through that door and you'll be in a hall with four rooms opening off it."

"Why, that's the entrance room."

"A hall is what I call it."

"Well, you say it's a hall and I say it's an entrance room."

"Oil's burned out in the lamp in there. Didn't I tell you?"

"Well, I'll replace it."

"Wake up at night, can't light my way to the kitchen to fix myself a bite to eat. If I can't sleep, might as well come in here as to lay in there thinking how I should have done differently years ago." She moved on out into the dark hallway, complaining to herself.

It's worse tonight, he thought to himself. It was his own nature to tolerate life and adjust to it, but she had trouble adjusting to change. "What you make of her, Papa?" he whispered. He believed in the presence of family spirits, that they moved daily through his world; his father was a precious companion. He could sense his presence often of a night about bedtime. Sometimes he sensed the presence of his brother Charlie, who first left home when he was sixteen. Their father had left Charlie nothing in his will, claiming no benefit derived from a son who traveled so much. Charlie was constantly moving on in the face of challenge, authority, kinship, affections, was probably now in California somewhere. Young resembled him in personality.

The wind howled, was very like a woman crying, he thought. Usually, not so much wind in a snowstorm. Now, who would have expected snow this evening, after a mild afternoon? Might be that Mavis wouldn't come tomorrow, and her absence might tie him to the house until he could find somebody else. Annie would not stay for long in a house alone. Must have somebody to criticize, to hold to. That new man, Jackson, his first wife had died in water—did Jack say that, or was it somebody else who reported it? Better than dying in a fire, Wright imagined. His father had died in the fire of his store when somebody set the store ablaze.

He spit into the fireplace. At least, he spit in that direction. Not careful of a night. Got sleepy and in a hurry.

Last time he had watched the train roll into Asheville was when Charlie said, all right, goodbye again, see you in a year or two, and there he went, to write a letter home from Oregon awhile later, the first of May, then one from San Francisco more recently.

Wright moved through the large entrance room where he kept his wool coats, leather boots and saddle, which he often said were worth more than he was. They were not often used. Seldom that he rode horseback nowadays. He walked wherever he needed to, or rode the store's truck. He stumbled over a boot. Annie had set it there to aggravate him, he had no doubt. She was expert at silly tricks like that.

He sat down on the edge of the bed. "I'll put oil in the lamp tomorrow," he said. "I keep meaning to do it. And I'll get a man to come over to shovel snow tomorrow so you can get about."

She breathed deeply. "I hope so," she said.

"I don't think the storm'll be too treacherous, Annie. Please, honey, don't hold the past against yourself. I tell you what I think: it's the snow that does it, that weighs down the air, makes words sound somber, and makes the mind heavy. It's whenever there's a storm, Annie..."

That same night, sitting near the campfire, Cole Campbell ate his birthday supper, deer tenderloin which his two companions had broiled on a stick over an open fire, and liquor. The three of them were camped on an upper branch of Collie's creek, about four miles north of Collie's house. He was with his cousin Skeet and his half-brother Harmon, companions on his hunt in such wilds as remained to the north. A handsome, auburn-haired giant, today turned twenty-one, Cole ate while he accepted gifts from his two friends: a pat of horse manure from Skeet and a six-inch length of rope, tied about with thongs to resemble an erect penis, from Harmon.

For supper entertainment Cole watched Skeet aggravate a wolf he had trapped, one safely bound and muzzled. Skeet admitted to a dislike of wolves. Weary of his teasing the animal, Cole finally asked him to stop, which Skeet refused to do. Cole, weary of his company anyway, said the snow was changing his plans, that he would ride on tonight to tend to a private matter. He winked heavily at his brother, who had often said Cole had a McGregor girlfriend, which Cole had not denied. Cole advised the others to return home tomorrow by the route through the Spiveys' tract, which was less dangerous in the snow.

He went off to saddle a horse, and Harmon, following, said no McGregor girl was worth a trip in this weather. "What sort of woman is she, to be worth this? What's she willing to do for you?"

Cole said he had about enough liquor left to see him safely through.

Left in camp, Skeet, who had been drinking since noon, pulled the wolf close and, without sign of concern or excitement, used his knife to sever the skin around the bound animal's throat until the neck skin was retained only at the throat. He then unrolled the flap of skin over the top of the wolf's head, covering its eyes. With his knife he cut the ropes, freeing the wolf's feet, then cut the muzzle. The delirious beast leaped into the air, howling, and began running in ravenous leaps, in circles, terrifying the horses and bringing Cole and Harmon on the run. Stunned, they stood at the edge of the circle of light watching the wolf leap in madness, in anguish, trying to throw off the brutal torturer of its throat and head. Fascinated, dismayed, Cole watched as the wolf staggered in a circle of decreasing size. Wobbly on its feet, it cried piteously until it fell into the fire, where its fur began to burn and smoke and stink. All the while Skeet proudly surveyed his handiwork, the knife in his hand wet and red. The entertainment over, he stretched his arms, yawned and walked into the woods to piss against a tree.

"God save his soul," Cole murmured.

The two pack horses, terrified by the event, had tried to break free. Harmon calmed them. Blood from the wolf had splattered three beautifully marked, spotted cat furs. "I'll carry these with me," Cole told his brother.

"What in God's name gets into him, tell me?" Harmon asked.

"Skeet blinded a dog that way once, and Young almost killed him. We were up in Papa's south cove, beyond the second bed of springs."

Harmon pulled the smoking carcass out of the fire. "You're a God-damned heathen, Skeet!" he shouted into the woods.

The snow had thickened by the time Cole got the three pelts rolled and tied. He would show them to his son. Not been any pelts like these in many years. He realized he wouldn't be able to see even a few yards ahead, but he trusted his horse; Skeet and Harmon had brought him his favorite of his father's stable. Lord, it knew the way home, and to her house as well. The splashing of the main creek was to his left as he rode out of the camp, and as he moved along he could hear other creeks join in, could hear their gurgling, thrashing voices.

He would ride to Collie's, where, thank God, he would find welcome, warmth, decent food and the pleasures of a passionate woman.

Wayland awoke. Must have dozed off sitting in the chair. He could see the clock face on the wall, the master clock without a case that he had hung there. Be ten o'clock in a few minutes. Collie was asleep on the bed. He rested his head forward in his hands, conscious of having over-celebrated this evening. Young had come by, and they had talked about selling clocks, and what needed to be done, and how the company was going to be a big success. Then he had shown Young how to swim in the creek. "Oh, Lord," he moaned aloud, remembering that Young wasn't accustomed to cold water, had had to be pulled up on the rock and pounded.

Later Young had started home, only to return at once. "You come with me, Wayland."

"Well, I'm warm here," Wayland had told him. "I have Collie's nightgown on."

"Listen, I've heard some things from Mavis that worry me. You better not stay here."

"No, I'll sleep with Paula in her rock room." He was drunk, and dizzy from the cold water, and still unnerved because Young had lost his strength in the water. He had heard of powerful men dying in a minute or two when the water was bitter cold. "No, you go on home, Young," he had told him. "I'll be all right tonight."

Wayland roused himself. He sat down on the bed beside Collie, pulled his nightdress close around his neck and listened to her breathe. He decided he loved her as much as anybody in his life, even Paula, which alerted him suddenly. Had he been neglecting Paula? he wondered. This afternoon he recalled he had left her with Jonathan, and had taken Collie to see how the clock tower was working out. Had he really left the baby with Paula to tend while he went away with Collie? And what had Paula thought about that? he wondered.

Sleepily, yawning, he pulled his shoes on and stepped outside. Snow. The world was covered with branch-clinging, fence-clinging white snow. The world was purified, remade, renewed; nothing jagged was left in view. Snow was still falling, too. At a mill somewhere in the sky, as he had often told Paula, elves were grinding out snowflakes at a cent a million, probably German elves with porcelain eyes.

He had to latch Collie's door from the outside in order to hold it shut against the wind. He located a yard board with his foot and walked its length, paused to find another and shuffled along toward the stone room. He managed to open the door without awakening Paula, and lay down on the bed beside her.

He was awakened by a man's voice, somebody talking in the distance. He lay motionless, listening. Probably Young's voice. Paula also awakened, and she confirmed that it was Young. She said she knew his laugh well enough.

He dozed off, but was awakened again by the same voice. He still couldn't make out what was being said, but after a while he decided it was not

171

Young, after all. He felt around for his shoes.

Paula was sitting up now. "Where you going?"

"What's he saying?" he asked her.

"Something about Young, saying Young has been here."

"But you said it *was* Young."

"Hush, Papa. Don't talk so loud."

"Hush?" he said, startled by the reprimand. "Hush?" he asked her.

"I think it's her husband."

The thought stunned him. For several moments it seemed he scarcely breathed. "She has no husband," he said.

"Be quiet, Papa."

"I'm not quiet by nature when I'm scared." He pulled his shoes on. "It's a wonder he came here tonight, through all that snow."

"Papa, please. I'm scared, too."

"Oh, honey." His confidence suddenly crumpling, he took her in his arms, rocking her like a baby. "You stay inside and keep this door shut. Can you latch it from inside?"

"No. Don't go out there."

He stumbled outside. The sight of the snow again startled him. The indentations of his footprints, made an hour or so earlier, remained visible, shadowed by light falling through the house window. He moved to the window, stopped close to it, peeked inside and saw the back of a tall, muscular man with reddish hair. The man was saying that three pelts ought to be brought into the house. "They're for the boy," he said. "Have my horse to stable and feed. Saddle's still on her." Suddenly the big man exclaimed, "If it's Young that's standing between us, Collie..."

Wayland moved to the house door. He pushed tentatively against the door. It held.

"Young has nothing to do with it," Collie was saying. "Your father would never allow a marriage." When the man began to curse her, she said, "It's all over between you and me, Cole."

"Over, my ass," he said. "My baby is in bed in the other room. That's my boy, Collie."

"It was an accident—"

"No God-damn fucking accident. Don't call my son an accident."

"Well, what are you going to do for your son, Cole? Do you mean to marry his mother?"

"Yes, I mean to, but not this God-damned minute."

"You can't and you know it. You don't dare ever ask your father, or mine, for that matter."

Cole went rambling about the kitchen, mumbling about when he would marry Collie, asking where was his bottle of whiskey. He broke open the chest.

"Why you bust it for?" Collie demanded angrily.

"Bust your ass in a minute. No need worrying about this here. More important worries. Come home, find the latch set on the outside, and you say it was not done by Young? Find a man's clothes drying."

"Maybe Young did fasten it when he left."

"Once said he would kill me if he caught me here again. He told me that, with Harmon present."

"Young wouldn't kill anybody."

"I have three as pretty pelts as I ever saw. They was so pretty, them cats, with all the spots on them. Something for the boy," he said. "I'm not a fucking angel, Collie, did you ever think I was?" he added suddenly.

"Cole, I'm talking about my own life."

"You got a fur on you. Softest fur. Let me see it, Collie."

"Go to hell, Cole."

"Used to show it to me all the time. Now you say go to hell, Cole."

"I'm through with you, Cole."

"Tell me who this other'n is."

"You leave him alone, too, Cole."

"No, I'd like to see him. Did you give him much of it yet, Collie?"

"None of your business."

"You're my business. You are my very own God-damned personal business. Don't you forget it. I'm not one of the local wags that comes around. I've been drowning in you for two years."

"Hush, for God sake—"

"You got me addicted. No other woman ever did that."

"For God sake, Cole."

"I miss it. Let's have some now, Collie."

"Please, Cole."

"Let's have some, want to or not. A little anger won't hurt you. Does that make it close up?"

Wayland knocked on the door.

Silence inside the house, the breathless silence of people interrupted in a personal conversation. For a long while there was no response at all, then he heard Cole say, "That you, Young?"

"No, not Young," Wayland replied.

Quiet for a long moment. "Collie, who is it?" Cole asked her.

No reply this time.

"Young, you come in here," Cole said, "and I'll whip your ass. You hear me?"

Wayland knocked louder. He heard heavy foot-steps approach the doorway, heard the latch turn. The door was allowed to coast open. Cole was standing near the table, rifle in hand, staring at the new arrival: a small man on the stoop, unarmed, wearing a woman's gown. "Jesus," Cole whispered. "Is it Christ hisself?" Mouth agape, he stared at the dressed figure. "Has he a name?"

"Name of Jackson," Collie said from the bed,

where she was leaning back against the far wall.

Cole smiled with relief, but he remained apprehensive even so, muscles taut. "I've opened many a door in my life, but never saw such as this. You from around here?"

"He's living here," Collie said, "in the stone room."

"That man?" Cole pointed at him carelessly with the rifle. "What's he do here?"

She hesitated. "He's—a clockmaker," she said.

"Stands there like a ghost looking at me. A what do you say he is?"

Wayland stepped inside, shut the door.

"He's a clock man," Collie said.

"He have a voice?" Cole asked.

"What's your name?" Wayland asked him.

"There's his voice. You an outlander, are you?" Cole lifted his hand in a mock salute. "Hail, Caesar," he said. "Where'd you find such a dear fellow, Collie? Look how he floats over the floor."

"He has shoes on, Cole—don't be absurd," Collie said.

"He floats before me. I feel the chill coming over me from his body. What you and him do together, Collie, pray together?"

Wayland pulled a chair out at the table and sat down. "You want to make coffee for us, Collie?" he asked.

Collie tried to speak, faltered. "You want coffee?" she finally managed to say.

Cole kept staring at Wayland, fascinated. With one big boot he pulled a chair out, sat down across the table from him, laying his rifle on the table before him.

"Cole, you want coffee?" Collie asked, busying herself at the stove.

Cole was studying Wayland intently, squinting at him. "Speak to me, great spirit," he said.

Collie splashed water into the kettle. "I washed

his clothes. He has only two pair of pants," she said. "That's why he has my gown on."

"You talk, great spirit," Cole said to Wayland.

"I think it's time to put all the cards on the table," Wayland began.

"We going to play cards?"

"He didn't mean that—" Collie began.

"Collie, let him talk. He can talk as well as any other spirit. I'm listening, spirit, ghost."

"Let her talk, too," Wayland said.

"What say?" Cole said, astonished.

"She's the one with the most to say, with a baby to—"

"My boy."

"Her boy," Wayland said.

The correction stung Cole. To Collie he said, "Jesus, where'd you find this?"

"Cole, you've been drinking," she reminded him.

"Shut up. I told you before."

"You asked me a question, Cole," Collie stormed out.

There was quiet in the room, in response to Collie's anger. Finally Cole said to Wayland, "You own that clock there?"

"Yes, my uncle and I made the works in Pennsylvania. I've not made a case for it here."

"Listen to me, ghost, get that clock out of my house."

"I won't do that," Wayland said simply.

"Don't be like that, Cole," Collie said. "He gave the clock—"

"Move the clock out of my house, move it off my wife's property." He shifted the rifle on the tabletop to point in the general direction of the clock.

"I want to talk to you about this family—" Wayland began.

Cole fired four times in succession, each shot a shattering, deafening, terrifying sound, the bullets

176

ripping the clock face and pendulum. After the burst of noise was over, the three people listened to the tinkle of glass from a broken pane of the window near the sink.

Wayland slowly rose to his feet, his face white, drained of blood. "Now, that was the destruction of a great clock. Nobody except an idiot would destroy a clock!" He shouted the words at the startled Cole, even as he began fumbling about the clock, examining the extent of damage. "Off and on I worked for eleven years to get as near perfection..." He turned on Cole, shouted, "What the hell you mean destroying something you can't make?"

The baby began crying in the back room.

"You trying to make me ashamed of myself?" Cole asked, astonished.

Collie said, "Cole, I swear to God, look what you've done." Her voice trembled with anger and fear. "I loved that clock."

Cole turned the rifle slightly so that it pointed toward Wayland. "Go ahead with what you was saying, spook."

"Why say anything to you? You're not listening, are you? You're a trigger finger. Go on and use the damn thing."

Collie said, "Cole, don't shoot. What in the world? Cole, don't shoot that gun."

"Tell him to shut up, Collie."

"Mr. Jackson, you'll have to be quiet now. Don't say another word."

Wayland helplessly studied the clock again. "Ah, Lord, look at it," he said.

"You can make another clock, Mr. Jackson," she said quickly, trying to settle the argument.

"It was a work of exact size, as near as I could come—"

"Collie, tell him to shut his God-damn mouth," Cole said.

"Yes, hush, Mr. Jackson." She put her finger over her own lips. "Please, God..."

Wayland slumped down in his chair, staring at the rifle before him. "A clock is like a human being, and nobody has the right—"

Collie said, "Cole, I don't know what gets into you."

"Oh, there'll come a time when I'm explained. I'm not all mystery." He leaned far back in his chair, drunkenly trying to focus on Wayland. "Now that the clock's settled, we come to you." Suddenly he turned to Collie. "Can a bullet strike a spirit or not? Does it have to be of silver?"

"You broke a window, too," Collie said. "This is my house, Cole, do you know that?"

"We used to meet up here to this place, her and me, sometimes Young as well," Cole told Wayland, speaking in a friendly manner, "and the house had no glass left in the window. Was a deserted, common place."

"Cole, let me have that gun." Collie was standing over him now, holding out her hands for it.

He looked up at her, calmly began reloading it. "Her and me used to make a fire on the hearth to cook. Had no stove. Then her womb took to Jonathan and her mother got mean, so her dear papa fixed the window glass and made the house livable, not knowing it was for me, that I got to bed with her."

Collie still was watching the gun. Cole's big fingers inserted the last cartridges, poked them into the chambers, slammed it shut.

Cole said, "And each time her and me'd celebrate a new possession by going to bed. You ever had a woman you was greedy for, ghost?"

"Yes."

"Who was it?"

"Collie."

For a long while Cole sat grimly considering that, the rifle on the table before him, aimed generally toward Wayland. "Jesus, you got nerve," he whispered finally. Then, distractedly, he said, "Kept trying to teach me to read. She'd say spell *bridge*, Cole. That's what she'd say to me, trying to make a gentleman of me. So I'd make a try at it, maybe get it right, and that would cause her to hug me and give me a kiss and take on over me. She'd just about play with my cock ever' time I got a word spelled right."

"Cole, for God sake," Collie pleaded.

"I'd say b-r-i-g-e. And she'd say no, no, Cole, you left out a letter, honey, now try harder. And finally I'd hit on it, you know how it is, and be getting hard all the while."

"Cole, you want to talk seriously?" Wayland said.

"She'd say spell *Santa Claus*, and I'd do it wrong. Hell, I knowed not to put an *e* on *Claus*, but I'd put it on there, delaying, you know, and when I'd get it right, she would take on over me, plead with me to let her have it."

"It's not so," Collie said to Wayland.

"It's all gospel," Cole said, his mind full of whiskey and ideas, whimsical in its unsteadiness, sodden with hurt and amusement. "She was a born teacher," he said.

Snow falling into the chimney sizzled into steam; except for that, there was no noise to rustle Cole's thoughts. He adjusted his big body to the chair, which threatened to give way under him.

Wayland said, "My daughter and me, our truck was on the ridge—"

"Ghosts have daughters?" Cole said. "They have baby ghosts? Is a baby ghost a boy or a girl? They come with no cock on them, that I'd say for sure. A ghost has nothing at all down there, no pecker, no pussy, which is one reason they're so spooky. Stand up there, ghost, lift up your dress and let me see if

179

you've got any proof at all."

Wayland adjusted his gown across his chest.

"Stand up, ghost."

Collie leaped forward, grabbed for the gun. Cole threw her toward the bed, where she struck her head on the wall. She cried out, then began to sob.

He poked at her with the rifle, said he was sorry. "You hear me, honey? I'm sorry."

"You no good son of a bitch."

"I said I'm sorry. What the hell you want? Just don't come at me with them claws."

"Those claws. Not them claws."

"I know, but I can't remember."

"Stop pointing that rifle at me," she said. "Cole, I'm through with you, honey," she said through her tears. "There's not any way that'll change, nothing you or me either one can do. I'm not in charge of what I feel."

"Well, I'm not either, then."

"I love him, Cole."

Cole cleared his throat, looked around for a suitable can to spit in, spit on the floor. He turned to Wayland. "Does he or she have a cock? I want to know. It's educational."

"Cole, look at that clock, see what you've done."

"I didn't say clock, I said cock."

"Jackson, Mr. Jackson, will you go, please, and let me talk to him alone?" Collie said.

Wayland got up to leave, but Cole said, "Don't be rude, Collie. He wants to talk to me."

"Oh, for God sake," Collie said, and buried her face in a bed pillow. "Jesus, help me," she said into the pillow. "Please God, I love him, Cole."

"Sit down, spook. That's right. Look, he sits down like a normal person. I suppose he don't eat food. Wouldn't eat meat, I guess. I'm hungry myself, Collie."

"Well, go home and eat," she said.

180

He smiled suddenly; it was as if a haze had parted. "You ever see my baby boy? Collie, go get me my baby."

"You're too drunk to hold him."

"Go get him, I said."

"No."

Rifle in hand, he staggered into the back room, returned with the baby dangling by its dress from his left hand. He made his way to the table, where he plopped the baby on its belly, then placed the rifle alongside him. The baby began cooing and gurgling, grateful for the journey. "His name's Jonathan, as was my grandfather's," Cole told Wayland.

"Jesus," Collie whispered, sitting up on the bed staring at Jonathan, who was trying to reach the rifle.

"I had a pony when I was a boy," Cole said, sitting back in the chair. One hand was resting on the baby's rump, his other entangled in his own heavy head of hair. "Grew up not so plain, as Papa said. Had a pony. I was the youngest son and nothing was too good for me. No hand-me-downs for little Cole, either. My brothers wore the same as one another, but not little Cole. My mummy made me clothes of silver threads, ghost, spook, whatever appar—appar—apparition you are, and embroidered them, put my initials on my shirts. Papa's got them over there to this day. Lord, I loved her, and when she died I cried, let me tell you, I slobbered all over my silver threads. I was five when she died, something like that. She lay on her bed, like that there, and hell, man, ghost...ghost...she lay in that bed and asked me to become a preacher when I growed up."

"Grew up," Collie said.

"Grew up. I said yeh, whatever you want, Mama. For you I'll preach, I'll stand in a pulpit and preach my guts out, for you, Mama, I'll go into the waters and be baptized and baptize in the name of God the

181

Father, the son and the . . . and the . . ." His mind settled on an idea, his hand lifted, a pointing finger
stabbed the air in Wayland Jackson's direction. "Is
that you?"

"I'm not, no," Wayland admitted.

"I wondered."

"No, I'm a clock man."

"You keep time, do you? I don't hear you ticking."

At the sink Collie ran cold water over her wrists
and splashed water on her neck and face. Now and
then she would hold her hands under the water once
more. Cole was talking on and on about growing up.
He was in a talking mood. Maybe he would talk
himself sober. She dried and on her way past him
thought to gather up the baby and take him to her
bed. Cole told her to bring his baby back to him and
put him where he was. She did so, she rested Jonathan on the table on his little belly, but he began
crying. Cole became disturbed when the baby would
not be quiet; he even tried speaking directly into
Jonathan's little face, ordering peace and quiet, and
finally he picked Jonathan up by his dress and carried him to the shattered clock, where he hung him
up on the stem, the neck of the dress pierced by the
hour hand. The child was left dangling there to
stare out at the world, bawling at the top of his
voice, his face turning scarlet, while Cole examined
critically the picture he had created, deciding it was
a masterpiece, calling on the ghost and Holy Ghost
and Collie to admire it with him.

Collie tore loose the baby's dress and carried him
into the back room, slamming the door almost off
its hinges. Once she had the baby quiet, she came
back, leaving him, and apologized to Wayland for
"my company being so loud around here." She
slumped down on the edge of her bed, listened to
Cole go on about growing up, being the favorite of
his sisters and father. When finally he was sleepy,

weary even of his own voice, he turned restlessly in his chair and drunkenly considered the room. "Don't hear ticking anywheres." His finger pointed at Wayland. "Say scripture for me, if you're the Holy Ghost."

Wayland said, "I hope to give Jonathan a home, give Collie a family, provide for them, see that the children are well educated ..."

Cole murmured sleepily, "My mother's mother was a Jackson."

"Your mother's mother was a Parker," Collie corrected him.

"I think she was," he admitted. "Her great-grandfather was a preacher to the Indians."

"Even though it's difficult for a man to give up his son to another," Wayland said, persevering, "and his wife—"

"Preached from horseback," Cole said.

"Coleman, listen to him," Collie said.

"When he called for them to come to the waters and drink, he was serious about it. A horse can go only a few hours ..."

Collie swept some of the window glass into a pile. She wearied of that, left the job half done. "When the baby was born," she said, interrupting Cole, who was droning on, "I should have told Papa whose baby it was, and told your own father. What I have now is a secret that has no meaning any longer, because I don't love you any longer, Cole."

As if this were fresh information, he turned in his chair to stare at her, astonished.

"You don't love me, either," she told him.

"Who asked you?"

"Never even knew what love is. I beat my head on a barn wall once, I was so lonely. I knew what you and me had wasn't lasting. Look at you, sitting there drunk, broken glass all over the floor, the clock busted. You ought to be polite, not even sit down in my house till I ask you to choose a chair."

"Listen to her," he murmured. "Talking away, like a river flows. I love the way the Wrights talk, especially her and her little brother."

She touched his hair, ran her fingers into the curls, untwined one lock between her fingers. "You're mean, Cole. And you stink."

Roughly he pushed her away. "I'll burn your ass, lady, come at me that way. What you think I am? Throw me aside. Nobody's ever done that."

"How long you going to stay this time, Cole?" she said. "An hour, or two hours?"

He slammed his hand down on the table. "Stop criticizing me in my own house."

Collie ran cold water on her wrists, then drank from her cupped hands, spitting the water into the sink.

"What you want me to do?" Cole asked. "All right, let me know the truth. What is it?"

Wayland waited for Collie to tell him, but she appeared to be too weary to repeat it all. "You know the answers by now," Wayland told him.

"I know a few more questions that's not been asked yet, such as who the hell are you to come here and tell me how to do with my own?"

"Your own what?"

"My own wife and son."

"Whore and bastard," Wayland replied.

The table came up and slammed against him, throwing him against the wall. On the floor he sat looking up at the giant above him, spoke dazedly to Cole and vaguely was aware of Cole's boot coming toward his head. Even after the kick, he was still conscious. He knew that he was lifted from the floor, was shaken, hauled roughly, thrown through the air. Wind was cold on his face, snow was cold all about him. A door slammed, and he was left in the yard in the dark.

184

Slowly, painfully, he forced himself to sit up. His head was aching, pulsing with sharp pain. He spit blood out onto the ground. Paula came running, slipping and sliding, and helped him to his feet, guided him to the stone room, where he sat down on the bed, spitting blood. "I was never more calm," he told her thickly. "I said to myself, better here and now."

Paula used a snow-dampened cloth to wipe his lips and chin.

"You want to go with me to find help for her?" he asked.

"I'll go," she said.

She spread the damp cloth over his face. His heart was thumping as loud as a boy's drum. He heard the door open. "Where you going, honey?" he asked.

"For Young," she said.

It was some time later that he heard Collie cry out. Painfully he pushed himself to his feet and managed to gain the yard.

Cole was shouting, "It's the cold blood in your God-damned Wright veins..."

Wayland moved along the boards, following the trampled path he and Paula had made. He got as far as the black oak tree when he heard Cole say, "No, lady, you tell me how you plan to get rid of me. You going to kill me while I'm mounted on you? You heard that Holy Ghost call you whore. Now prove it."

God knows, let Young arrive soon, Wayland thought. Blood on his chin, blood in his mouth. He scooped up snow and wiped it on his face, scooped up some more and chewed it, swished it about between his teeth.

Abruptly the house door was flung open. Cole stood in the yellow doorway light, a drunk giant gazing off in the direction of the barn. He listened for a few seconds, then went back inside, slamming the door. It stuck, but released itself, swung open an inch or two.

Wayland picked up a piece of sapling fireplace wood and weighed it in his hand, an oak club.

No new sounds of protest from the house; Jonathan was crying in the back room, that was all. Wayland decided he ought not even to look to see what was happening. He was going to wait for Young, had to wait for Young. Nothing he could do inside there. He stood motionless and cold for a moment, listening to the two argue. Cautiously he moved to the door. He would glance inside, he decided; he would draw as close to her as he could. He pressed his face to the crack in the door, just as Cole, with a deep cry of anguish and frustration, flung his arm wide, the back of his hand striking Collie, brutally toppling her onto the floor, the very sight of the blow sympathetically toppling Jackson backward into the snow. He scrambled to his feet, secured the club, approached the door, only to see Cole kneeling beside her, tears in his eyes blinding him as he patted her face. He was drunkenly telling her he was sorry, that he loved her, that he had not meant to hit her.

Wayland backed off. He heard Collie say something, but the words were garbled. Then he heard her say, "Where you going now?"

"Outdoors. I have them furs to tend to and a horse to feed. Why, you want to fight some more now?"

"You better not hurt him, Cole."

"Who? That ghost? He put a damp breath on me. A ghost can smother you, did you know that?"

Wayland backed farther away, trembling. He stumbled, turned, found his way to the rock room and hid behind it.

Light lit up the limbs above his head. Cole

stepped outdoors, cursing. "Still snowin'," he called back into the room. "I'll be back here directly. You be ready." He whistled for his horse, then called it by name. The saddled horse came to him, slowly, a step at a time, reluctantly, resentful of neglect. From the corner of the rock house Wayland could see Cole untie a roll of pelts from behind the saddle and fling them into the house. "Man wasn't made to suffer at the hands of a woman," he called out suddenly. He trudged through the snow toward the stone room, paused there. "You in there, ghost? Hey, ghost, come out. I want to see you have a turn with her." He slipped and slid awkwardly on his way back to the house. He held to the doorway with both hands, spoke thickly to Collie. "The ghost is not in his rock-pile, Collie. I think he's ascended. What we do now for a ghost to play with? Hey, ghost, come here!" he shouted to the snow-filled air. "Does a ghost leave tracks?" he called to Collie. "I'll find him in the air. I want to see him and you together, Collie." He went into the stone room and tore the bed apart, kicking the pieces about. That done, he led the horse to the creek to drink, and Cole drank as well, knelt on the rock and used his cupped hands, sucking water into his mouth. Suddenly he began to laugh, a raucous giggle filled with mirth. At the same time he began to slosh the water over his face and neck, and into his mouth, sucking the water. He was alive with drunken hungers.

Wayland walked down the soft path until he stood directly over him. He raised the oak club. With one blow he could fell him, but he could not bring himself to strike him.

Cole swung around, still crouched, alerted; his hand reached out, closed around the club. "You afraid to hit me?" he asked, rising slowly to his full height. "Why, God-damned," he said. He tore the club free from Wayland and brought it around in a

187

swishing arc, striking Wayland's left shoulder.

Wayland, with a cry of pain, backed away as the club once more swished through the air. "You going to run from me, ghost," Cole told him, "did you know that?"

Wayland backed off as Cole advanced. The club swung by, this time close to his head. The stone room was at his back. Cole, grimly smiling, moved on the snow. Bracing himself against the wall, with a lunge Wayland hurled his body forward against the giant, using his own body to push Cole backward across the slick rock, both of them landing in the water, Cole with a fierce roar of anger and surprise. Both were off balance in the water, neither at first able to gain a foothold. Cole began thrashing at the surface with the club, angrily, wastefully trying to assert himself. He swallowed a gulp of water, began coughing, and desperately, blindly he grasped hold of Wayland's arm, hurled him toward the middle of the creek. Grappling, Wayland sought to gain a hold. Cole, far superior in strength, was disadvantaged in the water by the coldness and coughing, and Wayland dove at him, managed to pull him underwater, held him down until his own lungs burned with pain. He and Cole turned once under the water, then, thrashing about wildly, Cole sought desperately to break free. Wayland held him. Both men were still under the water. Wayland held him in spite of a twisting pain in his neck as Cole tightened his hold. Wayland held him, his own lungs bursting.

Only when Cole stopped struggling, when he surrendered, did Wayland release him and make his way to the slab of rock.

He stood at the rock, dazed. He looked back toward where they had wrestled and made out Collie herself standing there in the water, holding Cole's auburn hair, keeping his head out of the water. A lantern was burning here on the rock slab.

"You help me," he asked her, "or help him?"

Cole's hair was floating on the surface of the water. "My good God," she said.

"You helping me or him?" Wayland asked again. He shoved himself deeper into the creek, braced himself against the current, waded to the hair and grasped a handful of it, pulled it toward the rock. "Cole, you better come out now." He pressed the head against the rock, told Collie to hold it there. "Hey," he said to it, slapping it. She held the head out of the water while he climbed out of the water, then helped pull Cole's body onto the rock. He slapped at the big man's mouth. Wayland worked with the body until Cole breathed. Cole belched water onto the snow.

"You about died," Wayland told him.

Cole's body was still a heap of sodden flesh. Wayland and Collie squatted on the rock, staring spellbound at him. There was no sound at all from the house, from Paula. After a while Collie took the lantern and returned with Cole's horse, which she led onto the rock slab. Wayland helped her lift Cole onto the saddle. At first he lay with his head forward against the mane. Snow matted his hair, melted on his head and shoulders. Wayland poked one of Cole's feet through the stirrup. Collie was working on the other leg.

Snow lay on the rocks of the stream, dark water flowing around them. The lantern light shone, glistened on the snowy rocks.

"Don't send him by the house," Collie said.

"Why not?" he said.

She led the horse into the water, led it down along the creek edge, making her way slowly.

Cole sat up. "What the hell?" he said, but he spoke in a weak voice, without defiance.

Wayland watched from where he crouched on the

landing stone, his body pulsing with warmth pressing in around him. By God, he had won. Or he and Collie had won. He didn't know when she had arrived. Together they had won.

Directly Collie came wading back up the creek. "He'll go home that way," she said, her teeth chattering. She accepted Wayland's help onto the rock. Wayland noticed the club, the stick of fireplace wood, and picked it up, weighed it in his hand, estimating its value. He tossed the club into the stream, then made his heavy, tired way to the path, where he waited for Collie. She was waving the lantern as she walked, which made his shadow tilt and turn against the tree limbs overhead, made him appear to be immense. "Collie, what did we do?" he asked her groggily.

"Need to warm," she told him.

"Not comfortable here," he whispered slowly. They helped each other to the house. "Where is Paula?" he asked suddenly. He sank down at the table, balanced himself on his chair, glaring at the fire. "He left those furs on the floor," he said.

"He scared me," she said, drying with a blanket. She gave Wayland a towel, but he dazedly stayed bent over the table, staring at the fire, marveling at the evening, at his winning over Cole. "Stranger than God's breath, what's been done," Collie said. "I'm thinking we'd best leave here soon as we can, go in the truck in the morning."

"Will the snow delay us?"

She began pulling Wayland's gown off over his head. "If you had been raised up here, you'd know how to protect yourself better, Mr. Wayland. This is a rough place to live. The men here make their own demands. There's not much gentleness."

"Well, I was born elsewhere," he said.

She wrapped him in a quilt, brought it up tight around his neck, then paused to examine the bruise on his face where he had been kicked. "It break any teeth or not?"

"Don't think so," he said thickly.

She touched his hair, fondled it. "Not your fault," she said. "You were brave enough. You were brave as I ever saw, let me say that. I never saw a more calm man as he walked into a lion's den. You were as direct with him as if you had a plow to sell."

"Hush, Collie. Don't talk so much."

"It took Cole by surprise. He was expecting more danger from you. Did he hurt you much?"

"Well, he's built like a spring, you know that. I imagine he has some trouble holding down whatever he's lifting." He laughed quietly. "Watching his boot come toward my head was the longest second I ever lived."

"Knocked your head against the wall." She crouched beside him, touched the bruise on his face lightly, gently. "I'm merely wondering if we should leave tonight."

"Can't drive that truck tonight," he said.

She retreated to the back room, emerged from there soon with the baby. She put him on the bed, over next to the wall, and sat on the edge of the bed, from where she disconsolately studied Wayland. "Can we leave tomorrow?"

"I'm not going anywhere, Collie," he told her.

She got out of a wall cupboard a bottle of buttermilk and poured herself a glass. "Papa says this is settling."

"I believe it might be. Did Cole get to you, Collie?"

"No. I've tried to stand him off ever' time since Jonathan was born, but tonight's the first time I succeeded."

"Might pour some buttermilk up you, I was thinking, if he'd got into you."

She laughed, a giggly laugh. "Please, don't. I'm exhausted."

"Lie back on the bed, put a pillow under your hips, and I could dribble some into you a bit at a time."

She went on giggling.

"Isn't there a poultice or tea or something you people have?"

"Let me worry about myself. What you mean by *you people?*"

"I do worry about your being with a man. I tell you, I don't mean to bring up another child born of that one—" He caught himself, turned away awkwardly.

She scooped the baby off the bed and ran into the back room, slamming the door.

Once the baby was quiet, he could hear her inside there weeping. "Ah, Jesus," he whispered. "Ah, Jesus, woman, stop crying, will you?" In there talking to the baby, too, crying while she comforted him. Ah, well, hell, he hadn't needed to hurt her. It was all part of the explosions of this certain night.

He stood straight up, pressed his hands down along the blanket, feeling the body of the new man, himself, a victor over Cole, a crusher of women, Collie.

For a moment he stood at the bedroom door and watched her as she fed the baby, then he went to the bed and knelt down beside them both, took out her free breast and kissed it.

He knelt there kissing one breast while she nursed Jonathan at the other one.

The McGregor twins brought Paula home, she walking along between them, her pig, Scarlet, following on the leash. They brought her directly to the house light, stood in the yard grinning in that exasperating McGregor manner which claimed rare knowledge known only to themselves. "Come up the house with that there pig," one of them said, "dogs got atter her."

Wayland, who was not certain what the boy had said, was equally unsure about what had transpired.

"What you doing here?" Collie demanded of them.

"A favor, ma'am," one replied curtly, "so be obliged."

Paula, wrapped in a blanket, sitting in the house, said all they'd done was pinch and feel her, which she guessed was worth the bother in order to be brought home on a night blinding as this one. Even the pig had lost its bearings, she said. At the start she had decided she might need the pig to guide her home, so she had led him along, but when Young wasn't at his house, she had started on to Milton's and got lost.

Collie kept asking what those twins had done. "What you mean by pinch? What mean by rub my stomach? Rub through the dress, was it?"

Wayland took a lantern down to the creek to stare at the place where he had beaten the big man. Never in his life had he excelled over another man in a struggle, and he was surprised, proud, distressed, full of wonder.

Gudger, making his rounds in the snow, he and his dog, heard an animal or a person in the creek, out near the mill dam. "Somebody out there?" Gudger called out. He lit his lantern and approached the water. A horse was standing in the creek, stymied by the dam, frightened by the light. While he watched, the animal stepped across the dam, into the pool below. By God, something was dragging from it. "Jesus, a man," he whispered. The man was trying to hold to the dam's logs, to pull himself out of the water. The horse, just below the dam, belly deep in water, was staring at the lantern. The man held out

193

his hand toward the light. His face was deathly white. Cole Campbell, sure as God lives, Gudger realized. His hands were grasping at the slick logs of the dam, his face deathly eerie in the lantern light. Flashing water was behind him, around him; the horse was neighing in fear, was trying to move downstream. Cole's foot must be caught in a stirrup. "Help me," Cole called.

Gudger moved slowly, carefully out onto the dam until he was within reach of Cole. He bent low, held the lantern in Cole's face.

"I'm slipping," Cole said between clenched teeth.

Gudger took firm hold of one of Cole's wrists to secure him. The current was swirling about the big man, but his head was out of the water. "Tell me about you and Collie," Gudger said, watching him carefully. "Cole, you hear me? I been thinking about you."

"For God sake, help me out of here."

"You got your leg caught in the stirrup?" Gudger asked, his voice even, unconcerned. "Cole, you got my sister pregnant, did you?"

"Jesus Christ, you son of a bitch, I'm dying."

"Cole, you tell me that you're the father."

"I'm the father, son of a bitch."

"And what are you going to do about it? Can't desert that little boy?"

"Jesus Christ, Mister, I'm drowning."

"What you offer?" Gudger said.

"To kill you, to burn you, son of a bitch."

Gudger released Cole's wrist and an expression of startled horror came over Cole's face as he was swept on downriver, water gurgling over him, drowning his last words even as he shouted them, the water claiming him, the horse, pulling him on down the creek. Cole once fought his way to the surface, shouted out angrily at Gudger, then was drawn under once more, while Gudger crouched on the dam, in the snow, watching the water in horror and disbelief, his heart pounding against his chest.

In the dead of night Benie Frazier heard a horse neighing; seemed to be right outside her window. She climbed out of bed quietly, so as not to awaken Young, and crept downstairs to the parlor, which was directly underneath. She held a light up to the window and tried to see past it, but without success, so she pulled her husband's boots on over her naked feet and tromped outdoors, carrying a lamp, to find the animal.

The horse was standing in the road where the creek washed under it. The horse was untied, but wouldn't budge from where it stood. She noticed that one stirrup was pulled tight, and then she saw that a man's foot and leg extended from it. She moved the lamp under the horse's belly and found herself looking down into the creek at the open-eyed face of Cole Campbell.

She stifled a cry. She felt herself spinning, fainting. Recovering, starkly afraid that somebody had heard her, that she would be associated with this incredible, awful corpse, she fled, stumbling blindly through the snow to her house.

Tell Young? Should she tell Young? No, please God, don't have him launch himself into this. Let the discovery go to somebody else's credit, not to his, nor to hers. Secret, quiet. Quiet. Lamp off. Boots in the closet under the stairs. Not a sound.

She fixed herself a cup of tea, hoping to quiet her nerves, but could not lift the cup, her hands were trembling so. The horror-filled face in the water, a dead giant in the creek beside her inn. God help us, she whispered. Should she leave the horse out there to freeze? Would it die, exposed to the road wind? Should she free the man's head from the rocks, or at least keep the horse from further pulling at the body. No. Please God, do nothing.

She felt so overcome with fears she began to weep and pray, seeking comfort from within and from God, and asking pardon from God for her uselessness and weakness, for she would not, could not do anything at all.

9

The entire rolling land was beautiful in the morning, white, pure, with mere shallow indentations left by last night's footprints. The cow returned to her shed after milking. The chickens stayed on their roosts, deceived by cloudiness. In the house the three people chatted, laughed. Wayland now and then would step outside in the fresh air to listen, as if for an arrival of someone. Collie would interrupt whatever she was doing to speak to him in passing, would say affectionate words to him. Paula followed him about, asking what had happened the night before, receiving scant notice and no information. When Wayland walked to the creek and stood there staring at the water as if transfixed, she followed along, pulled half a pail of water from the pool beside the rock to soak beans in. "You going to tell me what went on, Papa?" she asked.

"We chased him off finally," he told her. "Collie and me together."

"Chased him off how?"

"In the water. Best way we could. The cold water constricted him."

He was looking down along the creek. What was he trying to see down there? she wondered. By stretching she could see the little breakwater dam at the mill; she could see beyond that only for a brief, laureled piece. "No footprints left on the far side of the creek," she said. "Did Cole go home on our road?" She knew she had not passed him down that way.

"No, I don't think so," he said, preoccupied.

"Papa, your master clock is busted."

"Lord, yes," he said. "Put it in that clock box, will you? No, I'll come help you."

"Broke a window, something did."

"Need to buy a new pane at the store. Can stuff paper in there for the morning." He walked back to the house with her, testing his muscles. "Sore. Muscles I never knew I had—"

"That bruise makes your face look heavier on one side than the other," she told him. "Collie's bruised on the side of her head, she told me."

"But we came through the storm, anyway. It came at us suddenly, didn't it, Paula? It crashed in on us. A natural winter storm, I'd say."

The one who found Cole lying in the creek was Perry Lawrence, who with his family had yesterday evening been on their way to Tennessee. When snow started falling, they parked their car at the lot and spent the night inside the church, being unwilling to pay inn fees. They slept on different benches, he, his wife, and three young children. Much of the night he lay awake listening to a horse neighing, having no idea whose it was or where, knowing nothing about the lay of the land here, or placement of houses and barns. At dawn, however, he saw the horse over beyond the cemetery, a bay gelding only slightly larger than a pony, holding its head low against the wind. Now, what the devil? he thought.

His wife made breakfast tea and provided bread and butter, which revived him, got his blood flowing properly. He mentioned to her and the children that there was a horse over there exposed to the weather and it seemed to be in pain. As soon as was convenient he braved the weather, two of his children tumbling about in the snow after him, the other one bawling protests because he had been left behind. The troop of three advanced on the troubled animal, intending to move it to a sheltered place, and so they came one by one to see the corpse lying in the creek, and one by one they reached into the water and touched its chest and neck. Perry Lawrence could not bring himself to touch the agonized, desperate face.

So here they were, on their first morning in this isolated country community, discoverers of a dead man, the first dead person the children ever had seen. Mr. Lawrence called out to the nearest house, the inn where he had priced rooms the night before, and he thought he saw the woman's face appear momentarily at a window, then a man's, but he wasn't certain. When further calls did not attract a reply from anybody, he on his own released the corpse's head from the rocks which imprisoned it. He told his children to tie the horse's reins and run ring the church bell. They had very much wanted to ring it last night for fun. "Ring it now," he told them, and they responded with peals of laughter as they began their race to the church.

Lawrence, left alone, felt for the pulse of the body; of course that was perfunctory, for the eyes were open wide and confessed death.

The bell clanged, and soon the sounds reverberated, returning from the mountainsides, mingling, saturating the village even as a new *clanggggggg* was born, grew, extended itself outward to strike the mountain walls and return diminishing, all of this alarming wild animals in their dens and holes, and citizens in their houses. A dozen tolls went out before house doors began opening along the road. There came Mr. Wright from the direction of the river. Mr. Lawrence had tried to bargain for land with him; a kind man, and probably honest, but not generous in a trade. There came his oldest son, pulling on his coat, even though his shirt and pants were unbuttoned. "What is it?" the son called ahead, clearly alarmed.

How to tell him? Lawrence wondered. He remained silent, out of respect for the message itself.

He led the group, half a dozen of the first men to reach the church, to the place where his children had tied the horse. They found the horse gone and fresh tracks in the snow where it had turned upstream, had made a way for itself along the creek bank.

"We tied the reins to this bush," a boy explained.

"What's he dragging?" Wright asked Lawrence.

"A dead man," Lawrence said.

Milton saw the horse. It was just over there in the inn's back yard. The children rushed toward it, so the horse moved on away from them. "Don't frighten him," Sam Crawford bellowed, and his voice, which was tenor and shrill anyway, scared the horse yet again.

Once at the mill road, the horse turned uphill, moving toward Collie's house. Its pursuers, now approaching more stealthily, could see it in Collie's lower lot. "Scared by the bell," Wright said, "and all the yelling. Call your children back, Mr. Lawrence."

"What dead man is it?" Gudger asked Lawrence, his voice trembling.

"I don't know him."

They were in full view of Collie's house now. Wayland and his daughter were coming down through the yard, but they stopped on confronting the horse and the heap of cloth and leather it was dragging behind it. Wright called, "Go slowly up to take its reins, Mr. Jackson."

Wayland didn't move. The horse responded to

Paula's approach by bolting to Collie's barn, securing shelter for itself in the wagon stall.

"It was scared by that bell," Wright told Wayland as he approached him. His breath was white puffs of mist. "Who's it dragging, can you tell?"

Wayland, speechless, was staring at the barn. Collie appeared at the upper corner of the house. "Don't come here," he called to her. "Go back inside."

Gudger was trembling so fiercely that he had to sit down, and it was his younger brother Milton who took ears of corn from the crib and offered them to the gelding. Of course, once he had caught hold of his reins, he was able to secure the horse and disengage the corpse's boot from the stirrup. He turned the body over onto the snow even as the other men assembled, and they all stared down at the face, Cole's face, bruised, swollen, one eye open, the other closed, the mouth hung open in a ghastly, silent shout.

Gudger began murmuring bits of desperate, disjointed prayers. It was as if he feared the ghost of the body was lingering here, all about. Still other witnesses gathered and stared stupidly, nobody saying much of anything, the cold north wind stinging them as they waited. Sam Crawford, red-faced, struck breathless by surprise, turned away, murmuring to himself. To Wright he said, "It's that there Campbell, ain't it?"

Wright shook his head in disbelief, unwilling to accept what he clearly recognized. "It's Drury Campbell's best one, is it?"

Nobody spoke the dead man's name. Everybody present knew who lay there, his cold, bruised face entrapped by death. Wayland went off to himself and sank down on a box of clockmaking tools, his thoughts reeling into a world of disbelief. Gudger was still mentioning God; he was saying God and Jesus help us. He clenched his fat hands together,

201

repeatedly cleared his throat; he stared blankly at the flank of the white mountain rising above them.

Wright stared transfixedly at the awful face. "I wish I'd not seen it. Who found him?"

"I did," Lawrence admitted ruefully.

"Where is Young?" Wright asked suddenly, the implication of Cole's death taking hold. "Hey, Gudger—"

Gudger couldn't seem to bring himself to respond.

"It was in the creek near the inn," Mr. Lawrence said, "had its head caught between rocks, the head underneath the water, the eyes staring up through the current at me..."

Wright was seeking Young among the faces of the men who had assembled. "Where is he?" he said desperately. "Gudger, where is your brother?"

Gudger was lost to the day; he was helpless.

"...face looking up from the bottom of the creek at me, and with the snow on the rocks above it, so it was peeking up through, with the eyes round as big white marbles..."

"Milton, where is Young?" Mr. Wright called to him.

Mr. Crawford poked the corpse with the toe of one boot. "He's about stiff."

A man said, "The underwater parts will be limber for a while yet."

"Well, where are the women?" Wright asked, dismayed. "Somebody has to get him in better shape for— If his father sees him like this—" Everybody was distraught. Nobody could make sense out of the situation that had been thrown upon them. "Who's going to go tell his folks?" Wright asked, not expecting an answer. "That face is full of anger. Would you call it anger, Milton?"

"Or pain," Milton said.

"Collie's good at doing faces," Wright said. "You recall she did both the Tempest boys when they drowned. Go tell Collie to come out here, Mr. Jackson."

Wayland was sitting near the barn, stunned, awkwardly grappling with dread and quiet and fear. He seemed not even to know what was taking place.

"What's the matter, Mr. Jackson?" Wright asked, approaching him. "I say, go tell Collie, tell her she has to do the face."

"No," Wayland moaned, "no, she's not able to do that."

"She is able. I've had her do faces before. Go tell her."

"She doesn't want to do that."

"None of us want it," Wright stormed out, furious with the delay. He swung toward Mr. Crawford. "Where is your wife? She lays out bodies."

"I'm— Take that body down to the church," Wayland said, his words formed with difficulty. "I don't want it up here."

"Who is making the decisions?" Wright said. "Now go get Collie." He saw Mrs. Crawford, who had stopped on the hill road to get her breath. She was a round woman with jowled face and pudgy hands and a small mouth, which just now was exhaling puffs of mist. "Mrs. Crawford," he called, "you're to take charge of the body, but I'll have Collie do the face."

Mrs. Crawford approached the corpse, bent over it, moved the legs, found one willing, the other stiff, that one being the leg which had been caught in the stirrup. "It'll need breaking," she announced.

"Yes, I expect so," Wright said.

Gudger took his father aside. "You listen to what Jackson told you, Papa. The farther from here that body lies—"

"What you say?" Wright was confused by the interruption, as he was by the late arrival of others,

203

some of them calling out, asking questions. "What, Gudger?"

"We don't want that body up here, Papa," Gudger said hoarsely.

"Those children yelling, that bell frightened the horse—"

"Take him to the church," Gudger said. "Or send him to his father."

Wright had not seen such pain on Gudger's face in years. "Mr. Jackson, you come here," he called to him, and when Jackson had joined them he said to the two of them, "Is anything funny about this that I should know?" He watched their expressions carefully. Neither man would look at him. Finally he said, "You go to the house, the both of you. Where's Young?"

"I'll find him," Gudger said, still whispering, unable to get control of his own voice.

"Was Young— Is he the one you're afraid for?" Wright asked.

Gudger closed his eyes tightly. "I'd get that body off our land."

"Was Young to home last night? Do you know?" Wright asked.

"He wasn't home," Gudger said.

"This man died, Cole died near the mill, didn't he?" Wright said.

"Papa, get him off the land."

"My God," Wright exclaimed, realizing the dangers, then realizing there was no way to hide the presence of the dead man here, not even by removing him from the place; everyone would know.

Mrs. Crawford had Cole's leg in her big hands. Mr. Lawrence and his wife held the body while she pulled the leg until it snapped. She fell backward onto the snow, laughing.

More people were on Collie's road than had ever been there before. News of the event was passed person to person down the long way, and the rising excitement swept like a tide across the countryside, moving out from here, this piece of trampled ground. Wright murmured further instructions, first to one, then another, leaving much unclear, his comments now heavily distracted by worry; he made his way to Collie's house, half blind, groping along on the boards, or where he thought the boards ought to be, and came upon Collie, who was a full hundred feet from where the dead man lay but was staring in that direction, her eyes reflecting horror. "Honey, what are we to do?" he asked, and took her in his arms. Embracing her caused his eyes to well full of tears. "Ah, damn us," he whispered. "We're all damned. Young killed that Campbell heir, I'm afraid," he said to her."

They held to one another, supporting each other, both in tears. Many of the people who were present noticed all this.

"Need soda, if he's not to turn blue," Mrs. Crawford called out.

Other ladies had pushed their way through to see the corpse. "Lay him out in Collie's house," one of them said.

"No, keep him cold," Mrs. Crawford said. Then to her husband she said, "I have always done the faces as well as the bodies."

"Oh, I wouldn't make too much of that," he advised her.

"It's not customary for two people to do a corpse," she told him. "Someone must be in charge."

"Oh, let Collie do the face," he told her.

"Well, where is Collie? Where is the soda?"

"I'll go tell her," he offered.

"Why, yes, bring her out here," Mrs. Crawford said. "Remove his outer clothes," she told the other women. "Let's see what we're up against. Cut off his clothes. We'll get new ones, clean ones," she told them.

Wayland opened the house door softly. Collie was at the sink, staring out the window toward the creek. He didn't dare touch her; even her body had the appearance of brittleness. Her father was sitting in a corner chair, his hands clenched between his knees.

"Collie," Wayland whispered. "It's all come to our place."

"Who is it dead?" she asked, knowing all the while. "It's Cole, is it?"

"Why, yes, it's Cole."

After a while she said, "What is it Mrs. Crawford's been yelling for?"

"For soda."

"It's there on the shelf, in the yellow bowl."

"And for you to do the face."

She moaned and bent far forward, her hand shielding her eyes from light, a fist closing the scream that was rising to her mouth.

"Collie, they'll know," he whispered. He turned her body so he could hold her, and pulled her hands away. Her eyes were drawn deep into her head and were utterly pained and lost to life. "You have to do the face," he told her.

Together they walked through the yard, nodding to people she had known all her life, her countenance shrouded, her steps unsure, her hand grasping Wayland's arm to steady herself, arriving all too soon at the rock slab swept of snow, Collie nodding to Mrs. Crawford, whom she had never much liked, neither she nor her ravenous brood of children, nodding to the other women, listening, but not really hearing the thin voice of Mrs. Lawrence as she introduced herself and said she was journeying from

Charleston. "What is it?" Collie asked Mrs. Crawford.

"The face," Mrs. Crawford said. "You father said you'd do the face. It's pasty and past due."

Collie had not looked down at the corpse; she did not look at it now. She knelt beside the rock slab and asked for the pan of soda and water. She saturated a rag and laid it over Cole's face, wet his skin thoroughly, then in a sudden sweep, an angry affirmation of herself and her own right to life, she pulled the wet cloth away, revealing his blue, bloated, angry flesh, and looked straight, deep into his sightless eye. "Cole," she gasped, the only sound she allowed herself, spoken to his open mouth. Her lips went on forming his name.

"Well, are you begun?" Mrs. Crawford demanded impatiently.

Collie touched Cole's face with her fingertips, withdrew them, burned.

Mrs. Crawford was watching, and was talking. "Massage the face, if you're going to do it. Get the eyes both closed, and close the mouth afore it sets in that awful cry it's got. Then tie it closed. I say, Collie, we are short of time, we are working against time..."

Collie stared at the face of her son's father, her lover, the one she had loved once as close as breath, more than her own life...

"Your father said you was good with faces. There's his face, and a worse one I never saw, considering the way the water's mottled him..." Mrs. Crawford rattled on.

Collie laid her hand on his forehead. The skin was icy cold. She forced her fingers to touch the brow of his one closed eye, then move along the cold ridge of his nose, touching finally his upper lip, which resented the impression and resisted it. She sought out the muscle at the corner of his mouth, pressed

207

on it, began to rub in a circular motion to warm it, free it from its frozen bonds.

Mrs. Crawford, when she cut the clothes off Cole's body, had placed her own green-and-white bonnet over his genitals, the bonnet's artificial decorations turned so that the flowers were displayed appropriately. A circle of attentive, caring ladies was drawn tight around the bonneted corpse now, and surrounding them was a circle of other sympathizers, men curious about the laying out, wondering how the work was progressing; they were speculating among themselves as to what might have happened to produce the death. Most anything that was unusual, exceptional, was noted. For instance, a window was broken in Collie's house. For another, her new man had a bruise on his face that was caused by no slight blow. Then, too, one of them had noticed that Young had not used his house last night; at least there were no footprints left in the snow going to the door, except those of a child and an animal—looked like a pig's prints, but that was not likely. There were footprints of the child and animal going away from the house, too, then wandering about, aiming when last seen toward the McGregors' place. "That's all I need to know," one observer said profoundly. "The McGregors are bound to be into this."

"And Young's in it," another said. "Was a friend of Cole's for a while."

"Why'd they fall out?"

"Over a woman, I'd imagine."

The men wondered about it all, while enjoying the wonders of the unknown, piecing together the puzzle, all the while watching Collie's hands massage the dead Cole's cheeks. "Takes that even pressure, that warmth, don't it?" Mr. Strother Collins said. "Only a woman can do that."

208

"She's getting it, if she stays with the pressure."

Other people were walking about the yard, some just now arriving, talking, speculating, drinking a nip of whiskey to ward off further chill. Children were climbing, tumbling, slipping, wallowing, most of them thoroughly wet by now. Here and there babies issued loud protests of mistreatment or desertion. A life-sized snowman was being completed over near the barn rails; it needed only eyes, and they were being fashioned out of wood ashes.

Bleak sky overhead, befitting a day of loss, appearing especially desolate here in the cold, wet yard. "More sody, more sody," Mrs. Crawford called out periodically.

Collie tied a ribbon under Cole's chin and around the head to hold the jaw closed. "Not too tight," a woman advised her, "or he'll appear even more grim." Collie moved the ribbon the least bit, and his expression changed perceptibly. Mrs. Crawford commented favorably on the general impression. "But he's not looking like he's in glory yet." All Cole's flesh was shiny white, except for blue around the bonnet, where the women had not dared venture close with the soda. New trousers from the store were lying beside the body, as were a pair of socks, a white shirt and a jacket, one more formal than any Cole wore in life. Mrs. Crawford held up the pair of trousers. "Shall we cut them up the back or not?" she asked Mrs. Lawrence.

"I'd say yes."

"No, we'll be able to pull them on him whole," Mrs. Crawford decided, resenting advice even when requested. She set to work pulling the pants legs on, and asked Collie and Mrs. Lawrence for assistance in lifting Cole's buttocks off the rock. For a few scant moments the bonnet slid out of place, revealing a shriveled bag and penis, blue, emaciated by freezing cold and death. With haste the pants were pulled up

209

to cover him decently. Once the shirt was tucked in under his back, Mrs. Laura Lincoln, a prideful Virginian who had married Jack Lincoln a few years ago, thought to comment, "My father turned blue before we ever got him off his horse."

"What was he doing dead if he was on a horse?" Mrs. Crawford asked.

"Why, he died a-riding."

"I'd think sooner or later he would have fallen off," Mrs. Crawford said.

"No, he rode well all his life," Mrs. Lincoln said defensively. "Looked splendid in the saddle."

Mrs. Crawford stepped back to review the work, to get a fresh perspective on it. Both Cole's eyes and mouth were closed. His lips were less twisted than earlier, and the new clothes lent an air of accomplishment to the endeavor. She gave her view that the lips were too tight and that the frightened grimace of the mouth was not complimentary to a Christian.

Stung by the criticism of her own work, Collie replied in kind, said she thought the shirt collar was too tight, that the pants were too binding around the waist for a comfortable rest, and that the left leg was twisted, showing that it was broken.

These comments produced from Mrs. Crawford the opinion that the best facial she had ever seen had the eyes of the corpse open, looking toward Heaven, to which Collie replied that the corpse would, of course, need to have his shoes put on.

"I don't see why," Mrs. Crawford said. "Waste of money, shoes to be buried in."

"Is he not to walk about in Heaven?" Collie asked.

"Angels have wings," Mrs. Crawford said. "Let him use them."

"Is he to be an angel?" Collie asked, surprised.

"Why, if he's in Heaven, he is."

"In the Bible we are told of people and of angels,"

Collie said, "and I don't recall a place where it says people become angels."

"Gabriel was an angel, and he come to Mary of a night to announce the mating with the Holy Ghost. He spoke in plain words, in whatever language he was using, English or whatever—"

One of Cole's eyelids flew open. Mrs. Lawrence screamed, and several women shouted out. The bleak, bleary eye peered out, and Mrs. Lincoln gave a little whoop and cry and knelt beside Cole to begin massaging. Collie, in a trance, stared helplessly at the face.

"We'll need to put a coin on it when it's closed again," Mrs. Crawford said to Mrs. Lincoln. "She ought to have coined it before."

Collie rose to the attack. "I'm not saying an angel cannot be sent to Mary, but I doubt if the angel could become a person, or a person become an angel."

Mrs. Crawford turned on her, her own face reddening, jowls quivering. "When Cain killed his brother Abel and went into a far country, he took wives, and since him and his brother was the only two people born as of that date, as recorded in the Bible, then he could only—" She paused to await the undivided attention of the other women present. "He could only have bedded down angels."

The women murmured approval of that argument. It was, after all, unanswerable.

Collie waited for the ohs and ahs of these underlings to be finished, then quietly, hands folded, said, "Did the offspring have wings?"

Mrs. Crawford blanched noticeably. "I'd say not," she admitted.

Collie said, "The Revelation says there are streets in Heaven. Why do they have streets if people are not to walk on them?"

"To fly along," Mrs. Crawford said quickly.

"Why make them of gold, then?"

"Well, a body can light on them if he chooses to."

"Use planks to light on. No need for metal streets."

A number of men were crowding in closer, alerted by the sprightly debate. A duel by two women squaring off at one another always was promising, and retellable.

"I will want shoes, myself," Collie said. "I'm not one to fly about. I'm a person made for solid ground, and I'm of a mind that God is the same."

"Same as you Wrights, is he?" Mrs. Crawford replied at once, striking a quick, decisive blow.

"Not if he flies," Collie said.

Wayland had a silver quarter in his pocket. He set it on one of Cole's eyes, then stood back to study the effect. He took his remaining coin, a copper penny, and placed it on the other eyelid. The onlookers discussed the effect, one silver and one copper eye, one larger than the other, both shimmering. "Ought they to match?" he asked Collie quietly.

"Oh, I don't think it matters," she said, anxious to be done.

"I was right nobly born," Wright said, speaking to a room now empty except for Wayland and Milton. "I was not born to be a tinker door to door, a chimney sweep in autumn, an itinerant pruner of apple trees. I was intended to be an educated person who could think his way through tangles and could respond to the feelings of others. My father taught me to feel other people's passions, honestly to perceive, fairly to decide matters, and here I sit in loneliness, hearing that my son has slain Drury Campbell's son, and even rumors that— Where was the other report from, Milton, that you told me awhile ago?"

"A Tompkins and a Nyland—"

"That she, that my Collie was seduced by Cole, that he saw Cole coming through those woods across the creek, how many times?"

"He said twice."

"And that my grandson—did he say that my grandson—"

"No, he only said Cole was seen—"

"Would it mean my grandson was the grandson also of my father's enemies, is that the gist of it? I've always wondered if Drury was in any way involved in Papa's death."

"Oh God, Papa—" Milton moaned. "The weak lie about the strong, you know that."

"Lie? That she lay with her brother Young— you've heard it? That's what Drury Campbell's people have claimed, say openly—"

"Papa, she never did that."

"No," he said, gathering his thoughts together, more calmly considering his position. "They say Young was Cole's close friend for a year, two years—"

"I think that might be, Papa," Milton said.

"Go through friendships like that, young people will. If you tell a boy no, that boy's family is not worthy of us, is beneath us, is alien to us, is objectionable to me, your father, why, sir, Mr. Jackson, they will seek the boy out, they will hug him to their bosoms. For all I know, she might have opened up her body to him, seeking—some sort of—freedom, not knowing all she was doing was enslaving herself."

When he was prepared to leave, the old man paused at the bed, looked down at Jonathan, who was asleep. He lifted the corner of the blanket so he could see more of hs face. He lifted the blanket further so he could see his arms and belly and legs. He said not a word, but of course was questioning who it was lying here, the grandson of what other man.

He left the child uncovered and turned to Milton, who was exploring a small hole, a bullet hole he had noticed in the north wall; Milton was poking at it with his pocket knife. "Did Gudger go on his rounds last night?" Wright asked.

Milton nodded. "Stopped by the house, as usual."

"Did he see anything on his rounds?"

"Was nervous last night, so shaky he couldn't talk clearly. Couldn't hold his cup steady. I noticed that."

"He didn't mention seeing a horse and a man in Collie's creek?"

"No, but he wasn't asked, either. He's out there now in the yard, following Young around like a dog, ready to save him. You can ask him."

When his father had left, Milton poured himself a drink of liquor with trembling hands. "Campbells are about due here," he told Wayland. He poured Wayland a drink as well. "Never saw Gudger scared before. And Young's already drunk. Told Papa he wouldn't leave, go hiding from anybody. Collie's window's broke out, is it?"

Wayland picked up the sleeping baby, sat down with Jonathan held close to his chest. He rocked back and forth to comfort himself with the child, to comfort his own torn mind more than comfort the child. God, had he killed the baby's father? he thought.

"Young said he never killed him," Milton said.

"No, he didn't," Wayland said simply.

"Hell, no," Milton whispered, and swallowed the last of his drink. "No, it was the Widow Frazier done it." He set the glass aside, closed the knife. He looked into the wall hole that he had been exploring. "Sort of lead-looking," he said. He moved outside, where the people were waiting for the Campbells to arrive.

For several minutes it seemed that Wayland scarcely breathed. When Collie came in, her eyes

214

momentarily probed his, as if she thought he might have it within his province to understand and forgive her. He responded not at all. It was as if an incomprehensible maze had opened before him and he had stepped involuntarily into it and did not even know what was needed of him.

There were twenty Campbell horsemen in the yard, and other Campbells and their kind were approaching on foot, Drury himself among them. The horses were tethered here and there in the yard and near the barn, wherever a pole or tree or bush could be found, and twenty horsemen, sweaty from the ride, still sitting in the saddles, tough, hard, leather-clothed, furred men, their rifles and shotguns in the saddle holsters, their pistols bulging in their under-arm holsters and pants pockets. A truck loaded with Campbell women tried to climb the hill; its tires slipped on the snow and the truck was left near the mill dam, where a few wagons also had been parked. The Campbell women came up the snowy, mud-mired road, one of them from time to time crying out to Jesus. They were weeping aloud out of their sense of loss, and out of a fear of retribution. A vital nerve had been touched, old and buried, almost forgotten animosities had been laid bare; mindless were days like this one, and the fears arose out of the bowels, not the mind, and were vital, close to the quick. One death caused others.

Drury Campbell arrived, walking slowly, purposefully; he was seventy, stooped, intense, a preacher on occasions, the hunter who stopped killing bears at the age of sixty-one when he had killed two hundred and forty-six, so as not to surpass his father's score, his face reflecting a lifetime of rough weather, high elevations, long distances, kinship with the sun and wind. He moaned, almost fell, his rubbery legs faltering, refusing to support him in so deep a sorrow. He reached out a hand for a daughter, Miss Margaret, held to her arm until at last he stood near the swept rock guarded by a circle of women. He would not, could not bear to look at his boy. The women moved back, stood aside, revealing the corpse in a stark white shirt, tight black pants...

He stared down at his son, the twisted image of Cole, the present reminder of what he had been. A warped image. He looked down at the distortion of his son, which was more real than ever Cole had been in life, which was more final in its savagery than smiles in life, or laughter, or crying, or any other attitude; here was the final image of his son, his youngest and best, his favorite, the companion of his older years, his hope. Tears flooded his eyes and dropped onto the fur of his beaver coat. His hands, long and tough-skinned and scarred, clutched helplessly at his daughter Margaret's arm.

Around him now gathered his several children, in ages fourteen to fifty, and nearby assembled other powerful adults, flinty, watchful, careful, nephews and the like. William Wright stood nearby, his daughter beside him, neither of them uttering a sound. Milton Wright came forward and awkwardly began talking, greeting these warlords with words of sympathy, saying death was an inevitable occurrence, mentioning the storm of the night before, which had closed off even the moon and stars for light, mentioning the filled creek, the cold water, the winds, the many hazards resulting in accidental death. Drury paid only passing attention to him, and when at last Milton fell silent, Drury said, "Cole is gone, Margaret," speaking to his daughter, glancing at the corpse, taking brief peeks at the sight of his lost life left on the rock.

Mrs. Crawford approached, introduced herself by name, including her maiden name. She told him she had laid his son out for burial. She courted his approbation, recalled how distorted the body had been when she had taken charge.

Drury felt around inside his coat and came out with a purse; he sorted through it, selecting two coins, which he handed her. At first she thought they were pay, and not much pay at that, but she came to realize on inspecting them that they were identical to the two which lay on Cole's eyes.

Quiet. William Wright might have spoken now, but did not. None of the Campbells dared speak while old Drury stood silent. "Cole's body is set, is it?" Drury asked.

"It's set," Mrs. Crawford said. "I'll not say it can't be altered some, but it's come close."

"There's nothing more to be done about the mouth?"

"I didn't do the face, Mr. Campbell," she admitted quickly. "It was done by another."

Drury's present wife, a pretty, unadorned woman, perhaps thirty, came to him and took his arm with both her hands. Drury sobbed, patted her hands with his own. Loud sobs broke through him, which he didn't try to hide. His daughters and nieces began to weep, and his oldest living sister, Mrs. Kincaid, began to weep, and then so did Harmon, who had been the last of the Campbells to see Cole alive. When Drury had control of himself once again, he wiped his face with the fur sleeve of his coat. He sneezed, cleared his throat and spit onto the mired ground. "He's lost all his color."

"He was in the water," Mrs. Crawford said.

"You never thought to put a camphor cloth on him. He'd 'a retained his color."

"He had no color, Mr. Campbell. It was washed out."

"Them bruises on his forehead," he said to his wife, "you cover them, Helen."

She removed her scarf and, kneeling, laid it over the forehead, tucking it under Cole's head. She worked without disturbing the piece of ribbon that held his lower jaw closed, the ribbon circling his head. When she was finished she leaned forward and kissed the cold cheek. Others moved forward now, knelt and kissed the scarf or the cheek. Harmon was helped to the rock by his cousin Skeet, who did not bother in any way with the ceremony. While Harmon knelt, Skeet stood above the body, looking across the dead man at Young Wright, his gaze cold and insolent.

Drury wiped his eyes with his wife's handkerchief. One of Cole's sisters began sobbing aloud, and he paused to consider her, tenderly watched as her brother James put his arm around her, began whispering to her. Old Drury removed his greatcoat, laid the coat over his son's body, then he flopped on his knees beside the corpse and kissed Cole's face. "I'll swing them high enough to be seen, Cole," he said. "It won't bring you back, but it'll be done." He waited for the cry of a distant crow to cease, then asked Mrs. Crawford if there were any wounds on him.

"His leg got caught in his stirrup and was twisted, and it had to be broken."

Milton interrupted. "He was found in the creek, down at the main road."

"Who found him?" Campbell demanded at once, turning on him.

"Why, I think a traveler," Milton said, surprised.

"Not found up here?" he asked, looking about at the place.

"No, down at the creek, as I said," Milton told him.

"Why, then, is he here?" Drury asked.

"His horse was scared by the bell and young 'uns screaming," Milton said.

218

"Why not flee down the road, away from it?"

"The way opposite of the noise was up the creek," Milton said.

"But the road is the clear way. A frightened animal will choose the clear way, unless he's returning home," Drury said. "One grows up with animals, he knows the way an animal thinks, and it won't go, can't be driven up a creek unless it's the way home." Quiet in the yard, except for icicles dripping drops of water. Away off in the deadened woods a limb fell.

"The horse ran before us up the hill, we pushed it on," William Wright said, coming to Milton's rescue. "It's not unusual."

"Pushed it on from the mill?" Drury asked.

"From the road," Wright said. "No, it wasn't at the mill."

"Well, its tracks will be on the ground," Drury said, waving his hand, dismissing the Wrights and all such arguments. "God is not mocked, we'll see where it went, certain enough." The wind was whipping through his linen shirt, moving the black string tie at his throat. "Is he broke anywhere, Mrs. Crawford?"

"Yes, sir. The leg."

"Is he complete?"

"Yes, sir."

He wiped his nose with his hand, coughed. Harmon offered him his coat, but Drury refused it with a shake of his head. "No parts missing?"

"None," Mrs Crawford said.

"He was struck by a limb and fell," Milton suggested, trying to represent the family. "It was a stormy night. He fell into the creek and was able to get as far as our road."

Drury's gaze lifted. Coldly he said, "Cole fell?" The question was left clothed in its full irony. "Cole fell?" he repeated. Dismissing the idea, his attention returned to Mrs. Crawford. "You broke his leg?"

219

"Had to, if we was ever to coffin him."

"I see," he said. "You're Hiram Jones' daughter by the Flemish woman, are you? Your mother used to bake bread for my wife Matland, Cole's mother."

Mrs. Crawford beamed with pride.

"Matland," Drury called out suddenly, "he's with you now. Bless you, darlings, you are together." He wept, even as he sought to regain his composure. After a while, with a shrewd glint in his eyes, he said, "We will all die, Mr. Wright." He looked directly toward the silent, brooding William Wright, well aware that a lifetime of animosity lay between them. "We will all die, what say, Mr. Wright?"

"We will all die," Wright replied.

"It is written that the wages of sin is death. What say, Mr. Wright? Any sin here?"

"The gift of God is eternal life," Wright said, "through Jesus Christ our Lord."

"An eye for an eye, Mr. Wright," Drury said.

"Forgiveness is mine, saith the Lord," Wright replied.

Drury shrugged, a heavy frown settled on his face as he considered Wright. "We'll want to search the grounds all about," he said.

"Very well," Wright said.

Drury was done, but he did not leave at once, and nobody else of his company moved away, either. For a minute or so he seemed to have quite forgotten where he was, what the nature of his work was. His gray eyes settled on Wright once more. "My son left Harmon and Skeet to come through this way on a personal mission of some sort. What mission was it?"

"I don't know," Wright said. "You must ask them."

Drury nodded. "Do you know the reason for his death?"

"I know of no reasons for it," Wright replied.

Drury, with head bowed, considered that. "I have

a wagon at your mill. We'll need to carry Cole down to it."

"Borrow what you need," Wright said, still guarded in manner, somewhat unsympathetic, resentful of Drury and his people, even so knowing he was host and a caretaker of the corpse.

"I'll take a door," Drury said. "Harmon will see to its return."

They removed a shed door from its place and made portage down the hill, slipped in the snow and mud, one horse kicking at them, the people moving past the truck that was ditched, the women singing. Old Drury held to his daughter Margaret and his wife's arm as he followed.

Skeet lingered, waited near where the corpse had lain. He asked Milton where the McGregors were, why they weren't present. Milton claimed not to know what McGregors would do, where they would be. Skeet was last to leave, and he turned back when near the black oak tree to seek again to isolate Young Wright with his burning gaze.

Evening settled in. The cow was milked, the chickens were housed, the pigs fed. A duck wandered in from somebody else's flock and made a place for itself in the barn, near where Wayland once had stored his clockmaking equipment. How remote and unimportant, he thought, was making clocks, compared with the death. All day he had feverishly sought to make adjustments to Cole's death, and no matter what danger was assaulting his mind, underneath lay the agonizing awareness that he had killed him. People he didn't even know wandered about the yard, remnants of the larger gathering, talking with one another in reverent, mumbled sentences, cautious with warnings, repeating stories of past revenge, shootings of men from laurel, deaths in the river, falls from high

221

places, a disappearance in the trackless woods, all means of justice administered by the harmed innocent against the guilty.

Caesar Plover, one of the better cabinetmakers, was rehanging the shed door that had served as litter. It had come apart; one of the bearers had slipped, and the door had struck hard on the ground. Plover was using a board from a barn stall to mend it with. "Old man taking apart sheds, is that it? Is that what I've come to? Wood from a barn? I'll discard you if you split," he told the piece of board. "Working on the ground like a beggar. Will you split or not, I ask you? I'll discard you or cut you off. She'll have no stall doors at all if you don't hold together."

Wayland could see Campbell men moving up the creek, examining the banks, the bushes, going on upstream of the rock room. From time to time they would call to one another, their words muddled by echoes. The cabinetmaker stopped work to watch Wayland. Wayland turned toward the field and saw that five Campbells were moving along with the tracks made last night by the two McGregor boys and Paula and her pig. The five men were a row of black dots on a bed of white, slowly, patiently tracking.

"Collie want this stall door rehung on its leathers, or for me to use metal hinges, Mr. Jack?" Plover asked.

"Oh, yes," Wayland said, watching the Campbells.

"I have a set of hinges made by Milton, but they cost precious."

The five Campbells stopped up in the field, briefly conferred. Behind them, at the far border, two McGregors appeared, arms folded, watching them silently.

"You can be sure they have men in the North Woods tracking Cole from his last camp," Plover said, "I'll lay money on it." He nailed the leathers to the door frame, using chips of wood to help secure the nails. "I'm making you your clock case. Mr. Jack, you listening? Next one I can veneer out of as pretty a piece of bird's-eye maple you'll ever see."

"I don't want maple," Jackson said, watching the Campbells.

"Never saw maple like this here is. Of course, I've got walnut cured enough for a case more. Gudger says you'll want mantel clocks as well."

"I only want long cases," Wayland said. The searchers moved in a necklace pattern along the hillside, just beyond reach or questioning.

There had been over a hundred people in the yard most all day, and of course they had stirred snow and mud together into a froth, so that people slipped as they moved about. Wayland saw Collie, with Paula worrying along behind her; the two of them were scattering corn for the chickens. He found himself wondering about Collie; today she was a foreign tune to him, full of marvels, a single human being capable of bringing about this complicated repositioning of half a dozen lives, all simply done. Her own loss, the extent of her personal tragedy, attracted him strongly to her, even as it served to force him to one side as spectator. He wanted to forgive her and help her, to save her if he could.

Dear Paula, scattering corn to the chickens in the mud, this alien ground, too young to understand, too old to forget. What will become of us now?

When the door was hung, he walked up toward the breaking woods, stood near the embrace of the dead trees, stared into the snow-limbed maze, the arms and hands intricately mated, reaching though not searching, resting though not restful. The sunset, blood red today, cast a red glow over the woods, over the community all about. Even the river off in the distance was red. Near his feet the snow melted into red water. The red blood of the earth seeped away. The snow and trampled ground were sopped in it; wherever he trod, blood was left, he noticed. This was the way the earth was now, and was its promise.

Young was alone inside Collie's house. He was still drinking. He had been drinking since the confrontation with his father that had followed Drury Campbell's departure. The two men, son and father, had shouted at one another, defying each other, here in this room, their voices carrying out over the yard.

Gloria swept into the room, as bright as usual. She laughed pleasantly, and the sound cut the air strangely. "Shoo those sad thoughts away like flies," she told Young. She ran a finger over his brow. "Boo," she said, and cooed into his ear. "What you sad for? You fond of Cole?"

"Waiting for somebody to deliver me from my sins, Gloria."

"Can I help?" she asked.

"I'd imagine you'd do the opposite," he said.

Milton came inside, told her they would go home now.

"Young, come on, smile," Gloria said, ignoring her husband.

"Leave him alone, Gloria," Milton said.

"Well, I feel sorry for him," she said. "I never saw him so sad."

"Leave him alone, Gloria."

"Well, what am I supposed to do," she asked petulantly, "with you men making all the plans?"

"Do?" Milton said.

"Yes, what am I to do?" she insisted.

"Come home," he said.

Gudger came by as they were leaving, a morose, somber man, transformed in half a day's time, a tragic attitude lingering about him. He said the

Campbells were everywhere on the road. They had found that last night a man in boots had gone from the inn to the place Cole was found, and had returned running to the inn. The man must have killed Cole, the Campbells had decided. Gudger sat before the family of frowning listeners, worry heavy on his own brows and shoulders. "I'm very tired," he confessed.

"What they mean, somebody at the inn killed Cole?" Young asked.

"Man in boots. They say he walked directly to the place where Cole was found dead, some time during the latter half of the snowfall. That's all I can tell you."

"And ran back into the inn?" Young asked.

"They said he ran fast as he could." Gudger shifted his heavy weight on the chair, frowning at his youngest brother. "Middle of the night, about half-snow, the Campbells said. They were proud of having found the tracks so soon."

"Well, I never left my bed last night," Young said.

"Her bed, was it?" Gudger asked. "In the inn?"

Young poured whiskey into a glass, drank it down. "I don't know any her," he said.

"The Widow Benie, was it?" Gudger said.

"No, I don't know any widows," Young said.

10

At last the yard was empty of strangers, was returned to the family. Even so, each one, Collie, Wayland, Paula, moved in a trance. There were no stories told, there was no informality of any sort. Collie forgot about fixing supper. Paula finally mixed cornbread and, when it was baked, put it on the table alongside a dish of honey. "It's all going to be brushed over, this death," Wayland declared at one point, speaking soberly. "They'll leave us alone once Cole's buried." Whether he believed this or not, nobody asked. He did not believe it. He could not free himself of his own thriving guilt, which was unattached to Campbells or revenge. He was finding it difficult to relate this death of a stranger with himself, but he could not tear himself loose from it, either. He was infatuated with his enslavement to guilt. The murder of Cole clutched him just as tightly tonight as it had earlier in the day when Cole was lying on the swept rock.

He noticed that Collie carried the baby wherever she went, clutching it especially close to her body. Was she protecting the baby, or protecting herself with the baby? he wondered. He resented the way she held Jonathan. She said nothing to the baby, he noticed. She appeared to be unaware of the child. Whenever she spoke, it was to mention incidentals:

the repairs needed on Paula's blouse, of which there were several, her intention to plant an orchard in the spring, with reference to the kinds of trees and where they could be found. She complained that a bat which had hibernated in the copper tub stored in the back room, this certain bat which had been resting on a gourd inside the tub for months, had today of all days collapsed onto its back, was to-night lying on its back dead, one of its tiny arms missing. "Now, what could have got inside that tub? What would want a bat?" She kept repeating the questions, and others similar. "No animal knew it was there, did they? Could a mouse get inside the tub? Has there been a cat up here? Could a snake crawl inside the tub and get out again?"

"We have snakes inside the house?" Paula asked, distressed.

Collie said, "I swept a blacksnake out that door when I first moved in here, and he's stayed outdoors since." She talked on and on about that brief inci-dent, prattling on to occupy her mind, to relieve her deep distress. "What sort of country is it when noth-ing's safe?" Collie asked. "Can't have pets. My dog was killed." On and on, seeking to escape the yawn-ing questions themselves which lay unanswered, unanswerable.

But listen—a shot sounded off in the valley some-where. She stopped talking for a minute or so, wait-ing for another. "Why, that's nothing," she said. "It's shooting of a hog, it's the butcher killing a beef for tomorrow, it's a snake found in a grain bin, it's a horse too old to stand...nothing unusual about a shot around here, especially from the McGregors' compounds, or from the Campbells'." She paused, considered the validity of her argument. Then she turned to, sought out a new distraction. "Gloria made that soap last summer when the sun was hot, so it would sink the pine scent way into it...made it

227

on a rising moon, so it would harden..."

No, she did not hold the baby in quite the same way as yesterday; she was more possessive of him, Wayland thought, held him tighter, her fingers gripped him harder, she had a feverishness about her in regard to the baby, even when putting her nipple into its mouth and pushing its face against her breast to help start the flow of milk, even in the wrapping of her hands and arms about the child, as if to ward off offenders, snatchers. Wayland also noticed that Paula would stare at the baby strangely, as if studying his features, perhaps in connection with his father's coloring. Wayland realized he had only once touched Jonathan since the death of Cole. He had himself killed the baby's father, and now he was to be the baby's father. Before the death, what was his relationship? Was it that of a kind, benevolent father-stranger—that is, a stranger becoming a father to the child? Tonight he was the father surviving. Also he was the slayer of the father. The child he had seen himself as rearing, teaching, was now the surviving heir of the man he had killed in the water. Would the baby know that? Would there ever be transmitted to the baby actual information on the subject, explaining that the father who loved him day by day was the enemy of his father? Would Jonathan one day know that his mother had aided in the slaying of his father? Would Wayland not be conscious of it, regardless of the child's knowledge, and regardless of all explanations, all excuses a dozen years could provide?

Last night, he recalled, he'd told a story to the boy. Was it only last night that he had mentioned the events of a deaf bear? And what tonight would he tell him? Something more dire. Last night he had embraced Collie. Tonight they were joint criminals in Cole's death; it associated them closely, and it separated them as well. Last night he had been depending on her love of him; tonight he wasn't certain their love could survive their guilt. Was it the death or the guilt that worried him more? he wondered. Last night he had trusted her; tonight he was conscious that she had knowingly brought him into a place of dangers for which he was unprepared.

Paula went to bed in the back room, slept with the baby. Wayland sought her out, sat down on the bed beside her. He rubbed her back, which she always appreciated, and told her she should dream of sheep gamboling in snow. She kept saying that he would not leave here, would he, that the wounds would be healed here. Of course, he said, they would be. At last she fell asleep, and he was able to lay an extra quilt over her; she always insisted she didn't need more than one, but he thought differently. He kissed her, then he prayed, asked Jesus to watch over her.

When he did return to the main room, he sat bolt upright in a chair, attentive to Collie, respectful of her, but wary and critical as well. He watched her as she prepared for bed. She asked him if he wanted to come to bed now, and he said no, he would wait up awhile longer. He thought maybe he should go to the stone room, but that idea annoyed him; there was little pleasure in the prospect of being alone, or of deserting her at a time of need. Collie got into bed, moved over close to the wall, as she had done the night before, leaving space for him.

He had stashed the pieces of the broken clock, the one damaged by Cole, in a box under the bed. He pulled it out now, shoving the roll of pelts aside, and dragged it over to a place near the table. He spread a cloth over the table and laid clock parts on it. "Whenever I'm nervous, I work on tiny things. It keeps my mind occupied," he told Collie.

She was lying on the bed with an arm thrown across her face, as if the shallow light bothered her. Light, he thought, or thoughts of Cole, whom he supposed she loved, thoughts of his death, which was cruel even for an enemy, much less the father of one's child, thoughts of revenge, a cruel, cutting word here. "Collie, tell me what you're thinking," he said. "Collie, you awake? Be hard to get to sleep, I'd imagine."

She said it was, that it would be for a long while.

"Changes most everything, this death," he said. "I remember myself when my Uncle Fletcher died, the one I never liked, when he was said to be passing on, I hoped he would hurry on his way. You know how a child can think. And so he did. He died, Collie. And I missed him. I came to the point where I wanted him back."

"Well," she said softly, "I don't want Cole back."

"But you're not sure."

"Yes, I'm sure."

"You're confused, maybe. You might want Cole back, or it might be that you want him to die differently."

She turned onto her side and stared at him. "I don't want Cole back," she said, then she turned over, facing the wall.

"All right," he said. He decided that two bullets, maybe three had shattered the center of the clockworks. No way to repair it, either. "That little Jonathan, when he grows up, it'll all be told to him that his Uncle Gudger, or his Uncle Young, or that his papa Wayland killed his father."

"Hush," she said. "Please don't say who killed him."

"Jonathan can't hear me," he said.

She rested back on the pillows, staring at him. "Don't say that."

"Paula's asleep, too. So's Jonathan."

"Even so," she said. "They'll hear it."

He waited for her to continue. "They who?"

She nodded. "Out there," she said.

"The ones out there measuring the ground?" he asked. Later he said, "I used to read Shakespeare, then I would read the Bible, then Shakespeare some more. They're not unalike, they're not strangers to one another. Shakespeare was like God in a lot of ways, was willing to punish people."

"What you talking about?" she said.

"'Who hath measured the ground?' That's in Shakespeare."

Collie waited patiently for him to continue, but apparently that was the end of it.

"So I'm asking you who is out there measuring the ground."

"You going to sleep in here?" she asked him.

"Not going to sleep," he said. "Have to work on this clock."

"Tell me why," she said simply. "Will you work all night?"

"Can't sleep when there's a clock to be mended." That seemed not to satisfy her. "I'm a man of clocks, have to have order. Everything has to balance and move together."

"But everything doesn't now, does it?"

"Not recently," he admitted.

"Everything is off kilter around here," she said.

"I'd say so," he agreed, and went on working. He felt that he ought to explain but was not in command of his own thoughts just now, much less his feelings. "I don't want to add to your suffering, Collie," he found himself saying, "but you might have warned me more than you did, and told Paula about the danger as well."

"I was afraid you'd leave."

"I should have left, within an hour of arrival."

"Even if you went to Papa's to sleep, you'd soon be living down there. I was fond of you beyond what I'd expected to be."

"You were, you say?"

"Yes."

"You don't say you are. You say you were?" His hands moved quickly, dissecting the bits and pieces of the clock. "You mean it's all over now?"

"I mean I don't know anything just now. It's as if I'm not complete."

"You miss him, that's the truth of it."

"I miss him? No, but he didn't deserve to be killed."

"I agree with you."

"I don't feel sorry for him, even so. How can you feel sorry for somebody that's dead? I sorrow, but I don't feel sorry for him."

The clock had one hundred and forty pieces, he remembered, and he was finding about half of them sound. "Even when they appear to be sound, these parts, Collie, I ought to replace them. I'd never be satisfied."

She pulled a quilt up to her chin. "I don't feel sorry for Cole, for he's beyond what I can do for him."

He brought a lamp closer, held the wheel up to it, then he used a piece of paper to reflect light from the lamp through the wheel. "You meant awhile ago that you were fond of me and didn't want me to leave here, but not now."

"I don't want you to go now."

"That's what I mean, that you had affection for me earlier, but that it's over."

"No, I don't know what I think. If you left, I'd die, that's what I feel." She studied him for a long while. "I would go crazy if you left."

"Well, Collie, I've been wondering what to do. I mean, here you were as good as married to this man, and you said nothing to me about it, not so I understood, anyway. I didn't want to kill a person, Collie. I really don't take satisfaction in it."

"I helped *you* in the fight, you know that?"

"I saw that you were in the water, that's all I know."

"So you can imagine what I feel like."

"No, I can't imagine anything of the sort. I can see you'd be troubled more than me," he said.

"I think if it'd been any other time of the year," she said, speaking more assertively, "I wouldn't have kept you here in spite of the danger, and I wouldn't have helped you in the water, either, but it's the wintertime, the gloom and bareness, the loneliness—"

"Any other time he probably wouldn't have died, if the water were warmer," Wayland said.

"I don't know about water, but I know I wouldn't have helped drown anybody, except in the wintertime."

He considered that, wondering what had prompted such a thought and if she meant it or not.

"No, if I was you and Paula," she said, "I'd take that truck and leave here first thing in the morning, but it'd kill me if you left me."

"Leaving you? Maybe you could leave with us."

"Well, I can't go. I can't go and let them kill Young, which is what they'd do."

"How can you stop them, whatever they decide to do?"

"I'm not sure yet," she said, "but I'll have to."

He went on working over the pieces, squinting and studying. "Need a magnifying glass for the little ones," he told her.

"Papa has one," she said.

"If you left, wouldn't they decide you'd done it?"

"No, not a woman. No woman could kill Cole alone, they'd say."

"No woman ever killed a man up here?"

"They don't want a woman to have done it," she said. "They want a man to have done it."

"If Young tried to leave—"

"He'd not get far. You might not, either. Paula

233

could go, I think." She had been talking away, not thinking about the deeper meanings of what was being said. Suddenly she said, "Don't leave, please."

Her manner told him how vulnerable she was. He had always thought of her as being self-sufficient and competent, but just now she was bent under a weight heavier than life. "Collie, don't press on me," he said, speaking directly to her. "I have Paula to think about, as well as myself, and I don't know that I can stand up under all this."

She closed her eyes tightly.

"If Paula wasn't with me, I might be of more help. You might as well know the truth."

"You going to leave me alone?"

"I don't say that. But I'll have to decide, once the full weight is lowered."

"You did leave me alone just now."

"No. Here I am."

"But you're not here to depend on. You're not thinking about me as much as about Cole dead—"

"I don't care about Cole dead."

"Working on a clock—"

"I care about killing Cole. And it bothers me that you allowed it, that you put me in that place—"

"Hush," she said sharply, finally.

"Well, God damn it, Collie, you are the one who caused all this worry. Everything has to be traced back to you, so don't get critical of me for drawing away."

She stared at him, perplexed, her mouth open. "What you say?"

"You go out there and whore around with Cole Campbell, have a baby, get me to your bed, help me kill Cole—"

"No!" she screamed out at him. "I never," she said, throwing a pillow at him.

He dropped the pillow onto the floor.

"If they hear what you say," she reminded him,

"you'll not leave. I told you that before."

He reflected back on what he had just said to her. "Who would hear us?"

"Why, they're out there," she said.

He went to the window and looked out. Nobody was in sight.

"Mr. Wilkins, who lives in the third cove, he crossed a Campbell once, and they spooked his house for seven nights," she said, "then they came with lanterns, dug up his yard. He got so nervous, he was about crazy. They began to dig at the edge of his yard, kept digging. This was at night. Finally his wife worked up enough courage to go ask what they were doing, and they said they were digging her husband's grave."

"Did they kill him?"

"Not that night. The grave was full of water by the time they killed him. By then he was so frightened he could scarcely breathe, anyway."

"How'd they kill him?"

"I don't recall," she said evasively.

"Now go ahead and tell me," he said.

"No," she said. "It's too painful." She propped herself up on an elbow and watched him. "I'm sorry, Mr. Jackson. I am," she said, "for all the trouble."

"Well, so am I," he said. He put more wood on the fire and returned to his work. Only a few logs left indoors, he noticed, not enough to last all night, not to keep the room warm.

Some noise outside. Sounded like somebody tilted a yard board, the board slapping the ground. He noticed Collie freeze in place on the bed.

"Hear that?" she said.

He got up slowly from the table, pulled on his coat.

"Where you going?"

"If I sit here for all night, I'll need more wood."

"You're going out there?"

"Collie, it's our yard," he said. "You want to lock the door after me?"

She pushed her legs over the side of the bed, sat up. "Don't go out."

He pulled open the door. Nothing unusual in sight. He stepped outdoors, closed the door, then waited for his eyes to adjust to the dark. The woodpile was just there, nearby. In one arm he stacked a big load of wood, then picked up an oak sapling, a limb-log, in his right hand, to use if he needed to. He tapped on the door with one foot until Collie opened it. He dropped the wood down beside the fireplace, watched her as she fidgeted with the lock on the door. She was so nervous she could scarcely lock it. "Don't stand there and catch cold," he suggested. He was amazed at how frail she appeared, here at night in her gown, and how frightened she was. "You scared for me?" he asked, attracted to that thought.

"I never saw anybody as likely to do crazy things in my life."

"Nothing crazy about getting firewood," he told her.

"Why, there's people out there."

She was in a flannel gown, low cut in front, and he could see the roundness of her breasts, see them rise and fall with her frightened breathing. She was vulnerable just now, was in need of care, affection, he realized. Reluctantly, in a way cruelly, he returned to his chair at the table, resumed working on his clock parts, marking on a slip of paper which ones were broken. His uncles might be able to replace some of them from what was left of their stock. Ought to write them tomorrow, in any case, tell them where he was, and where Paula was. They had always loved Paula. And ask them for their special notice of her at this time, in case something happened to him suddenly.

Collie went back to bed, rolled over with her face

to the wall, pulled covers over her head. He realized she was in agony. Well, even so, it was an agony born of her own actions. With a file he made repairs to a few of the larger pieces. He would file them some more in the morning, when he had better light—that is, unless he and Paula decided they ought to leave here. If Collie weren't so vulnerable just now, and in need of him, he would, he just might leave. He was of two minds about it. Later he could come back and would try to mend the break, could ask about her life and their prospects of a family. Nothing like that could be decided with circumstances as they were.

Once more he heard a walk board move out in the yard, this time near the stone house. He went on working, listening. Later there was a sound just outside the window. He carried the lamp to the window and tried to see out, but the glass merely reflected the light. He set the lamp aside, then pulled the wad of paper out of the broken part of the window and, as he bent down closer, found himself staring into the face of a Campbell only two feet away. The man's lips curled in surprise and anger. Wayland snarled a challenge at him, and the Campbell fled, blinded by the light. He fell on the path that led to the creek, crashed onto the rocks, waded across the creek noisily, calling out, cursing.

Wayland poked the wad of newspaper into the window hole and sank down on the edge of the bed, trembling.

Collie turned over. "Who was it? Did you see anybody?"

He jumped away from the bed, from her, as if she might sting him. When she looked over at him, he pretended to be engrossed in his clock work again. He wasn't sure what more he could say to her, how to explain that he was frightened of being close to her, or of being committed to her.

"What time is it?" she asked.

"Lord knows," he said. "Paula took my watch into the back room with her."

"One time I loved him, the next time I didn't," she said abruptly. "It was only about a year and a half I knew him at all well, Mr. Jackson. I met him casually a long while ago, but it was only a year and a half since I first went with Young to meet him at the falls. Cole and Young were to go there and hunt. I loved him so much, first day. I fell in love so crazy. All my emotions swung on hope of him. Young was furious, said not to fawn over him, not to fall all over him, either. But if I love somebody, I do that way. As I did with you."

"Did you fall all over me?" he asked.

"Yes. Didn't you notice? Lord, yes. I'd been wanting somebody pleasant around here to take on over me. Cole never would. He would put me up against the wall, that was about all he would do. He was rough, especially when he drank."

"I'd say so."

"First day I ever agreed to meet him alone, I went up to that falls scared to death. I hadn't told Young a word about it. I crept up to the pool, sneaked my way in, and was going to wait for him secretively, and maybe not reveal myself, maybe hold on to my virginity, and first thing I knew, he was atop of me, and leaped onto me, had me pinned to the rock, was kissing me, devouring me like a starved man. He had followed me most of the way."

"Did you manage to fight him off?"

"Lord, no."

"Was he careful with you?"

"No."

After a while Wayland said, "I owned a cathedral skeleton clock once. My father had two cathedrals, but that was during his second marriage, and when he died, my stepmother took everything for herself and her three children, except I got a cathedral clock and a Swiss chronograph, with it missing its friction spring and column wheel."

"First time I had ever been with a man at all, and there I was spraddled on the rocks. But I had plenty of room, I'll admit that, and I didn't have a right to complain about him." She brightened abruptly. "But don't you know my back ached."

"How high a falls is it?"

"I don't know. Man fell in it once. Was night. He was missed, and the Campbells finally were called to help trail him, since they're expert at that, are as expert as the McGregors, Gudger says, and they followed a trail four days old. Can you imagine?"

"Found him in the pool?"

"Sitting at the bottom with his hat still on his head."

"What held that hat on, I wonder?"

"A man name of Bolton."

He got so sleepy pretty soon that he couldn't hold his eyes open. He cleared off a place for his head on the table and rested that way. She kept saying he ought to lie on the bed, that she wouldn't bother him, but he stayed where he was. Have to write his uncles tomorrow, he thought, ask for enough money for Paula to come home. If he could send Paula away, he would feel more free to act on Collie's behalf, as well as his own.

Next morning Paula was first one out of bed, so he went into the back room and used the cot she and Jonathan had slept on. It had a wet spot in the middle of the mattress, but he didn't mind. He heard Paula, on her return from the outhouse, say the woodpile had been disrupted overnight, that logs were left strewn about. He was wondering vaguely about what that might mean as he fell asleep.

That morning Benie Frazier was taking from her springhouse a jar of milk when she saw a Campbell

239

man, by name Horace McIntosh, standing beside the corner of her inn where the wood drainpipe ended, waiting for her. She cried out and dropped the jar, which broke. "What in heaven's name?" she said.

He held out a piece of oak firewood. "Your'n?" he asked.

"I didn't see you there," she told him.

"See hit?" he asked, and approached until he stood only two feet away. "Crushed on both ends. The bark's been crushed."

"Well, what of it?" she said. "I didn't see you, and you frightened me."

"Hit's been crushed," he said. "Was in that there creek."

"Well, you will please get off my property. I am weary of seeing men tramping up and down that creek. Now, if you please—"

"Is hit your'n?"

"What?"

"This here log?"

"No, I don't think so. Most of my wood is cut shorter, is for stoves." From her kitchen window she watched the same man kneeling at her woodpiles, examining the ends of the logs stored there, his forefinger going over them, moving slowly, seeking identity. She bolted herself inside the house, even locked the windows, and, full of fear, listened to the stairs and swing creak, and to the voices she imagined in the tall rooms.

11

About eight o'clock that morning Gudger came up to Collie's road, walking heavily, wearily, stopping from time to time to inhale deeply. He was stifling, inside his body he was suffocating. Collie heard him call hello and came out to meet him. He apologized at once for intruding, said Milton had roused him from his own house and had led the way to Young's; they had got Young out of bed.

"Was he at his own bed?" Collie said.

"In his own bed," Gudger said. "They'll be along directly."

"Somebody been in my yard," Collie said, noticing footprints.

"I was here for a while last night," Gudger said, shrugging. "I couldn't sleep, Collie."

"Why didn't you come inside?"

"It was my mind that wouldn't stay still. Couldn't rest enough to visit."

"You want to come inside now," she said, "and wait with us?" Collie cleared a place on the bed for Gudger to sit; she knew he preferred the bed to any of her chairs, which were small for him.

Paula brought him the baby to hold, as he requested. "I'll teach this boy to hunt before much longer," he claimed, smiling at Paula. "Killed a bear with my hands once," he told her. "Wrestled him."

"How do you wrestle a bear?" Paula asked him, unsure whether to believe him or not.

"Grab him wherever you can," Gudger told her.

"What does Milton want?" Collie asked.

"Lord only knows," he said, instantly nervous once more.

He was rather dear, Paula thought, the big man holding the tiny baby, perched on the bed, not now engaged in argument, not showing the slightest sign of ambition, not representing his enormous will; merely another intimidated person being shoved about by circumstance.

Milton arrived, Young following along, claiming he had not got any sleep. Wayland came in from the back room, rubbing his eyes; he watched the brothers guardedly, unsure of them just now. Milton took a piece of folded paper from his pocket, unfolded it, looked it over. "I made notes," he told them, his first announcement.

Every eye turned to him. "What you talking about, Milton?" Gudger asked.

"Papa sent for me at seven o'clock, said Mavis has a list of items. Papa wants me to report to you on them." He smiled, pleased by his newfound prestige. "I never asked for it."

"Where'd Mavis get her information?" Young asked.

"She told it all to Papa. Some of the Campbells had sought her out, knowing she would see him."

"Why not go to Gudger?" Collie asked. "Why'd Papa go to you?"

"I asked that, asked where is Gudger, and Papa said Gudger was one of the accused."

"What the hell?" Gudger blurted out, sitting bolt upright, the tiny baby a forgotten appendage of his arm. "What the hell you say?"

"It's all here." Milton tapped the piece of paper in his hand. "It's their current ideas, that's all it is, the pieces they've come up with."

"Jesus," Gudger whispered. "What the hell?" he whispered feverishly.

Milton said, "Papa said to talk with the three of you." He paused, looked at Gudger, then Young, then Wayland. Simply he spoke, calmly, without hint of danger, but the meaning fell heavily.

"Campbells never do what's expected," Gudger said. "It's best not to help them," he added. "I'd tell them not a damned thing." Then he said bluntly, "Well, what are you about, Milton?"

Milton studied his penciled notes. "I'm getting ready to tell you. They found evidence that their son Cole was at the mill dam about third-snow, as they now term the time of night."

"Where was he?" Gudger asked, his voice trembling.

"At the mill dam. There was a struggle there, they say, or an incident at the dam. His horse crossed the dam."

"How can they tell that?" Gudger asked.

"Marks on the rocks, in the snow, I'd say," Milton said. "Cole held to the rocks, they say. That's item number one. You want me to continue, or for us to talk about these as we go?"

"Go on," Collie said.

"Item two is about Young's whereabouts. He wasn't home during the snow, he didn't go in or come out, but he was seen the next morning coming out of the inn. This was soon after Cole's body was found."

Everybody looked to Young, who said nothing and made not even a gesture.

Milton put a check in the margin of his paper. "Item three is the matter of footprints from the inn to the place Cole was killed to where the creek flows under the road."

"What footprints from the inn?" Young said.

243

"Was he killed there?" Collie asked.

Milton drew back, considered Collie's question first. "I don't know. It's where he was found next morning." To Young he said, "There was a man left the inn at half-snow—" He referred to his notes, found the proper place on the dirty piece of paper. "His bootprints go down the inn steps, across the yard, then are lost in among others on the road. They are picked up again hurrying back to the inn, across the yard, up the steps. They say the man who made them had to have been inside the inn, as best they can tell. You, Young, were inside the inn, and so far as they know now no other man was inside there."

The words fell like weights, leaving Young staring wearily at his family. Milton made a marginal check. "No comment yet, Young?" he asked.

Young appealed suddenly to Collie. "I never rolled over that night, damn them..." His voice was thick with hurt. "I never made any such walk," he insisted.

"Then there's a stick of firewood, that's a fourth item," Milton said, referring to his paper. "They called it a club. Said it was in the water at the road, near where Cole was found. They showed it to Mavis and said it had been gripped hard by somebody, and the other end had struck somebody." He frowned at his two brothers, waited patiently. "That's an item," he said. "No comment?"

"So they think I left the inn and clubbed Cole, is that it?" Young asked heatedly.

"I'm going to list the items," Milton told him calmly. "I didn't make up these here. I'm telling you what the Campbells say." He studied his notes. "Then there's the matter of the girl and a leashed pig. She was at Young's. Which girl is it, they asked Mavis, and she said she didn't have any idea." He paused to look at Paula, who was sitting on the bed

244

next to Gudger; Paula was having trouble keeping her emotions under control just now. "Whose pig was it, they asked, and they said who is the girl staying at that sister Collie's house, and Mavis said she didn't know her name—didn't know your name, Paula."

"How do they know she had the pig leashed?" Wayland asked.

"The leash whipped the snow now and then, as she walked. Now, there was no trail left of the girl or the pig between here and Young's house, where people trampled up here yesterday, but there was a little trail going up to Young's door, and they say she went inside there. Is that so?"

"Yes," Paula replied.

"So you went inside and out, and then went wandering about, they said."

"Yes, I guess so," Paula said, "trying to find your house."

"I said to Mavis, did she go onto the mill dam, and she said no."

"No, I never went out there," Paula said.

"But you went to the McGregors', onto their property, the Campbells decided."

"I must have," she said.

"And then met two men along the way and walked with them to the top of Collie's field, and entered the field, where the wind covered over the prints somewhere in the field. So—" He looked from face to face, pausing on Wayland's, who was staring at his daughter, agony in his eyes. "So," Milton said softly, "that's an item."

"I never dreamed they'd bring Paula into this," Wayland said.

"It's item number five," Milton said.

"Why did they tell you all this, to scare us?" Wayland asked.

Milton calmly, silently considered him. "I don't know."

"Well, I don't know, either, bringing a girl into it," Wayland said.

"They're not gentlemen," Milton conceded. He referred once more to his paper. "Here's item number six. They could trace Cole through the woods from his and Harmon's campsite as far as the falls, where they lost the trail. They picked it up somewhere after the falls, then lost it in that big woods, where the snow was wind-whipped, covering up the trail, so they lost it, but thought they saw signs of the trail in Collie's field, right up there, but the snow had drifted over them so bad they weren't sure. Then they found prints of Cole's horse at the barn and in Collie's yard, and they asked Mavis if the horse had walked through the yard and barn when it dragged Cole's body up here, and she said—she told them—" He looked over his notes carefully, both sides of the piece of paper, while nobody else in the room dared to breathe. "She told them it had."

Everybody released the breath he had held. "That's clever of her, Milt," Gudger said.

"That's an item," Milton said.

"When did the horse go into the barn itself?" Gudger asked.

"They said there are hoofprints inside the far stall," Milton said, poring over his notes. "Item seven is the rock room. It's that room right out there."

"What about it?" Wayland asked tensely.

"It's busted up right much inside there, they told Mavis. Is that so?"

"Yes," Wayland said.

"They asked her how did it get that way."

"It's been that way." Wayland said, helplessly seeking a reply.

Collie said, "List the items now, we'll talk later."

246

Milton nodded, referred once again to his list. "Item eight is the bruise on Wayland's face, and a swollen eye." He paused for comment. Hearing none, he went on. "Item nine is a broken window in Collie's house."

"Well, we can explain that," Collie said at once.

"How?" Milton asked.

"Go on and list all the items first," Collie said nervously. "Lord, how many more are there?"

"Two more," Milton said, pleased with the effectiveness of his recital. "This next to last one is about Gudger."

"What the hell they item me for?" Gudger said angrily.

"It's a bootlace that slashed the snow-top, so they could trail that lace to your house."

Everybody, including Gudger, looked down at his bootlaces. One lace on the right boot was left dangling even now.

"They said Gudger left his house in the snow, about third-snow, went past the inn but didn't stop there, and went on to Young's house but didn't enter there." He looked up for confirmation from Gudger, who only glowered at him. "Then you went to the mill and stopped at the mill dam."

"No, by God, I never did that," Gudger said.

"About third-snow."

"No, no. God, no, I never stopped at the—at the dam."

Milton patiently considered the emotional reply. "They say you walked out onto the dam."

"No, by God," Gudger said, "I never did that."

"Then stepped back to the bank, where you lit a lantern."

"I never did any such damn thing—How'd they think that?"

"They said the lantern left a mark."

"No, hell—" Gudger said, waving the arguments

aside. "They get so clever they can't be believed."

"Well, they told Mavis there was a lantern lit and that you crouched down near the middle of the dam—"

"I wasn't out on the dam," Gudger said defiantly.

Milton allowed the effects of the outburst to subside before going on. "Next item is three pelts. They say Cole had three pelts."

"What pelts they talking about?" Young asked.

"They didn't say more than that," Milton said.

"Well, where are they? Who is supposed to have them?" Young asked.

"I don't know," Milton said, most patiently, calmly refusing to be intimidated by anyone. "They say Cole had three pelts with him."

"All right," Gudger said, suddenly, waving that consideration aside. "You finished, Milton? Are you done?"

Milton nodded.

"So that's it, is it?" Gudger said, glaring angrily at his brother, then at Young, then at Wayland. "My God," he said suddenly, helplessly, realizing all that was known.

Young sat in his own front room, swatting at a newspaper on a table, swinging a fly-swatter; there were no flies, he was merely occupying time. "Don't ever marry," he told Paula. She had been sent down to see that he didn't drink too much; she had followed along behind him on Collie's orders, as he knew. "How old are you?" he asked her.

"Thirteen, almost fourteen."

"When you're thirty-four, think about marrying. That gives you twenty more years not to have somebody poking your tits or feeling of you."

"I'd like to have babies of my own," she told him at once.

"Yeh," he said, "that's a good idea." He was drinking brandy, had already drunk too much of it for best use of his reasoning. "No, they see it as a big scheme, a plot we made up. They think we're clever, always have thought so. That's one reason they dislike us so much. They think Cole was trapped out there on the creek, that you carried the message to alert me and Gudger and even the McGregors, to say the time had come. We were all conspiring to kill one man."

"You want me to make you some tea?" she asked him, worried about him.

"You can. Why not?" he said. "I always like to have a drink in my hand."

She put water for two cups of tea into the iron kettle and set it on fireplace coals. "There's no fire in your stove," she explained.

"No, never is," he admitted. "I go down there to the inn, let the widow take care of me." He appeared to be making mild fun of the widow's considerateness.

"You don't like Mrs. Frazier?"

"Yes, I like her."

"Then you don't love her," Paula concluded.

"I can't love her if I like her?" he asked.

"You won't marry her," Paula said.

"I think not," Young said. "Though if we can get clocks made, I might marry and settle down. Tell me about the bed, Paula."

Paula looked up at him, surprised, unsure what he meant. She knew enough about men, having been warned often enough, to be wary of them, even of ones she considered to be friends.

"You know," he said, his mind groggy. "Oh, God," he moaned, disappointed with his loss of powers. Suddenly he pulled himself together. "On that list of Milton's— Did you know Milton could write?"

Paula had to laugh at the ludicrousness of the question.

"He never writes, but there he was reading what he had written. The bed that was broken," he said, focusing once more on the problem.

"I don't know how it got broken," Paula admitted.

"Cole broke it? He was up there for how long, Paula?"

"Until I came to find you, to tell you. It was an hour or more."

"And he fought your father, you told me."

"And threw him out of the house."

"I don't doubt it," Young said. "I warned Collie as late as yesterday, day before— What day is this?"

"Then I left," Paula said. "I decided to take the pig so I could find my way home again."

"Yeh," he said, murmuring. "Good idea. Wonder what happened then. I'd ask Collie, but hell, there's so many people around, can't talk secrets. Everybody has secrets, you know that?"

"I don't have a one."

"You don't?" he said, seriously concerned. "Lord knows," he murmured sympathetically. He said no more for a while, but watched the steam rise from the kettle, all the while trying to think through the puzzle that he was caught in. He began to hum a melody borrowed from old times, one he might not know the name of himself, and that Paula had heard only once before. "That window," he said, "was it broke before you left?" He paused. "Tell me what you know happened."

"Cole and Collie were arguing. Papa went in. Later there were several shots inside the house, and I thought Papa was shot, but in a few minutes he was thrown outdoors into the snow. I don't recall the window, when it was—"

"Pelts. You remember any furs?"

"I saw some in the room after it was all over."

"Are they up there now?"

"I don't know," she told him.

"You better go see," he suggested. "Look around the house, get them out of there."

She busied herself making tea, unwilling to leave him alone.

He was lost to his own speculations. "Once I had a girlfriend among the Campbells, did you know that?"

Paula looked up at him, startled. "You never."

"Pretty one. Cousin of Cole's. I met her at a revival. Cole was there, several dozen Campbell people, and I watched only her. Prettiest thing I about ever saw, and it was dangerous even to look at her with her relatives about. She saw me watching her, of course, and knew the danger, enjoyed it. Name of Laurel. When she went off in the woods, I followed. Spent the better part of the afternoon with her, and when she came back her papa beat her, or so Cole told me."

"What—did you—what did you do in the woods?"

He laughed gently. He reached forward and tousled her hair, smiling at her, but then he became serious all in a moment. "Papa was angry when he found out. Of course, Gudger heard about it and told him. Gudger is a big son of a bitch, if you want my opinion."

"Well," Paula said helplessly, seeking a way to converse with him, "that might be." She poured tea into a mug and set the mug on the newspaper he had been swatting. "You ever get frightened?" she asked, noticing that his hand trembled as he lifted the cup.

"Now and then," he told her.

"You enjoy danger?" she asked.

"Not here lately," he said.

"When I'm eighteen, if I marry then, will you come to my wedding?"

"No, you wait longer than that."

"I might not be able to," she said, astounded at her brazenness that she would make such a confession.

He watched her thoughtfully, nodded briefly. "Anyway, I went to see that girl a time or two. She was crazy to meet with me. Cole would arrange it. He liked intrigue and secret meetings and special names. He was curious about the Wrights, too. When I took Collie to meet him, he was crazy for her. I didn't know she would fall all over him, though. I thought she would be reserved, but hell, no, she had as crazy an interest in Campbells as he had in us."

"As you had in Campbells, too," Paula reminded him.

"I know," he admitted.

"And you and Cole were friends, when your family said not to be."

"I know." He sipped tea and, when that cup was finished, asked for more. "You don't want any?" he asked her.

"Not just yet," she said.

The windows on the east side had lost the sunlight by now, and the south window was shaded by a grapevine that had been trained on a trellis, so even without leaves on the vine the room was somber. "Mavis is a Campbell," he said. "I love Mavis best of all."

"Why wouldn't you come to my wedding?" she said.

"Oh—" The question interfered with his train of thought; he shook it off. "Won't be long before they put everything together, Paula, you know it? The bruises on your father's face, the broken bed—"

"The log taken from the woodpile, from Collie's—"

"The log, the broken window, the bruises—"

"You counted the bruises already."

"Put it all together, so they know Cole stopped up

252

there. Then they realize he came down that creek, where Gudger saw him."

"He says he didn't."

Young nodded. "Then to the road where, I suppose, Benie heard his horse and ran out to see what was the matter."

"She did?"

"If somebody did. She was the only other person there."

"Tell them, then. Say it was Mrs. Frazier."

He tapped the fly-swatter against the tabletop. "Don't think so," he said.

"But if you don't love her," Paula began.

"Don't think so," he said. "And I do love her." He threw the fly-swatter aside, moved to the window, looked out over the road, then walked to the back room and looked down at the creek, returning almost at once, taking the same chair, studying the pretty girl sitting on the floor near the fire. "Not my style," he said.

"But if you don't tell them—" Paula said.

"Not believe me, anyway," he said. He was up again, wandering about, wrestling with what he could do, would do to free himself and the others. He returned to the chair and accepted more tea. The tea was helping to clear his thoughts. "Last night I thought of a way," he told her. "What you think of this, Paula?"

She crawled closer so she could listen even more attentively.

"One of the Campbells follows me into the North Woods. Let's say I pack a few things and go off, and he follows, thinking I'm running away. Say it's Skeet that follows. So Skeet and me fight, and I win. Then I put my clothes on him, my belt, my pocketbook, my watch, a few coins, then I burn Skeet's body, part of it, and put on his clothes, and go on to Boone or Asheville. What say to that so far?"

"Well—" She was flabbergasted by it all. "What you mean? You wouldn't— What if you didn't win?"

"Oh, I would win," Young said simply. "Then he'd be me, you see?"

"But who would you be?"

"The point is, I would be dead and could be thought guilty of Cole's death. You would have a funeral for me."

"I don't think so," she said.

"All the while I'd be in Asheville, or maybe California. Somewhere safe from all this."

"Is Asheville safe from Campbells?"

"No, not far enough," he admitted.

"But you'd have to stay away from here, wouldn't you?"

"Oh, yes," he said. "But it would all be over for everybody else. Papa could announce I had done the killing of Cole, explain some reason for it, and then it would be over. And there'd be a funeral. I want them to sing 'Rock of Ages,' Paula."

"I'll try to remember," she said, smiling at him, amused now even by his seriousness.

"And I want the ten commandments read, and the other commandments. Did you know there was more than ten?"

"No."

"Must be thirty of them in all. They go on and on. Tell you what kinds of lawbreakers to execute, what to do with sexual deviants, tell you what—"

"Sounds like quite a funeral," Paula said, relaxing, resting back on her stiff arms, smiling at him, content to be with him, realizing he was serious but that his scheme would surely topple. "Could you kill him?" she asked.

"Kill who?" he asked.

"Kill Skeet Campbell?"

"No," he said. He walked about the room, worrying about that. He was frantic with concern. "It's crazy, I know," he whispered. He shrugged. "Used to shoot birds; can't do that any longer. Benie got after me about it." He turned to her. "Did you ever hear what Skeet likes to do to animals?"

"I've heard all about him from Collie," she admitted.

"Wouldn't think it would be hard to kill somebody like that." He knelt near her. "Not sure that's even a sin." He put both arms around her, pressed her close to his chest. Her body was quivering, her little hands were pressed against his shoulders. "Yes, I would have to kill him, Paula, if there were only the two of us," he told her, rising to his feet.

12

Early morning, Young was lying on the bed in the upper room at the inn, watching a couple of wasps crawl on the south wall, where they had been awakened from winter sleep. They were trying to find their nest, he imagined. Well, so was he, he thought.

Benie flounced into the room, naked from the waist up. She enjoyed being naked from the waist up, going about that way, with her pretty, firm tits standing up. "You must be tired by now," she said.

"I slept an hour or two. We slept an hour or two, didn't we?"

"We made the house rock," she said, and laughed. "I do think we rocked the house. I know it rocked me back and forth."

"You were reaching out toward the stars several times, Benie," he said, smiling fondly at her.

"I touched them three times." Then quietly she said, "Young, when are we marrying?"

"Oh, God," he moaned, clouding over at once.

"I don't want anybody else. You're going to make me honest, aren't you, Young?"

"You're honest, Benie."

"No. I don't think so."

"What you told me last night wasn't honest?"

"What did I say?"

"With your body, what you told me. Whenever you go tender, trusting me."

"Yes, that was honest," she admitted.

"When the defenses go," he said.

"I want a baby, Young. I've told you that." She pulled a gown around her shoulders and allowed it to fall across her breasts. "Young, don't you know I'm in misery?"

"In the mornings, you mean?" he said, watching the wasps.

"I'm in misery, Young," she said. Tears in her voice suddenly. "Oh, God damn you."

"Come here and lie down," he said.

"No. I want to marry you and have babies before it's too late."

"Come here and lie down, Benie."

She lay down beside him and pulled the gown over her breasts, but he removed it from her body entirely and tossed it onto the floor beyond her.

She lay there whimpering beside him. "I'm not going to marry you this morning," he told her, whispering to her, kissing her ear, her neck. "This is all there's going to be this morning, Benie."

"But is this all there's ever going to be?"

"I've been designing my funeral, Benie," he told her suddenly.

"Hush, please," she said.

"I'll write it out and give it to you. I want it to be held high on the mountainside, so the village lies below, and I want a stone altar to be raised."

"What on earth are you talking about, Young?"

"Then I want Papa to read from the Bible the commandments. And when he gets to 'Thou shalt not commit adult'ry,' he's to call Collie by name, and when he reads the one, 'Thou shalt not kill,' I want him to call my name, then everybody will decide I killed Cole. Do you understand? I want it done at night, this first service, with all the sins laid before the people, and names called, and have people come to the altar where the dead lambs are bleeding and confess, pray for forgiveness. Have it held at sundown."

"Young, what on earth . . ."

"Then at dawn let the people know they're forgiven. Have the women take off their black dresses and put on white, and let the food be uncovered and the cider, let there be a celebration up on the mountain, up there beside Collie's woods, the one that's to be cleared this summer, where you can see the village below."

She was staring at him strangely, tears in her eyes. "Young, what are you saying? Please, Young, tell me."

"Have them sing hymn one twenty-four, Benie."

She began to weep, more from frustration than from any certain knowledge of what his rapidly moving thought might mean.

"Do you need to write the number down?" He sang softly:

> *Even now the dawn is breaking.*
> *Soon the night of time shall cease,*
> *And in God's own likeness waking,*
> *Men shall know eternal peace.*

"Then have them sing one twenty-one," he told her.

She began weeping, sobbing aloud, unable to fight back the wretched fears that broke through her body.

"Oh, now," he whispered into her ear. "Now, now," he whispered tenderly, moved to tears by her agony.

"Talk about leaving," she told him through her sobs.

"It has to be faced, I imagine somebody's funeral has to be held, Benie."

She clutched at him. "Please, help me," she

prayed to the guardian angels of her life. "Please, Jesus," she prayed, seeking release from the torture she felt.

He stroked her hair, gently caressed her neck, her lovely shoulders, her back. "It'll probably be either Wayland or me," he told her, speaking calmly, objectively. The wasps were seeking their home still, even yet, he noticed. "Two of us," he told her. "Or three, if Gudger's to be included. It'll be one, or maybe two of us before it's over, I predict." Like a mathematician, he recited the figures, unmoved, not yet frightened by them, figuring on the statistics, the probabilities, while his hands lovingly touched her body and aroused her, Young kissing her finally, tenderly, then passionately.

Noontime, old Wright sat in the dining room at his accustomed place, with the west wall to his back, before the paneling which closed off the double window that had faced the Campbell territory. "And it is Cole's child, is it?" he was saying, complaining, a whine entering his voice, his emotions threatening to break. "The boy is at war with himself from birth."

His wife, Annie, the only other person in the house, waited at the doorway, holding to the door jambs with both hands, a haunted smile on her lips. "Never let it be said—"

"She might as well lie down with a hog in the pen and be done with it," Wright said.

"Never let it be said—"

"Crawl into the slop of a pig trough and give birth."

"Like I said," she said.

He heard Gudger enter from the porch, saw him lurking just beyond the door in the kitchen. "I'll tell you, Gudger, it's come a blow."

"I never wanted to tell you, Papa," Gudger said.

"Tell me? When did you know?"

259

"I guessed it. I wasn't sure until—here lately."

"When did you guess it?"

Gudger came into the room, sat down in one of the six straight-backed chairs. "Had to put two and two together, eliminate, and a few times at night Cole was on his way across the road near the inn. I thought at first he was there to see the widow, for she's nothing but a whore, in my opinion."

"Go on, go on," Wright said, interrupting him impatiently, knowing with that sort of comment he was trying to hurt Young, that was all.

"But I added it up finally, a week or so ago."

"And never told me?"

"Hurt you? I want to hurt you?" Gudger scratched at his chin with greasy fingers, then belched. "Sorry, Papa." Whether he had apologized for the indiscretion or for holding the secret wasn't clear.

Milton and Young entered the house together, Gloria following, talking about being cold, about winter being the only time of year she simply could not get her blood circulating. "My feet freeze even in the bed, and Milt won't allow a foot, even a toe to touch him anywheres," she said, giving a firm nod in the direction of Milton, who was giving his mother a lingering hug, one of a type reserved for the more serious days of meeting.

"We'll come through this all right. The Wrights always do," his mother was saying.

"Tried to take their temperature with an outdoor thermometer," Gloria was telling Young. "Feel my hands. Feel my fingers, Young," Gloria told him.

Milton propped his rifle in the corner nearest the dining-room door. He made his way through the dark hallway to the front door and locked that. He came back through the hallway, murmuring about all the windows in this house, stumbled over one of his father's boots, viciously kicked it against a door, stopped in the pool of kitchen-doorway light, groaning, covering his face with both hands, considering the mire the family had sunk into. He noticed Young, now coatless, had a pistol in a shoulder holster, a bone-handled .30 caliber revolver.

"You ever shoot that at anybody?" Gloria asked Young.

"Used it to shoot birds with, long ago."

Milton said, "He could shoot birds in flight with it."

"Shoot a bird for me," Gloria said, then giggled. "I'm always asking Young to do something or other," she explained to Milton, "and he never does anything."

"Damned nuisance," Milton said to her.

Young put his arm around her. "No, she's dear. I'll have to take your foot temperature sometime, Gloria."

"Oh, Jesus," she whispered, and nudged his chest with her chin.

Milton, grumbling, threw himself into the dining room, took a chair. He listened to his father talk about having sent Mavis home for the day, being unwilling near her to discuss Collie's relationship with Cole. "So Annie made a stew, that's about all, and a pan of biscuits."

Young moved about from place to place, like a caged animal. Suddenly he turned from the kitchen's north window. "My Lord, she's coming now." Collie was approaching, carrying the baby, with Paula beside her and Wayland following.

His mother crossed the kitchen, walking faster than she normally admitted she could, and delivered the news to her husband and Gudger. "Collie's on her way through the lot."

"Now, let her be, let me tend to it," Wright warned Annie at once.

"Come here to my house with that child—" Annie stationed herself at his big rocker, the one near the kitchen fireplace, and picked up a book, one Wright had left open on the table nearby, *Poems of Keats*. She let it lie in her lap.

Collie came indoors, brushing her hair back from her face, flinging cold drops of moisture off of it, wiping her face with her wool-gloved hands, murmuring gratitude for the warmth of the kitchen. Young embraced her, even as she held the baby. "Papa's in the dining room," he said.

Wayland came indoors after wiping his boots repeatedly on the porch mat, and closed the door carefully. Young came forward to bolt it. "Put your gun where you can reach it," he told him, then noticed that Wayland was unarmed. "Better borrow one of Papa's," he told him.

Wayland smiled at him. "Coming across that field, I was thinking a Campbell could shoot me from any tree."

"They can shoot as far as you can see," Young said.

"Shoot from behind a bush. How would I know?"

"Shoot back," Young said.

"If you're dead, how do you do that?"

"Won't die all in a minute," Young said. "Most people live a little while."

"What difference does it make, if you're going to die?" Wayland said.

"Even so," Young said doggedly, "it deters them. It's best to go armed from now on." Paula came to stand near him. He hugged her, gave her a kiss on her forehead.

Wayland was watching Collie, who was trying to talk with her mother and was being ignored. "She wanted to come here," he murmured to Young.

"Collie, you want to help serve?" Young called to her, trying to save her some further embarrassment.

Their mother barked angrily at him. "You're not to decide such matters as service in this house."

262

"Well, we all know you're crippled, Mama," Young said.

"When did you care about that?"

"All right, all right, Mama," Young said. "For years I've cared—"

"You have problems enough without setting my table, Mister," she told him.

"If they only get their nerve up," Young said, winking at Gloria, "they'll kill me."

Gloria clouded over instantly. "Not my baby," she said.

"There's those with nerve on both sides of the river," Gudger called to him from the dining room.

Collie asked her mother if logs were laid in the parlor fireplace. Receiving no answer, she went through the dark hallway, carrying Jonathan, calling for Paula to bring her a cup of coffee. The door closed behind her, then the kitchen was quiet.

The five men sat at the dining-room table and Gloria waited on them. They talked about Gudger's smallest worry: who was going to pay for the suit of clothes put on Cole? "He wore his own boots, did he?" Gudger asked.

It was Milton who brought the conversation back to the quick. "We're going to have to point to somebody, Papa. Maybe two."

Wright nodded toward the door, and Young reached out a long arm and pushed it closed. Wright drank half a glass of buttermilk, wiped off his mouth, then his mustache. "Would a prayer help us?" he asked. Patiently he awaited his sons' opinion. The five men lowered their heads and he led them, asking God to identify the guilty and protect the innocent, in Jesus' name, amen.

"Somebody in this room has to be guilty," Young said, speaking softly, awed by his own observation.

Gudger buttered a biscuit. "Might have been an accident."

Young said, "What time was it when you saw him, Gudger?"

Gudger glared at him across the table. "Saw him leaving your place about ten o'clock."

Wright looked sharply at his oldest son, grunted critically. "Don't muddy what's already muddy enough," he said.

"They won't accept an accident. Not with Cole," Milton said.

The Wright appetite began exerting itself, except for the old man's; he was lost in thought, in wayward journeys. "Could call the law. Tell them a man's been killed. They'd send somebody, maybe today or tomorrow."

"Law would hang one of us, Papa," Gudger warned him.

"Hang? They don't hang here any longer, do they?" Wayland asked, surprised.

"No, sir," Young whispered.

"Electrocute a man to death in Raleigh," Milton told him.

"Or a woman," Gudger said, glancing at Wayland meaningfully.

Wayland paused, his glass near his mouth, his eyes darting to Gudger, seeking all the meaning in what he had said. He set the cup down beside his near-empty plate and wiped his mouth. "They'd not execute a woman, would they?"

"Not if she's pregnant," Gudger said. "They'd give her time to deliver."

"No, they don't execute women," Milton said abruptly.

After a minute or so, Wright said to Milton, "Do the Campbells know that Cole was the father?"

"No. Might guess it later," Milton said.

A cough broke in Wright's throat, fluttered in his mouth. "You say Drury doesn't know?"

"No."

"Does Drury Campbell know Cole was at Collie's house last night?"

"Not yet," Milton said.

"And later was at the mill?" Wright said.

"He knows that much."

"And was alive at the mill?" Wayland asked.

"Yes," Milton said.

"And Gudger met him there," Young said confidently.

"Take care, Young," Wright said, shaking his head ruefully. "Hush now," he said softly, then sat quietly for a long moment, seeking a thought he dared to say. "Milton, it looks like they'd accept Young, or Gudger, or Wayland."

Wayland frowned at him, at the others. "Take us for what?"

"To even the score, to quieten the fire-headed ones among them, and there's a parcel of them over there, believe me, that Drury has to handle. I'll say this for Drury, he's a strong man. I'm not as strong. No, don't interrupt, Young. I know I'm not. It has been some years now since I could draw the long lines when they are needed. Drury's still able to command."

"They say he killed one son," Gudger whispered.

"He might even go that far," Wright said.

"Are we supposed to designate somebody?" Wayland asked tensely.

"Unless we want *him* to choose," Wright said.

"Choose a McGregor," Milton suggested, whispering, staring at his plate.

"That's possible," Wright said.

"They're not far from the mill," Milton said.

"Wayland has three furs that Cole was carrying," Gudger offered. "Could let the McGregors have them."

"I don't have any furs," Wayland said.

"Well, where did you hide them?"

"Collie might have them," Wayland said finally, reluctant to talk about them.

Quiet for a long moment around the table. Gudger spooned preserves onto an open biscuit, closed it, tidied up the sides of the biscuit with his knife before biting into it. "The widow lives near the mill," he said simply. He looked innocently at Young.

Young glared at him.

"And Collie," Gudger said, biting into the biscuit, "lives close."

"That new Englishman, the stranger," Milton said softly, "might have done it."

"I had three children on that creek last night," Wright said, ignoring Milton's suggestion. "It's a matter of the devil's work that three were on that creek last night. And they're lined up for a conviction. A funeral hymn is sounding in my head." Then at once, more businesslike, he said, "I don't think the Englishman did it, and after all he's merely a stranger. It doesn't reply to the blood of Drury's son. It's too much an evasion, the Campbells will decide."

"Then there's the McGregors," Milton said. "We come back to that."

Young sat staring at his plate, his face pale as death itself, no sign of life twitching or molding his flesh. Old Wright's gaze moved on past him and settled on Wayland, silently asking him for comment.

"I don't believe they did it," Wayland said.

Gudger said as he ate, "Collie will probably go along, whatever we decide. She knows the difference it'll make. You're not a stranger either, not any longer, Wayland."

Wayland said, "What you talking about?"

"We took you in this family as one of us, and the Campbells know that. You had reason to kill Cole, none of us had as good a reason as you."

"What are you telling him?" Young asked tensely.

"I'm saying Jack's one of us, that's all," Gudger said in his insistently casual manner. "He's got a clock business that depends on this community, has a daughter that's been all over the trail this Cole made, her and that pet pig, has a wife-to-be, has land in sight, has a house already made, has even a factory building, for I'd say it'll never be a mill, has kinfolk to help him, so he's one of us now and not better'n we are, not above doing as we decide here today, can help the family same as I can, as you can, that's all I'm saying."

A long quiet as the family considered all that.

"And so he should do what?" Young asked.

"Be part of the family. Help us as we decide," Gudger said.

Young fairly shouted at him, furious with him, "What you saying, damn you?"

Gudger threw up his hands, angrily turned away, began grumbling to himself.

"Somebody ran out of the inn," Milton said calmly, "and struck Cole down at the creek. That's the best possibility. Somebody did go out of the inn, all right. Even this morning I could see the tracks across the yard."

"They're not my tracks," Young told him.

"Then whose are they?" Wright asked.

Young stared blankly at the wall. "Benie's husband's boots made them when she walked out to see why a horse was neighing."

Gudger started to speak, but Wright cut him short with a glance. "How do you know that, Young?"

"She told me. She wants to tell the Campbells, too."

Gudger groaned. "Why not let her?"

"It's none of your concern," Young told him.

Gudger glanced up toward Heaven, as if seeking relief. "Jesus, forgive us our stupidity."

267

Wright murmured, "I doubt if they would take a woman like Benie, anyway."

"Take Collie?" Milton inquired simply.

"Possibly," Wright said. "In a way, she's the one responsible for all this."

"I'm the one brought them together, Papa," Young said.

"You're as guilty as she is, are you?" Wright said firmly. He drank some buttermilk. "Milton, what do we have in the way of possibilities?"

Milton itemized them. "There's the McGregors. There's the widow. There's Young. There's Gudger—"

Gudger furiously, nervously blurted out a denial.

Wright waved him down. "I suspect you saw Cole in the water, Mister," he said sternly. "You didn't walk out on that mill dam for nothing, not in the snow."

Stunned by his father's rebuke, Gudger didn't dare risk a reply.

Wright said, "Then there's Wayland Jackson here. And there's Collie."

"There's the girl, too," Milton said, "Paula."

"So then, including Paula, how many suspects are there, counting the McGregors?"

"Seven," Milton said.

Wright nodded. "Of the seven, three are present in this room, and the girl and Collie also are in the house. Five are in this house."

"That Englishman—" Milton began.

"No, they won't accept a stranger," Wright said. "It all seems to me to continue to rest on three of you in the room here. I suspect the Campbells will decide one or two of you killed Cole."

Nobody said a word, not a muscle moved.

"We can choose, or we can let the Campbells choose," Wright continued.

"Young is the only one without a family," Milton said.

"I can more easily leave, Papa, that's so, can confess from some other place," Young said. "Can keep traveling for a few years."

Wright accepted that silently. He looked over at Gudger. "What about you, Mister?"

"Good God," Gudger said. "I've got a family, have a store to do. I can't run off."

"Was Cole dead when he was at the mill dam, Gudger?" Wright asked patiently.

Gudger began profanely to deny seeing him at all.

Wright, suddenly, angrily told him to be quiet. "Now, just hush. Your denial is so passionate I'd call it a confession, wouldn't you, Milton?"

Milton lowered his head, nodded.

"Was he alive, I asked you," Wright said to Gudger.

"No," Gudger said.

"You say he was not alive? Then you saw him dead."

"I never saw him."

"Did you kill him?"

"No," Gudger said.

"Did you let him die?"

That question caught Gudger off guard. "Papa, why you come at me for?" he shouted, deeply pained.

"Did you let him die?" Wright repeated.

"No. God damn, Papa, why you come at me?"

"Did you tell him you knew about Collie?"

Gudger began to sob, big, tearing sobs, even as he returned his father's stare. "Papa, you help me," he managed to say.

"Did you let him drown?"

Still sobbing, he sat there at the table staring at his father with large, round, wet eyes.

"All right, then," Wright said finally, turning away from him, settling on Wayland. "Jack, we come to you now. You fought Cole, you told me, in that creek."

"And I put him on his horse and he rode off."

"But he might have fallen off the horse and drowned, wouldn't you say?"

"God knows, I think so. I worry about it every minute," Wayland said.

"How long could a man live in that cold a water?"

"Two or three minutes," Wayland said.

"That's a fair estimate, is it? Then he could very well have died in short order if he'd fallen off his horse."

"Yes. If his body was mostly immersed."

"And you knew that when you put him on his horse."

"I didn't know he was going down the creek. For some reason Collie—" He hesitated, decided not to continue.

"Go on. What about Collie? She didn't want his horse to go along her road past the mill?"

"Yes," Wayland admitted, "leaving tracks past Young's and the inn, with him maybe being seen."

"Probably the way Cole usually went home, down the creek," Milton suggested. "Did Cole choose the creek? Or was it Collie who chose the creek?"

"Yes, Collie chose it," Wayland said. "Cole was groggy from the fight. He moaned a good deal, but that was all."

"He never spoke?" Wright asked.

"No, he never spoke, not clearly."

"Then you might have suspected he would fall off the horse," Wright said.

"I didn't go with him."

"Who did?"

"Collie went with him."

"How far?"

"Well, it was dark. Not far."

"I see," Wright said simply. He closed his eyes, sat silently for a moment. "Jack, I want you to understand where we are in this discussion. I've concluded for myself about what the Campbells will conclude in a day or so. I've come out with you and Collie. My guess is that the Campbells will select you two from this group."

"Select?" Wayland asked.

"Mark you for it."

"That's the truth," Gudger murmured.

Wright said, "So, unless we can get you out of here—"

"I think so," Milton said.

"Anyway, that's where we stand, Jack," Wright told him. "You can decide if you want to mention any of this to Collie. She's not likely to be of much help in making a decision like this."

"What decision is it?" Wayland asked.

"She might prefer to leave as well, Papa," Milton said.

"The Campbells would go around the world to find her, once Drury realized whose baby she has with her. They'll not let that baby grow up untouched, whether she stays or goes." Wretchedly he looked about at the family, each man trying to block out the horrors of the family's plight. "I'll ask her, if you like, Jack, as to which of you."

"No, it'll do," Wayland said.

"Will you want to discuss it with her on your own?"

"No."

"Then what do you decide?"

"I'll go."

"You mean to take Paula with you?"

"Yes."

"Might be best for us to take Paula another way and meet you later in Tennessee. However, you'll need to keep moving on, can't stay that near."

"I understand."

"You arrived here a stranger, just a little while ago..."

"I'll leave in flight, I can see that."

"A stranger, to move on, keep moving on. Gudger can supply you with cash to make a start, if you need it."

Young had not spoken for some time. He had sat hunched over, biting into his lip, tears in his eyes. "Papa, I'll go," he murmured.

"No, you won't, and I'll tell you why," Wright said evenly. "You never fought Cole that night and put him half unconscious on a horse and sent him down the creek in winter—"

"No, but Wayland didn't send him down the creek, either."

"Collie did, in his presence."

"Wayland didn't even know where that creek went—"

"No, and Cole might not have known there's now a mill dam on it, but Wayland was present, was involved, and you were not, never fought him, never killed him."

"Collie as well as killed him." Young said, blurting out the charge.

"Yes, well, you want her dead, do you?" Wright shook his head irritably. "I told Wayland to make a choice, himself or Collie. What you want him to do, let her take it on herself?"

"I'll take it on myself," Young said. "She's my sister. God knows, she's my mother."

Wright sank back in his chair. "Mr. Wayland, you heard what he said. You decide between the two: you or Young. Which one do we try first?"

"I decide for myself to go," Wayland said.

"Of course," Wright said simply. "Of course, you would."

Young said, "Papa, let us have another choice, for

272

God's sake. Don't tear everything up Jack and I have here."

"You tore it up, sir," Wright said. "I didn't tear it up. You tore it up when you brought Cole into friendship—"

"Let us have another choice."

"You mean the widow?" Milton asked him.

"No," Young said, recoiling from that.

"The girl, Paula?"

"No."

"The McGregors?" Milton asked.

"The McGregors," Young whispered between clenched teeth. "Yes, what about them?"

For a minute or so the family was silent. "Very well," Wright said finally. "Are we prepared to choose the McGregors? I take it you have those three furs, Jack."

Jackson nodded. "Collie has—"

"Well," Wright said softly. "Give me your advice."

"What would you do, Gudger?" Wayland asked. "Put the furs on their barn walls?"

"Let them steal them," Gudger said. "Let them barn them up themselves. They have to cure them that way, don't they?"

"So all we would do is allow them to steal the furs?" Wayland asked.

"That's all," Gudger said. "Fair enough?"

"Then there are other ways, as well, to hang this particular bell," Milton said.

Finally, Wright said, "I admit to you I have no hole card worth holding on this hand, Jack. I want you to move first. If you say you want to use this McGregor ploy, I will—I will put it on the table before us all. It appears to have supporters here. However, in case you are unwilling to do this with the McGregors, I would prefer not to have the matter on the family record at all."

273

Wayland stared intently at him, seeking some hint of guidance from him.

"Would you like to talk with Collie about it?" Wright asked. "It's her life as well."

"I understand," Wayland said, "whose lives are at stake."

Wright said, "I can see some reasonableness on both sides of the decision. If I were in your place, I don't know, I just don't know what I would decide. After all, what is best for the most people? The losers would be the McGregors, but they hate the Campbells with every breath, and they are not defenseless or powerless, are they, Milton?"

Milton said, "No, sir," a mere whisper. Then he turned to Wayland. "It's the way McGregors always have lived, here and in Tennessee."

"If they steal, it's their crime," Gudger reminded him.

"It'd be a crime to leave us, Wayland," Milton told him, speaking slowly, with a painful sincerity. "We're talking about ending everything you're doing here, Wayland, and that matters to all of us."

"I'd be a fool to give it all up, I agree." Wayland arranged his fork and knife side by side on his plate. "If McGregor came in that door, I'd tell him the same thing. It'd tear my life apart to leave this place."

"Then it's settled," Gudger said.

"It's been the best part of my life so far to be here." Wayland's throat closed on him and he couldn't continue.

"Well, I understand," Wright said.

"It's not a trap in a path to break a man's leg; it's a death trap for several, as I understand it," Wayland said.

"It might be all of that," Wright said at once.

Gudger said, "Papa, he has decided."

"Very well," Wright said, "I asked him to decide."

"He has said," Gudger insisted.

"I say no," Wayland said.

For a while nobody spoke. Young shuddered, moaned. All of them settled into the wake of the decision, considering their own lives now that the life of the family had been rearranged. Wright, breathing huskily, deeply, studied the faces of his sons. "Thank you," he said to Wayland. "Milton, have the Kraft brothers take Paula to Asheville tomorrow at noon. Gudger, ask Crawford to drive Jack to Tennessee about two o'clock, using his car. Arrange a meeting in Knoxville day after tomorrow for them. Get Jack's truck to Knoxville by then. Is that all we need to decide?"

Silence. Not a word.

"God help us," the old man murmured. Wearied by the moment, utterly saddened by this form of death, he lowered his head onto the table before him.

13

The evening dragged like an old whip song, Collie
found, it droned and whined no matter what she
wanted it to be. Distraction did not relieve her of
the heaviness in her chest and the thickness of her
thoughts. There had been the meeting at her father's
house; nobody afterward confided in her about
what had transpired, which encouraged fears, then
there had been her mother's final burst of anger at
her and the long walk home with Paula, with every
breaking limb in the woods a warning to them.
There had been Campbells on the road near the inn,
near Young's house and his mill; also, Campbells
had been on the road up to her house and two were
waiting when she and Paula and the baby arrived,
one of them insisting she come into the barn with
him, which she refused to do, and two others trying
to show her a stick of firewood that matched another stick they held in their hands. They were as
exultant as if they had discovered the hinge of a
great door. Oh, my God, help me, she thought, she
prayed, trying not to allow Paula to know how deep
was her worry. "What'd they decide at the meeting?" she would ask Paula. That child knew not a
whit more than she, had sat with her in the parlor,
had watched her while she nursed her baby, had
brought her a bowl of stew finally, had insisted she

eat something, though Paula ate nothing herself. "Well, I'm not feeding two," Paula had told her.

When night fell, the Campbells had stopped measuring and tracing and pacing the yard, had stopped asking about the broken window, the broken stone-room bed, had finally left, no doubt to confer with others of their breed and take further steps tomorrow toward disrobing the means of Cole's death.

Wayland arrived about an hour past nightfall. There was not a bite of food cooked, but he said nothing about that. He got out the brandy and pulled a chair up to the fireplace, mentioned needing to go soon to the stone room, or maybe to Young's house, admitting he was tired tonight. Lord, yes, she thought, with the weight of the world on his shoulders, life and death dangling over him, as it was over her, judgment, pain ahead as certain as pain lay behind by two days' time. "Ah, Jesus," she moaned, standing at the sink staring at the broken window, which was misted over, sweating. "Mr. Jackson, tell me what Papa said at the meeting, will you?"

"Nothing much to say," he replied.

Paula stood in the bedroom doorway, leaning back against a jamb, watching them, wanting to be near them and to tend the baby, too. Everybody needs company tonight, Collie thought. "Well, what did he decide, what did Papa say? You met for a long time."

"Oh, yes," Wayland replied, not looking at her. "A long time," he repeated.

"Did he decide on any message for Mr. Campbell, a warning of any sort?"

"I don't think so," Wayland said.

"Tell him to keep his people home?"

"No," Wayland said. "Nothing like that."

"Oh, Lord, they're everywhere," Collie said, shaking her head in agony.

Paula said, "They went through a pile of our cut logs, Papa, found one that matched a log they had with the same rings. Said they'd be back."

Collie said, "Did Papa decide which one of us is guilty of the death?"

"Well, no," he said finally.

Paula said, "And they were in the barn, said Cole's horse had been stabled there some weeks ago."

"I wondered if they'd see that," he said simply.

"What does that mean, Papa?" Paula asked, speaking so quietly she could scarcely be heard.

"It's all pieces of a puzzle they're working on," he said. "You know, it's a wonder how hunters can do, how they can read signs in the dirt and on tree bark and even under the water, or on the stones of a creek bank. They go by little flecks of evidence."

"Will they come back tonight?" Paula asked.

Collie moaned. "They might come back and shoot the treetops to scare us."

"I don't know," he said to Paula. "Probably they're not in any hurry."

"New clock case has arrived, Papa," Paula told him.

"Has it?" he said, at once interested.

"It's set under the overhang at the mill, with a tarp thrown over it."

"Which family finished it?"

"It didn't say on it anywhere, but it's pretty work."

"Maybe I can assemble a clock tomorrow. I'll have to do it in the morning."

Collie turned toward him slowly, sought to read his thoughts. "What you say? Why only in the morning?"

He scratched at an itch on his neck where his collar had rubbed his skin. "I have something to do tomorrow afternoon, Collie. I have something to do is all. It's a gift, one might call it."

278

"For me, Papa?" Paula asked, watching him.

"For all of us. For Jonathan, too," he said softly.

When Jonathan began crying, Paula went to see about him, and Collie brought a chair close to the fireplace. "What did Papa say?"

"He kept trying to find out which one of us had killed Cole. I told him my part in it. It went round and round the table, Collie. You can imagine."

"And what did you decide?" she asked.

"I'm not able to recall anything."

She tasted the brandy, put a few drops on her tongue. "Mr. Jackson, I know Papa better than that."

"Gudger talked about the McGregors, letting them steal the cat furs so they could become involved. I said no, that wouldn't do."

"You said no to Gudger, did you?"

"And Milton, and even Young. I took a stand against it."

Collie clenched her hands together, intently stared at the fire, which was glowing hot with hickory. "Did he say which one of us it'd have to be?"

"I'm asked not to talk about what he said," Wayland admitted.

"Is it you or Young or me or Gudger that's to be offered first?"

For a while he remained quiet, then he said, "I'm not to say."

At once she went to the sink, busied herself there, fighting back tears. When she came back to the chair, she brought a cup of tea for each of them. "When are you to go?"

"I didn't say it was me going anywhere."

"Will you come back later? Was that discussed at all?"

"No, I'm not able to talk about it, Collie," he said.

"I'll go out now, tonight, and find Young and ask him, if that's what it takes, or ask Papa, but I mean to know. You might as well tell me."

He considered that thoughtfully, nodded finally. "It came down to us, Collie, to you and me. We fought Cole and put him on the creek, and I suppose he drowned. It was an accident, as I see it, but the Campbells won't believe I was able to kill Cole fairly, will they? That won't satisfy their loss. So one of us has to leave." A moment later he told her, "I'm to leave tomorrow."

She waited patiently, hoping for other words, for a second view, an alternative, but when there was none, she seemed to accept what he had said. She sat back in the chair, appeared to relax. "It seems as if you've just arrived here, you know? A few days ago I went out into the yard while you called and there was so much hope in my heart, for I'd wanted somebody of my own so much. I can recall the very moment, and every moment since that we've been together."

"I believe I can, too," he said.

Later she said, "When are you to go?"

"Well, Paula's to go at noon to Asheville, and I'll go west an hour or so later, and we'll meet in a few days over in Tennessee."

"It's dangerous, is it, to leave?" she said.

"I don't know yet," he admitted. "Not so much for Paula."

"Oh, my God," she whispered. Suddenly she couldn't hold the tears back. She wept for a few minutes, then drew herself together. "There's that second clock body to be mounted, so that'll require your morning," she said. "The case is down at the mill, Paula said."

Agony settled on Collie, came in like a cloud of shame and desperate whispers, possessing her. Time after time she went into the back room and took the baby in her arms, held it close, rocking it, tears flowing. She would speak softly so as not to awaken Paula, who had fallen asleep in Jonathan's room.

"You might never know. Maybe you won't ever know. Dear little boy." She carried him into the front room, sat on the edge of her bed with the child on her lap. "No, maybe you'll never know." She was almost grappling with his little body. "Please don't you worry. Why, it'll be all right." She kissed his little face, then carried him into his room and laid him on his bed, sank beside him on her knees and feverishly asked God to remove the bitter cup from her. "I can't do this, please, God." She wept and prayed. She grasped at the bedclothing and at the little body of the child, her fingers digging into his clothes. "Ah, Jesus, help me, please, God," she whispered.

Time after time Wayland came to her, sought to comfort her, but she was beyond sympathy, it seemed, was wrestling within her own body with forces that were strangers to his own. "I must do this," she would tell him, and tell her child. "I have caused this." She stayed awake for hours, clothed in such misery.

During the night the wash of depression came over Wayland as well. It had been easier during the day while he had been given decisions to make and was the center of activity; now he was isolated and had begun to tear himself away from the one woman, the one place he wanted. Leaving was for him a form of dying, he told himself. Last spring he had moved close to despair after his wife walked away to die. He had been shocked away from living his own life. Here he had emerged from that stupor, but now, tomorrow, he was again to fall backward, to break himself once more, and go staggering in a daze about the countryside.

He would have Paula. Thank God for her. They would make their peace with whatever the world offered in Tennessee, and maybe he could sneak back a time or two and see Collie and Jonathan, or maybe they could all go to California together, sometime. That truck might get to California, given tires enough, time enough for him to stop to fix clocks. God knows, it was an idea, anyway. It cut his soul to think there was no hope for him, and no hope for her, either, except to draw back into this log house with her baby and let the days pass by, one day after another, with the Campbells watching both of them.

It was all a prank, seemed to him suddenly, it was God's game with him, the hot breath of God was punishing him again. Sitting at the little table in Collie's kitchen, he wept in his heart for her, dear Collie, and the baby born on a family cross, the red-headed baby sleeping on its cross, and for Paula, who was being taken away from her new mother and brother, and for himself.

Next morning Collie noticed they packed nothing to take with them. This was according to Gudger's instructions, she supposed. There were no goodbyes. The family acted out a scene of evasion. They moved close to one another without touching, they spoke without clear meaning, or merely to ask for a cup, a dish, the soap, a towel, a diaper for Jonathan. Wayland left first, stopping at the barn to finish packing up his tools for shipping. Later he paused at the barn door, held his hand up to her. She shielded her eyes with her hand, watching him as he walked down the hill.

Paula began to cry as she left, and Collie held her in her arms, said she loved her, then told her to get along.

All this time Collie was patient, was thoughtfully waiting, but once they were gone she became alert and purposeful. She washed her face and arms, then put on her blue dress. She dressed Jonathan in his

282

prettiest dress as well, one of the two on which she had embroidered flowers. For a few minutes only, she hesitated, lingering over him lovingly, calling him baby names, kissing him, nudging him, making him laugh his sweet, raucous laugh. Finally she wrapped him in blankets and, carrying him, walked down along the creek, choosing her way carefully, crossing the creek by stepping from rock to rock. She tried not to think of her mission; the weary, weary, long mission. Even so, the half-hidden thoughts weighted her shoulders and legs, made the steps slow and measured, her eyes vacant.

Across from the mill dam she paused, considered the struggle Cole must have had there. She wondered if he had died at the dam or not, and how Gudger had contributed to it. Slowly, reluctantly, she turned from there, moved downstream of the mill and Young's house and the back yard of Benie Frazier's inn, stopping at the place where Cole's body had been found.

Collie walked west from there, taking the main road. Now and then she would shift Jonathan from one hip to the other, and along about the Krafts' farm she paused to nurse the child; she sat on a rock that was said to be the very place that Mr. Tinkler Harrison had died long years ago. He had eaten too big a dinner and had jumped a ditch, or so the story went.

As he sucked, the baby's little eyes darted up to see her face, to be sure she was there.

Her pace slowed as she passed the McKinneys'— there he was out in the back yard with the three sisters he was living with, married to the oldest one. She passed the Fletchers' farm road, which had washed out the previous winter and was in need of more dragging. She passed Gouge Cove, moving nearer step by heavy step to the place of sacrifice. She stopped in Mrs. Crawford's yard and waited to

283

be noticed. She asked for the loan of a boy and the boat so she could cross the river. One of the middle children came running, anxious to be of help. He rowed her across and said he would wait, but she told him she had no idea how long she would be and to go on home. She walked up the hill toward Drury Campbell's house. People, turning to look at her, stopped their work to ask what the Wright sister was doing over here.

She came upon Harmon Campbell sitting on the porch of the big house, talking with two other men. He agreed to go indoors to find out if his father would consent to see her; meanwhile, she waited with the baby near the water trough, where a yoke of oxen was hitched. Several women had followed partway up the hill and were watching her from vantage points along the way, women in yellow or brown bonnets, most of them wearing a leather or wool coat over a long dress.

Harmon reappeared. "He's inside, Papa is," he said. He led her into a hallway where she could make out a dusty pump organ set against a wall, and a number of deer horns with leather coats and hats hanging from them. He pushed open a far door, which she saw led to the kitchen, a large log room, almost square, with clay chinking between the logs, with scores of bags of provisions hanging from iron hooks embedded in wall logs and beams. Sitting near the hearth was Drury himself, surrounded by dogs and grandchildren, ensconced in a big rocking chair upholstered in raccoon skins. She approached him, the baby in her arms, her eyes squinted to keep tears and fear from showing. She stopped near the main table.

"You surprise me," he said simply. "Sorry we have nothing fine here to offer you."

Her throat was closing with dread and fear, which she fought back, realizing it was to Jonathan's advantage she represent herself well.

"Come to mourn Cole with me?" Drury asked. "Was buried this morning. Big gathering."

She selected a chair across the table from him.

"Only ones from your side of the river that attended was the Crawfords. Is that right, Harmon?"

"I'd say so, Papa," Harmon said. He was leaning back against the hall door, his gaze on Collie and the child, his mouth routinely chewing a wad of tobacco.

"That Mrs. Crawford said she wanted to see how Cole looked. He looked about the same, I told her."

She laid Jonathan on the table between them and folded one corner of his blanket to make a pillow for his head.

"That inn widow you got across the river sent me a letter. Where is it, Harmon?"

"I think you put it in your pocket, Papa."

He rummaged about through his coat pockets, gave up finding it there. "Hard to read her writing, anyway. Said she wore men's boots that night of Cole's murder. Was a short letter. You know about it, do you?"

Collie shook her head. She was pressing her teeth tightly together, clenching her hands.

"What is it, Miss Wright?" Drury asked, noticing her intense nervousness. When even then she said nothing, he called across the room to Harmon. "Harmon, what does she have in mind to tell me?"

"She was standing outside the house, Papa," Harmon said. "That's all I know."

"Well—it's pleasant to have company, Miss Wright," Drury said. "Are you mourning for Cole?"

"Yes, I've come about Cole," she said, her voice tight as stretched wire.

"What did she say, Papa?" Harmon asked.

"She's come about Cole. Well, I knowed she must be, on his burial day. He was a great man, Miss

Wright. I was telling my daughter Margaret that he was always into something new, never was one to settle for what was offered, was flinging outward into the world, seeking, yet he wasn't a stranger to old ways, he could sit here at the table and enjoy his fare and laugh and tell stories, be the finest company. Nothing grand about Cole. Did you ever know him, Miss Wright?"

"I loved him."

"He was one to travel, stay away for . . . yet . . ." His voice trailed away. He was left staring blankly at her. "Ah, now, lady," he whispered, "I don't know." His lean fingers scratched at his neck. "You knew him, you say?" He pushed away a granddaughter, one who was trying to crawl onto his lap.

Harmon from across the room said, "What did she say, Papa?"

"She said she loved Cole."

The children were quiet now, respectful of secrets being discussed. Their little faces peered at Drury, then at Collie, then at Drury. Drury licked his lips, swiped awkwardly at his eyes. "Ah, Lord God," he whispered, and pushed a grandchild away so he could lean closer to the woman. "Was he dear to you in some special way, is that it?"

"Yes, he was dear to me."

"I didn't know he come on your side of the river, except now and then to hunt, as the case of the other night he was in those North Woods—" He turned to look at Harmon. "You said Cole had a personal matter to attend to, is that so?"

"He came to my house, Mr. Campbell."

The old man's head jerked backward as if he had been struck. He was clearly dismayed by her. "Harmon, did you know that?"

"No, sir. I sure as hell didn't."

"Harmon, I asked did you know it?" the old man demanded.

"No. Didn't you hear me say no?"

"Am I the only one in this family that's been kept in the dark?"

"Papa, I told you by God I didn't know it," Harmon declared.

The old man settled back among the cushions. His grandchildren, shocked by the outbursts, had retreated to the window couch, where they waited breathlessly, the troop lined up like dolls. Drury blew his nose into a blue handkerchief, a woman's handkerchief; he noticed that Collie was looking at it strangely. "It's my wife's. I use all mine, then I use hers." He told a grandson to put the dogs outdoors, and waited for that commotion to be over, using the time to try to gather his thoughts. All the while he kept glancing at Collie, evaluating her, measuring the possibilities that occurred to him. "Your people never have claimed to love anybody over here before," he told her.

"That's true," she said. Her words were quietly, patiently uttered. There was a sparseness about her efforts to talk with him.

"I never did follow him too close, never put him on a tether," he said. "He wasn't the sort that could be led that way." He paused for her to say something in response, but she only sat there staring at him with her haunted eyes; it was almost as if she were not present here, were living somewhere away off, looking back at him. "His mother died and that freed him from her care, so at an early age he was free to kick up his heels." He waited. "I had this pretty wife back then, and she bore him in that room off the kitchen, where we could keep it warm. Cole was a winter baby, did you know that?"

"January twenty-ninth," she said.

"That's the day, yes," he said, surprised.

"Claimed he was too late to be a Christmas present," she said, smiling wanly.

287

"Cole and his mother breathed the same air for a year or so, same breath," he said, speaking informally but watching Collie carefully. "I'd go in there and look him over, try to attract him to me, but he was in her arms and was lying with his head pressed under her chin, his little arms and legs against her body. She would show him to me, but he was hers, and that was the way it was till he was two and I started insisting on my father's rights. His mother fell ill of pernicious anemia soon after that. Did you know her?"

"No."

"Did you know she died?"

"Yes. Cole was five."

"Was he? I don't know. I thought he was three."

"No, he said he was five, and would stand by her bed and listen to her breathing, which was sometimes loud enough to be heard in every room of the house."

"Uh-huh." Drury was persuaded to examine her thoughtfully, scarcely daring to take his eyes off of her. "As pretty a woman as ever lived," he said.

"Was Cole a handsome baby?" Collie asked.

"Oh, Lord, yes. Redheaded baby, not fiery, but it was there, the red was. Cole stood here at the table next to my elbow to eat his meals. He was three, or maybe he was younger. Harmon, how old was he?"

"I don't know, Papa. Would you think to ask her about Cole's dying, Papa?"

"Call Margaret. Get your sister in here."

"Papa, for God sake—"

"Margaret!" He shouted so loud the chinaware on the shelves rattled.

Margaret was heard in a room above. She came hurrying down the stairway, came through the hall, burst into the kitchen, fearful of a catastrophe. "What is it? What is it?" She stood there confused, surveying her father, then the Wright woman and her baby. "For God sake, what is it?" she said.

"How old was Cole when he first stood up to the table to eat?"

"You didn't call me down here to—What you say?"

"He nursed till his mother was so weak—"

"He nursed until the month before she died, but he also ate from a spoon. I fed him myself," she said.

"I just recalled him standing at the corner of the table near my elbow—"

"He was three years old when he done that."

"There was no chair for the littlest one in the family, Miss Wright."

"No, and he stood there until he was old enough for a chair."

"Until Greg married and left the house, and then there was a chair."

"He stood right here, and you sat at the end, and over there is where Harmon sat—"

"For God sake," Harmon moaned.

"I remember it now just as clear as if it was yesterday," Drury said, beaming with pleasure. "The boy would eat and make the damnedest mess of his food."

"It had to be mashed for him," Margaret said. "Ever' child—"

"Applesauce I remember he liked—with the inside portion of a biscuit—"

"He had applesauce and mashed cornbread, too, and potatoes, and a bean or two. And of course he had an egg of a morning and stood there while you had your eggs and ham . . ."

"I can't recall everything," Drury said, critical of her taking hold of the conversation.

"Well, I recall that," Margaret said defensively.

"She's made that way," he said, speaking directly to Collie. "Ever' date, birthday, anniversary. You go to church with her and she'll stand at the door and

289

say happy birthday next Tuesday to so-and-so, and is your little one ready to be five this week, on and on, so that it's humorous."

"Well, I just do that," Margaret said, flustered.

"Miss Wright has come to visit, to be with us on the funeral day, Margaret."

"Well—" Margaret considered the woman and the baby. She pulled a chair back a few feet from the table, so as not to impose on them, and sat down on the edge of it. "Cole wasn't the sweetest of the children," she said briefly, quickly, merely glancing at Drury, "but he was the strongest and most daring."

"He was sweet enough," Drury said.

"He had a good deal to learn about sweetness, if you want my opinion, but he was courageous, and was athletic."

"Never lost in any contest," Drury said to Collie. "He was sweet enough, Margaret," he told her.

"And he was a hard worker."

"Oh, Lord, yes. He got in the field—my Lord, we used to plow that hillside above Aunt Hannah's house. Now, that's steep. That's steep. That's rocky, too. Harmon, what you say?"

Harmon said nothing.

"He'd plow that, using that little mean mule named Dorchester. He as much tanned that mule himself, but only for his own bidding. Plow it deep. None of this scratching the soil. He'd do it driving hard. Then he'd take a double yoke of oxen—"

"Took four oxen one time," Margaret said.

"He'd snag stumps, pull them out of the ground, roots and all. Break chains, but never break him. Timber. My Lord, think of the logging we've done, Harmon. If I could get out there once more, just another day. I can see to it, but can't do it. I worked side by side with that boy when he was fourteen, and he wore me out. He could drive an eight-yoke

290

team when he was fourteen. Timbered five thousand acres a year—"

"That big poplar that was at the south fork—" Harmon began.

"He dragged it to the field and burned it. Four days burning. Oh, I've witnessed sights in my time. Nothing too demanding for Cole, nothing too dangerous—"

All the while Collie was watching, listening, her hand resting on her baby's body. Patiently she was waiting for the eulogy to end.

One of Drury's other sons came into the room, peering about suspiciously. He took water from the sink, where a pipe delivered springwater continuously. "What's she doing in here, Papa?" he asked brusquely.

"Oh, this woman come by to mourn for Cole with us."

"She know Cole?" the son asked.

"Says so," Drury murmured, leaning his head back against the chair, looking at Collie through half-closed eyes. "You go finish your hauling," he told the son. He waited, saying nothing, until the young man had gone, then he said, "How old is your baby, ma'am?"

"Six months." She pushed the blanket-wrapped baby toward him, across the table, and Drury quite happily took Jonathan in his bundle and set him on his lap. He unpeeled the layers of blankets. "Why, look at that. Is a pretty one."

Margaret had leaned closer and was beaming at the child.

"See the baby, Harmon? Look at those cheeks on him. I like for a baby to have a round face. I want size on a baby, like this one has." He opened the inner blanket and stared down at the baby's dimpled knees. He touched one of them, and the baby smiled at him. "That's a million-dollar smile,"

Drury said, laughing gently. "Margaret, did you ever see a better smile?"

"Why, he's healthy," Margaret said.

"There'll be work to do, sonny, you hear me?" Drury said to him. "Your mummy will have to get you a pony one of these days, too. I had Cole mounted when he was three—"

"Four," Margaret said.

"Bald pony. Little mare."

"You might want to cover his legs up, Papa, or he'll catch cold," Margaret said.

"Why, it's hot enough in here." He peeked under Jonathan's diaper to check if he was wet or not. "As true as holy writ," he said and laughed. "My Uncle Charles was in the war on the South's side, Miss Wright, was a renegade sort of fellow, anyway—my people fought for the Union, Miss Wright, most of them. Charles was with Vance down east some'ers, and this soldier—"

"Papa, what are you telling about that for?" Margaret asked, flushing red all in a moment.

"Papa, ask about Cole dying," Harmon suggested.

"This soldier come into the headquarters and said he was not a man, he was a woman, and had decided war wasn't for him, or for her, and he wanted to go home, and Vance said he didn't believe him. So then and there the soldier dropped his pants and leaned back and showed him what Vance later called proof as true as holy writ." He laughed, his voice bellowing out his pleasure at the story, and at Margaret's embarrassment. Jonathan was frightened by the noise and began to whimper, so Drury put the baby on his chest and patted his back and talked to him, cooed to him. "Didn't mean to scare you," he whispered into his ear. "What's his name?" Drury asked Collie.

"Jonathan," Collie said. The room was indeed hot and she was especially dizzy in it.

"No need to cry around here, with as many hands eager to hold you."

"Papa won't let anybody else hold him, only himself," Margaret complained to Collie.

"Leave him be, Margaret," he said. "I'm not hurting the baby. He's got a lifetime to grow up in."

Margaret ground her hands together anxiously, then suddenly laughed, relaxed. "I know it."

"Mr. Campbell," Collie began, seeking to exert herself. She hesitated, but only for a moment. "I am here to say something to you."

Drury stopped rocking. He sat stiffly, his full attention on her. "What say, then?"

"I'm here to bargain, that you let the matter of Cole's death go by, without taking revenge on it."

"Miss Wright, I've done a world of trading in my time, and I learned early on that a man can't bargain with a woman. It's not the same, their minds don't work the same way. One is not any better than another, but they're not partners in a trade."

"I have no man to stand for me," she said.

"No offense," he said. "If you was to offer me the North Woods, which your family's part I take to be about fifty, sixty thousand acres, I wouldn't deal with you, for there's always the rumor that I took advantage of your family. They have held me in disrepute for all my adult life, claiming even death and maiming—"

"Mr. Campbell," she said, interrupting firmly, "I'm asking that you listen to me, to what I have to say."

The old man sank back slowly in his chair, staring at her, his mouth still open, other thoughts rising to be spoken, but he held quiet, waited for her, respectful of a guest.

"There's nothing to be gained by causing more deaths," she said simply.

"I have lost a son, Miss Wright, and that was of pain to him, and is to me. At the funeral dinner this noon, his brother Joshua said to me—"

"Another death will cause more suffering."

"Miss Wright, your people and mine are so different— Why, good heaven, I couldn't convince this pack of men around me, couldn't tell them we will let it all slide by. Why, no."

"No, sir," Harmon said, agreeing emphatically.

"There's seven older brothers, not to mention sisters and other kin," Drury said.

"I loved Cole as they did," Collie said, conscious that Harmon was glaring at her unkindly.

"Even so," Drury said, dismissing that possibility. "I'd say it's two brothers of your'n that killed him, or helped with it."

"There was the three men, Papa," Harmon said, "including the one she's been living with."

"All three, is that it, Harmon?"

"I'd say it's all three," Harmon said.

"A life for a life," Drury said. "I'll settle for one of the three, if you'll tell me which one killed him, Miss Wright." When she remained silent, he said. "An eye for an eye, a son for a son. That's Biblical. Don't try to take religion away from us. I've promised to obey, and it'll be done as certain as the sun rises. Maybe a day, a week, a month—"

"Be soon," Harmon told him.

Collie said, "A life for a life, Mr. Campbell, does that have to be a life lost?"

Drury's brows knotted, his head tilted to one side, and he squinted at her curiously. He shifted the baby slightly to relax his shoulder. "Don't follow your meaning."

"Does the life have to be shot?"

"In the war they was shot, as a rule. But there's been death by falling from off mountains, there's been drownings, there's been burnings. There's different ways of death. Stranglings, hangings."

"No, sir," Collie began, but found herself unable to go on.

Drury kept his gaze on her. "A life for a life is what my Bible says, and it'll be your brother Young, I imagine, if there's but one chosen."

"There's three of them, Papa," Harmon said firmly. "We found the identical oak stick, took it from that woman's own house," Harmon said. "Then she comes over here trying to trade. Ask her which ones killed Cole. She can tell you."

"A life for a life, Mr. Campbell," she said, then fell silent, unable to say the words that were needed, to proceed with the declaration. "It doesn't have to mean a death for a death," she said.

The old man watched her carefully. "What— Margaret, what does she mean?" he asked. "Lady, what you saying?" he said, taking the baby from his shoulder and laying it on the table before him, his gaze remaining on Collie's agonized face. "There have been sacrifices made that are of a person's own life, I've heard that said. You offering me yourself?"

"Why, it's Cole's baby," she said.

Margaret and the old man stifled cries. Instantly tears welled up in his eyes, and he began to fight them. "No, I don't think..." He looked down at the round little face before him. "Harmon, did you hear her tell me?"

"Papa, she'll say anything," Harmon said tensely.

"I was sitting here talking to these children, trying to remember pleasantries about Cole. I can't talk about Cole any more today."

"I know, Papa," Margaret said sympathetically.

"And here comes this—this woman..." With his sleeve he wiped his nose and mouth, swiped at his eyes awkwardly. "You tell me this is Cole's?" He viewed the baby for a minute or so before tentatively touching the child's hair, rippled his finger through it. He ventured to touch Jonathan's forehead, his cheek. He folded the blanket down from the little body and bent over it, seeking proof somewhere on his person of his parentage. The baby was cooing, smiling at him, was trying to touch his face. One of the other children came close, and Drury had to ask him to stand back a ways, "so's not to smother him." He folded the blanket lower and lifted Jonathan's dress, considered his diaper and stomach. The idea Collie had presented was too precious to him to be dismissed, but he couldn't bear to accept it. He proceeded to undo the baby's dress and to stare dumbly at the naked chest and tiny shoulders. The baby smiled, its toothless little mouth opened with a gurgle. With his finger he wiped the drooling spit from its chin. He turned the baby over, examined the back and legs. He ran his fingers through Jonathan's auburn hair for a second time, the baby's eyes darting about, seeking its mother. On one of Jonathan's yawns, Drury took occasion to peer into its mouth.

"Well, I'll tell you," he declared, "there is something about him I like." He kept staring at the baby, his fingers resting on Jonathan's stomach. "What you have in mind, Miss Wright?"

Collie spoke in a whisper. "I can't have my brothers killed, or Mr. Jackson killed, for something I got myself into."

"What is it you propose?" he asked.

"You must set the bargain, Mr. Campbell."

"You've come here to me. I never come to you. What are you proposing, Miss Wright?"

"It's the baby," she said, unable to express the complete thought.

"Yes, I see the baby," he said.

"Papa, before you get yourself lost, you might as well know no mother can sacrifice a baby," Margaret told him, speaking swiftly so as not to be cut off by him.

"She's making the proposition," Drury told her. "She's the one come here. She has to put her proposition on the table, Margaret."

"That is a baby on the table, and she's its mother," Margaret said.

"Then let her take him," Drury said, upset by Margaret's interference. "Now, when a trade is being made, Margaret, you stay well away from it."

Nobody moved for a little while, not even the children. Then Drury rested back in his chair, got his shoulders comfortable in among the pillows. "There was a scar on Cole—there were two, actually, Miss Wright. Where were they?"

Collie closed her eyes tightly. "Please, God," she whispered, disappointed to be pressed further. She said to him, "On his right side, and there was a long scar inside his right thigh where he claimed a stob ripped him."

Drury stared at her for a long while, revealing nothing. At last he nodded. "That other'n come from a fence post, did you know that?"

"Thrown from a horse," Collie said.

"No, he was not. He was throwed three times as a boy, but never again. His horse fell agin a fence."

"On the upper side of the river lot, where he had the longest stretch to ride," she said.

"Yes," Drury said, watching her carefully with his glinting trader's eyes. "Now tell me where you and him would meet."

"Meet with Cole?"

"Yes."

"Yes, sir," Collie whispered. "In the North Woods, some several places near the falls."

"Were you ever seen by anybody?"

"I don't think so, though he sometimes said the McGregors had been close by."

"Did Cole come to your house many times?"

"On—several occasions."

"How many times?"

"I don't know."

"More than a dozen?"

"Yes."

"Was it you that he was coming to visit when he left Harmon and Skeet?"

"Yes, I'd say so."

"Did he— Was he injured at your place?"

"Yes."

"Was he killed there?"

"No."

"Who injured him?"

"Mr. Jackson."

"That little one?"

"In the water. He's a better fighter in the winter, in the water—"

"He killed him?"

"No. But he almost killed him, and put him on his horse, and I led it into the creek, headed it toward the mill."

Drury scratched his face with his long fingers. "Used that oak club on him?"

"I don't know which one used it on the other."

"So he was put on a horse—"

"Yes, sir—"

"And he was left to ride home. Then he was troubled at the mill by somebody."

"I don't know."

"Your brother Gudger and a dog, I'd say. Then he was killed, either there or by Young. I'd say both brothers killed him, laid in wait."

"No, I don't think so."

"And that little girl took a message to them that Cole was in the creek."

"Why, he would have ridden past before she could reach—"

"She went ahead to give word that Cole was in the neighborhood."

"Nobody was down there when she arrived," Collie said desperately.

"So all of them, they all killed him."

"No," she said, speaking distinctly, "I know that's not true."

They were quiet then, contemplative. Jonathan was cooing on the table, his eyes moving from the old man's face, which he found interesting, to his mother's.

"Harmon," Drury said, "it was the three men, did you say?"

"That's what I've been saying," Harmon said.

Drury nodded. "What other men you ever slept with, Miss Wright?" he asked her.

She blanched. "No other men."

"My experience is that an unwed woman who will lie down with one man can be had by others as well."

"I never had any other man."

"Then you contend that it has to be Cole's, could not be any other person's."

"I never came close to any other man," Collie said.

"Young, for instance?" he said.

"Why, no. I never."

"I've heard it that—"

"It's not so," she said.

"Well—" he said, allowing that matter to settle quietly, gently to be allowed to rest. There was a kettle on the stove that had been boiling for some time, making hissing noises in its spout, begging mercy. Margaret got up, set the kettle off the stove lid and returned to her place.

Drury said, "Jonathan has the same color hair as Cole had as a baby. Margaret, did you notice that?"

Margaret nodded tensely.

Drury was in a dilemma, obviously was struggling with himself because of the trade he was discussing. "He's your sole heir, is he, Miss Wright?"

"Yes, sir," she said, on guard at each new swing of the conversation.

"You not making plans to marry, are you?"

"I might, yes," she said.

"So Jonathan is an heir, but not a sole heir."

"Yes, sir."

"What is your father planning to leave you?"

"He says he'll leave me most of that North Woods, but I don't know what the will says."

"He's not showed you a copy yet?"

"Gudger keeps it at the store, but won't show it. It gets changed from time to time."

"What is this boy Jonathan down for in your father's will?"

"Papa says he's to be put down for a full part."

"And it'll be left that way, will it?"

"What will be left that way? Who do you mean?"

"Will Jonathan still inherit?"

She hesitated. "I don't know what Jonathan is down for," she said.

"Does your father know the boy is Cole's?"

"I— I think so."

"Well, it's important. It matters thousands of acres of land."

"It matters more than that, Mr. Campbell."

"You will urge on your father that the boy remain a full heir?"

"Yes," she said.

"And you think he will agree?"

"I think in time he will," she said, speaking more confidently, "though my brother Gudger won't like it."

"Gudger stands to gain his life by having a trade made, Miss Wright. I think your father will agree, with two sons marked. Are you understanding what I say?"

"I know what you say, but I can't speak for other people."

"Well, you're here to trade."

"I'm not here to trade for somebody else. If you want to trade with somebody else, you'll need to see them. I'd be curious to know what you're going to leave Jonathan in *your* will?"

Drury froze in place. Even his expression was set as he considered her direct thrust. "Anything I say would be subject to his proving to be like Cole as he gets older," he began.

"We're making a trade today," Collie said, "not some time in the future."

"If he turns out to be Cole's," Drury said, measuring the words, "I'll leave him a fair part as a grandson. Then he'd have your family's part as well, so he'd be a wealthy man. As I say—"

"How much is your part going to be?"

"I don't mean to talk about the Campbell business with you."

"Will it be an equal part?"

"It'll be a fair part. I don't leave equal parts, for some children please me more than others, and some don't please me at all. Take Harmon's full brother Stacy, he's gone from here, lives in Kentucky. Well, I'm not leaving him a cent. I might leave him a few personal things, like a picture or two ..." He wearied of that thought. Once more his manner became contemplative and he sought the baby, leaned over him and examined him. "Now, all right, then. We come to it. What are you offering?" For a while he watched her thoughtfully, his expression unrevealing. "You're not intending to offer me the right to visit him, are you? I won't accept that."

Margaret said, "Papa, she's a woman, and in years to come—"

"We are talking about murder. We are not talking about minor matters."

"A life for a life, you said," Collie said.

"Papa, don't be mean," Margaret said.

301

"Miss Wright, you fell into bed with my boy, and you have a problem left you. You have people to save. You don't think I'd settle for a little?"

Collie shook her head.

"Did you say yes or no?" he asked.

"No," she said. "I don't know what you want."

"Well, I'll tell you. I'll take the boy."

Collie's hands were resting on the table, both palms on the table, and the only change about her was the clenching of the hands, which took a long time for the flexing and the closing of them, and finally the knuckles turned absolutely white.

"You'll need to leave him here and go home yourself. Your union with my son was not one I respect. As a minister, I have standards to uphold in my household."

"Until you die—" Collie whispered.

"Until I die, you say? Did she say until I die?" he asked Margaret.

"Papa, please don't be cruel," Margaret pleaded with him.

"Very well. Until I die. I accept that, Miss Wright. So we have our deal, Miss Wright. I agree. What do you say?"

"It's his life for his father's," she said, her voice failing on her. "For my brothers and for Mr. Jackson, who never ..."

"I know all that. Three men. What say?"

"Agreed," she said.

He carried the baby in his arms as he accompanied her to the front porch. They waited there for Margaret, who had gone to get a wrap. From the porch they looked out over the village itself, and down along the rocky bank of the river, and across the river at the wide, rich fields of the Wrights and Crawfords and others, and beyond the fields of the

302

main Wright road, where just now a farm truck was rolling slowly toward Tennessee. "How does his birth certificate read?" Drury asked her.

"Gudger never has sent one in," she said, looking neither at him nor at the child. "Was waiting for the father's name."

"I'll take care of it myself," he said

Her arms were strangely light. Light arms. By now, as she could tell, word had gone out, Harmon probably having delivered it, and most every yard had people waiting, men as well as women and children, to see Collie pass. Light arms, she thought, strangely light. One old woman wearing several layers of dresses and no coat hissed at her, but Margaret told that one to stay away, not to come closer.

Light arms. Collie didn't pause as they walked past a dozen houses. Light arms, useless, dangling. Most of the women averted their eyes whenever she came close. She walked through the cemetery, using the stone path, her legs trembly by now, so that once or twice she had to grip Margaret's elbow. Her eyes had glossed over as well, and she couldn't see clearly. Even so, she moved resolutely past the new grave, the one without even a headstone to mark it. Light arms. As in a dream she heard Margaret tell two boys to run to cousin Cliff's house and see if his wagon still had its team hitched, so they could drive her to her house.

She waited there at the place of the row of Balm of Gilead trees, in the sunshine, which was unusually bright and somewhat warming on the flesh, and when the wagon came, she climbed into the back unaided and lay down, pulled her legs up close to her chin and was like a child unborn, bouncing in the back of the wagon on the long trip.

She climbed down at her father's store and went inside and sat down near his stove, took the ladder-back chair Gudger usually used, which had a folded blanket nearby. She covered up with that. Paula and Wayland had seen her drop off the back of the wagon, and they came hurrying inside, and her father and Gudger were there, and everybody present was curious about her and why she had approached the store from the Campbells' territory. And where was her baby? Paula asked that first.

She told her, "Over to the Campbells'. To Drury's house."

There was something strange even about her way of speaking. Paula noticed that. They all did. Her father sat down near the stove and asked her pointedly where Jonathan was, and she told him he was now staying at Drury's, that he was Cole's son. That was the coldest moment in his entire life, Wright said later, but he didn't show it then. He nodded, that was all; he was more concerned about her than about the child or himself. He could see that she was strange and ill. "Honey," he whispered to her, "honey, are you all right?"

"I'm tired, Papa," she admitted.

"I imagine you are tired."

Wayland had been watching from near the pay counter, and he was beginning to realize what she had done, seeing even then that it was all she could have done, yet it had not been foreseen by him. He realized slowly, as thoughts unfolded one after another, that he was free because of her, and she was in bondage deeper than any other, as deep as her life could go, and was now about to break apart before them all, cry out, strike down herself before them, whom she loved, for whom she had lost her baby, and he went forward suddenly and extended his arms to embrace her, to hold her tightly, to try to save her even as she began to fall.

14

She lay in the bed in the parlor in her parents' house for three days and nights, Wayland sitting up with her most of the time. He talked to her, trying to break through the searching stares with which she viewed the world around her. He told her all there was to know about clocks. He told her about the clock tower, too, and that the top of the tower was to be a ball carved of wood and banded by Milton with iron straps. As to the three dials of the clock, one would face the store, which was her father's directive; another would face the church, so that a person leaving the building could judge the time but the clock could not be seen from the pews, another of her father's decisions; and the third would face the cemetery, but, of more practical consequence, would be visible from the school. Next year a bear might be installed, but nothing as grand as Young had wanted; at most it would be three feet tall, would be carved out of a light chestnut wood and stained dark brown. He suspected that it would be clothed, he told her, but in furs. There had been talk of casting the bear at the forge, but such a piece of metal would be too heavy to maneuver. He admitted to feeling somewhat pretentious because of having a bear at all, but he would not lose family friendships because of it, particularly Young's. "Has

305

he been here today to see you?" he asked her.

"Why, I've wondered where he was, if I'd offended him."

"He's just returned. He's been off in the North Woods. Day before yesterday your father got so worried he sent six men to trail him, and that oldest boy of Gudger's found Young twelve miles past the falls, hiding from the Campbells who were out looking for him. Several men had trapped him up there."

"They are not to hurt him," Collie said sternly.

"No, they weren't able to catch him." He pulled a rocker up close to the bed, pleased by her show of feeling. "He'd not slept for two, three days." Whenever he found a subject that appeared to break through the protective scrim around her, he pursued it. During these days she had held his hands tightly whenever he offered them, and sought affection from him and Paula, and her father as well, but she had not appeared willing to enter into conversation. "Young wants his funeral service used one Sunday," Wayland told her.

"Why, how can you do a funeral service for a live person?"

"He said we would use it Easter, and he'll officiate."

"What service?"

"The one he wrote out and left with Benie. He has the different Bible passages lined out for each member of the family, and even for the Lawrence family. Said something about being kind to strangers, that was their part. Had himself down for verses about lying. Keeps making changes."

"What was mine?"

"Oh, I don't recall, Collie."

"Now, you tell me. What was it?"

"Thou shalt not commit adult'ry."

"Why, I don't know—I never committed adult'ry, did I? Cole wasn't married."

306

"It's with me, I imagine he has in mind."

"Well, you're not married either."

"I'm not the one saying it, Collie. It's Young that has the verse for you."

"I'm not very pleased, as you see."

"Yes, I can see that." This was the first time she had shown real spirit in the three days since the trade, and he was enormously pleased.

"What was yours?" she said. "Your commandment?"

He cleared his throat uneasily, even stopped his rocker in place. "Thou shalt not steal another's wife, something of the sort," he said simply. He was thoughtful for a while, examining the marvels of Young's plan, and of the way his mind worked. "The family has broken all ten commandments, at one time or another, all in a single winter, Young contends."

"Thou shalt not kill," she said. "Who gets that one?"

"He has it down for Gudger just now."

She moaned heavily. "Gudger'll not like that."

"He never said a word when it was all read at dinnertime yesterday. Your papa read it all out, lined it out, and Gudger never said a word. I think that surprised all of us. He never questioned it. And Young has Milton down to kill the lambs. Said his papa would splatter blood all over himself, couldn't do any butchering. And Paula has offered her pig, Young reported, said she would make a personal sacrifice, but Young said pigs couldn't be used."

"Well, sometimes I think Young's crazy," Collie decided.

"Altar's to have a fire lit, is to cook the meat. I guess it's all to be skinned—I don't know. Do you?"

"I have no idea."

"We'll have to ask somebody that knows the Old

Testament better than I do. Are we to eat any of the meat?"

"I wouldn't think so."

"Maybe a virgin could," he said, and laughed, and was pleased to see her smile. "If we can find one."

"Oh, hush," she said. "I was a virgin past twenty years old myself."

"Altar has to be of uncut stones, without mortar."

"Paula's a virgin. There's plenty of them."

On impulse, without any planning at all, he said suddenly, "Paula told me she was pregnant, said so, anyway." He was startled to hear the words spoken, but pleased to see the reaction. The declaration got Collie up from the bed.

Pulling her gown down over her knees, she demanded to know if he was serious and who the man was. She was feverish about it.

"Why, she won't tell me who it was," Wayland said, a grin working at his lips in spite of his efforts.

"She'll tell *me*," Collie said, and flung herself toward her clothes. About halfway to the chair where they were folded, she began to realize the possibility of a prank existed, and when she turned on Wayland, she saw a big smile on his face and heard his laugh start down in his chest. So she sank back in the chair and laughed herself.

However, the next few times she saw Paula there in the room, sadness came over her; always the same question came to mind at once: Who is watching Jonathan, if one of us is not? But on the fifth day, which was a Saturday, she stopped mourning. At least, she stopped showing her pity so openly, and she put on clean clothes, Paula helping by bringing what Collie wanted from the house, and she went out into the kitchen, where her mother welcomed her without protestations. She fixed herself coffee and a few eggs and opened a can of Stokely's cut green beans, then went into the dining room and sat at her papa's chair and ate by herself, Paula hovering about, bringing her toast, even though she hadn't said anything about toast. Her mother brought her some sausage made just yesterday and asked her opinion of it.

Then about noon Young came by, expecting a meal, and he sat at the table with her.

"Well, are you married yet?" she asked him, and there was not much biting criticism in her question. It carried a suggestion, really. "You said she wanted a baby."

"She's always told me that, Collie," he admitted, watching her carefully. "She wants a family."

"I hope she's given all the help she needs to get one," Collie said. Slowly she made her way to the door, felt for the door jamb for support. She turned to look back at him. "If we ever get a minister, we can all get married together, but you better tell her I mean to start soon. Tell her I don't want to wear white." She moved into the kitchen, poured half a cup of coffee from the steaming pot on the stove, came back to the door. "You tell Benie I know about the note."

"What note?" Young said.

"Ask her." Collie drank down the coffee, set the cup aside. "You've always needed somebody to mother you, Young, and I expect you've found her."

From time to time Wayland tried to talk to Collie about his own feelings. He would lie in her bed of an evening and hold her, talk to her. He was bound to her by chains so strong he couldn't think of parting them now. "I never was sure Ruth loved me," he told her. "She'd say she did, but she never sacrificed anything. She gave me herself, but she gave me what she had to give some man, didn't she?" Now here, as he explained to Collie and to himself, was a wife who had given up her child for him, as well as for her brothers, even for the McGregors. That was staggering to his sensitivities, and mystified him; at the same time it satisfied his soul, he told her, in spite of the pain he felt for her and Jonathan. It was a short distance beyond his comprehension, he told her. "Just as Cole's death was almost beyond my strength to endure," he told her, "took me to my limit, as on the last night we were together at the house, before you went on and gave up Jonathan."

"It wasn't for you," she would tell him repeatedly, "nor Young, nor anybody else. It fell to me to complete what I had started. There wasn't any escape left to me. Don't think it was for you, when it was all I could do ..."

All the rest of that winter and spring none of the Wright family saw Jonathan, not a glimpse of him, not any word about him except what Mavis brought, which was favorable. Collie on several occasions after her marriage to Wayland had gone down the shadowed path to the river, had stood behind rhododendron, anxious for a look at him. All she saw was women beating clothes clean on warm winter afternoons. Old Wright prayed for Jonathan every church service, mentioning Jonathan Wright in his prayers, stressing the word Wright. Of course, he knew from Gudger that the boy had been registered at the County Seat as Jonathan Coleman Campbell.

Then in March, on a Friday, Wright was sitting in the store writing a letter to his sister-in-law Hattie, who lived in West Asheville, when Drury Campbell arrived in the yard out front, his son Phillip with him. The two men wandered about, pausing to consider some old iron wares that Sam Conaway was offering for trade. Gudger came heavily down the store steps, approached them, said good morning to Phillip, whom he knew in passing, nodded to old Campbell, whose attention was now concentrated on the rock tower that was being fitted with three round faces. Wayland, working inside it, appeared at one face opening, which surprised and amused Drury. "What in the world is he a-doin'?" he asked Gudger.

Gudger shrugged his heavy shoulders. "Why, it's to be our clock."

"Clock?" Drury said, astonished. It was about fifteen feet high and was built in three tiers, the faces set in the top tier, under a domed roof. It was a major clock indeed. Drury walked all the way around it, marveling. He called for Wayland—that man inside there—to show himself again, which Wayland was happy to do. Clearly, Drury was impressed.

He approached the store at a leisurely pace, stopped to inquire about brooms that Mrs. Smith Taylor had for sale, paused before a display of quilts, holding one hem up in full sunlight so he could evaluate the quality of the stitching. He climbed the porch steps slowly, casting glances back at the tower, spit onto the store's porch floor before going on inside, where he again paused, this time to allow his eyes to accustom themselves to the gloom. "Well, where are you, Mr. Wright?" he inquired impetuously.

"Half in the grave, I reckon," Wright replied, peering at him from his chair near the stove. "Come back, if you want to."

Drury and the son Phillip, a handsome, smiling fellow well over six feet tall, took seats on a bench near where Wright was sitting. Two old visitors who had been dozing there got up at once and went to stand along the wall. Even Gudger waited for his father to invite him to join them. "And you better call Wayland inside," Wright said.

"I'm here about the boy," Drury said, dropping the words quietly into the dusty air.

"How's he getting along?" Wright asked, speaking calmly.

"Oh, he's growed. Has no belly on him, but has weight enough. Is a round-faced baby, but remains slender of limbs."

Wright said, "I think his mummy was like that. Wasn't Collie slender-armed even as a baby, Gudger?"

"I think so, Papa."

Wright said, "I get confused, trying to keep memories straight, I have such a rich supply. Suppose you can remember well, like your father could, can you?"

"I never forget what's important to me to remember," Drury said.

The men paused in their conversation while Wayland took his seat.

"This here is Wayland Jackson. He's a clock man," Wright said.

"Yes, I saw him inside his clock, looking out."

"And he has married Jonathan's mother."

Drury stared at Wayland for a moment, nodded finally, accepting the information warily. "One of my daughters can remember ever' detail of the family. What I recall is only what I need to; although I do remember everything I see. It's a natural trait for me to recall what I see. I can remember my first wife, the first time I ever saw her."

Wright took a pipe out of a tin cup and lit it.

"Saw her near Newport. Had on a blue-dyed dress. Now, I'd not laid eyes on many of them, not in blue. As a boy I saw browns, greens, yellows, and now and then a reddish color, which was about half brown, and once in a moon I'd see a black."

"I never saw many blues, either," Wright said.

"Well, sir, it set me back. And she had raven hair, and she had on a white lace collar and cuffs, and a gold necklace."

"I never saw a gold necklace till I was forty-some years old," Wright said.

"I never had met her before, and I introduced myself, told her where I was from, asked her if I could talk with her father about her, and she said yes, he's right over there by the crib. And I said I'd treat her right, that I had a house and plenty of land and stock, and she'd never be harmed in any way, and she said she knew me, had heard of me. And I told the same to her father and said what's her dowry look like, and he said mostly quilts and spoons, and I asked about land, for that was all as a young man I ever truly loved, and he said no, there's no land, the sons have that, and I asked about stock, and he said no, not any stock, except maybe her mama will give her something. And I said, well, when you've thought it over, let me hear from you. That was the gist of the conversation, and along toward Thanksgiving he drove up with her in a red wagon with a Guernsey cow and a right pretty horse and a deed to fifty-one acres in Tennessee. If I'd knowed how steep and rocky the land was, I might not have wanted it, but by then I wanted her. I did. She had on a chestnut-dyed dress with German buttons, and patent-leather shoes that buttoned, and she had that still, small smile, as if she knew secrets about me that I never would know without her, and it was all settled there in the yard."

Wright nodded. He lit his pipe and blew a whiff of smoke toward the cat, Othello. "She was a McDavidson?"

"No, she was a McDaniels. She was a good worker, too, as fine as the world ever made. Was Phillip's mother. He has some of her features."

Wright studied the old fellow thoughtfully. "How many wives have you lost so far, Drury?"

"Lost two," he admitted. "Phillip's mother, and Cole's."

313

"I'll not tell you about my courtin'," Wright said. "It'd be embarrassing to Gudger and Wayland." He laughed softly. "That baby of Collie's has his birth registered, has he?"

"I sent in the papers by way of another preacher," Drury said.

"Lives at your house?"

Drury nodded. "Sleeps just off my room. On my south side I have three rooms in a row, two with fireplaces, and he's in the middle."

"I wouldn't mind getting a look at him now and then," Wright said. "Expect he misses his mummy."

"Oh, Lord, yes he did, but now he's content. We have plenty of women in my house, living there and visiting. He's everybody's favorite, too, let me tell you."

Wright said, "The youngest is usually preferred."

"Never a hand been laid on him in anger. I don't believe in hitting youngins. I never have done it."

"I agree with you," Wright said. "We're all Christian people, I know that."

"Christian people," Drury whispered, nodding. "What you going to leave the boy in your will?"

Wright said at once, "I've about forgot him."

"He's your blood-kin grandson. Do you deny it?"

"I've not thought about it. No, I don't deny it."

"Your daughter said he was to be listed for a full share."

Wright nodded toward Wayland. "Her husband's sitting here. She's up at the Millers' house, if you want to talk to her."

"No, I want to talk to you," Drury said.

"If you traded with her, you'll want to see her about it," Wright said. "I would have been pleased to be asked at the time, but was not."

"She said she expected to get more'n half of your

property in the North Woods. That'd be everything up to the ridgecrest, I'd imagine."

"Oh, I own beyond that, to the forked river, and across that to the top of the next ridge."

"Does she get more'n half of it, I'm wondering?"

Wright considered it. "She's moved down the hill recently, seems to be more a part of the community. Young has moved on down the hill to the inn, and she's in his house. She's not as near the North Woods as she used to be, is more interested in the community, I'd imagine, in land down this way."

Drury said, "How many acres in the North Woods?"

"The tax book lists twenty thousand."

Drury snorted, then tore off a bit of tobacco with his teeth. "I can see more'n that."

Wright said nothing more about it. He appeared not to have much interest in continuing the conversation.

"Heard you was making clocks over your way," Drury said.

"Have started out at it," Wright admitted.

"My boy here has an interest in woodworking. Has made gun stocks and a gun case as pretty as you ever saw. Had a glass door. Is burled pine, the likes of which I never saw. You wouldn't think pine could be that pretty."

Wright nodded. He glanced at Wayland. "We can use him, I imagine," he said simply.

There was another pause, an admission of Wright's disinterest.

"Been timbering," Drury said after a while. "Been spending the colder months at it. Timbered this year for the Pattersons to the south. Got timber rights from them for five thousand acres, more or less, but, law, it's been a long haul to the railroad."

"You've finished there, have you?"

"Close to finishing."

"Need more timber to cut?"

"It was all oxen, no flume. Timbered some in Tennessee last winter. Now, that was easier, because we had a fair road, not too steep where we was cutting."

"Virgin timber, was it?"

"Some of it." He spit into the stove box. "I find timbering is the best I can do, now that game's scarce. How often do you want to see Jonathan?"

"Every weekend," Wright said at once.

"No, he's bound to go to church with me."

"Then I'll take him every Saturday and on alternate Sundays."

"Now, he has to go to church with me."

"Let him go with you on alternate Sundays. Your preaching's powerful enough to span two weeks."

Drury paused, seemed to be listening to a voice heard only by himself. "She'll get him back anyway when I die, you know that," he said.

Wright nodded. "She told me."

"And I won't live forever."

"Well, we wish you no harm," Wright said.

"You'll have him soon, won't he, Phillip?"

Phillip said not a word. His gaze kept moving from his father's face to Wright's and back again.

After a few moments Drury said, "I could timber the North Woods, and I'd share one third with you."

Quiet. Not even a rocker moved in that big room. A cat meowed, then stretched out in the sun that was pouring in through the south window. "Young won't want his part timbered yet," Wright said.

"It's past time, Lord knows. It'll rot," Drury said.

"That's virgin timber. I'd say there's eighty thousand acres in all."

"Then I'll timber forty thousand and quit," Drury said. "Over eight years—"

"For half the value of the logs delivered to the mill," Wright told him.

"Half is a dear price, considering the distance."

"You are able to start on it? You have the men and oxen ready, do you?"

"I have two teams of oxen, eight to a team, with chains enough, and I'm thinking I can make a flume from the top of the ridge to the field out there, using Collie's creek for wetting it, then I can float the logs from the field, except for the biggest ones. I don't know how to handle those yet."

Wright scratched at his neck. "Leave them standing," he said.

"No, I'll get them out, if I have to set up a mill myself."

Wright cleared his throat, glanced at Gudger, then at Wayland. "What say, Mr. Jackson?" he asked.

Wayland looked up. "I imagine Collie'd be pleased."

Wright nodded to Gudger. "What say?"

Gudger had some difficulty deciding, apparently. "It's what Collie'd want, I guess," he said. "But the profit ought to belong to all of us, what you get out of cutting it, Papa."

"No," Wright said. "It'll go to her. What you say?"

"Papa, it's yours, so it belongs to all of us. It's not hers yet."

"Well, I'll keep half of it, then," he said evenly. "What say, Gudger?"

Gudger stared at him, his lips trembling.

At once Wright said to Drury, "I'll mark off twenty thousand acres here directly. We'll make a start with that, see how we get on."

"In such place as I can flume the timber," Drury said.

"Some of it. Mr. Jackson and Young will mark it. I'll reserve ten acres near the falls."

Drury turned to look directly at Wright. "I'll agree to ever' other Saturday and ever' other Sunday, one day a week."

"Every Saturday and every other Sunday," Wright said, "and I'll turn over to you my oxen, at least six, and two little donkeys that are steady as mountain goats." When that offer seemed not to be adequate, he added, "And I'll have you here to preach in our church two Sundays every year."

Campbell's eyes clouded over at once. A smile began to work its way at the corner of his mouth. "I'd put the fear of Almighty God in the Wrights and Crawfords," he said. He laughed suddenly. "Is it done then?" he asked, standing, peering down at Wright. "Is it done or not?"

"Why, it's all agreed, so far as I know," Wright said. As Drury started to leave, Wright called after him, "You deliver him and I'll bring him home."

"To your house, or to his mother's?" Drury asked, stopping near the door.

"You bring him to my house tomorrow breakfast, and I'll bring him back to you Monday breakfast."

"Now you're taking an extra spate of time," Drury said angrily, turning on him. "I'll want him back Sunday night."

"Twenty-four hours is a day," Wright said, "that being the way God made them. Now, let's not split days. And you preach on Sunday next, if you've a mind to. We have a Davidson who was to try out again on Sunday, but he can stand aside. He's an accommodating person."

Drury hesitated, seemed to be debating the matter further, apparently was still upset about the Sunday night being considered part of the day.

"Pour him a drink of brandy, Wayland," Wright murmured. Wayland knew where the brandy was kept, and he poured a glass about half full for each of the elderly gentlemen, gave Wright his first, then took the other to Campbell, who rejected it. Wayland left it on the counter before him.

Wright said, "What about using the text 'The

318

church is the bride of Christ'? That would be a fine text for this side of the river."

A smile began working at the corners of Drury's mouth once more. Suddenly he laughed, then he took up the glass of brandy and drained it in a big swallow. Tossing the glass onto the counter, he walked out of the place.

Making his afternoon tour of the trading lot, Wright grasped Wayland's arm, held firmly to it. He stopped at Silas Gouge's wagon, where he noticed a cage full of wild rabbits for sale. He fed them through the wire, watching their little mouths chew hungrily, appreciatively. He paused at the stone clock tower, which had its faces and two sets of hands in place. He moved past it to where Young had dragged an old chestnut stump. "Don't you mention that baby to Collie, you hear me?" Wright whispered to Wayland. The stump was about five feet in diameter.

"I couldn't keep that a secret," Wayland said, startled.

"I'm asking you to. Tomorrow before noon you bring her over to the house. Tell her I have two ducks caught and want her to have them. Don't mention the baby to her yet."

"Mr. Wright, a secret like that is impossible for me—"

"No, now, it's grandparents doing this. I bought the rights to the boy, and I mean for Annie to get to know him. I want Annie to feel somewhat responsible for him, don't you see?"

"And what about Collie?" Wayland said, anger rising in him suddenly.

Wright turned to him, searched his face for his meaning. "I suppose it would be sort of sweet of me, as women say, to make him a gift to Collie, but we get what we buy, if we're fortunate, and I've bought my grandson. I mean for his mother to have a hand in the rearing of him, but he's going to be his grandfather's for some years to come." He looked deeply into Wayland's eyes. "I can't give the boy to his mother, then take him back once a week. You see that."

Wayland hesitated on the verge of replying. "What do you want Collie to do?" he asked finally.

"She sold him. That was her trade. Now I've made mine. I'll deal fairly with her."

"You can't buy and sell human beings."

"Why, that's what a family is."

"So Collie will come to visit her own son?"

"And her son when he's older will visit her. That's until Drury dies, that'll be the way. Drury and I will bring him up. You will understand it better later on."

"Your wife doesn't like the boy," Wayland reminded him.

"That's so," Wright admitted. He took out his pipe and tapped tobacco into it, returned it unlit to his pocket. "Don't give up on her, though. She might respond, given a new chance." He moved closer to the stump, studied it. "What on earth you going to do with that?"

"I suppose it's not for me to say how you and Collie will rear the boy, anyway," Wayland said.

"No, probably not," Wright said. "What you plan for this stump?"

"Could be a playhouse, could be a bear's den."

"Lord have mercy," Wright murmured. "Young had too much freedom as a boy, and he hasn't settled down even yet." He saw Gudger approaching from a distance, his big body bent forward, his meaty hands swinging heavily by his side. "He's still buried under worry, Gudger is. You think he did kill Cole?"

320

"I wonder. I'd say so, if it were required to say."

"He walks in his sleep nowadays, his wife tells me. I been considering sending him out to see Charlie, to visit."

Gudger stopped nearby, stood balanced on slightly spread legs, staring at the clock tower. "It's the best one I ever saw."

Wright laughed contentedly, shaking his head with pleasure. "I'd say so, too. Best one around here." He took firm hold of Wayland's arm, squeezed it and led him on over to Zacharias Taylor's truck, where Taylor had a few tools for trade. "Don't you worry about that boy Jonathan," he told Wayland confidentially. "There's worse ways for a boy to grow up than being the prize of both his grandfathers."

Next morning was warm, about as warm as a March morning can be in the mountains. Wayland sent Paula down to Milton's house to get two sets of weights. He supposed she would surely hear about the baby there or at the store, and he told her to keep the secret. He sat around the house for an hour or so, talking with Collie. It was when he heard the church clock strike ten that he led her up through the field, past the breaking woods, into the North Woods. They were both content to be here, there was no asking about why they had come or where they were going; the sun was playing with them, was casting beams down through the massive trees high above their heads, the limbs like the beams of a cathedral.

It was a bright, cloudless day, this special Saturday. He followed the sound of the falls, reaching it sooner than he had expected, a shimmering sheet of glass with foam in a big pool at its base. He climbed up the west bank to a place above the pool, to a mossy place near a big rock. She said near here was where she had met Cole that first time.

They swam together for the better part of an hour, then lay on the warm ground and sought one another, the union of their bodies seeking the beginning of another life.

At noon he took her to her parents' house. Collie went on inside to ask what her father had been talking about; there were no ducks penned up that she saw. He waited in the yard. Paula, who had been standing at the kitchen window, looking in, joined Wayland and took his hand.

He slipped his arm around her. "Did you see them meet?" he asked her. He decided he would not go in there just now, he would leave her alone with her child for a few minutes. "Why, it's all right," he told Paula, "it's all right," he told her, taking her in his arms.

There's an epidemic with 27 million victims. And no visible symptoms.

It's an epidemic of people who can't read.

Believe it or not, 27 million Americans are functionally illiterate, about one adult in five.

The solution to this problem is you... when you join the fight against illiteracy. So call the Coalition for Literacy at toll-free **1-800-228-8813** and volunteer.

**Volunteer
Against Illiteracy.
The only degree you need
is a degree of caring.**

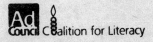